JUN **1 3** 2017

THE
AUEN
FOUNDATION

The purchase of this book
was made possible
by a generous grant from
The Auen Foundation.

PLAIN
MISSING

Center Point
Large Print

Also by Emma Miller and available from
Center Point Large Print:

Plain Killing
Plain Dead

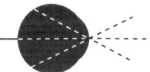

**This Large Print Book carries the
Seal of Approval of N.A.V.H.**

PLAIN MISSING

Emma Miller

CENTER POINT LARGE PRINT
THORNDIKE, MAINE

This Center Point Large Print edition is published
in the year 2017 by arrangement with
Kensington Publishing Corp.

The text of this Large Print edition is unabridged.
In other aspects, this book may vary
from the original edition.
Printed in the United States of America
on permanent paper.
Set in 16-point Times New Roman type.

ISBN: 978-1-68324-381-6

Library of Congress Cataloging-in-Publication Data

Names: Miller, Emma, author.
Title: Plain missing / Emma Miller.
Description: Center Point Large Print edition. | Thorndike, Maine :
Center Point Large Print, 2017.
Identifiers: LCCN 2017004026 | ISBN 9781683243816
      (hardcover : alk. paper)
Subjects: LCSH: Amish—Fiction. | Missing persons—Fiction. | Large
type books. | GSAFD: Mystery fiction. | Christian fiction.
Classification: LCC PS3613.I536 P569 2017 | DDC 813/.6—dc23
LC record available at https://lccn.loc.gov/2017004026

PROLOGUE

Stone Mill, Pennsylvania . . .

Dathan Bender flicked the reins over the horse's back and urged him into a long, striding pace. The wagon lurched forward, and Elsie Hostetler, riding beside him on the wide board bench, gave a small cry of excitement and grabbed onto the seat to steady herself. "Fast," she said. "He's not only pretty to look at. He's fast."

In the darkness, the horse was a moving shadow ahead of them, hooves thudding rhythmically on the pavement.

"Me or the gelding?" Dathan's tone was low and teasing.

Elsie laughed. "I meant the horse, *dummkopp*."

"But you have to admit, it does apply to both of us."

She giggled. "Better not let my father hear you talk like that. He's not too fond of you."

"Aaron Hostetler isn't fond of many people."

"That's true," she agreed, now smiling. "But *Dat* and your father had some kind of feud a long time ago. He says you're cut from the same cloth. Not someone he wants around his daughter."

"How can he say that when he doesn't know me? I'm taking baptism classes, right? I'll soon be a baptized member of the church."

Her smile grew wider. "You're taking the classes because I told you that I wouldn't go out with you if you didn't."

Dathan's baptism was the first step to overcoming her father's opposition to their being together. Elsie had joined the faith at eighteen, two years after she'd left school. It had been her choice, but her parents had urged her to join as soon as she was old enough. One daughter like her oldest sister, Mary Aaron, was enough for any family, her father said. Mary Aaron was nearly twenty-five and still *rumspringa*.

Dathan and Elsie were both quiet for a moment, enjoying the steady sound of the horse's hooves on the pavement and the creak of the wagon wheels. Then Dathan spoke. "I hope you're not mad at me over what happened tonight. I'm sorry I lost my temper."

"*Ne*." She shook her head. "I wish it hadn't happened, but it's over now."

"It's just that . . ." He was quiet and then went on. "I care about you, Elsie. And I couldn't stand—"

"Don't. It's not important." She looked up at him. The moon was just beginning to rise and it illuminated his face. "He and I weren't . . . I mean, I didn't . . ." She nibbled her lower lip. "We're just friends now."

"But he obviously wants to be more than that," Dathan insisted.

"I don't care what he wants. That isn't going to happen. Not now." She wanted to put the whole incident out of her mind. What was important was being alone with Dathan, riding beside him, sitting close to him. She was so happy now that she felt as though she would burst with joy.

"He isn't really mine, of course," Dathan said, wisely changing the subject. "I borrowed the horse and wagon from my brother-in-law because I wanted to ask you to ride home with me. But I mean to buy my own rig soon. I've been saving to buy a good horse at the auction."

"*Dat* says you can find good horses at the auction if you know what you're doing."

"I want a dependable animal, but one still young and high-stepping. I thought maybe I'd buy a retired racehorse. Then I could call him Flash."

"Flash is a good name for a driving horse," she agreed.

"Unless you'd rather call him something else." Dathan reached over and closed his hand over hers. It was a warm, strong hand, callused from hard work.

His touch made her go all shivery inside. "He'll be your horse," she replied. "Not for me to name him."

"But if we wed, he'll be *ours*. The horse and everything I own will be half yours."

Elsie drew in a sharp breath, looking up at him. "Is that supposed to be a proposal?"

"*Ya*, I guess it is. I never felt like this about any other girl. And . . ." His voice deepened with emotion. "I want you for my wife, Elsie."

"And I want to marry you," she said in a rush. "But my father—" She looked down and then back up at him again. "I'm afraid he'll never give me permission to marry you, Dathan."

He squeezed her hand. "We'll change his mind."

"You don't know him. Once he decides something, he's like an . . . an oak log. Solid. You can't budge him."

"I'm not a penniless suitor asking to court his daughter. I'll be a full member of the church soon. I have a good trade and a job. And when I marry, I'll inherit my father's farm. My mother says it's silly to wait until she dies for me to have it."

"God grant her a long life," Elsie said quickly.

"Of course I hope she'll be with us for a long time. I'm just saying that I'll have a home to take you to. I can support you and any children we might be blessed with."

She felt her face grow hot as she thought of babies that might be born to their marriage. The physical side of having a husband was a delicious and scary thought. "So what you're offering is a home *and* a fast horse," she teased.

"And a fast horse." Dathan pulled back on the reins. "Whoa, boy," he said. The horse came to a stop. The wagon wheels squeaked to a halt, and from both sides of the road came insect song.

"Elsie?" Dathan turned to her, still holding her hand. "Do you think you could be my wife?" He went on quicker than before. "You must know how you feel about me. And it's not like you haven't known me all your life."

She smiled, wishing she could capture this moment and keep it forever. Here in the moonlight with Dathan, her heart pounding, she'd never been happier. Three years ago she'd thought that she had no chance with Dathan, and she'd almost promised her heart to someone else. But that was in the past. She'd secretly longed for Dathan to cast his eye on her since she was fifteen, and now they were together. It seemed almost too good to be true.

"Last year you were taking Sadie Troyer home from singings. Marriage is forever, Dathan. How do I know you won't change your mind?"

"Because I promise you that I won't. Because you're the only girl I've ever asked to be my wife." He leaned close and brushed her lips with his. The kiss was sweet and tender and left her breathless.

"Because if you won't say yes," he whispered, gazing into her eyes, "I'll throw myself into Indian Creek and end it all."

"Into Indian Creek?" She couldn't help giggling as she leaned back. "Indian Creek is six inches deep."

He groaned. "I could hardly jump into the quarry. You know I can't swim a stroke."

She laughed and he laughed. They kissed again. From the woods across the field, a nighthawk cried, and the lonely sound sent a shiver down her spine. For a moment Elsie felt odd, as if a goose had walked over her grave. Far in the distance she saw headlights from an approaching car. "It's getting late," she said. "You'd better get me home before my father comes looking for us."

"Not until you say yes," he persisted. "Or into the creek I go."

"I can't marry you without my father's approval."

"We'll get it. Once he knows that I'm able to take care of you and how much we mean to each other, he'll come around."

"I wish it was that easy."

"I promise you, I'll get his blessing."

"Then I'd better say yes," she answered, sliding away from him on the wagon bench. "And I warn you, there will be no more kissing until after our wedding."

"Don't you like my kisses?" he asked.

"I do," Elsie replied. "And that's the problem." She couldn't hide her smile as she pointed ahead. "Drive on, Dathan Bender."

CHAPTER 1

"You shouldn't have insisted on supervising the sauerkraut making," Rachel fussed as she tucked her mother into bed. "That's why you're worn out. You know what the doctor said about getting your rest."

Esther Mast laid her head back on the pillow with an audible sigh of relief. Rachel smiled down at her before bending to kiss her cheek. Her mother's pale skin was warm against Rachel's lips, and her eyes glowed with the affection she found it impossible to show.

"Need another pillow?" Rachel asked. Her mother shook her head. "Want me to rub your feet?" Again, her *mam* signaled in the negative with a slight shake of her strong chin. Rachel smiled at her again. "Good night, then. I love you."

Esther's mouth tightened into a stubborn line. She closed her eyes and turned her back to her eldest daughter.

"Don't forget your prayers," Rachel admonished teasingly. There was no answer, but she didn't expect one. Her mother hadn't spoken directly to her in nearly seventeen years. Not since

Rachel left her Old Order Amish family to become an Englisher.

Rachel crossed to the nearest window and pulled down the shade. Dusk was falling over the farm, and the dark shadows had already laid claim to the valley, sheltered by the mountains. Glancing around the peaceful room with its wide-plank floors, plastered walls, and old walnut dresser, her gaze kept being drawn back to the iron double bed. How small and vulnerable her mother looked, how unlike the strong, vigorous woman Rachel had known all of her life. The white elders' *kapp* that tied under her chin and covered what hair she had left made her appear even more fragile. "God bless and keep you, *Mam*," Rachel murmured.

Straightening her shoulders, she left the *borning room,* the downstairs bedroom that always smelled of mint and served for childbirth or sick or elderly members of the family. It seemed strange to see her mother sleeping there, rather than in the upstairs chamber that she'd always shared with Rachel's father. But everyone had agreed that the steep stairs of the old farmhouse would be a challenge for Esther just now. And it was easier for Rachel to care for her without climbing the steps.

Her *mam*'s battle with breast cancer had made it necessary for Rachel to leave Stone Mill House, her bed-and-breakfast in town, to come home and help while her mother recovered from her latest round of chemo. But Esther was doing well; the oncologist said so. With prayer and the best medical treatment, there was every reason to believe that her mother would beat the disease and remain at the heart of her family for many years to come.

Rachel wrinkled her nose as she made her way down the hall and back to the kitchen, where her sisters were washing and drying dishes. The kitchen, unlike the other rooms in the house, was piled with clutter. No trash or dust accumulated, but empty canning jars stood on the counters, lids and rings filled bowls already holding pens, notepads, and recipe cards, and soup kettles and cast-iron frying pans rested on wide window-sills. More pots filled the cabinets, threatening to spill out when a door was opened. One of the cabinet doors always stood ajar.

"This whole house stinks of sauerkraut," Rachel observed. It had been a warm day for September, and the breeze had failed them. She wished she could turn on the central air. But in a house without electricity, there was no air-conditioning and no fans. Not that she didn't love her mother's sauerkraut; she did. But the smell was over-whelming. "Mind that pitcher," she warned her sister Sally. "If you drop it, *Mam* will have your head on a platter."

Eleven-year-old Sally, freckle-faced and full

of herself, rolled her eyes. "I'm not going to drop it."

"She didn't dry it properly," their sister Amanda reported in a patient, matter-of-fact tone. "She just whisked the towel over it. See, Rachel. Water dripped all over the floor. And I just mopped it this afternoon."

Sally stuck out her tongue at Amanda, but Amanda simply went on rinsing off a long-handled dipper. "I told her to be careful. That spatterware pitcher came from *Mam*'s grandmother," Amanda said. "It's one of the few things that survived the fire."

Tattletale, Sally mouthed silently.

"Hush, now, both of you," Rachel interposed. "Do you want *Mam* to hear you quarreling and come out here to settle things? I just got her into bed." She tugged tenderly at one of Sally's thick auburn braids, which had come unpinned from under her rumpled *kapp* and dangled down her back. "And you mustn't be so quick to snap at Amanda. She wasn't being mean. She was just thinking of *Mam* and how much she treasures that pitcher."

"I'm sorry," Sally said, "but she's such a goody-goody."

"Am not," Amanda retorted. "You know you're clumsy. I just didn't want you to get in trouble." She placed the ladle in the drying rack beside the dishpan.

"I am not clumsy!" Sally flung back. "You're always trying to be the boss of me."

Amanda's chubby face crumpled into an expression of hurt. "I'm your older sister. It's my duty to help you see what you've done wrong. And yours to listen to what I say."

Sally tossed her head. "You aren't my mother."

"All right. Enough," Rachel insisted. "I'll finish the drying. Sally, you run out to the chicken house and make certain that Levi fastened the door tightly. Aunt Hannah lost a hen to a fox last night."

Sally didn't need to be told twice. She flung off her apron and dashed barefoot out of the kitchen, her *kapp* strings flying.

"You shouldn't give in to her," Amanda said as the screen door slammed. "Because she's the youngest, everyone spoils her. But you'll do her no favors. What kind of wife and mother will she make?"

Rachel looked at Amanda and tried to hold her peace. Amanda was the model of what a properly-brought-up Amish girl was supposed to be: quiet, hardworking, a skilled seamstress, and more concerned with the next life in heaven than this earthly one. But since Amanda had been small, Rachel had found it difficult to appreciate her strengths. Amanda should have been born a Hostetler, Rachel thought. She would have fit in perfectly with their mother's family. The Masts, their *dat*'s family, were mostly easygoing; they

15

didn't break the rules so much as find more comfortable ways to follow them. Not that their *dat* wasn't solid in his faith, but he wasn't as quick to judge the Englishers or those of his own church who were a tad more liberal.

But here was Amanda, looking for all the world as if she might break into tears, while helter-skelter Sally had forgotten the fuss and was happily doing her thing. Rachel didn't expect to see Sally before evening prayers. If she knew her little sister, she had a romance novel stowed in the hayloft, and as soon as she made certain the chickens were safe, she'd be searching out her book. It wasn't exactly a forbidden pursuit, since Rachel, having bought the paperbacks for her, knew that they were Amish romances and suitable reading material for a girl her age. So why was it so much easier to find charity in her heart for the independent little sister than the dutiful one?

Feeling a pang of guilt, she gave Amanda a quick hug. "Sally's young," she murmured. "And you know she's always been more like *Dat* than *Mam*."

Amanda shook her head. "But she gets away with everything," she said. "*Mam* never let me—"

"You were a different girl," Rachel interjected, giving her another squeeze. "Being good comes easily to you. Sally is a wild rose, prickly and unpredictable, but every bit as sweet as you."

"I worry that she will stray from the fold when

she becomes *rumspringa*," Amanda said. "Or leave us altogether, like you did."

Regret settled over Rachel's shoulders like a damp sweater. There was the nut of it. Amanda resented Rachel for choosing a worldly life rather than an Amish one, and Amanda feared that she would lead Sally to follow her, as their mother also clearly feared. And there was no answer that Rachel could give that would comfort either their *mam* or Amanda, because she'd often thought that if one of her siblings left the church, it might be Sally. Sally, who had such a desire for books and what lay beyond the boundaries of their family farm and the church community. "Each of us has the right to choose," she answered softly. "And I haven't left you altogether, have I?"

The cell phone vibrated in Rachel's apron pocket. "*Mam* may be awake still," she said to her sister. "She might like it if you went in and read the Bible to her. You know how she loves to hear you read the Psalms. She always says that you have the most soothing voice of all her children."

Amanda brightened. "I can do that. I'll just finish wiping down the counters."

"*Ne*," Rachel urged, falling back into the *Deitsch* dialect they usually spoke at home. "I'll do it. You go to Mother." Her phone vibrated again. She glanced at the clock that stood on the mantel. *Could it be Evan calling?* It was Friday,

17

and she hadn't spoken to her fiancé since the beginning of the week.

The screen door squeaked, and boys' boots thudded on the porch. Rachel heard the raucous voices of her younger brothers, Levi and Danny. "Any more of that blackberry pie left?" one of them called.

Obviously, there would be no privacy for her to answer her phone here in the kitchen. And as the cell vibrated again, Rachel made a beeline for the bathroom, a last line of defense in her mother's busy household.

Rachel slammed the door, flipped the slide bolt, and answered her phone. "Hello?"

Nothing. *Missed Call* popped up on the screen. Evan. "Wriggling cabbage worms," she muttered, using her mother's favorite exclamation when something went wrong. She dialed back, but it went straight to voicemail. He must have tried to give her a quick call between lectures.

She wished she could have answered the phone when she'd felt the first vibration. There were no rules against her having a cell. She wasn't Amish. Not anymore. But her mother disapproved of the phone, and Amanda would have been certain to have reported the call to her. So she'd been a coward and not answered, and now, who knew when Evan could call back?

Rachel slid the phone back in her pocket and opened the bathroom door. She went out, and

Danny rushed in. She returned to the kitchen, wiped down the counters, and tidied up as best she could. When she was certain that all was in place, she drew the white curtains and went out to take the laundry off the clotheslines, a task that should have been completed hours ago. How her mother did it all while raising nine children was more than Rachel could comprehend. And Rachel wasn't cooking nearly as much as her mother usually did. Neighbors were sending over casseroles, pies, hams, and roast chickens almost daily.

When all the clothes were folded and placed securely in the basket, Rachel stood a moment in the soft twilight, gazing over the fields and woods as her mother's favorite orange tabby rubbed against her bare ankles. Taking a deep breath, she let the familiar sounds and scents of the farm seep into her bones. Years ago, all she'd wanted to do was get away, but now the old patterns tugged at her heart. She swallowed, amazed at how easily she'd slipped back into her old life in the past few weeks.

There was peace here. And as much as she loved Stone Mill House and as much as she looked forward to marrying Evan and building her business at her B&B, she had to admit that being here was almost a vacation from her busy schedule. That thought was so crazy that she laughed out loud. A vacation? Caring for her mother, overseeing the house, canning green beans and corn, cooking for her parents and siblings, and keeping track of her brothers should have had her sound asleep before dark. But, strangely, it hadn't. She'd never minded physical labor, and it was fun being part of a large family. It almost made her wonder if she could have been happy remaining Amish and following the path everyone had expected her to.

From the meadow came the *crack* of a bat striking a ball, a dog bark, and excited shouts. Some of her cousins and probably her brothers Danny and Levi were playing ball. If she closed her eyes, she could imagine herself fifteen and there with them. English people believed that the Amish led austere lives, and that the children grew up without playtime. That was far from the truth. She couldn't think of anything sweeter than being an Amish child in the midst of a loving and faith-filled family. Their home had always been a place of prayer and hard work and laughter. She'd never gone to bed hungry or heard her parents argue. Even today, being here on the farm made her feel safe and cherished.

Soon it would be too dark to see the ball, and the kids would scatter to their own homes. Her father expected them in the house by nine for evening prayers and then bed. Morning came early on the farm, and breakfast was at seven, after milking and first chores. It probably wouldn't do her any harm to turn in early either. There were lima beans and late tomatoes to be picked, and the best time to work in the garden was before the sun was high enough to make it hot.

"There's that *kitz*. Your mother was asking where she was." Her father's voice cut through her thoughts. She looked up to see him strolling across the grass from the direction of the barn. He was a tall man with a long-legged stride and a short-cropped beard that was just starting to show streaks of gray. "You know how she is about her children and her cats. Wants to know where they are at bedtime."

Rachel smiled at him. She and her father had always shared a closeness, that in spite of the love she felt for her, her *mam* never experienced with her. Her *dat* was easy. He said what he thought, and he was always tolerant with ideas other than his own. "I imagine she's asleep by now."

"*Ya*, probably is." Her father spoke to her in English, as he usually had when she was growing up. He'd always wanted his children to be comfortable in the outer world, and she was certain that her familiarity with the language had helped her transition from an Amish farm to corporate America. "She looks *goot*, don't you think? Better than after her first round of chemotherapy?"

"Yes, I do," Rachel agreed. "She's going to beat this."

"I think so, too," her father said. "I believe it." He picked up the basket of folded clothes. "I don't have to tell you how much it means to her to have you here helping out while she recovers . . . means to us all."

Rachel shook her head. "You don't have to say it, *Dat*. I know, and I know that she loves me, but . . ." She shrugged. "You know how she is."

He smiled back at her. "And you know why she does it. You were her firstborn, and always dear to her."

"But we've always butted heads."

He chuckled. "And you think we haven't? My *grossmama* warned me, 'That Esther is a Hostetler. She won't be easy to live with for sixty years.' "

"But she's been a good mother," Rachel defended, keeping pace with him as he walked back to the house.

"And a *goot* wife. We're a team. Sometimes she pulls harder, sometimes me, but we pull the load together."

Rachel nodded. "I hope that it will be like that for Evan and me, too."

"He's a *goot* man, that one. For an Englisher. I'd rather he was Amish, but parents don't get to choose. Your mother was just asking me if you'd set a date for your wedding. You've been walking out with him quite a while."

"And I'm not getting any younger?" She said it lightly, but she knew that in her thirties, she was getting a little long in the tooth for a first-time Amish bride.

"I didn't say that."

"But I'll wager *Mam* has said it," Rachel replied with a chuckle. "But to answer your question, no, we haven't set a date. The English have longer engagements than our people. Evan has a friend who's gone with his girlfriend for six years."

"Sounds like a waste of time to me, time that could be spent making a home together, giving me grandchildren."

"Whoa." She laughed, throwing up her hands. "First comes love, then comes marriage. The babies come last, or they should."

Her father carried the basket of clothes into the house and returned to the porch to sit with Rachel. They talked about the day, about crops, about one of her father's cows that was feeling poorly. As evening became night, one by one, the Mast children went into the house, and soon it was time to start thinking about turning in. Everyone was up early on the farm; there was no sleeping in past six for Rachel. There would be breakfast to make, and a dozen other things to do come sunrise.

Her father was just moving toward the kitchen door when he pointed. "Here comes Lettie." He indicated the figure coming up the dark driveway. "Hostetler girls must have let her off at the end of the driveway."

"It's early for her to be home," Rachel remarked, though it was close to ten. Her sister had gone to a singing with some of her cousins. As pretty and popular as Lettie was, it was unusual for her not to ride home with one boy or another. She wasn't serious with anyone yet, but she enjoyed the attention.

"Tell your sister that we're having prayers soon," their father said as he went into the house.

"I will," Rachel promised. "I'm coming, too."

She waited on the back porch for Lettie, but her younger sister seemed self-absorbed and in no mood to share news about her evening. Whatever had caused Lettie's early night, she wasn't talking. The two of them joined the rest of the family in the parlor for a short prayer, and then Lettie went directly up to bed.

But Rachel was wide awake. After her father and siblings had turned in for the night, she went back to the porch and sat in her mother's rocking chair. It was a beautiful night. The September air was still warm; the mosquitoes were almost nonexistent, and the chirp of crickets was comforting. Moonlight tinted the farm-scape in a soft glow, and the quiet was so soothing that she could feel every muscle sighing with pleasure. She knew that when the alarm went off the following morning, she'd wish she'd gone to bed earlier, but it was so nice out here that she couldn't bear to leave just yet.

As it grew later, the stars came out, one by one, bright and clear as they had never been in the city, brighter even than they seemed to her in town in the backyard at Stone Mill House. There was something about a soft September evening that rejuvenated the spirit and enriched the soul.

Minutes passed and then an hour and still she sat, rocking, remembering, and making plans for the future. When her mother had completed her treatments and was well on the way to recovery, Rachel thought, she would find a professional to redesign the website for the craft shop at the B&B. She'd done an okay job with a basic site when she didn't have two pennies to rub together, but the Amish craftsmen and women she supported deserved the best chance to reach the widest market for their creations. A professional-looking, easy-to-navigate website would lead to more sales. Mary Aaron's quilts were museum-quality, and Coyote Finch's pottery deserved a space on the shelves of New York's finest retailers. Of course, her friend Coyote wasn't Amish, but she was local, and Rachel was delighted to have the opportunity to show some of Coyote's hand-thrown pieces.

A shooting star streaked across the sky. Another flash gleamed in the darkness, lower on the horizon. Rachel peered into the night, trying to get a better look. But then she realized that it couldn't be a shooting star. It was too near the ground. She rose from the rocker and walked to the edge of the porch, trying to figure out what it might be. And then she realized that it was a bobbing lantern. Someone was coming across the meadow from the direction of Uncle Aaron's farm.

Rachel was puzzled. It was late. Few Amish were abroad so late. Even courting couples would be home by now. She left the porch and walked across the damp grass toward the source of the light. "Hello?" she called.

"Rae-Rae! I'm so glad you're awake." Her cousin's voice.

"Mary Aaron?" Rachel lowered her voice, not wanting to wake the dogs or disturb her mother, whose bedroom window faced the meadow. "What are you doing out at this hour?"

"Have you seen Elsie? She didn't come home from the singing." Mary Aaron lowered the lantern and set it on the ground. Her face was pale and worried in the yellow glow of the lantern light.

"Lettie was home by ten but that was hours ago." Rachel glanced up at the sky. It had to be after midnight.

"Did she say anything about Elsie? Joanna said she thought Dathan was driving her home."

Rachel shook her head. "She didn't say much at all."

"I just can't imagine where she would be so late. Elsie listens to *Dat*. She should be home by now."

"She and Dathan are getting pretty serious, aren't they? I imagine they just parked somewhere. To talk," Rachel added hastily.

"Not our Elsie. She follows the rules. And you know how our father is. He told her to be home by ten at the latest."

"What did Joanna say? Did she know if Elsie was with Dathan for sure?"

"She didn't see them leave, but John Hannah left after eleven, and he took one of the Stutzman girls home. He didn't see them anywhere on the road."

John Hannah was Elsie's twin and took his obligation to look after his sisters seriously, even though he was at an age when he was cutting a swath through the hearts of the Stone Mill girls.

"Maybe John Hannah just missed them for one reason or another," Rachel said. "They may have had trouble with the buggy or—"

"*Ne*." Mary Aaron's tone was becoming more agitated. "*Dat* sent him out on horseback to retrace the route to the singing. They weren't anywhere, and none of the other boys had seen them. I'm frightened, Rae-Rae. And I have a bad feeling. Elsie isn't late. She's missing."

CHAPTER 2

"I don't think we should panic," Rachel said. "Why don't we take my Jeep and drive the route from your house to where the singing was held? Elsie might have come home while you were walking over here."

"All right," Mary Aaron agreed. "I was hoping that you'd offer. *Dat* is pretty mad, and *Mam* is close to tears. It's just not like Elsie to do anything like this. I've probably bothered you for nothing, but I didn't know what else to do."

"Let me go in and get my shoes and keys to the Jeep," Rachel said. "And it's no trouble. How many times have I needed your help?"

Minutes later the two of them were trudging down the long lane to the road. Rachel kept her vehicle parked across the road in a grove of trees on an old logging trail. The land belonged to her father but was far enough from the house that her mother wouldn't complain about it. She hadn't wanted Rachel's Jeep in the yard, in the shed, or even behind the barn, saying that it set a bad example for the younger children. Rachel knew that if she'd held her ground, she could have parked closer to the house. Her *dat* would have supported her. But it was easier to let her mother have her way. With her *mam*, it was best to pick her battles.

Once in the Jeep, Rachel and Mary Aaron went to Mary Aaron's house, which wasn't far away, being the next farm over. Both Aunt Hannah and Uncle Aaron were up and came out into the yard with a lantern when they arrived. Rachel's aunt was wearing a long nightgown and robe, and her usually pleasant face looked drawn. Her graying hair was hanging down her back and she hadn't bothered to cover it, which normally would have brought criticism from Uncle Aaron. But there had been no sight and no word of the young couple, and her uncle was clearly more concerned about Elsie's whereabouts than his wife covering her head.

"Where's John Hannah?" Mary Aaron asked her mother.

"Putting the horse up." Uncle Aaron was fully dressed, but he'd come out of the house without his hat, an omission that Rachel couldn't remember ever seeing before. Tufts of hair the same shade as his bushy eyebrows stood out from his head. He was a big man, but tonight, he appeared even larger and more imposing.

Whenever the preachers had preached about Moses in the Old Testament, Rachel always pictured Uncle Aaron, with his long white beard and forbidding countenance, denouncing the sins of the Israelites. He was a good man and she'd always loved him, but many found him difficult and taciturn. And when it came to his children, Uncle Aaron was definitely a strict father. Rachel's own mother, Esther, was one of the few people who went out of their way to spend time with him. Rachel could see the state her uncle was in tonight, and she almost felt sorry for her cousin Elsie.

"Elsie told Joanna that Dathan was bringing her home," Aunt Hannah explained, referring to one of Mary Aaron's other sisters. "And John Hannah said the two of them left long before he did. I don't know what could have happened to them."

"Whatever the reason is," Uncle Aaron said, "that Dathan Bender's excuse had best be a *goot* one. He'll be fortunate if I don't take a horsewhip to him for keeping our Elsie out so late."

"Elsie's a sensible girl," Rachel soothed. "I'm sure this is all just a misunderstanding." She doubted that her uncle would harm Dathan; the Amish were nonviolent. But with Uncle Aaron, you never knew. "Maybe the wagon threw a wheel or the horse went lame," she suggested.

Her uncle scowled at her in the lantern light. "She'd have had time to walk to the Troyers' and back three times by now."

"It won't hurt for us to double-check their route

home." Mary Aaron glanced meaningfully at Rachel and then back at her parents. "We'll be back soon," she promised.

They climbed back into the Jeep, and Rachel drove cautiously out of her uncle's farmyard. \ The home where the singing had been held wasn't far away. They passed only one vehicle and no Amish buggies on the twisting country roads. When they reached the Troyer place, all was dark and quiet. Rachel stopped halfway up the lane and listened. There were no lights and no voices coming from the house or yard. If anyone was still awake, they were already in bed. "I don't see any reason to bother them," Rachel said. "I think we'd better check the spots where boys like to park."

Mary Aaron frowned. "Elsie wouldn't go there. She's not that kind of girl."

A dog began to bark, and Rachel grimaced as she backed carefully out of the lane. "Elsie thinks she's in love with Dathan, doesn't she? Under the right circumstances, we're all that kind of girl."

They drove to Allen's Pond and found two buggies parked there by the edge of the water. One held a young married couple who'd stopped to listen to forbidden country-and-western music and find privacy from a crowded multi-generational household. The other buggy concealed a young man from another church district. His date remained in the buggy and didn't show her face, while he assured Mary Aaron that he hadn't seen Dathan or Elsie, and neither had he seen any wagons on the road tonight.

"Where could they be?" Mary Aaron exclaimed to Rachel as they returned to the blacktop road. "They couldn't have just vanished. Maybe we should go to Dathan's house."

"I was thinking that," Rachel agreed. "But we'll check out the old schoolhouse on our way. I've seen buggies parked there pretty late when I was coming home from Evan's." She glanced at Mary Aaron. "Seat belt."

"*Ya, ya,* will do."

Seat belts were an issue when Amish rode with her in her Jeep. Rachel was adamant, but most of them couldn't see the need. "It's all in God's hands," was the usual argument. Even Mary Aaron tried that one when she thought she might get away with it.

"I think we're all making too much of this," Rachel said. She kept her speed down so that she could scan both sides of the road. "Who hasn't gotten into trouble with their parents for coming in too late?"

"Elsie."

"There's always a first time," Rachel countered.

The Bender farm was farther away, near Bear Ridge. According to Mary Aaron, Dathan lived with a widowed mother, and a married sister and her husband. When they pulled up to the house, Rachel saw a light on in the kitchen. Mary Aaron was just getting out of the Jeep when an Amish woman with a crying baby in her arms opened the back door.

"What do you want?" she called in heavily accented English.

Mary Aaron answered her in *Deitsch*. "Sorry to bother you this late, but we were looking for Dathan. Is he here?"

"*Ne.* He didn't come home tonight. He's not come to harm, has he?"

"*Ne.* Not as far as we know." Mary Aaron went up to the door, introduced herself, and asked another question. Rachel couldn't quite hear her or the answer that the woman gave because they'd lowered their voices. After a brief exchange, her cousin returned to the Jeep. "Not much help there," she said as she slid back into the seat beside Rachel. "That was Dathan's older sister, Agnes. Apparently he stays at one of his friend's houses sometimes after a frolic because it's so far out here. She said she didn't know which buddy, but she didn't seem too concerned that he hadn't come home."

"So she wasn't sitting up waiting for him?" Rachel asked.

Mary Aaron shook her head. "She probably knew who Dathan usually stays with but didn't want to say." She shrugged. "She wasn't too friendly. Said her baby's cutting teeth and she hasn't had a wink of sleep."

Rachel knew that the Benders belonged to a different Old Order Amish Church community, and they weren't a family Mary Aaron knew well.

"It just doesn't make sense," Mary Aaron said, buckling her seat belt again. "I don't know what to do now. Maybe we should check that logging road off Noah's Creek. Tim wanted me to go there with him once."

Tim was Mary Aaron's steady, or at least he had been. Rachel hadn't seen much of Tim in the last few months, and Mary Aaron had resisted any questions about the state of their relationship. "Did you go with him?"

"None of your business, Cousin. It's enough that I know that spot and the best way to get there."

The idea had proved promising. When they got there, Rachel saw the light of a campfire and several figures gathered around it. But there were no wagons and no Elsie. A group of English teen boys had pitched a tent and were sitting around the fire drinking soda pop and grilling hot dogs. None of the boys had seen an Amish couple in a wagon or anyone else since they'd set up camp before dark.

"I think we should go back to your house and see if Elsie is there yet," Rachel suggested. "She probably is, but if she isn't, I think we should get John Hannah to show us where his friends go with their girlfriends. He's closer in age to Dathan, and he probably knows all the hot spots."

"My father won't be pleased to hear you say that," Mary Aaron replied.

"I don't suppose he will." Rachel yawned and rubbed the corner of one eye. She was beginning to be genuinely concerned for Elsie. Even if her absence was innocent, she'd be in a huge amount of trouble with her parents. "Maybe we should have wakened someone at the Troyers'."

"Maybe," Mary Aaron hedged, "but I doubt we would have learned any more." She looked at the clock on the dashboard. "It's awful late. I've got a bad feeling, Rae-Rae. What if Elsie's come across bad men?"

"Elsie has Dathan with her. Wherever they are, it's their own doing, not someone else's. If something bad had happened, we'd know it by now." Rachel hesitated, then asked the question that had been on her mind for the last hour. "You don't think there's a chance they could have run off together, do you?"

"Run off how? You mean, to leave? To be English? It's not possible. You know how Elsie is. She's like *Dat*. She's the stuff of martyrs. You could burn Elsie at the stake and she wouldn't give up her faith."

"We'll probably find her there in your kitchen," Rachel said, although she was beginning to have her doubts. *Pray God she is,* Rachel thought.

But she wasn't.

When they reached Mary Aaron's, Elsie's twin, John Hannah, was sitting on the back step. Of all of her cousins, John Hannah was Rachel's favorite after Mary Aaron. He was sweet and sensitive, and he had a real head for figures. Although he wasn't the eldest son or the youngest, Rachel was sure he would be the one who ended up taking over his father's farm when it was time to pass the property from one generation to the next.

"Get in the Jeep," Rachel said to John Hannah. "We need you."

When she explained, he quickly agreed to go with them, and the three of them drove to several places that John Hannah knew, including the old quarry, a lonely and foreboding place at night. But each stop proved as futile as the schoolyard had been. There was no wagon and no Dathan and Elsie. And after another hour of driving around, Rachel took her cousins back home.

Her uncle came out to the Jeep. He looked even worse than when she'd seen him earlier. "Time all of you got to your own beds," he said brusquely. "Whatever mischief Elsie has gotten herself into, she'll have to pay the consequences."

Mary Aaron said, "I think we should call the police."

Rachel inhaled sharply. This would not be well

received. Her uncle didn't like Englishers, and he liked the English authorities even less.

"*Ne*, we'll not call the police. Do you want to shame our family? Bad enough that your sister has no regard for her reputation. Her I will deal with when she comes sneaking home. You have done all you can for one night."

"*Dat*," John Hannah began.

"Is there something wrong with your hearing?" Uncle Aaron demanded. "Or have you forgotten who is the head of this house?"

Without another word, Mary Aaron's brother got out of the Jeep and went into the house. Mary Aaron climbed out of the back. "Thank you," she whispered to Rachel.

"Let me know when she gets back," Rachel urged. "I don't care what time it is."

"I will," Mary Aaron promised. "I'll send one of the boys to wake you."

Uncle Aaron stopped with his foot on the first step of the porch and glanced back over his shoulder. "Mary Aaron. Are you coming?"

"*Ya, Dat*. I am," she said quickly.

Rachel caught a glimpse of her aunt's pale face at the kitchen window. *Please, God, let Elsie be all right,* she prayed silently. *And have pity on her when she gets home.*

When the rooster outside of Rachel's window woke her early the next morning, it took a superhuman effort to get out of bed and dress. It had been so late when she'd snuck into the house, and then she'd lain awake listening to the clock ring out the darkest hours. She thought she'd be wide-eyed until dawn, but she'd fallen off sometime around four a.m. Now she could barely get her eyes open.

Her first lucid thought was of Elsie. Surely her cousin had gotten home by now. If she hadn't . . . Rachel tried to shake off her apprehension. Yawning, she hurried to get downstairs. She could hear voices from the kitchen, so she knew that her family was already up ahead of her.

Her mother and father were seated at the table drinking coffee. Her *mam*, fully dressed down to her starched *kapp*, was directing the preparation of breakfast from her chair. Her mother's complexion was pale and waxy, but her eyes were bright. She glanced up at Rachel and gave a small nod of acknowledgment.

" 'Morning, *Mam*," Rachel said in *Deitsch*. "*Dat*." She greeted her three sisters in turn, and they murmured a reply. Lettie was frying bacon and flipping pancakes, while Sally put out the dishes and silverware and Amanda slid lopsided biscuits off a baking stone into a bread basket.

"A good morning to you," her father said warmly.

Danny and Levi came in the back door, hair

and faces damp from where they'd washed up at the outside faucet after morning milking and feeding the livestock. Danny was grinning as he took a place at the main table. Rachel lingered by the door, wondering if she should ask about Elsie but not certain she should say anything about her absence last night. "Has anyone been here for me this morning?" Rachel asked.

Her father shook his head. "*Ne*. Not today. But it's early for company."

"Girls?" her mother said, clapping her hands together once, her signal to eat.

Amanda carried the biscuits to the table and slid onto the back bench. Lettie brought the bacon and eggs. Sally placed the pancakes in front of her mother. Rachel noticed that she'd forgotten the maple syrup and retrieved it from the cabinet, before taking her own place at the smaller table near the window, where Sally and Levi joined her. Their *dat* closed his eyes and lowered his head for silent grace. Rachel did the same, trying not to feel annoyed that, in spite of Levi and Sally's support, she was still technically isolated from the family.

In most Amish homes, she was invited to sit with everyone else. Even at Uncle Aaron's home, her aunt bent the rules and insisted she join the family at the main table. But here, in her mother's house, she was forced to be separate from her parents because she had left the church and become part of the world. It was the reason her mother wouldn't speak to her, and it rubbed like a pebble in her shoe. Strictly speaking, the ban shouldn't apply to her, because she'd never been baptized, never joined the faith. She should have been no different from any English guest. But after all these years, her mother still hoped and prayed that she would return to the fold. Refusing to eat with her and avoiding speaking directly to her were her mother's arsenal in the silent war between them.

Her father, she knew, would not have been so strict. He spoke to her. He invited her to eat with him when her mother was in the hospital or away. But by Amish tradition, at least here in Stone Mill, the house was her mother's domain, and her father would not contest her decisions. "Amen," he said aloud.

Rachel tried to calm her fears about Elsie as breakfast proceeded with the usual discussion of the day's activities and the state of the garden. Unlike many Amish households, mealtimes were family time, and everyone chimed in with tidbits of news and teasing exchanges. Rachel was pouring syrup on her second pancake when her cell phone vibrated in her apron pocket. She slipped a hand under the table and slid it out. Levi, who never missed a trick, nudged her ankle with the toe of his shoe and grinned. She scanned the caller's number and kicked him back in the ankle. The number wasn't one she knew, so she put the phone back.

"Daughter?"

This time it was Sally who kicked her foot. Rachel realized that her father was speaking to her and looked up expectantly.

"Your mother wants to know if you'll be available to help with the canning this afternoon."

"I think so," she answered. So long as Elsie had turned up and Mary Aaron or her aunt and uncle didn't need her. "I do have to pick up that prescription for her in town." That would give her an opportunity to stop by Stone Mill House and see that Hulda and Ada had everything under control at the B&B. Hulda had been a lifesaver in offering to take the reins at the business while Rachel was here at the farm. Otherwise, she would have had to cancel guests' reservations, and fall was a busy time.

"Tell your daughter that we need to do more tomatoes," her mother said to her father. Rachel's father nodded patiently. He was used to this. They all were.

"Whatever she wants," Rachel said, without waiting for her father to repeat her mother's statement. "*Ya,* I'll be glad to." She didn't really mind canning. Sewing had always been her least-favorite chore in the house. As the oldest girl in a family of eleven, there had been a lot of clothing to make and a lot of trousers and skirts to hem and patch.

Her cell vibrated again.

Maybe it was Evan, Rachel thought. Meals in the Mast household were not to be interrupted, but this might be an emergency. Rachel deliberately swept her nearly empty glass of apple juice into her lap. "*Atch*," she exclaimed, wiping at her skirt. "See what I did." Amanda started to get up, but Rachel waved her back to her seat. "*Ne*, sister, I can get it." Rising, she mopped at the table, excused herself, and hurried to the bathroom.

The cell had stopped vibrating, but there was a message. It's me. Call me back at this number. Rachel punched in the number, and Mary Aaron answered at once. "I didn't know you had a phone," Rachel said. Cell phones were definitely on the *not allowed* list in their church community.

"I don't. I borrowed this one from John Hannah. Can you come over right away?"

Rachel's stomach clenched. "Elsie's not home, is she?" Rachel kept her voice low.

"*Ne*, and I don't know what to do. *Dat*'s sure she has run off with Dathan. He's furious. Says he's through with her. Whatever she's done, it's on her head. But *Mam*'s been crying her eyes out. She wants to call the police, but he won't let her."

"Did you check at Dathan's house again? Maybe his mother—"

"*Ne*. She doesn't know anything," Mary Aaron said. "John Hannah rode over there at six thirty this morning. She's worried sick. And she says the same thing."

Rachel tried not to think about all the young women who disappeared in the United States each year . . . women who had never been heard from again. "What about his sister?"

"She agrees with their mother. Claims Dathan would never run away. They're afraid something bad has happened to the two of them. I think we should go back to the Troyers'. Someone must know something."

"I agree. Let me get things settled here. I haven't said anything to the family yet."

"You might as well. You know the Amish telegraph. It will be all over the valley by now. Can you pick me up at the end of our lane in half an hour? I'd rather *Dat* didn't know I was going. That way he can't forbid me to leave." "Amish telegraph" was the uncanny way the Plain people from one end of the valley to another seemed to pass on news quickly without the aid of phones.

"I'll be there," Rachel promised. The bad feeling she'd had earlier was getting worse by the moment.

When she reentered the kitchen, her father and the boys had already finished eating and gone out to the barn. Amanda was clearing the table. Her mother and Sally were nowhere in sight.

Lettie had gathered up the napkins and dish towels into a laundry basket. Rachel took hold of Lettie's arm, put a finger to her lips to signal silence, and pulled her onto the back porch.

"What is it?" Lettie asked.

"Keep your voice down," Rachel warned. "Did you see Elsie and Dathan at the singing?"

"There were a lot of people there. I don't really remember."

"But she rode there with you and Joanna, didn't she?"

Lettie nodded. "*Ya*, but I wasn't keeping track of her. You know how it is; we all scatter once we get to a singing."

"And you said that she and Dathan left before you and Joanna?" Rachel pressed.

Her sister shrugged. "I think so, but I'm not sure. Elsie runs around with a different crowd."

" 'Runs around'?" Rachel studied her sister. There was something about Lettie's expression that made her think she was the one getting the runaround. "I had the idea that Elsie was something of a goody-goody."

"She is. Usually she sits with the older women in church. And she never plays any of the barn games at the frolics. Joanna says Elsie says they're too close to dancing."

"So you didn't see anything odd, nothing that would make you think that Elsie was nervous or upset about anything?"

Lettie's pretty cheeks glowed pink as she frowned. "Why all these questions about Elsie? Is she in trouble?"

"I hope not," Rachel answered. "I'll tell you, but you can't tell anyone else."

"I won't."

"I mean it, Lettie." Rachel held up her finger. "Not a word."

"You can trust me. I'm not a total loss as a sister."

Rachel smiled at her. "*Ne*, you're not a total loss. But I don't want to make this worse for Elsie, so it's important that we keep it hush-hush."

"I'll be as quiet as a fence post," Lettie promised.

"Elsie never got home last night, and no one knows where she is."

Lettie's eyes widened. "She didn't? What does Dathan say?"

"That's the thing," Rachel said. "He didn't get home last night either. They're both missing. And if Elsie doesn't show up soon, I'm going to the police."

CHAPTER 3

Two dogs ran back and forth in a wire enclosure and barked as Rachel drove up the Troyer lane and parked near the back door of the large, white frame house. A girl, about nine years old, got up off the porch and darted into the house, carrying a toddler. Rachel made certain that her head scarf was in place as she got out of the Jeep. She didn't know this family, and hoped that they were friendly.

In the farmyard, a stocky young man climbed a ladder propped against a windmill. Mary Aaron gestured in his direction. "That's Titus," Mary Aaron said to Rachel. She waved to Titus and he waved back. "I know him from the farmers' market. He's a friend of Dathan's."

A middle-aged Amish man with a mass of curly beard pushed open a screen door, stepped out of the house, and pulled up his suspenders. He was barefoot and not wearing a hat. There was a towel around his shoulders, and Rachel suspected someone had been cutting his hair when they arrived.

" 'Morning," he called. Behind him, Rachel noticed a woman in a dark scarf peering through the kitchen window.

"Asa Troyer?" Rachel asked in *Deitsch* as she approached the porch. Mary Aaron had already shared the names of Titus's parents with her. "I'm Rachel—"

"Know who you are," Asa replied in the same dialect. "You're Elsie's sister, aren't you?" he asked Mary Aaron.

She said that she was. "I suppose you've heard that she and Dathan never got home last night?"

Asa nodded. "Heard that. Don't know what to think about it. I know your parents must be worried. And Dathan's mother. Not like him to do something foolish." He came down the steps into the yard. "I expect you're looking for them."

"We are," Rachel said. "We don't want to bother you, but we were hoping you could give us some information."

The dogs kept up a loud barking, and Asa shouted at them, "Quiet!" When they quieted down, he turned his attention back to Rachel. "Don't know what I can tell you that you don't already know. Big crowd here last night. Wife and I were outside for the singing, but after, we went back into the house. Some young people went home; the rest moved out to the pasture for a bonfire." He spread his hands in a gesture of finality. "Nothing out of the ordinary."

The woman whom Rachel had seen through the window came out to join them. She was a head shorter than her husband but was as stocky as her son. Rachel recognized her from the farmers' market as well. "Arlene."

"Rachel Mast. Mary Aaron." Asa's wife's voice was small and squeaky for such a hearty body. She seemed more reserved than her husband, but Rachel had never heard any negative gossip about her and thought her probably shy rather than standoffish.

The door opened again, and a girl peeked through.

"We're trying to find out anything we can about Elsie and Dathan's behavior last night," Rachel explained.

Arlene removed wire-framed glasses and cleaned them on her apron. "My Titus is a good boy. Never caused us any trouble. And his friends are good kids, too."

"Did either of you go out to the bonfire?" Rachel said.

"Didn't see any need to." Asa gestured toward a pasture behind the house. Rachel could see a blackened ring and some smoldering logs and assumed that was the remains of the fire. "All them out there are of age to know right from wrong. And like I said, Titus is trustworthy."

"Could we talk to Titus?" she asked. "I know he's working, but I'll be quick."

"No reason not to," Asa replied. "Mary Aaron, you tell your father and mother that we're praying for them."

"I will," Mary Aaron answered. "And I hope you will keep this private, at least until we find them."

Asa's wife folded her arms. "Not in a habit of gossiping about other folks' troubles." She glanced toward the windmill. "Don't keep Titus long. And I pray you'll find the both of them safe." She went back into the house and her husband followed. The dogs took up their yapping, and Arlene shouted at them through the screen, "Hush up!"

Rachel and Mary Aaron crossed to the foot of the windmill. "Could you come down for a minute?" Mary Aaron called.

A barefooted boy whom Rachel guessed was a little younger than her brother Levi came around the corner of the barn, leading a gray mule by the halter. He stopped just within earshot and watched his brother climb down the ladder.

"Ussi, get me a drink of water," Titus ordered. "Just tie Whitey to the back of the wagon. And make certain the rope is knotted tight. Last time, you let him get into *Mam*'s garden and she blamed me for being careless."

Ussi made a face but did as he'd been told. Once he was far enough away that he couldn't hear the conversation, Titus looked at Mary Aaron. "Guess you're looking for your sister."

"We are," Rachel said. "Did anything unusual happen at the singing last night?"

49

"You mean, did anybody know Dathan and Elsie were going to run away together?" Titus asked.

"What makes you think they ran away?" Mary Aaron put in.

He shrugged. "Where else could they be? They didn't just vanish with his brother-in-law's horse and wagon, did they?"

"Did they come together?" Rachel asked. She knew better, but she wanted to hear Titus tell it in his own words. "To the singing?" Titus's light brown hair was neatly cut in a longish shag, barely acceptable to most bishops. He was a nice-looking boy in spite of his receding chin, and he was well dressed for working on a windmill. She was sure he was popular among the other young people. He was bound to know something.

"Elsie's always been kind of quiet. Him, too," Titus said, not answering her question. "But Dathan and I have been pals since we were kids. They're the last two I'd expect to go English, but you never know, do you?"

Ussi returned with a quart jar of water. Titus drained half of it in two long gulps, removed his straw hat, and poured the remainder over his head. He handed the mason jar back to his brother.

"Sorry. Did they come together?" Rachel pressed.

"I don't know. Doubt it. But I know they left together. Saw them go."

"What time was that?"

He exhaled loudly. "I don't know. I wasn't checking my pocket watch. Nine, maybe? It was dark. But not late. I know that."

"Can you tell me anything else you remember about them?" Mary Aaron urged. "Even something you wouldn't think would be important. It could be a big help to us."

Titus glanced at his little brother. "What are you waiting for? Get that mule hitched up to the mower. They didn't come to talk to you."

"But she said that anything we know could be a help to finding them." Ussi rubbed the ball of one foot into the dirt and glanced up at Rachel through mischievous brown eyes.

Rachel took a harder look at him. "That's right," she agreed. "Is there anything you could tell us?"

"He doesn't know anything. He wasn't anywhere near the singing or the bonfire," Titus said. He waved toward the mule, who was chewing steadily at the rope. "Go get that animal before we have to end up chasing him."

"Was too," the boy corrected.

"If you snuck out of the house to spy on us, you'd be in big trouble with *Dat* and *Mam*," Titus warned. "Maybe I should say something to them. For your own good." He took a step toward Ussi, and the boy reluctantly returned to tend to the mule. "He's a real pest," Titus said. "That's one my mother needs to quit spoiling and take a switch to."

"Are you sure there isn't something that you remember?" Rachel asked. "Something they might have said or anything that would make you take notice?"

"They oughta be talking to Rupert Rust," Ussi called.

"What did I tell you?" Titus said. "Do you want me to speak to *Dat*?"

Ussi muttered something under his breath and led the mule away.

"Little brothers," Titus exclaimed with a shrug. "But there is one thing I can tell you. Early in the evening, Elsie and Dathan had a disagreement. Dathan got a little loud, and somebody shushed him so my mother wouldn't hear. But I'm sure it was nothing. You know how couples are. They fight and make up. It must have blown over quick enough, because one of the girls said that Dathan had told her he wanted to marry Elsie and they were trying to figure out a way to get Elsie's father to give his permission."

"Who was it that told you that?" Rachel asked.

"I'm not sure. It was later, at the fire, and there were a lot of girls there. Probably not worth mentioning, because everybody knew he was serious over her, but you said anything."

"Did you hear what the argument was about?" Mary Aaron asked.

"*Ne*, but by the time they left, it was all patched up."

Rachel considered that. "You're certain they'd made up?"

Titus shrugged again. "I guess. I wasn't really paying attention to Elsie and Dathan." He glanced at Mary Aaron for confirmation. "You know how it is at a frolic. Noisy. Lots of teasing and horseplay."

"Did Elsie and Dathan come to the fire?" Mary Aaron asked.

"I don't remember seeing them there, but it was dark." He looked up at the windmill blades. A breeze was picking up, and they were beginning to spin faster. "I need to get those bolts tightened before the whole thing sails away," Titus said. "I'm sorry this happened, but you can bet the two of them are fine. They probably ran off together. What are the chances that your father would welcome Dathan as a son-in-law?"

"Not good," Mary Aaron admitted.

"I suppose that's the most logical explanation," Rachel said, hating to think that was the answer, but almost hoping, at this point, that it was. "That they ran away. But it just doesn't seem like something Elsie would do."

"It isn't," Mary Aaron insisted.

"Sorry I can't be of more help." Titus picked up his tool belt and put one hand on the ladder.

"Thank you for talking to us," Rachel said. "We'll let you get back to your work."

"So, what now?" Mary Aaron asked when they reached the main road again.

"We go back to your house and hope for the best."

Mary Aaron looked as though she might cry. "And if they aren't there? What then? Tomorrow's visiting Sunday, and word will spread through the whole valley. Elsie's reputation will be ruined."

"Maybe not." Rachel kept her eyes on the road. There were a lot of potholes along this stretch, and she didn't want a flat. And there were more deer than usual this year. Even in the daytime, they would run across the road. "Maybe your father is right. Maybe they did run off and they're sitting somewhere eating pizza and drinking root beer and planning a wedding."

Mary Aaron covered her face with her hands.

Rachel reached over and patted her cousin's knee. "I'm going to have to tell my parents."

"That's fine. They should know." Mary Aaron hugged herself. "Rae-Rae, I'm so scared. What do we do if they're still missing?"

"What do you want to do?" Rachel asked.

"What I wanted to do when she didn't come home last night. Call the police."

Two hours later, Rachel stood beside Trooper Lucy Mars's patrol car in the shadow of her B&B, Stone Mill House. Lucy was a tall, slim woman in her late twenties, with the sleek look of an Olympic swimmer. Her well-scrubbed face was devoid of makeup and her sandy-blond hair cut in a stylish pixie. Rachel considered herself of more than average height for a woman, but Lucy Mars, in her Pennsylvania State Police uniform, boots, and hat, topped her by nearly a head.

When Rachel and Mary Aaron had gotten back to Uncle Aaron's farm from the Troyers', they had found what Rachel had feared. Elsie still hadn't appeared. Rachel and Mary Aaron had made a final effort to convince her uncle that there might be a real reason for concern and that they should call the authorities. And as usual, their arguments fell on deaf ears. Uncle Aaron was nothing if not consistent.

Mary Aaron had asked Rachel to drive her to the B&B. Rachel agreed that they weren't getting anywhere on their own, and it was time to call in professional help. Trooper Mars had come to Stone Mill House, and Rachel and her cousin had spent the last twenty minutes stating their case.

"I'll do what I can," Trooper Mars said as she made final notations in a little notebook. "But honestly, Elsie Hostetler hasn't been missing for twenty-four hours, and both she and her boyfriend are over twenty-one. I can certainly make inquiries. Check hospitals, accident reports, that sort of thing. I know this isn't what you want to hear, but I think you'll find that this is another case of Old Order Amish just walking away from the life. The outside world is a big draw. You can't really blame them for wanting to experience it."

"If it wasn't Elsie, I might be inclined to believe that," Rachel said. "But as Mary Aaron told you, neither she nor Dathan are the type to run off. And if they had run away, would they take the horse and wagon with them? A horse and wagon belonging to someone else? They didn't drive over the mountain to the highway in the wagon, did they?"

Trooper Mars looked unconvinced. "I don't know where the wagon is. It could be anywhere. It could be in someone's barn or carriage shed. They probably just caught a ride out of town; you know how it's done." She looked meaningfully at Rachel.

Rachel shook her head. "It simply doesn't make sense."

"I understand your concern, but just last spring we had a complaint from an Amish mother that two Englishers in a car had forcibly kidnapped her son. Once we investigated and located the young man, we found that he *had* been picked up at the crossroad in a car. But he had planned to leave, already had a job waiting for him and a place to live. The supposed *kidnappers* were two ex-Amish boys he used to work with on a construction crew." She tucked her notebook in the breast pocket of her uniform. "I don't want to sound unsympathetic. But I know you know there's a whole network of ex-Amish across the country dedicated to helping young people leave the order and acclimate themselves to twenty-first-century life."

Rachel didn't say anything.

Trooper Mars hesitated and then went on. "I didn't mean that as disrespectful," she said. "The Amish are good people, a credit to our community and state, but they certainly can't be called main-stream."

"No," Rachel said. "They aren't, and I'm sorry if I took offense where none was meant. It's just that I've heard a lot of disparaging remarks by outsiders who don't know them. Most outsiders think the Amish are quaint, great subjects for postcards and drawing tourists, but not quite as bright as the English."

"As I said, I'll do what I can to find your cousin." Trooper Mars removed her hat. "I've got your cell number."

"And you can get me at the B&B number we gave you," Mary Aaron said. "Or leave me a message. I'm here several days a week."

Trooper Mars nodded her assent. "Do you mind if I ask why you're dressed Amish?"

"My parents are Amish, and I've been staying with them while my mother has chemo treatments. It's just easier to dress this way around them."

"I'm sorry, I didn't mean to pry." She looked younger without the trooper hat. "I just knew you weren't Amish."

"No, but I was raised Amish," Rachel explained.

"My family are all from this valley, and they've all remained in the church. But I'm one of those who wasn't content with the life. I wanted to experience the outside world."

"But you came back to Stone Mill."

"I came home, yes. But I never joined the faith. You have to be baptized to be one of them. I spent seventeen years living the American dream, and then I came back. I wanted to feel some of the security and the peace that I knew as a child. I went to Wharton and worked in finance, but I'm happier here than I ever was out there." Rachel hesitated, then went on. "You work with Evan Parks, don't you?"

"Detective Parks?" She nodded. "I do."

"Evan and I are engaged to be married."

"So you're the Rachel he talks about. I'm sorry, right. I just didn't put two and two together. The long skirt threw me off." She chuckled. "I have the greatest respect for your—for Detective Parks. I admire him. Being picked for the Homeland Security course will be a feather in his cap."

"One of the reasons that I came home to Stone Mill, other than the personal reasons, was to try to help the valley by encouraging tourism and making this a welcoming place for small businesses. If we can create jobs and a strong economic base, we can keep our young people from moving away." Rachel gestured at her Plain attire. "This makes it easier to interact with the conservative members of the Amish community, sometimes. It's not my normal business attire."

"I understand."

Rachel didn't know if she did. She doubted if the young trooper had ever had experience with the Old Order Amish until she'd transferred to Stone Mill. And her people could certainly be difficult to understand if you were a stranger. "Are you going to ask around about Elsie and Dathan's disappearance?" she asked.

"Yes, I can do that. If I don't get any calls, I could stop and speak with Elsie's parents this afternoon. And the boy's family, of course."

"You may find it difficult to get cooperation," Mary Aaron said. "We Amish can be a little standoffish with Englishers."

"I'm not English," Trooper Mars replied. "I'm Swedish and Ukrainian, or rather my grandparents were. Not an Englishman in the bunch."

Rachel smiled. "Around here, if you aren't *Deitsch*, you're English. I'd be glad to come with you, if you'd like. It would be easier. The Amish don't like to be questioned."

"No, thank you, that's not necessary." Trooper Mars got in the cruiser, which she'd left running. "Please call the troop if Miss Hostetler contacts her family or comes home."

"We will," Rachel promised her. "But you have my number. Don't hesitate to call if you need me."

"I'll be fine," Trooper Mars assured her.

Rachel watched as the officer went down the driveway, then spotted Ada coming across the grass with a laundry basket of clean kitchen towels she'd just taken off the line.

"You best check on the girls, Mary Aaron. Those rooms need to be ready. Lazy as toads, both of them."

Mary Aaron nodded and headed for the back door.

The girls in question were two of Ada's nieces and not lazy, at least by English standards. Rachel knew better than to touch that either. "Is Hulda still in the office?" she asked Ada.

"*Ne*. She had to run next door for something. Some problem with that useless grandson of hers."

"Which one?" Rachel asked.

Ada shrugged. "Does it matter? None of them worth their salt." She shifted the wicker basket of towels to her other hip. "That English police going to find Elsie?"

"She said she's going to try."

"Going to talk to our people?" Ada's dour expression showed plainly what she thought of the whole business.

"*Ya*."

"She taking you with her?"

Rachel shook her head. "Said she would be fine."

"Good luck with that."

CHAPTER 4

The Mast family was just finishing supper when a Pennsylvania State Police car pulled into the yard. "Whoever is that?" Esther said. "It's not Evan, is it?"

Rachel rose to her feet and went to the window. "*Ne, Mam.* It's a woman officer."

"A woman policeman?" her mother remarked to her husband. "Samuel. *Vas* is this? Why would an Englisher police come to our house?"

"I'll go." Rachel's pulse quickened as she rose from her chair. *Did Trooper Mars have word of Elsie? Was it good news or bad?*

"Could be she's looking for someone," Rachel's father said. "If she doesn't know the valley, she could be lost." He motioned to Rachel's brothers and sisters. "Stay in your places. Finished we are not with our meal."

"This is Rachel's trouble," her mother said, taking a bite of biscuit. "Count on it. Always, to our door, she brings the world."

Rachel grimaced. She wanted to protest that this wasn't her fault, but she still hadn't told her parents that Elsie was missing. It was easier just to leave it until she knew what Trooper Mars had to say. Rachel hurried out of the kitchen to the back porch. The policewoman was walking toward her.

"Good. I wasn't sure that I had the right house," Lucy said.

"Did you find out anything?" Rachel called.

Lucy shook her head.

Rachel glanced back over her shoulder toward the house. "I'd rather not involve my family," she said to the trooper. "Could we speak at your car?"

"Certainly."

Trooper Mars still carried herself purposefully, but Rachel thought that the woman lacked some of her earlier confidence. "I don't have anything new," she confided when they had walked away from the porch. "I went to the Bender home, but I couldn't find anyone to question. It was the strangest thing. I saw a woman watching from an upstairs window, but no one would open the door to me."

Rachel nodded. That was the response that many of her people gave to the English, especially to the authorities. "The Amish are shy around strangers," she said. "It's what I warned you about." She could have added that where police were concerned, some Amish were almost para-noid. But that was probably more information than the trooper needed.

Lucy Mars frowned. "When I turned off the

road, into the driveway, I was sure I saw a man cutting wood. I even heard it through my open window. But when I got to the house, he was gone. There was a clothesline and a clothes basket on the grass beneath it. Only half the clothes remained on the line, the others in the basket. It's as though they all ran when I pulled in. Extremely suspicious behavior for a family expecting a missing member to reappear. I can't help but suspect they're hiding something."

Rachel sighed. "Surely you've had people refuse to open the door for you before?"

"That's true, but I guess I wasn't expecting it from such religious people."

"It's complicated. Amish people don't trust Englishers they don't know. And they don't trust me as much as they do Mary Aaron because I left them for the outside world."

Trooper Mars removed her aviator sunglasses. "I came to ask for your help, Ms. Mast."

"Please. Call me Rachel."

She nodded. "I want to go back to the Benders' and I'd like you to go with me. I've got questions for them. Otherwise, I can't help you. I'm walking on thin ice here, as it is. My desk sergeant thinks it's all a wild goose chase, that this is nothing more than another young Amish couple who didn't want to live in the sixteenth century."

"I'll be glad to go with you. Let me just tell my parents that I'm leaving."

Trooper Mars nodded and got into her cruiser to wait.

Rachel returned to the house for her shoes. "*Mam, Dat*," she said from the kitchen doorway. "I have to go out. Trooper Mars needs my help to speak to some of our people."

Amanda rolled her eyes.

"Can I come with you?" Sally asked.

"You certainly may not." Their mother fanned her pale face with a napkin. "Samuel, ask your daughter if she's being arrested again."

"Rachel—" he began.

Rachel moved to the table and gazed over it to look directly into her mother's eyes. "I'm not getting *arrested*. I didn't want to tell you before because I didn't want to worry you, but Elsie never came home from the frolic last night. Both she and Dathan are missing."

Amanda gasped.

Lettie clapped a hand over her mouth. "Missing?"

Their mother turned to Lettie. "Well, where are they?"

"I don't know," Lettie protested. "I thought they'd just stayed out late. I didn't know she didn't get home at all."

"None of us knows where they are," Rachel said, trying to hold her temper. "That's why they're missing."

Her mother looked at her father. "I don't

understand, Samuel. What is your daughter trying to tell us?"

"Rachel, your mother wants to know—"

"I heard her, *Dat*," Rachel interrupted. "And she heard me. Elsie and Dathan left the frolic and vanished. No one has seen or heard from them since last night. And wherever they went, they apparently took the horse and wagon with them. Trooper Mars is helping search for them."

Her mother dropped back into her chair. "Have mercy," she managed. "Poor Hannah."

"I'm going with the policewoman to question Dathan's family," Rachel explained to her father. "I'll be back as soon as I can."

Her *dat* nodded. "Of course. You must help. Don't worry about us. We'll manage here." He followed her out of the kitchen. "Have patience," he said. "Remember that what your mother does is done out of love."

"I try to, *Dat*," Rachel replied and walked out of the house. She blinked back what must have been a speck of dust stinging her eye as she walked to the police car and got into the front seat.

"I hope the Benders are more cooperative this time," the trooper said, surveying Rachel's mid-calf navy dress and head scarf from the shadows of her sunglasses.

"Me too," Rachel agreed. Privately, she wasn't sure that they would be. She supposed that Dathan's mother would answer as best she could, but the cooperation of his sister and her husband was anyone's guess.

She leaned back against the seat and fastened her seat belt. The interior of the vehicle was spotless. It smelled of leather and gun oil and, oddly, of bubble gum. She closed her eyes. "This time, why don't you wait in the car until I talk to Dathan's family first?" she suggested. "Just tell me exactly what to ask."

"That's not how it works."

Rachel opened her eyes and turned to the policewoman. "It may not be how it works where you came from, but if you want answers from the Benders, and any other Amish, you'll have to trust me. And it might be better if you didn't even pull into the driveway. Let me walk up the lane and see if they're willing to talk to you. Some-times it works that way. One of us introduces one of you, and it's as if I'm saying it's safe. That you're . . . trustworthy."

"I thought you weren't one of them."

"I'm not." Rachel gazed out the window. "But I am."

"This isn't procedure," Lucy said. "I thought that if we went together maybe they'd be willing to answer my questions."

"No." Rachel shook her head. "You've been there once today. By going back when you've been refused, we're already taking a chance. The Benders may look at it as harassment."

Lucy stiffened. "You don't think they'd file a complaint, do you?"

Rachel tried not to laugh. "No, they aren't going to complain to your superior, and you don't have to worry about a lawsuit. It's our world you're entering. And you either follow the rules or you run up against a stone wall. Believe me, there's no one as stubborn as a *Deitschman.*"

Trooper Mars didn't answer, but neither did she turn the vehicle around and take her home, so Rachel thought that maybe some of what she'd said had gotten through. They'd gone about three miles when the cell in her pocket vibrated. She looked at it, didn't recognize the out-of-state number, and let it go to voicemail. She and the policewoman didn't speak again until they reached the Benders' place.

"I'll walk up from here," Rachel said. "You can park at the end of the drive, and I'll wave to you to come up if they agree to talk to you. Will that work?"

Lucy's lips tightened and she gave a slight nod.

Rachel found Dathan's sister and husband in the barn milking. One of the cows was a black and white Holstein; the smaller one, a reddish Jersey. Rachel made her presence known and waited in the doorway until the woman gestured for her to enter. The man kept his head pressed against the Jersey cow's belly. Rhythmic hisses echoed against a stainless steel milk bucket, and

Rachel smelled the scents of warm milk, sweet feed, and fresh manure. She stepped carefully around a dark, steaming mound on the dirt floor.

"You've heard nothing from Dathan?" she asked his sister.

The dour woman shook her head and gave a few last tugs on the Holstein's teats. "*Ne*. Nothing. And what's Charles to do? Our horse and our wagon gone." She rose off the three-legged milking stool and carefully backed away from the cow with a bucket half-full of milk.

"Loaned it to him," Dathan's brother-in-law muttered. "Said nothing about him not bringing it back." Charles's cow swatted a crusty tail, and Rachel felt a few drops of something she'd rather not think about strike her bare arm.

Hungry cats mewed for milk, and Dathan's sister poured a generous amount in a crockery bowl that stood against the wall. The cats pushed and crowded around the container. The woman sighed and glanced at Rachel. "Our mother's worried near out of her mind."

"English woman came here in a police car this afternoon."

"I know. That's why I'm here. She's helping us look for Dathan and Elsie," Rachel explained.

The barn was dark and shadowy with huge, dusty cobwebs that hung from the overhead beams. It smelled of damp, nothing like the high-ceilinged, whitewashed interior of her father's big cow barn. The animals seemed healthy and well cared for, though, even the collection of multi-colored cats. Apparently, Dathan's sister and brother-in-law cared more for their live-stock than strangers. The thought that Lucy Mars would have been creeped out by this barn passed through Rachel's consciousness. It creeped *her* out, and she was used to old barns.

"Don't care whether he comes back or not," Charles said, pausing in his milking. "Not much loss if he don't. But my horse and wagon had better show up by tomorrow. I need them to bring a load of stock feed from the mill."

"Would you be willing to speak to Trooper Mars now?" Rachel asked.

"No reason," Charles said brusquely. "Got nothing to say. Boy claimed he'd take good care of my horse and wagon. You see how much store he put by that promise."

"Never called any English police," the sister said. "The two of them aren't hiding in this barn. Where they are, God alone knows. But wherever they are, you can be certain that it's not decent."

Rachel tried to look sympathetic. "I under-stand why you're angry. But what if something happened to them—something beyond their control?"

"What?" Charles demanded, taking a step toward her. He was a smallish, whip-thin man with small eyes and a scraggly black beard. "The horse threw a shoe? They got lost?" He made a sound of derision. "Sin, I say. They run off together. And without the Lord's mercy, they'll both be roasting in the fires of hell."

When Rachel walked out of the barn and back into the soft light of early evening, she found Dathan's mother waiting for her. The woman's tear-streaked face was wan, both eyes sunken and bloodshot, and she held tightly to a crying, squirming baby that Rachel supposed must be her grandchild. "Have you news for me?" she begged. "News of my boy?"

Again, Rachel had to explain that they hadn't and that Trooper Mars had asked if she could question her about Dathan's behavior on Friday. "You wouldn't have to ask her into the house," Rachel said. "She's only trying to find them."

"He's a good boy, my Dathan. He wouldn't do this. I don't care what they say." She gestured with her chin toward the barn. "Something terrible has happened to him. I feel it in my bones."

"Trooper Mars—"

"*Ne*!" Dathan's mother insisted. "Not the Englishwoman. You. You have to help us find him. Find my boy and bring him home."

A little after nine that evening, soon after she'd tucked her mother into bed, Rachel's cell vibrated in her pocket, and she went out on the front porch to answer it. Everyone in the house knew she had a phone, but even her father preferred that she not use it in front of her younger brothers and sisters.

"Rache."

Evan's voice made her smile. "Hi," she answered. "How are you? How's everything going there?" She sat on the steps. "I've missed you." In her mind's eye she could see his familiar face with his brown eyes and short-cropped dark hair.

"I'm good. Classes are good. Intense. Sorry I couldn't call earlier in the week. This is an accelerated course. It's a lot to keep up with. So far, I've passed every class, though. Keep your fingers crossed. Two guys went home already."

Happiness bubbled up inside her. It was so good to hear Evan's voice. And he was upbeat, which was good. When he'd first been told that the mucky-mucks were sending him to this Homeland Security course, he'd been worried that he wouldn't make the grade. He'd worked so hard to gain a place with the state police that he sometimes doubted his ability. Finishing this program with high marks was bound to give him a boost in self-confidence, as well as being a real asset in his career advancement. His temporary assignment as detective had been great, but that had only lasted until a more experienced officer transferred in, so any advanced training would be advantageous.

The bad part was that it was a six-week course, without an opportunity to come home. And he wasn't able to have visitors. They hadn't been apart this long since they'd started dating seriously. She'd really missed him. "Okay, so how are you, really? Are you enjoying the program?"

Evan laughed, a deep, masculine laugh that always made her toes curl. "I wouldn't say that I'm enjoying it. But I am learning a lot. We have to be ready for acts of terrorism, even in Stone Mill."

She shivered at the thought. "I hope not. I like to think that we're out of the line of fire."

"So would everyone in every town in America. In the world. But anything is possible. I'm just learning all I can to be in the best possible position to protect people if something bad comes down." He cleared his throat. "But I don't want to talk about that. How are you doing there with your family? You haven't gone completely *Deitsch* on me, have you?"

"I don't think so."

"Heard that before." He chuckled. "What are you wearing? That awful denim skirt that comes down to your ankles?"

"No, I'm not." Actually, she was wearing one of her mother's dresses because her denim skirt was in the wash. Or rather, on the clothesline. She made a mental note to bring in the wash before it got dark. She was a little behind on the chores despite her best efforts.

"I know you have something interesting on your head," Evan said.

Rachel's hand went involuntarily to her sister's scarf. Again, there were no rules that said she had to dress Amish, but things went easier among the Plain folk if she dressed modestly and covered her head. She wasn't trying to look Amish, simply not stand out as different as she would have if she'd worn her customary jeans and tees. And when she made the effort to accommodate Plain customs, she could interact smoothly with the more conservative Amish like her Uncle Aaron. It was a small sacrifice to make. After all, she'd grown up wearing full Amish garb and sitting through three-hour church sermons.

"Caught you," Evan said. "*Kapp*, scarf, or kerchief?" he teased.

Rachel groaned. "Lettie's scarf."

"Black?"

"Navy blue."

He laughed. "Knew it. Could be worse, I suppose. You could have grown a beard."

Now he had her laughing. "I do miss you," she said.

"Say the word and I'll chuck this program and come home tonight. We can pick up a license and be married by . . . I don't know. Tuesday? Friday at the latest."

"You'd just give it all up? And what would we live on?"

"I could buy a few acres and a mule. Maybe grow organic turnips."

"We could plow up the front lawn of the B&B," she ad-libbed. "Put it all in arugula and radicchio. And you could teach classes in Amish yoga on the side."

"Is there such a thing as Amish yoga?"

She chuckled. "Not yet. But anything's possible."

"I could do that with my little mat, leotards, and a straw hat. And if we were married, I'd have to grow a full beard. How would I look in tights?"

She laughed. She knew that Evan wouldn't quit his job and she wouldn't leave her family when they needed her. Both of them would do what was right. They were responsible people. "My father's been asking if we've set a date for the wedding."

"Did you tell him that you're the one we're waiting on? Didn't I just say that I'd marry you Friday if you'd agree? We'll be in and out of the courthouse in half an hour. Mr. and Mrs. Parks."

"Can't do that. We have to have a real wedding to satisfy my parents."

"Speaking of your parents, how's your mother? Treatments going okay?"

"She's weak when she comes home, but you know she's plucky. A week or so and she'll bounce back. The doctors say she's making tremendous progress on these drugs. They expect her to be cancer-free soon."

"I hope so," he replied. "Tell her that I'm praying for her."

"I will. I know she'll appreciate it."

"I spoke to Lucy earlier." Evan's tone became serious. "She filled me in on your missing cousin."

"I was going to tell you about it. We don't know what to do. Poor Mary Aaron. I can't imagine how awful I would feel if it was one of my sisters."

"I hate to be the voice of reason," Evan said, "but Lucy's probably right. Elsie probably *did* run off with her boyfriend."

"So, where's the horse and wagon? No one's seen it. They wouldn't run off with Dathan's brother-in-law's horse." Rachel hesitated. "It just doesn't feel right to me, Evan. I've called the local police departments and hospitals, even one in State College."

"Rache." He didn't sound pleased. "You're playing detective again."

"I don't care. She's my cousin. Elsie would never worry her mother like this."

"I'm sorry I'm not there with you," Evan said. "Maybe I could be of help. But you should listen to Lucy. She's got good instincts."

"Maybe she does, but she thinks we should wait until Elsie either comes home or contacts her family. I don't agree. I'm afraid something terrible has happened to them."

"I don't suppose there's anything I can say to

convince you not to become involved in this?" he asked.

"I'm already involved. And besides, there's no official police investigation, because they're both of age and there's no sign of an accident or a crime." She drew up her knees and wrapped her free arm around them.

"Why does this always happen to you, Rache?"

"I don't know, but I can't just sit here and do nothing. Elsie's practically a little sister. And the police aren't going to do anything as long as they think Dathan and Elsie just ran away to be English."

He groaned. "We're not going to argue over this. If you're determined to hunt for Elsie, I'll do whatever I can, from here, to help you. It's against my better judgment, because I'm guessing Elsie and Dathan did leave voluntarily, but you've been right before."

"Thanks, that means a lot to me."

"Don't make me regret it."

"I'm not taking any risks. I'm just asking questions of people who might know something about what happened last night."

"I'd feel a lot better about this if I was there in Stone Mill," Evan admitted.

"Me, too."

"Hang on," he said. Then his voice moved away from the phone. "Just a minute," he called. "I'm coming." And then to her, he said, "I've got to run. We do three miles every morning and evening."

"All right," she said. "Call again when you can."

"Will do. Love you, honey."

"Love you, too," she said.

"Love you more." There was a soft *click* and the line went silent.

Rachel turned off her phone and sat there in the soft darkness, listening to the crickets and the night insects. She was relieved that Evan wasn't going to oppose her in trying to find Elsie. But she still felt at odds. What should she do next?

There was one lead she hadn't followed up on yet. It was a long shot, but sometimes, that was the one that paid off.

CHAPTER 5

This Sabbath was a visiting Sunday for the church community that Rachel's family belonged to. Traditionally, services for the Old Amish were held on alternating Sundays in a member's home. Alternating Sundays were a day for family and friends. Rachel had intended on *visiting* Rupert Rust, but instead, she was caught up in assisting her mother in welcoming the stream of guests who came by to lend their support in her battle against cancer and to hear the latest news about Elsie.

No work and no cooking were done on Sundays, but guests expected to be served refreshment. Due to her mother's illness, each visitor brought a little something to tide the family over in the coming week. Buggy by buggy, friends and neighbors arrived, and cake by cake and pie by pie, the pantry began to look like the new bakery in town. A few brought soups and casseroles, which could be heated in the woodstove her father kept burning. No one in the house was cooking, andif the soup grew hot and tasty while the pot rested on the top of the cast-iron range, so much the better.

Aunt Hannah left Mary Aaron to care for her

younger children and came from next door, and she sat all afternoon with her sister-in-law, Esther. Aunt Hannah looked a sight. Her normally full cheeks were sunken, and there were dark shadows under her eyes. She spoke little, merely cried quietly or sat rocking herself back and forth. No word had come from Elsie, and Hannah was inconsolable.

It was half-past five by the time Rachel was able to get away. She walked down the lane, retrieved her Jeep from the trees, and drove to the Rust farm. She found Rupert near the road in the center of a paddock some distance from his father's house. Rupert had a long training whip in one hand and a lunge line in the other. At the end of the rope was a nervous yearling colt. Rupert was trying to teach the horse to obey instructions, to move at a trot, and to walk around the ring, reversing direction on command.

Rachel approached the paddock fence quietly. The young horse caught her scent and shied, rearing and bolting across the enclosure, coming dangerously close to its trainer. It appeared to Rachel for a moment as if the colt would run Rupert down, but he stood his ground and the animal veered around him. Rupert snapped the whip over the horse's rump, and the nervous horse resumed its circular pattern in a swift canter.

"Sorry," Rachel called in English. "I didn't think—"

"Didn't think much." Rupert kept his eyes on the bay colt. "Whoa!" he shouted. "Easy." And when the animal skidded to a halt, Rupert ordered, "Walk on!"

Because it was Sunday, strictly speaking, Rupert had no business training a horse on the Sabbath, but his place among the Amish of the community was complicated. He'd been shunned for leaving the church after baptism, when he'd joined the military. But Rupert had returned to Stone Mill and his Amish roots six months ago, a wounded man, and allowances were made for his youth and possible redemption. They were also made for the damage done to him in some desert battlefield. Those allowances were evident in the way he was dressed. A worn U.S. Marine T-shirt stretched across muscular shoulders, and a cowboy belt with a large silver buckle was cinched tightly around a lean waist.

The baby-faced boy whom Rachel had known was gone, replaced by the scarred, chiseled features and haunted eyes of a man who had seen too much bloodshed. Rupert's hair was buzzed military-short, and his mouth was set in a hard line. How old could he be, Rachel wondered. He must not be any older than Mary Aaron, yet life had marked him with the weight of at least ten more years.

Sympathy for the Amish boy who had gone off to see the world and returned an empty shell made Rachel's throat tighten. *God help him,* she thought. If there was peace anywhere for Rupert, it might be here in this valley with his own kind. "I was hoping you'd help me!" she called to him. "Could we talk?"

"Nothing to say." Rupert kept his gaze on the horse. "Trot!" He cracked the whip in the air, and the colt leaped forward. "Steady."

"You don't even know why I'm here."

He didn't respond.

Rachel glanced away and then back at him. "You were at the singing the night Elsie and Dathan disappeared, weren't you?" she asked. For a while she thought Rupert intended to ignore her question, but then he glanced in her direction.

"What if I was?"

"We're half out of our minds worrying over Elsie. If there's any way you can help me, Rupert, I'd really appreciate it."

"Said I didn't know anything." He turned to look at her. His expression was as hard as the fist that held the end of the lunge line. "You some kind of cop in disguise?" He began to shorten the rope, gradually pulling the colt closer to him, still putting the animal through its paces.

"Just a cousin worried about Elsie's safety."

He drew the horse even closer, and then led it step by hesitating step to the side of the paddock, where he snubbed the rope tight to a post. Ignoring her, Rupert reached through the wooden fence to retrieve a burlap bag tied shut at one end with corn string. Rachel moved to within a few yards of the man and colt.

"I heard that Dathan and Elsie had an argument at the singing," Rachel said. "Did you witness it?"

Rupert turned his back to her and slapped the bay's rump gently with the bag. The animal started and kicked out at Rupert. He was speaking to the horse now. She couldn't make out what he was saying, but his tone was low and soothing. He shook the bag against the colt's belly, and it kicked again and shied sideways. Rupert followed the animal, still talking, and repeated the action, brushing the burlap sack against the colt's neck and chest and over the withers. The colt's eyes rolled to show the whites, but he'd quit kicking. Rupert kept up the same process until the horse stood still, and then he began to rub the animal, stroking and massaging.

"You know what you're doing," Rachel said in an attempt to form some sort of rapport between them. It was true; he obviously had skill when it came to working with young horses. "So you don't know anything about the disagreement between the couple that night?"

"Didn't say that." He regarded her coolly, as if looking down a rifle sight. Rachel felt a chill run down her spine. "Said I had nothing to say to you."

He dropped the sack and took hold of the horse's bridle. Then he untied the colt and led it out of the paddock. Feeling foolish, Rachel trailed after them. Rupert abruptly stopped and glanced back at her. "Did Lettie tell you something happened?"

"Lettie? What's Lettie got to do with anything?"

"My point. Keep her out of this." His eyes narrowed. "Nothing happened that you need worry about." Dismissing her with a nod, he *clicked* to the colt and walked on.

They'd gone no more than twenty yards from the paddock, when a passing pickup backfired. Rupert let go of the horse's lead line and threw himself facedown on the dirt. He gave a cry of utter distress, half howl, half wail, and curled into a fetal position with his hands over his head. The colt took off across the field at a dead run with the rope trailing behind him.

Rachel's first instinct was to run to Rupert and try to help him, but fear held her paralyzed. What if he took her for an enemy soldier? Would he strike out at her? She'd heard of returning soldiers who suffered from PTSD, post-traumatic stress disorder. Some suffered severe anxiety attacks, even violent psychotic incidents.

She knew that the elders of Rupert's church community had taken into account personal information when they were considering lifting the extreme ban against him. What had they been told that caused them to alter centuries of practice of refusing to allow unrepentant, excommunicated people to associate with church members? Normally, even Rupert's family wouldn't be permitted to eat with him, invite him into their homes, or even speak to him. What trauma had Rupert suffered? And how dangerous to himself and to others was he?

Rupert's hoarse cries had faded to convulsive sobbing, but he still lay in a trembling posture on the grass. Feeling helpless and unsure, Rachel hurried back to the barnyard. Rupert's father, Eli, was just coming out of the carriage shed. She'd known Eli all her life, but he was nearly as forbidding in appearance as his son.

"Rupert needs you," she said. "He's having some sort of incident."

Eli frowned. He was a dour, thick man with hands like Rupert's. "Leave him to himself," he said. "He'll come 'round."

"But he needs help," Rachel insisted.

"Go home," Eli said. "And if you would help my Rupert, you will keep what you saw to yourself. He's been through enough. He need to be left alone to heal and find his way back."

"There must be something you can do for him," she argued. "Go to him, at least?"

"And shame him further? God will judge him. And God will restore his sanity if only interfering do-gooders would leave him alone."

That night, as the house grew quiet, Rachel sat on the edge of the bed and watched her sister Lettie brush out her hair. They were in Lettie's bedroom, a square, unadorned room with tall windows. The bedroom had once been hers. Sally and Amanda shared a room, as did the boys. But four of the nine Mast children were already grown and on their own, so Lettie, as the oldest girl at home now, had the privacy of her own bedroom. And in her mother's active household, having any space to claim your own was a blessing.

"Where could they be?" Lettie asked. She glanced over her shoulder at Rachel. "I know I fuss about Elsie, but I do love her. She's sweet and funny and she's never critical of other people . . . like I am. Oh, Rachel, I'm so worried about her."

"I am, too," Rachel admitted. Lettie was wearing a long, white cotton nightdress, and Rachel wore one of a similar style made from linen. The linen was old and had been washed many times. It felt soft against her skin. She'd given up nightgowns when she'd fled the Amish years ago, but after feeling how comfortable this material was, she might be tempted to see what she could find in a slightly shorter version.

Lettie came to sit on the bed beside her and

held out her brush. "Would you?" she asked. "It feels so good when you brush my hair."

Rachel smiled and drew the brush gently through Lettie's thick hair. It was good to have a chance to get to know Lettie better. She'd missed this little sister's growing-up years, as well as Amanda's and most of Sally's. A pang of guilt registered and she tried to shake it off. But the thought returned that she'd missed Elsie's as well, and now she might not have the chance to make up that lost time.

Evan would say she was being overly dramatic. Elsie was of legal age to go and come as she pleased, and she was with a responsible man. If they hadn't located Elsie and Dathan, it was probably because they didn't want to be found. Logically, assuming that something terrible had happened to them was premature. But logic had little to do with the gut feeling that something was wrong, a fear that grew greater with each passing hour.

"*Dat* said that you went to talk to Rupert." Lettie's statement interrupted Rachel's sentimental musing.

"I did." Rachel kept brushing. Lettie's reddish-brown hair was thick and wavy and hung nearly to her waist. As far as Rachel knew, her sister had never had it cut. In public, Amish girls and women wore their hair braided and pinned up or in a bun that the *kapp* covered. Only in private moments did Amish women let down their hair, but that didn't mean that they didn't take care to keep it well tended.

"You didn't mention me, did you?"

Rachel didn't answer.

Lettie grabbed the brush and got to her feet. She shrugged and chuckled, a forced sound if Rachel had ever heard one. "You know, Elsie and I rode together to the singing. I was there. I hope you didn't give him the idea that I'd told you to talk to him about . . . about anything that happened."

There was something in her sister's tone that made Rachel suspicious. Of what, she wasn't sure. "I heard that there was an argument between Elsie and Dathan at the party, a disagreement that several people witnessed. I thought possibly that Rupert might have been one of them."

"I don't know anything about that. There were a lot of people there. People I didn't know." Lettie frowned. "Why are you asking all these questions anyway? Boyfriends and girlfriends have disagreements all the time."

"So Dathan and Elsie *did* argue Friday night?"

Lettie watched Rachel. "Who told you that? Did Rupert say anything about an argument? Or . . . about me?"

Rachel averted her gaze. Lettie was smart. If she wanted to learn anything of importance, she'd have to be cautious. "Rupert did mention you."

"He did? What did he say?" Lettie curled her fingers into tight fists and tucked them behind her back.

"You think he's interested in you?" When she didn't answer, Rachel went on. "Lettie, you have to be careful. Rupert Rust is . . . he's not in a position to court anyone. Not to mention what *Mam* and *Dat* would think. He's barely out of being banned, isn't he?" She hesitated, but felt she had to say what was on her mind. "And I'm not sure he's emotionally stable."

"Now you sound like Uncle Aaron. You know he's never liked the Rusts. He didn't want to lift the ban on Rupert. He holds it against him because he left and joined the Marines. He's got a scar, you know. On his back."

Rachel thought about the scene in the Rusts' yard when the truck backfired. "It's not a scar that troubles me. I'm concerned that he has other wounds, ones that don't show."

"I heard Uncle Aaron tell *Dat* that he thought Rupert should never have been allowed to come back here and that he's dangerous. You don't believe that, do you?"

"I don't know," Rachel admitted.

"He's a hero. Did you know that? He even has a medal to prove it. He saved another soldier's life. People say bad things about him, but they don't know what a decent person he is," Lettie defended hotly.

Rachel studied the back of her sister's head. The old nightcap on her head. "I never said I thought Rupert was a bad person. I don't think that. I don't know him well enough to know whether he's good or bad."

"He wants to join the church again. He wants to be Amish. He's no different than you are. You went out in the English world and then you came home."

"What I heard was that he was discharged on medical grounds."

"What did I just say? He was wounded while he was saving another soldier. Everyone in their group died but Rupert and the boy he carried out on his back. Is it any wonder that he has nightmares?"

Despite the warmth of the evening, Rachel felt a chill run through her. "You *have* been talking to him, haven't you? Seeing him?" What had he told her? Rachel wondered. Lettie had led a sheltered life. How much could she grasp of the atrocities of war?

"I'm not *seeing* him. I just . . . see him around. He doesn't talk much. But he is really a sweet person."

"And you care for him?"

"What if I do?" Lettie returned to the bed. "I'm not a child, Rachel. I know that Rupert has been through a lot. But all he needs is a second chance . . . a chance to forget what happened over there."

"And does he feel the same way about you?"

"I thought he did. But then he got into this stupid fight with Dathan over Elsie at the singing, which means he still cares for her. They used to see each other now and then."

Rachel turned to her. "So you're telling me that Elsie was dating Rupert?"

"Sort of." Lettie looked up, wide-eyed. "You can't say anything. Not to anyone. Aunt Hannah and Uncle Aaron don't know. But it's all over. They broke up when he ran away to join the Englisher world."

Rachel took her sister's hand. "And Rupert still likes her?"

"She's been courting Dathan secretly for months, so I guess Rupert didn't know."

"So the argument wasn't between Elsie and Dathan? It was between Dathan and Rupert? And it had to do with Elsie?"

"I didn't see the fight. I just heard kids talking about it. And you know how it is. Everybody's got their own idea of what they heard or what caused it. And Elsie and Dathan did disagree. Over Rupert, I'm sure. But I didn't see that, either."

"And what was the outcome?"

"I don't know. But they must have settled it, because Dathan and Elsie stayed for a while after that." Lettie sighed. "I wish Rupert could understand that it's over between him and Elsie and that she was never serious about him."

"I wish you'd told me about Rupert and Dathan sooner."

"Rupert doesn't have anything to do with them being missing. I thought if I said anything, you'd be suspicious of him. No one understands him."

"But you think you do?" Rachel asked.

"Why can't he see that I'm a lot better for him than Elsie would ever be?" There was an innocence in Lettie's voice that worried Rachel. Her younger sister knew so little of the world, of people. "He needs someone who appreciates him," Lettie continued. "He doesn't need a girlfriend who is ashamed to be seen with him. And I'd never do that. No matter what *Mam* and *Dat* think. If we were walking out together, I'd want everyone to know it."

Every instinct told Rachel to warn her sister against becoming involved with Rupert. After what she'd seen happen at the Rust farm earlier, she wasn't certain that the young man was mentally stable. But she knew Lettie was like many young women. She saw Rupert as a tragic figure, a man she could save and redeem. Any criticism of Rupert would only make her defend him all the more. "But did you—"

Rachel broke off as something hard flew through the open window, hit the wooden floor, and bounced. Lettie gasped and Rachel scrambled off the bed as a second missile lobbed off the side of the dresser. Rocks. Rachel ran to the window, taking care to remain out of the line of fire in case of additional incoming. "Who's down there?"

"It's me. Jesse. Mary Aaron sent me. I need to tell you something." Jesse was Mary Aaron's youngest brother.

Rachel peered out the window at Jesse.

"What was that?" Amanda's sleepy voice came from the hallway.

"Go back to bed," Lettie told her. "I just knocked something over."

"I'll be right down," Rachel called out the window. Grabbing Lettie's terry-cloth bathrobe off the hook by the door, she scooped up her shoes and the clothing she'd been wearing and made for the hall.

"That's my robe," Lettie protested. "What am I going to wear?"

"Stay here," Rachel ordered. "Please. I'll tell you as soon as I find out what Jesse wants. If you come, Amanda's bound to hear us and then everyone will be up." She didn't wait to hear her sister's protests but hurried down the stairs as quietly as she could.

Once she'd dressed in the bathroom, Rachel slipped out of the house. She found Jesse on a pony at the edge of the yard.

"Sorry about the rocks," he said. "I tried calling to you, but you didn't hear me. Mary Aaron said I shouldn't come back without you."

"Have they found Elsie?"

"*Ne*," he said. "It's nothing to do with Elsie." The pony tossed its head and danced sideways. Jesse was riding bareback. None of the Hostetler children owned a saddle. "But Mary Aaron said you need to come. Timothy was just at the house. He said they need you out at the grave-yard."

"The graveyard?" Rachel stared at him, confused. "Now?"

Jesse's eyes widened in the moonlight as he nodded. "They found a grave."

"A grave? In a cemetery. So?"

"*Ya*," Jesse whispered excitedly. "But this is a grave that's not supposed to be there."

CHAPTER 6

They saw the lights—headlights, lanterns, and flashlights—as they turned off of Bee Tree Road and onto the dirt lane. It led up the hill and through the woods to the Amish cemetery. Mary Aaron released her seat belt and leaned forward on the seat. "You don't think that that grave could be—"

"Don't go there," Rachel interrupted. She patted her cousin's arm in an effort to comfort her. Elsie's disappearance had shaken Mary Aaron to the core. Rachel had never known her to be so emotional. Rachel could understand her best friend's worry. Bad things had happened to Amish girls in this valley before, but what were the chances? "Trooper Mars and Evan both think that Elsie and Dathan ran away together. They think it's the most logical explanation. Maybe they're right."

"They're wrong." Mary Aaron's voice was soft. She sounded so vulnerable.

It was a side of her cousin Rachel rarely saw.

"I know my sister." Mary Aaron stared straight ahead. "She'd never leave the faith. She'd never do that to our mother."

Her words made Rachel think back to what she had done to *her* mother when she left Stone Mill as a teenager. What she'd done to her father. And her siblings. And—she refused to go there right now.

It had rained the previous week and the road was rutted, both by buggy wheels and what appeared to be truck or car tires. The Jeep was capable of taking the driveway at a much faster speed, but there was no sense in tearing the road up worse. The cemetery was private—owned, maintained, and financially supported by the Amish.

Rachel made the final turn and saw a disorganized assortment of Amish buggies, pickup trucks, and cars parked haphazardly along the cemetery fence. One truck she recognized—a red pickup with a cracked windshield. A barking dog lunged back and forth in the piled-up truck bed. "Roy Thompson," she said, turning to Mary Aaron. "He's a ways from home. What's he doing here?"

"Let me out," Mary Aaron said.

"Wait. I'll park." Rachel looked around. The burial place was an old one, and the original section, going back to the early nineteenth century, was surrounded by a stone wall. The area to the left of the parking lot, however, had been cleared from woods when she was a child and held fewer graves.

Bobbing lanterns, flashlights, and the high

beams of at least one truck illuminated the darkness. Rachel could make out two figures huddled in the front seat of a Honda sedan, an older model with a Stone Mill High softball sticker on the window. As she drove past at a crawl, Rachel noticed that the car was blocked in by a pickup parked at an angle. She knew that truck, too. Not wanting the same thing to happen to her, Rachel backed up and left the Jeep just off the road at a wide spot in the lane. Mary Aaron jumped out, and with flashlight in hand, hurried toward the group of milling figures in the new burial area.

Seeing an Amish woman whom she knew climbing down out of the back door of a buggy, Rachel stopped to speak to her. There appeared to be several other women still in the buggy, but she couldn't tell who they were because it was dark. "What's all the excitement, Gertie?" Rachel asked in *Deitsch*. She already knew, of course, but the best way to get information was often to play dumb and let the other person talk.

The woman was middle-aged, but contrary to mainstream American custom, the Amish didn't use the titles of "Mr." or "Mrs." among the Plain people, similar to the practice of the Quakers; calling older people by their given name didn't show a lack of respect. That was another of those traditions that Rachel had stumbled over more than once before she got it right when she first made the transition from the Amish world to the English.

"Desecration of the dead," Gertie exclaimed in the same dialect. "Either that, or a new grave where no grave should be."

Rachel tried to remember the woman's husband's name. Elah? "Is Elah over there?" She waved in the general direction of the bobbing lanterns.

"*Ya.* We were coming home late from my daughter's lying in. She was safely delivered of a beautiful little boy, God be thanked. Their second boy and she's already up on her feet. Anyway, we were driving home and Elah saw the truck pulling in here. He's on the cemetery committee. No one should be in here at night, especially not the English. So he drove up to tell them they had no business here, and found all this."

"You say it's a fresh grave?" Rachel asked.

"Only know what I heard somebody say. Elah told us to stay with the horse and buggy, and that's what we're doing. You won't catch me wandering around in a graveyard at night. Stepping on people's final resting place. It's not decent."

The Amish, Rachel knew, had an aversion to the dead. Burials were quickly held after a passing of one of their own. The grief was genuine, but afterward it wasn't considered quite right to speak too much of the deceased. This earthly life was only considered a brief stop in the journey to eternal life in heaven. To the devout, a loved one who had passed on had truly gone to a better place.

"I was asked to come," Rachel explained to Gertie. "Is Zebadiah here?"

Gertie nodded and pointed toward the newer section of the cemetery. "He had a lantern. Don't know which one is his. I imagine Elah is with him."

Rachel nodded. "Thank you." As she started toward the others, another pickup came roaring up the lane. When the driver pulled up next to her, he slammed on his brakes. "What's going on?" he asked.

All she could see of him was that he was big and wore a plaid shirt or jacket and a ball cap. "Not sure what it is," Rachel answered. The voice sounded familiar. Definitely a younger man. "Buddy? That you?"

He flinched. "Was passing by on the way back from my grandfather's. Saw all the commotion." He shut off the engine and left the pickup in the drive, blocking everyone in but the Jeep.

Mary Aaron had her flashlight, so paying no more attention to Buddy, Rachel made her way carefully over the muddy ground. But Buddy came up behind her, and his long stride quickly left her behind.

There were more people in the graveyard than she'd expected. Amish men and boys were gathered in a knot in one corner of the cemetery. Four, no, five Englishmen and one woman stood on the other side of a section of freshly disturbed dirt. All of the grave sites in this new cemetery had small, almost flush, granite headstones engraved with the name of the deceased and dates of birth and death. Grass and moss grew between the graves, but it had been dug up in the place where everyone was gathering. A lantern stood at one end of the mystery mound, and the yellow flickering light revealed that, unlike the others, this spot had no headstone.

Ahead of her, one of the Englishmen swore. "You think it's that missing Amish girl? Somebody whacked her and buried her here?"

"Shut up, Roy," another retorted. "That's some of her people over there."

"What do you think it is, Zeb?" someone asked. "Don't look like a fox to me." The speaker was an older man in a cowboy hat. Rachel thought he might be a farmer from the other side of town. She wasn't sure of his name, Merle something. He wasn't Amish. She went to the Amish group.

Someone recognized her. "Here she is," a man said in *Deitsch*.

That person she did recognize. It was Eli Rust, not surprising because, as the crow flew, the Rust farm was the closest to the cemetery. She looked more closely at Eli and realized that the taller man with him, shoulders tight, hands jammed in his pockets, was his son, Rupert. He didn't speak, rather kept his gaze on the disturbed earth, seemingly oblivious to the people around him.

"Rupert," she said, hoping that he wasn't angry with her for witnessing his breakdown in the pasture. She didn't want Lettie to become involved with him, but she did feel compassion for the changes that war had wrought on an uneducated boy from an isolated Pennsylvania valley.

Rupert raised his gaze to her. She couldn't see the expression in his eyes, but his chiseled features seemed cut from the same stone as the granite wall behind him.

She blinked to accustom her eyes to the lights and saw Mary Aaron with Timothy hovering protectively beside her. Mary Aaron's face was pale, and she looked as though she might burst into tears.

"I sent for Rachel," Timothy said to Mary Aaron. "Zebadiah wanted her to come."

An Amish man standing in the center of the group waved her closer. It was the caretaker, a barrel of a man in his mid-seventies who appeared younger than his years. Zebadiah had been taking care of the Amish cemetery as long as Rachel could remember, and his long beard had always been pewter gray and stringy. He motioned to the turned-up area of ground. "Take a look," he told her. "*Vas* is, do you think? Not a groundhog or a fox."

The mound was raw, with fresh clods of dirt, and was irregular in shape. No grass grew on it. Small for a grave, Rachel thought. She swallowed, refusing to follow that thread. There must be another explanation. Maybe they were all jumping to conclusions. People usually saw what they wanted to see, didn't they? "Have you called the police?" she asked him.

"*Ne*. Not sure what to do." Zebadiah stared at the ground, kicking at it with the toe of a heavy, black work shoe. The heaped-up dirt was slightly sunken on one side. "Few years back, we had something like this happen. People wanted me to call in the Englishers, so I did."

She waited.

"Came in a big police van. Put up ropes to keep us out. Wouldn't let me in. Even put up a tent around it. Trampled all over everything."

"What is it?" Buddy demanded. "Is it a grave?"

Rachel tried to ignore that and the array of comments now coming from both sides. "And?" she said to Zebadiah.

He glanced at her and then back at the fresh earth. "Turns out what was buried here was somebody's dog. Made us look foolish."

"And this isn't one of our people? It's not possible that someone died and the family buried them here without telling you?" That sounded ridiculous even as she said it. There were ways that things were done among the Amish, the way they'd always been done. "Or maybe someone died recently? Headstone hasn't been brought in yet?" It wasn't likely, but she was trying to explore all the possibilities beyond the obvious. She'd been attending funerals here since she was a girl; this didn't seem like any of the neat, respectful burials she'd ever seen. It looked like it was hastily dug.

"*Ne.* Know my graveyard." He pointed to the nearest grave to the right. "John Beachy. Nobody supposed to be on this side of him."

"And you're sure this was done in the last few days?"

Zebadiah kicked the dirt again. "Was out here Monday last," he said patiently. "Cut down some poison ivy off those trees." He pointed. "You can't let poison ivy get a start. It would be all over this cemetery."

She looked around. "How did all these people get here?"

Zebadiah hitched up a suspender that had started to slide over one shoulder. "Timothy there was driving by in his buggy. He saw the car lights. Knew people shouldn't be here, so he came to the house to tell me. I got my English neighbor to bring me down. Chuck brought his son Mike along. Mike's a strapping young man.

Backup in case the trespassers were unfriendly."

The neighbor, Chuck, and his son joined them. "Zeb asked me to bring him here to tell those folks, whoever they were, that this was private property," Chuck offered. "Rachel." He tugged at his ball cap. ALLAN'S HATCHERY was stitched across the hat. "Mike, you know Rachel Mast? Runs the B&B in town." Strapping son Mike, who topped at least 250 pounds and was at least six feet, three inches tall, mumbled his assent. "Anyway . . . we drove over and found this young couple—"

"Englishers," Zebadiah clarified.

"Their car was stuck in the mud."

"Didn't say what they were doing here," Zebadiah continued. "But I can guess. Young man and a young lady. Thought I oughta take a look-see around to make sure they hadn't thrown any beer cans around. Or done any mischief."

"You know the Baptist cemetery had stones overturned and graffiti written on the monuments last summer," Chuck said. "If these two had caused any trouble, we wanted them to answer for it."

"Which is why you blocked them in," Rachel said. "But . . ." She glanced around. "That doesn't explain why everyone else is here."

Chuck looked sheepish. "I imagine my wife called her brother. They're close and he doesn't live far away. I suppose Dale and his wife decided to come out and take a look for themselves." He motioned toward the English onlookers. "That's them over there." The woman was wearing a pink raincoat over poodle pajama pants.

"That explains two more people," Rachel said. "Not . . ." She scanned the scene. "Not all these."

"Salmon Peachy saw Timothy driving out of the cemetery lane in a hurry. Stopped him to ask what was up. And—" Zebadiah shrugged and spread his hands in a *what can you do?* gesture. "Amish telegraph, I guess."

Rachel nodded. "So what are you going to do now?" she asked, glancing at an Amish man holding a long-handled spade. She didn't want to try to make that decision. She supposed this could be another dog or someone's canary, complete with cage? Or it could be some gruesome prank and the couple in the Honda could be responsible. The papers carried stories about all sorts of weird behavior. In any case, Rachel did not want Mary Aaron watching anyone dig, thinking this might be her sister's grave they were opening.

"Thought about digging and seeing what's in there," Zebadiah said.

"He dug down about a foot," Chuck said. "But whatever or whoever buried something, they went deeper. That's why he wanted Timothy to send for you. He thought maybe that friend of yours . . . Detective Parks, isn't it?"

Rachel nodded. "Evan Parks, yes."

"We thought maybe he could take an unofficial look," Chuck explained. "So as not to make your people—"

"Look stupid," Zebadiah finished for him. "Still hear about that dog down at the feed store." He looked around at all the people. "Wasn't my thought to make so much fuss. Maybe would have waited until morning if I'd known all these people would come up here."

"But that would mean letting the couple leave," Chuck put in. "If there is something criminal going on here, we shouldn't let that happen."

"Right . . ." Rachel glanced over her shoulder in the direction of the Honda containing the detainees. "That's another thing that worries me. I don't think you have the legal right to hold them," she said. "I think, technically, that's kidnapping. If it turns out to be nothing, you wouldn't want to end up in police trouble yourself. Can't you just ask for their names?"

"Did that," Zebadiah grunted. "Wouldn't give them."

"You can take down the tag number of the car."

"Wrote it down," Chuck said. He tapped a small notebook in his shirt pocket.

"But you also prevented them from leaving," Rachel pointed out.

"Not stopping them from going anywhere," Zebadiah said. "Not pulling their car out of the mud either. Didn't put it there."

The sound of other motor vehicles coming up the drive caught Rachel's attention. She turned to see an SUV followed closely by an oversized truck with HOWDY'S GAS & TOW painted on the side pull up behind Buddy's green pickup blocking the road. The driver laid on the horn. "Looks like your trespassers called for help," Rachel said. Roy's dog began barking at the boys who climbed out of the SUV.

Chuck and Mike started toward the tow truck; the brother-in-law and his wife did the same. Timothy and Mary Aaron came to Rachel's side.

"What do you think we ought to do?" Zebadiah asked Rachel. "You think your police friend would help?"

"He would," Rachel answered. "But he's out of state."

"So, what should we do?" Timothy asked.

"I'll call another trooper I know."

"What if it is a grave?" Eli Rust asked. "Shouldn't disturb the dead."

Rachel looked back at the spot where they had dug. *Was it a grave?* Gooseflesh prickled her arms. "I don't think we have a choice," she said. "In light of Elsie and Dathan's disappearance, I don't think we can handle this ourselves. We have to call the police."

"Thought we might," Zebadiah admitted. "Appreciate it if you'd do the calling. They might be inclined to pay more mind to you."

Rachel nodded and walked back to her Jeep, where she'd left her cell. Ahead of her, several town boys pushed at the Honda in an effort to loosen it from the mud. Roy Thompson's dog was still barking, and a horse was shying at the noise and lights of the tow truck. Lucy Mars had given Rachel her personal cell number and asked her to call if she had any news on Elsie. Evan would have been the best choice. She could trust Evan's judgment, but he wasn't here. She'd have to trust Lucy to decide on the wisest course of action.

Dig it up and see was the sensible and immediate solution. But Rachel didn't want to do that. That it could be Elsie in that grave was one possibility she couldn't bear to consider.

She moved over to stand beside the wall and called Lucy. The sleepy-sounding trooper picked up on the third ring. Rachel identified herself and apologized for the hour. "Something strange has turned up out at the Amish graveyard," she explained.

Instantly, Lucy's voice became alert and professional.

Rachel told her what the situation was and that she'd been afraid to wait until morning to call, in case this should turn out to be a crime scene.

"And this caretaker?" Lucy asked. "How old is

he? Do you consider his statement valid, that there was no disturbance there Monday?"

"Zebadiah is absolutely reliable," she assured the policewoman.

"And there's no possibility that this could be the work of an animal?"

"Absolutely not." Growing up on a farm, Rachel had a lifetime of experience with seeing ground-hog burrows and fox dens. There was no open hole on the site. Whoever had dug there, he or she had two hands and a shovel.

"Thanks for calling me. I'll get dressed and run out there now. If this looks like something that needs our immediate attention, I'll call my desk sergeant."

"I'll wait here for you," Rachel said.

There was hesitation on the other end of the phone. "I'd rather you didn't. Go home. If I need you, I won't hesitate to call. The caretaker can show me. The fewer civilians at the site, the better."

"Thank you," Rachel said. And then, "You don't think this could have anything to do with Elsie's disappearance, do you?"

"That's what we're going to find out," Lucy said. "Now, please, if you want to help, tell everyone to leave. What we don't need is a three-ring circus."

Rachel wasn't ready for the sun to come up the next morning. She definitely wasn't ready to get

108

out of bed. All night long she'd lain awake, staring into the darkness, going over and over the scene at the cemetery and the conversation she'd had with Lucy. Rachel had expected the young trooper to be skeptical, but she'd been much more receptive than she'd expected.

Rachel had sent everyone home but the caretaker and then, in spite of Mary Aaron's efforts to persuade her otherwise, she had taken her home and gone home herself.

I shouldn't have asked Lucy if I should wait, she thought as she pulled on her clothing in the faint light of dawn.

Then she would have known firsthand whether her worst fears were real or just another nightmare. And the nightmares had come. Bad dreams where she and Mary Aaron searched a foggy swamp looking for Elsie. They could hear her voice calling to them, but they never actually saw her. And whenever Rachel had drifted off to sleep, the same dream would return to haunt her.

Rachel kept her phone under her pillow, half expecting a call from Lucy. She wondered what had happened. Had Lucy gone out there and had someone dig up the grave, only to find nothing? Or was it someone's deceased pet, like what had happened before?

She couldn't bear simply lying there or waiting for the phone to ring. Waking Lettie, she told her that she had to go out and that Lettie and Amanda would have to manage breakfast. By seven thirty, she was down the lane and in the Jeep. She wanted to go back to the graveyard, but going against Lucy's orders might ruin whatever rapport she and the policewoman had formed. If this disturbance at the cemetery had nothing to do with Elsie, she might need Lucy's help again.

Rachel forced herself to turn right instead of left and retraced the route that Dathan and Elsie should have taken the night they went missing. This time, instead of driving all the way, she parked the Jeep and walked a quarter mile. The only things that she found out of the ordinary were an empty soda can, a single worn sneaker, and a chain of beer bottles that some jerk had been throwing out the window, possibly at mailboxes. The first two empties she found about halfway between the Troyers' farm and the Hostetlers' were smashed, the third intact. They were all the same cheap brand of beer popular with local rednecks. Vandalism and throwing trash by the roadside might be common in the outer world, but it rarely occurred in Stone Mill.

Annoyed, Rachel returned to the Jeep, got a trash bag out of the back, and retraced her steps, picking up the bottles. Then she checked every mailbox along the road. She discovered a couple of bottles in the ditch, but they were old and their labels faded. There were two more newer ones smashed against stone walls.

What was the fine for littering? she wondered. Whatever it was, it wasn't enough. Anyone so thoughtless should lose their driving privileges.

Walking the better part of the route and picking up trash, she'd still covered the distance by nine. She'd been patient long enough. If the graveyard had been a false lead, Lucy should have had the courtesy to call her. "So much for being patient," she muttered to herself. She threw the bag of bottles into the back of her Jeep, to add them to the recycling bin at the B&B, and headed for the Amish cemetery.

CHAPTER 7

Rachel stood beside Lucy, trembling. "Yes, that's her. That's Elsie." She closed her eyes and put one hand on the door of the white van to steady herself. She gripped the vehicle frame and took deep breaths.

"Can you state positively that the body is that of your cousin, Elsie Hostetler?" the coroner asked. His soft voice held the echoes of a Georgian boyhood.

Rachel nodded. "Yes. That's definitely Elsie Hostetler." Dead, Elsie appeared oddly peaceful, though no one could have taken her for sleeping. Her eyes were closed. There was black dirt clinging to her eyelashes. There was a filthy bandage around her head. It looked like strips ripped from a pillowcase.

"How did she die?" Rachel managed, fighting tears as she stared at the pretty girl, wrapped in a dirty, fitted bedsheet, dead on the stretcher.

There was no reason for her to fall apart. She'd known this was a possibility from the moment she'd seen the new grave the previous night. But she hadn't wanted to believe it. She'd prayed that it wasn't so . . . that she was jumping to conclusions. And all the time, her little cousin was already gone beyond their help. *God keep her,* Rachel thought. Her next thought was of Mary Aaron and her family.

"Come on," Lucy said, not answering Rachel's question. "Sit in my car. Give yourself a moment. Then we'll talk."

Rachel reached futilely toward Elsie, feeling a little dizzy. "I—"

"She's in good hands," Lucy said, clasping her hands and steering Rachel away. "They need to take her to the morgue now."

"She should go home to her family," Rachel protested. "In the Amish faith, the family will keep vigil all night and then she'll be . . ." She trailed off. What was she saying? There would be a full inquest . . . an autopsy.

Lucy pushed a bottle of water into her hands and led her to the patrol car. She opened the passenger's front door and motioned for her to sit. Rachel took a drink of the water. It was cold and she concentrated on the sensation of the liquid sliding down her throat.

"Better?" the trooper asked.

Rachel nodded. "Better. Sorry, I—"

"No need." Lucy leaned on the open door. "That was hard. I've seen cops faint when they had to identify a relative's body. I know that it wasn't easy for you. But better to shoulder this than the immediate family. Her sister? Mary, is it?"

"Mary Aaron," Rachel supplied. She took another drink. The dizziness seemed to have passed. "I'm all right," she said. "Really. Thank you for your kindness." Evan had been right in his assessment of Lucy Mars. She had the makings of a superior policewoman. Who would have thought that there was so much compassion behind that rigid exterior?

Lucy walked around and slid into the driver's seat. "By rights, I shouldn't be here," she said. "This sort of case is usually taken over by a detective. But we're shorthanded at the troop, with Evan in D.C., and Detective Starkey tied up in court today. So it falls to me to do the best I can with the initial investigation without making any serious goof-ups."

What difference did it make if procedure wasn't followed precisely? Rachel wondered. It was too late to save Elsie. There was no urgency now. Eventually everything would work itself out, wouldn't it? It wasn't as if what they discovered would bring her back. Her mother would say that Elsie was in a better place, and maybe she was. Rachel hoped so. She hoped it was someplace where a bright young woman could ride home from a frolic without vanishing like smoke and ending up in a hastily dug grave.

"Why the bandage on her head?" Rachel asked. The question was mostly Rachel thinking aloud. She didn't expect Lucy to have the answer. "She didn't die immediately after the injury, did she?"

Lucy had removed her Canadian Mountie–style hat; she placed it on the seat. "We're not supposed to speculate. The autopsy will tell us what happened."

"But it looks like head trauma to you?"

"These aren't questions I'm qualified to answer."

"You certainly are. You saw them remove her body from the ground, didn't you? Was there a lot of blood?"

"Almost none. The wound appears to be located at the back of the skull, but the site was covered with the wrappings. I didn't get a good look."

"So it could be anything? She could have been shot?" Rachel's mind was scrambling for a sane explanation. "We have a lot of hunting accidents in this county. Poachers often take deer at night. Is it possible that someone accidentally shot her?"

Lucy shook her head. "Stop. There's no sense in making yourself even more upset by trying to do the coroner's job. Wait for the report. Until then, your main concern has to be for Elsie's family. Helping them get through this. Losing a child is the worst thing that can happen to parents."

But Rachel couldn't let it go. "The makeshift bandages. They prove that someone tried to help her. But if they were concerned enough to bandage her, why weren't they concerned enough to call 9-1-1? Why didn't they take her to the emergency room? And where was Dathan when this happened?"

"Hopefully the investigation will answer those questions." Lucy keyed a few words into her phone. "But obviously the boyfriend's part in all this is a concern."

Rachel worried at a thumbnail with her teeth. It was a childish habit that she'd worked hard to rid herself of, but under stress, it came back. Even when she was at Wharton, she'd had to keep her nails unfashionably short to keep from biting them during exams and term papers. "You don't want to refer to him as 'her boyfriend' if you interview her parents. Stick to 'the young man who drove her home from the singing,' if you want to use anything other than his name. Uncle Aaron is a strict father. He likes to believe his daughters aren't typical young women. For Old Order Amish, that is. Elsie wasn't the type to go parking with a boy."

"I'll keep that in mind." Lucy looked up from her phone. "Do you know if Elsie had been injured before going to the singing? Did she have the bandages on that night when she went with Dathan?"

"Definitely not," Rachel said, shaking her head slowly. She thought about the old sheet that had been partially wrapped around Elsie's body. It looked like it had been white or beige . . . with blue cornflowers. "From what I've read, victims who are killed by someone who cares about them are more likely to be treated tenderly after death. Is that true?"

"Mm-hm." Lucy was reading a text that had just come in. "Yes. We often see that in child homicides when a parent is involved in the crime. But again, you can't jump to conclusions."

"So I guess Dathan is still your main suspect." Rachel rubbed her forehead. A dull pain throbbed behind her eyes. She hoped it wasn't the beginning of a migraine.

"I wouldn't say 'suspect'," Lucy corrected. "More *person of interest*." She glanced at Rachel. "Anything I say to you here can go no further than this moment. It's not my place to speculate. If I *was* going to speculate, though, I'd say this was a lover's quarrel gone bad. Maybe it got rough. She fell out of the buggy. He tried to take care of her, bandaged her head, but he couldn't save her. When she died, he did what you do with a body. He buried her."

"Okay, so where's Dathan? Where's the horse and wagon? Maybe Dathan took off, but you don't disappear with a horse and wagon. Not and not be seen." Of course that wasn't entirely true. There were hundreds of horses in Stone Mill, the majority of them bays. And there might be a hundred wagons like the kind they were looking for. "It's all farms along the route they took home from the singing. Someone must have seen something, even at night."

"How serious were they? Dathan and Elsie?"

"Nobody's parents knew it yet, but from what I hear, he wanted to marry her."

"And did she feel the same way?" Lucy asked.

"I believe so. But her father would have objected. He wouldn't have felt that Dathan was in a position to support a wife, certainly not one of his daughters. And Elsie was young, twenty-one."

"I thought Amish girls married young."

"Younger than most English women, maybe. Most weddings that I've been to since I returned to Stone Mill, the girls were in their mid-t wenties. A young woman like Elsie, from a respectable family, would never run off to be married. First of all, she would have to be married by her own bishop. Someone who hadn't known her or didn't know the family or the community would never consent to performing a marriage."

"They could be married anywhere in the country if they were both of age and could prove it. They wouldn't need to go to an Amish preacher. Not if they weren't going to be Amish anymore. A justice of the peace could marry them," Lucy argued. "Or they could have not gotten married at all."

The white, unmarked transport van with Elsie's body drove past them and out of the cemetery, followed by the coroner's vehicle. Zebadiah got into his buggy. His back was as straight as ever, but Rachel noticed that his nephew Cyrus was driving. Zebadiah, she realized, must have been here all night. She glanced back at the graveyard. The roped-off area with the crime scene yellow tape looked deceptively innocent, with fall sunlight filtering through the trees and squirrels scampering along the top of the stone wall.

"I need to put out an APB for Mr. Bender," Lucy said when the van was gone. "The sooner we talk to him, the closer we'll be to finding out exactly what happened to your cousin. I appreciate your help. Will you be all right to drive home? I imagine you want to be with her family."

"What about them? I have to tell them . . ."

"Someone is with them now. The officer was just waiting for your identification. As terrible news as it will be to deliver, it would be nearly as bad to tell them that Elsie was dead and then find out that it wasn't her at all."

"*Ya*, I should go to them," Rachel agreed. She turned to look directly at the trooper. "If Dathan was involved, it could have been an accident, couldn't it?" She wondered if she should tell Lucy that Elsie and Dathan had quarreled at the party. Or was that just hearsay?

"If you don't think Dathan did this, who do you think is responsible?"

"Responsible for what? We don't even know how she died."

"It's likely that whoever was involved in her

death, whether it was accidental or purposefully committed, buried her." Lucy said it kindly, but she wasn't sugarcoating it either. "It just makes sense, Rachel."

Rachel exhaled slowly, staring out the windshield at nothing in particular. "It's possible that they might have quarreled, Elsie and Dathan, but it's not possible that a boy like Dathan could bury a girl he loved in the graveyard. That he could put her in a hole in the ground and throw dirt on her face. *Ne*." She shook her head. "The Amish like to stay as far from the deceased as possible. He would never do that. Not without prayer or the wake or the people she loved bidding her farewell. He would probably believe that that was a greater sin than harming her, which I'm not convinced he did."

"Okay, so tell me, who do you think did it?"

"Me?" Rachel looked at her. "I don't know. But I think you need to talk to Rupert Rust."

"Why Mr. Rust?"

"He was at the party. He knew both Elsie and Dathan. And I suspect that more went on at that frolic than anyone's been willing to share with me."

Lucy removed her sunglasses and cleaned them. "But why Mr. Rust in particular?"

"Because I overheard something," she answered. "I don't know if there is any truth to it, so I'm not comfortable giving you details, but . . ." She looked away. "I'd question Rupert. You're going to have to do it carefully, though. And if you intrude too deeply into personal affairs, you'll find yourself facing a *Deitsch* wall thicker than stone."

Lucy looked at her for a moment. "I'll be sure and pass that on to the detective assigned to the case."

"Not you?"

Lucy shook her head. "I'm just a trooper. You know how this works. I know couples talk. A detective will do the interviews, now that this has become a possible murder case."

"You don't think it could have been an accident?" Rachel asked.

"It's possible. Not for me to determine."

Rachel put her hand on the door. "You're right. I need to be with Mary Aaron and her family. My parents, too. They'll all need me."

Rachel drove the pitchfork into the straw and goat manure with more force than was necessary. In times of stress, she craved physical work, and cleaning out her goat stall was definitely a way to get her exercise in. She'd spent hours with Mary Aaron, Aunt Hannah, Uncle Aaron, and her cousins, leaving only when Bishop Chupp and several of the church elders arrived to pray with the family. She'd called Stone Mill House from her cell and relayed a message through one of the cleaning staff to Ada, her housekeeper.

Rachel had wanted to ask Ada if she could possibly make an evening meal for the Hostetlers on this short of a notice. Communicating with Ada from a distance was difficult though, since Ada refused to use a telephone. Ada was the cook as well as housekeeper for the B&B. She ran the kitchen with the cool efficiency of Vito Corleone. In return, Rachel paid her well and stayed out of her way. Ada in a tiff was not something she wanted to face. Evan accused her of being terrified of her cook. Maybe he was right. So long as Ada was absolutely dependable and honest, produced fabulous meals and desserts, and provided an endless supply of nieces and granddaughters to clean and do the laundry, Rachel was happy to leave the details to her.

Fortunately, Ada's good heart surfaced in any emergency, and she promised something fitting for the Hostetlers by five, which left Rachel with more than an hour to kill an excess amount of nervous energy. At a B&B, especially one that tended to collect stray animals, there was always work that needed doing. Rachel had changed into a pair of jeans and T-shirt, her muck boots, and leather gloves. She'd locked the goats into a smaller stall and was busy heaping her wheelbarrow with material for the garden compost pile.

Earlier, when she'd had to hold Mary Aaron in her arms and stand beside her aunt and uncle, she'd held in her tears. But she couldn't do it any longer. Here, with no one but the goats to witness, she gave in to the grief and sorrow from Elsie's young life lost in a foolish accident. She had to believe that what had taken her from them was an accident. If she thought that someone, anyone, had deliberately struck her little cousin hard enough to cause her death, she wasn't certain she would be able to forgive that person or contain her anger.

And so the tears welled up and spilled out of her eyes, splashing down her cheeks and causing her nose to run. And the harder she cried, the more furiously she dug at the soiled bedding, scooping up and flinging the straw into a wheelbarrow. After a while, she had to stop to blow her nose and dry her eyes. Elsie was in heaven. It was what Aunt Hannah believed and what she had to accept. Elsie was beyond pain or harm. From tears, Rachel moved naturally to the prayers of her childhood, and in them she found comfort.

When she finished the stall, covered the floor with fresh bedding, and put away the wheelbarrow and pitchfork, her sense of helplessness had been replaced with a determination to find out what had happened to Elsie. And if there was blame, if Dathan or anyone else had intentionally harmed her, she would hunt him down and see that he was made to pay for what he'd done.

She was luring the goats back into the stall when her cell rang. She fumbled for her phone with one hand while shooing the mischievous animals with the other. One of the younger goats made an attempt to squeeze between Rachel and the door frame, but she blocked the way and tossed a withered apple into the clean straw. She answered the call; it was Lucy.

"Rachel. I just wanted you to know that I started the investigation of the case, under a detective's supervision. I went out to the Rust farm and spoke with Mr. Rust."

"With Rupert or his father?" Rachel interrupted.

"Mr. Rupert Rust. He says he didn't witness any argument at the party and had no confrontation with Mr. Bender or Miss Hostetler at the party or at any other time. He claimed he wasn't aware of any problems. He says he can't even say for certain that he saw Mr. Bender that evening."

He was lying, but Rachel kept that to herself. She wondered why he would lie. Was it just because Lucy was English, because she was a cop, or was it something more sinister?

"Still nothing on Mr. Bender's whereabouts." Lucy paused and then went on. "I know you don't want to believe it, but everything points to Mr. Bender. You have to look at the facts. Best guess, as I said before, the boyfriend accidentally killed her. She died of a cerebral hemorrhage—blunt force trauma, according to the preliminary autopsy. Miss Hostetler—"

"Don't call her that," Rachel said. "No titles,

remember. Her name was Elsie Jean Hostetler."

"Elsie had been deceased about twenty-four to thirty-six hours at the time of discovery. The most natural assumption is that the boyfriend got scared, tried to bandage her up. And when she died, he panicked. She's Amish. They both are. The natural place to bury her might be an Amish cemetery. Once he did, he took off. He had to feel guilty, because even if he wasn't at fault, he should have called for help immediately. That delay might have caused her death. But that's only conjecture. The final autopsy report will be more detailed."

"The family needs to arrange for the funeral," Rachel said. She shot the bolt on the goat stall gate. "How soon will Elsie's body be released?"

"I don't know."

"Could you find out? It's really important for her body to go in the ground as soon as possible. For religious reasons," Rachel added, hoping that would help her case. And it was true. The Amish didn't embalm their dead. They usually buried them within twenty-four hours.

"I'll see what I can do," Lucy said on the other end of the line. "Please convey my deepest sympathy to the family. I'll be speaking with them in the next few days. Well, me or Detective Starkey. I really am sorry that this terrible thing happened to your cousin."

"If there's anything I can do, don't hesitate to call," Rachel reminded her.

"Be assured, I want this case behind us as much as you do."

Once Lucy hung up, Rachel rang Evan's number. She expected to reach his voicemail and she did. She left a message telling him that they'd found Elsie's body and that Dathan hadn't shown up and appeared to be the most likely one respon-sible. She asked Evan to call her as soon as he could.

She was halfway to the house when her cell rang again. The caller ID showed *Wagner's Grocery*.

"Hello, Rachel? This is Polly. Down at the grocery. I'm so sorry about your cousin."

"Thank you." Polly was the owner-manager of Wagner's and a lifelong staple of the town. Rachel could hear registers ringing and the clatter of the market.

"George O'Day put in an order for our deluxe lunchmeat and cheese tray to go out to your aunt and uncle's place. It turned out real nice, with pickles, olives, and little rosettes of kale. Looks too pretty to eat. Anyway, George wanted it to be there by suppertime. He knew they'd have a houseful to feed."

Rachel guessed that Polly had called for some-thing specific, but like most of the natives of Stone Mill, she wouldn't be hurried. "How is George?" George was a friend in the last stages of cancer, and Rachel had meant to stop by one evening.

"Poorly," Peggy said. "Ell was in to pick up some milk and two deluxe Reubens and those big dill pickles we have in the barrel in the deli section. George loves our pickles. He eats one every day. Says it's one of the few things he can still taste."

Rachel waited.

Peggy caught her breath and went on. "I wouldn't trouble you, but we're shorthanded here. Customers stacked up at every register, and the boy who does our deliveries didn't show up for work today. So the aisles aren't getting swept and deliveries aren't going out. I'd do it myself, like I said, but we're swamped. Would you mind picking up this platter for the Hostetlers and running it out to them? I hate to disappoint George. He's such a good customer."

"Who does your deliveries? Buddy Wheeler?" Rachel asked.

"Yeah, Buddy. But you know how he is. Sober today, hung over tomorrow. Typical of him to tie one on over the weekend and call out."

Rachel had seen Buddy at the cemetery the previous night. She didn't remember thinking he was intoxicated. He said he'd been out to his grandfather's. But anything was possible. Maybe he tied one on after the visit. Or maybe he really was sick. "Sure," she told Polly. "No problem. I'll be there shortly."

CHAPTER 8

George's prediction was right. By the time Rachel returned, the Hostetler home was overflowing with people. Rachel's parents, the elders and their wives, and most of the members of Aunt Hannah and Uncle Aaron's church community had come to sit with the grieving family. Men and the few younger people who had stopped by clustered in tight groups outside, while women and older folks, including the elders, sat in the parlor and living room and dished up plate after plate of food from the kitchen. This was exactly what Amish custom called for in Stone Mill. From the time of death of a family member until that lost one was buried, there would be a constant coming and going so that those closest to the deceased never mourned alone.

The majority of the callers wore their black go-to-worship clothing, making Rachel look almost festive in her blue denim skirt, brown long-sleeved blouse, and navy head scarf. Choosing what to wear to visit more conservative Amish families in the valley was difficult, but picking the right dress for a wake was daunting.

When she was growing up, picking out clothing

had been simple, Rachel thought as she sliced hard-boiled eggs into a wash pan full of German potato salad while close to a dozen women in starched white *kapps* and aprons bustled around her. Every day, Rachel mused, she wore a dress just like every other Old Order Amish girl. She usually had four to pick from: her best dress, black; her everyday dress, blue; her go-to-town dress in dark green, or the brown go-to-town one, depending on the season. Now, she couldn't wear something too close to what Amish women wore, because that might have looked like mockery, and she wasn't free to choose what she did every day at the B&B. Sometimes it felt to Rachel as if there were two invisible lines dividing the Amish world from the English and she inhabited the shadowy no-man's-land in between.

"She should use more eggs," her mother commented to no one in particular.

"I will," Rachel promised. "There are more waiting in the refrigerator."

"Shell another eight eggs," her mother ordered her daughter-in-law Ruth in *Deitsch*. "Potato salad needs more egg."

"I'll do it," her Aunt Hannah said.

"No need for you to be in here," Rachel's mother said soothingly. "The bishop is leading prayers in the front parlor. Go sit with them."

Rachel glanced at her aunt and saw her shake her head in protest.

"*Ne*, I need to keep busy with my hands."

"Esther, let her be. Each mother grieves in her own way," murmured another neighbor. "When I lost my last babe I didn't sleep for a week, but I finished all the winter's mending in three nights."

"It's hard," someone else interjected. "Lord knows it's hard, sometimes nearly more than a body can bear. But you have to remember, your Elsie's in a better place. Death doesn't discriminate. It takes the good along with the wicked."

A broad-faced woman in a black elder's *kapp* nodded. "You'll see her again in heaven. Be certain of it."

"It's not for us to question the will of God," Rachel's mother pronounced.

"I can finish this," Ruth told Rachel. "Someone needs to cut the cakes, and I'd make a mess of it. Would you mind?"

"*Ne*," Rachel replied. "I can do it." Cake slicing she could do. Rachel wasn't much use when it came to cooking, but Ada had taught her how to slice cakes and pies like a pro. She moved to confront a four-layer hummingbird cake that towered over three other cakes and a bounty of pies and sweet buns at one end of the scarred trestle table.

Although there were no stoves going and the windows were open, Rachel felt sweaty. Aunt Hannah's spartan kitchen was spacious, but too many women, too much rich food, several crying babies, and a whining toddler made the room stuffy. The migraine that had been threatening Rachel all week hovered like a cloud over her. Not everyone in the room had remembered to shower before coming, and Rachel had a highly developed sense of smell. She swallowed, determined not to become queasy. Not all Amish women had recognized the necessity of deodorant, an omission that had troubled her even as a girl.

She eased a slice of cake onto a saucer and looked around the room. Where was Mary Aaron? She wouldn't have expected her to be amid the devout sitting with the bishop, but she hadn't seen her since she'd arrived. Aunt Hannah could have used Mary Aaron's calm strength. She looked exhausted, almost as if she were going to faint. Rachel was just removing a second slice from the cake when she heard her aunt gasp. She turned to see her clutching her hand to the front of her apron. Drops of blood were dripping down onto her spotless apron.

"Oh, Aunt Hannah," Rachel exclaimed. She put the cake and the knife down on the table and went to her aunt. "Let me see. How did you do that?" When she slipped an arm around her, Rachel could feel Aunt Hannah trembling.

"Stupid. I was slicing an egg and . . ."

Someone handed Rachel a damp washcloth

and she took her aunt's hand and examined the finger. "I think you tried to slice the tip of your finger off." It was bleeding like a typical finger cut. Fortunately, despite the amount of blood welling up, the wound didn't seem to be too deep. Rachel wrapped the washcloth around it. "Are you all right?" she asked. Her aunt's face was ashen.

"*Ya*, such a foolish mistake. How many times have I sliced eggs?"

"Once we clean this up, I think you need to go and lie down for a while," Rachel suggested. Her aunt nodded, and Rachel guided her toward the bathroom.

Visitors spilled out of the parlor and living room into the hall. From somewhere, Rachel heard her uncle's voice raised indignantly. She could make out only part of what he was saying. ". . . Not right. We should have her body to bury decently. They want to embalm her. Put chemicals into . . ."

Aunt Hannah's pale face blanched to a ghastly gray. The bathroom door opened and Rachel tugged her aunt inside and locked the door. Someone knocked, but Rachel ignored the intrusion. "Sit down." She put the toilet seat down and guided Aunt Hannah onto it. She ran her a glass of water and handed it to her before soaking another washcloth with cool water, wringing it out, and pressing it to her aunt's forehead. "Let me tend to that finger and then we'll get you upstairs and off your feet. I imagine you're exhausted."

"Her father doesn't want them to . . . to do that to her body. That embalming. He says it's a desecration. And Aaron's right. Elsie should be here in her home, where I can wash her and dress her in white before . . ." Aunt Hannah broke off and rocked silently, her grief too deep for tears.

"I'll speak to the coroner," Rachel offered as she soaked a cotton ball with peroxide and patted her aunt's injury tenderly. "Even call a lawyer if I have to. We should be able to get a religious exemption. I'm certain Trooper Mars will help." Blood was still seeping from the cut but not enough to be concerned about. Rachel smeared it with an antibiotic cream, wrapped it in gauze, and then taped it securely. "There. Would you like a moment's privacy?" Her aunt shook her head, so Rachel took a deep breath and they ventured out into the crowded hall.

Eli Rust's wife stopped them with a hand on her aunt's arm. "Oh, Hannah, we are so sorry. We've been praying for you." Other women, some Amish, some English, offered similar words of comfort.

Rachel thanked them, repeatedly mentioned her aunt's need for a little quiet, and managed to extricate her from the mourners and up the stairs to Aunt Hannah and Uncle Aaron's bedroom.

There, she helped her aunt into bed, untied her shoes, and massaged her feet. Aunt Hannah lay back on the pillow and closed her eyes. Rachel smiled. Her aunt's kitchen, parlor, and other downstairs rooms were devoid of any color or decoration, painfully plain. But her linen sheets and pillowcases were daintily embroidered with a pattern of yellow roses and green leaves, and the folded quilt at the end of the bed was a colorful rainbow.

"That feels so nice, Rachel," her aunt admitted. "You're a good girl."

"The police suspect Dathan killed her, probably by accident," Rachel said quietly. "But he was a decent boy. I can't believe that he would hurt her. You and Uncle Aaron didn't know that they were walking out together, did you?"

Her aunt gave a small sound of disbelief. "You think I didn't know? A mother knows these things. I know that my Elsie cared deeply for that boy. But don't tell your uncle. Elsie didn't want him to find out. He would have forbidden her to see him again, you see. And Elsie was an obedient daughter, but the heart wants what it wants."

Rachel thought it was interesting that her aunt would quote Emily Dickinson. She couldn't imagine Hannah had ever read Dickinson. "Why wouldn't Uncle Aaron have approved of Dathan?"

"His father was a terrible provider. Lazy, your

uncle called him. And his father before him. But our Elsie was a sensible girl. If she believed in Dathan, then I think he would have proved himself different from his family. And he wouldn't have been starting with nothing the way some young folks have to these days. His great-aunt told me that Dathan's mother meant to give the farm to him once he settled down and took a wife. Aaron would have come around in time."

"Do you think he's to blame for Elsie's death?" Rachel asked as she gently rubbed her aunt's instep. "You're a good judge of character."

"Your uncle thinks Dathan killed her. The Bible tells us that the husband is the head of the house." Aunt Hannah turned on her side. "He says that if our daughter hadn't left the frolic with him, she would be alive, so she's partly to blame for what happened."

Rachel moved to sit beside her aunt and rubbed the back of her neck and her shoulders. "But you have your own thoughts," she prompted.

"I do."

"Tell me, Aunt Hannah."

Her aunt sighed. "I don't care what the English authorities say, and I don't care what my husband says. At least not about this. I listen to my heart, and my heart says Dathan is innocent of any wrong." Her voice dropped to a whisper. "Some things a mother just knows."

Rachel waited for her aunt to say more, and

when she didn't, Rachel leaned over and kissed her cheek. Then she went to the windows and pulled down the shades, darkening the room. She stood vigil until she heard Aunt Hannah's breathing slow as she dropped off to sleep.

"Back to the fray," Rachel muttered, half under her breath. At the bottom of the stairs, she was confronted by a twenty-something woman in tight jeans, a leather jacket, and more teased hair than Rachel had seen on one human in a long time. The hair was unnaturally black and had enough hair spray on it to withstand a tornado.

"Hi, I'm Wynter. Wynter Feathers. I just stopped by to say how sorry I am."

Rachel was certain she'd seen Wynter before and tried to place her. Maybe it was at Wagner's Grocery. No, how could she have forgotten Wynter's performance in last year's talent show? She sang a country-and-western song off-key and played the guitar . . . after a fashion.

Wynter balanced a plate of food on the banister and blocked Rachel's way. "I know who you are," she said. "You're that Rachel who owns the fancy B&B in town."

"It was kind of you to come," Rachel murmured, wondering how the girl knew the family. She didn't *look* like someone the Hostetlers would keep company with. "Were you a friend of Elsie's?" she asked.

"I used to buy pies off her at the farmers'

market. My mom sells plants and stuff there sometimes. She's Mennonite. She and my dad used to be Amish, but they left before they had any kids. My granddad, he's Amish. He's got a farm on the other end of the valley. We live there to take care of him, me and my brother."

"So you and Elsie weren't really friends?"

"Yeah, I guess you could say we were friends. We used to talk music. She liked the oldies, you know, the classics. Johnny Cash, Merle Haggard, Hank Williams Jr. The Grand Ole Opry stuff, not these fake studio-generated wannabes you hear on the radio today."

"Right." Rachel forced a smile and tried to squeeze past.

"So, I was wondering"—Wynter blocked Rachel's escape—"about where they found poor Ellie's body."

"*Elsie,*" Rachel corrected.

"Yeah, I know," she said. "Right . . . I just always called her Ellie, like a nickname. Not so old-fashioned, you know. But that was awful, somebody burying her like that. Not even in a box, just in the ground. I guess the cops have a good idea who did it."

Rachel tried not to show her impatience. She had no reason to dislike this girl. "They're doing a thorough investigation. I'm sure they'll find out exactly what happened."

"I heard they're doing an autopsy. That's when

they cut open the guts and everything, isn't it? I saw that on *CSI*. That show that used to be on about Las Vegas?"

"I've seen it, yes."

"They showed all that stuff. Crazy, isn't it?"

"Forensics. It's invaluable in solving crimes."

"So they think a crime has happened? They think she was murdered?"

An Amish woman standing near them picked up her plate and fork and moved away. "I'm sorry," Rachel said. "Today is a day of mourning for the family. We shouldn't really be discussing Elsie's death."

"Sure, I understand," Wynter said.

Was that a ring through her eyebrow? Rachel tried not to stare. "If you'll excuse me, they need me in the kitchen," she said.

"Oh, sure. I was just curious. I guess the cops are looking for the guy she was with."

"Do you know Dathan?" Rachel asked.

"Me? No." Wynter shook her head, and the pouf over her forehead swayed precariously. "It's just that usually the first one the cops look at when a girl gets killed is the husband or the boyfriend. They're always the one. You know, one little argument and *bop,* somebody loses their temper. Such a shame, her being so sweet and all."

"Yes," Rachel agreed. "She was a sweet person and whatever happened, she didn't deserve it. No one deserves this."

"I didn't mean anything," Wynter said. "Not to be disrespectful to the dead, you know. I'm not like that. I just wondered if they'd caught the boyfriend yet."

Rachel noticed Elsie's oldest brother coming out of the parlor where the elders were gathered. Paul had his father's stern look, but Aunt Hannah's sweet disposition. "There's Paul," Rachel said. "That's her brother. Have you met him? Paul, can you come over here for a moment?" Rachel motioned to him. "This is Wynter Feathers. She told me that she was a friend of Elsie's." Using Paul's solid form as a shield, Rachel ducked around him and made her escape. *Weird people,* she thought as she went out the front door and onto the porch.

Jesse, twelve, Elsie's youngest brother, was sitting at the edge, his legs dangling over, an uneaten plate of food in his lap. "Hey, Rae-Rae," he said. His flat-crowned straw hat was pulled low on his forehead, probably, she guessed, in an attempt to hide that he'd been crying. A brindle collie with a chunk missing out of one ear lay beside him.

Rachel lifted his hat to its proper position and tucked a stray lock of hair out of his eyes. "It's all right to mourn for her," she said. "You don't have to be ashamed of loving your sister."

Jesse's fair, freckled face flushed and he averted his eyes. Rachel winced, knowing that his childhood had ended today and that nothing she could say or do could take away the pain. She'd always had a special place in her heart for Jesse, who liked peach ice cream and Boxcar mysteries. "We have to think Elsie's in a better place," she said, repeating the old phrase that so many had said to her today. "She's safe."

"But she's not here. I want her here," the boy said.

"Me, too." Rachel gripped his shoulder.

"Find out what happened to her," he said. "Promise me you will."

"I will."

"If that Dathan hurt her, I'll . . . I'll—"

"Don't think that way," Rachel cautioned. "She wouldn't want it. If someone, *anyone,* hurt her intentionally, the police will find out and that person will face the full force of the law."

Jesse sniffed and wiped at his eyes with the back of his hand. "I just . . . I feel like I should be doing something. I'm not a kid anymore." Absently, he stroked the dog.

"You can pray for her. That's what your mother and father would want and that's what will bring you peace."

He nodded. "I can do that."

"Good. Have you seen Mary Aaron? I can't seem to catch up with her."

"I saw her a little while ago," Jesse said. "I

think maybe she's out in the yard with some of the young people."

"Thanks." She descended the steps and started around the house. When she reached a secluded alcove between three lilac bushes, she removed the cell phone from her skirt pocket and called Lucy.

"Rachel?"

Some children appeared, laughing and kicking a ball, and Rachel turned away, hoping that they hadn't seen the phone. "Sorry to bother you, but I need your help," she said. "Can you tell me what I'd have to do to get Elsie's body released as soon as possible? It's important in the Amish religion that she be buried quickly. If we could get it back tonight, we could hold the funeral tomorrow."

"Autopsy's done. Let me call the coroner's office," Lucy said. "If they give me the runaround, there's a judge I know who would be sympathetic. His wife has Amish relatives. Nothing like a court order to speed up justice."

"Thank you," Rachel said. "I appreciate it. It would mean a lot to the family."

"I don't suppose Dathan has turned up?"

"No one has seen him."

"Would they tell you?"

"Most people aren't inclined to give him much leeway at this point. I think I would hear if he'd been seen."

"If you do get any leads on Dathan's where-abouts, call me right away. No playing detective," Lucy cautioned.

"I'll call you." Rachel thanked Lucy again, turned off the phone, and continued through the side yard. When she reached the farmyard, she saw several clusters of Amish. Among a group of young adults was Lettie. And as she neared them, she realized that Lettie appeared deep in conversation with Rupert Rust. She almost hadn't recognized him because he was dressed Amish, a wide-brimmed black hat pulled down over his close-cropped hair. She was still looking at him when Rupert caught sight of her. He spoke abruptly to Lettie, then turned and strode away. Rachel hurried toward her sister, but before she could reach her, Mary Aaron waved from the other group.

"Rachel! Over here."

Rachel gave Lettie a final glance and then went over to Mary Aaron.

"Were you inside?" her cousin asked. "How's my mother?"

"Worn out. I think the crowd and confusion is too much for her," Rachel explained. "She needed to take a break, so I convinced her to lie down for a nap."

"Any word about Elsie? When she will be released to us?"

"I just spoke with Trooper Mars. She's going to

see what she can do to speed things up. I told her that it was a religious requirement that Elsie be buried quickly."

Mary Aaron nodded. Her dress was a deep blue, so dark that it was almost purple. There were dark shadows under her eyes, and she looked awful, as if she hadn't slept in days, which Rachel supposed she hadn't.

I probably don't look much better, Rachel thought. "We're going to find out who did this."

"*Ya,* we will." Mary Aaron's usually smiling mouth was a taut line, her shoulders stiff. "An accident, I could almost understand. But why did he have to bury her like that? Like she was a dead dog? Only you wouldn't put a dog in a cemetery, would you?" Tears filled Mary Aaron's eyes.

Rachel took her arm and led her through a gap between the shed and chicken house to a swing under the grapevine. "Sit," she ordered, and Mary Aaron sat. Rachel sat beside her and they pushed off with their feet, swinging as Rachel remem-bered doing here as a child. For minutes, they didn't speak again, but gradually the swing drifted to a stop.

"Do you think it's our fault she died?" Mary Aaron asked.

Rachel turned to her, surprised. "How could it be our fault?"

"Not you and me specifically, but all of us. It

keeps going through my head that my sisters and my little brothers are so innocent of the world that they don't fear what's out there. They don't understand the evil in some people's hearts. They don't know that there are men, and women, too, I suppose, who take pleasure from pain."

"You mean the whole Amish thing? Remaining apart from the world?" Rachel said.

"Exactly. Only you can't, can you? Because the world is all around us. We keep our kids apart to protect them from sin, but maybe we make it impossible for them to recognize it when they see it."

"I don't know, Mary Aaron. Uncle Aaron wouldn't agree."

"*Ne*, he wouldn't. Only—"

Shouts broke the quiet of the grape arbor. "Fight!" a boy yelled.

Rachel and Mary Aaron, simultaneously, scrambled off the swing and ran toward the farmyard. When they burst through the passageway into the open, they saw a knot of young adults. And on the ground, amid a cloud of dust, two men wrestled and pounded each other. Rachel didn't know who the guy on the bottom was, but the one on top, landing the most punches, she knew. Rupert Rust.

CHAPTER 9

Aaron Hostetler's deep baritone rang out from the porch, and in seconds, Rachel saw her father and uncle ordering the young Amish men in the gathering crowd to separate the two on the ground. "There is no fighting on my farm!" Uncle Aaron roared. "What is wrong with you that you must resort to violence on this day of mourning?"

John Hannah and Alan dragged the English boy up off the ground, his shirt torn and bloody. Once Rachel got a good look at him, she recognized him as Zebadiah's neighbor's son, the football player. Mike made no further effort to lash out at Rupert, but his opponent was clearly out of control. Her brother Moses got between the two of them and extended his arms to block any effort to renew their fight.

Paying no attention to Moses, Rupert wrenched off one of the Amish men holding him, shoved the other away, and made a lunge for Mike. Moses and the others grabbed him, not striking, but pinning his arms and legs. Rupert cursed and struggled, but long hours in the fields meant that the peacemakers were nearly as strong and fit as he was. Trembling and sweating, eyes wild, he gradually subsided.

"Rachel! Help him!" Lettie cried. "Don't let them hurt Rupert!"

Mike was standing quietly, face red, obviously embarrassed. "Sorry," he said to Lettie.

Rachel glanced from her sister to Mike and then back to Rupert. What did the boys' fight have to do with Lettie? She looked at her father to see if he'd heard Lettie defending Rupert. Her *dat* stood stone-faced, arms folded, shoulder to shoulder with her uncle. "Best you leave, young man," Rachel's father said. "You fellows can let him go. He'll cause no more trouble. Isn't that right?"

"No, sir," Mike said. He wiped his nose with the back of his wrist and someone handed him a handkerchief. He pressed it to his face and put his head back, trying to stop the bleeding.

At that moment, Mike's father, Chuck, came out of the house. He crossed the yard at a trot. "My apologies," he said when he reached them. He glared at his son. "And you, into the truck." His son obeyed without argument. Chuck started the truck, and people stepped aside to let them drive out of the farmyard.

Rachel approached Rupert. "Get in my Jeep," she said. "I'll take you home."

"No need for that," Rupert said. "I walked here. If I'm not welcome, I can walk home."

"Please," she said, looking up into his eyes. "Just get in."

Two minutes later, they were rattling down the driveway. Rachel looked at Rupert and saw a bruise over one eye quickly turning dark. He had a swollen lip and another bruise on his chin. Altogether, he looked a lot better than Mike, although Mike outweighed him by a good forty pounds. "What was all that about?"

Rupert stared at the floor. "He made some wisecrack about Lettie and I hit him."

Rachel braked at the mailbox to allow a car to pass before turning onto the blacktop. "And you believe fighting helped? It won't help Lettie's reputation. You should know better. Adults talk out their differences; they don't hit people."

"I lost my temper," he admitted. "I shouldn't have taken a swing at Mike there. I should have waited."

"You shouldn't have fought with him at all," Rachel said. "Look at you."

Rupert's black wool hat lay, dirty, on the floor of the Jeep, the crown crushed. "Not much of an Amish solution, was it?" He wiped blood from the corner of his mouth.

"No, it wasn't. And if you really hope to fit in here, if you want to be part of the community again, you have to control yourself."

"Yeah, I know it. But . . . it's hard. D—" He bit back what she thought might have been a curse.

"Mike's okay. I know him. He thinks he's a jokester. But I don't like jokes about Amish girls. Especially not today, after . . . after Elsie."

"Why would Mike say anything about Lettie? Has she done something inappropriate?"

"No, she's a good girl. One of the few who seemed to want me to come back."

"So, there's nothing romantic between you?"

"I think you should ask her. She's not a kid."

Rachel shifted gears. She came to the fork in the road that should have taken her to the Rust farm, but instead of taking the right turn, she took the left. She proceeded until she came to a dirt drive leading into a farm field and pulled over there.

"Thought you were driving me home."

"I am. I'd just like to ask you a few questions."

He exhaled loudly. "Not promising answers."

"Fair enough." She put down her window and then twisted to look at him. "Why did you lie to me about the fight at the singing the night Elsie disappeared?"

Rupert folded his arms. "Who says I did?"

She sighed. "I'm not playing games with you. Either you're interested in what happened to Elsie or not. That's all I'm trying to find out. I'm not trying to blame you."

"No?" He looked back at her and his eyes clouded over with either anger or sorrow. "Sounds like you are."

"You lied to me, Rupert, and I want to know why. You said you couldn't remember if you'd even seen Dathan that night. But that's not true. Because you and Dathan fought. And my guess is that you were fighting over Elsie. Is that what happened?"

He didn't answer.

"You and Elsie used to like each other, didn't you? Before you left to go English."

"Maybe we did. We were both kind of young then."

"But not too young to care about each other?" Rachel suggested.

Rupert shifted in his seat and ran a swollen hand through his short hair. Dried dirt sprinkled down his face. "I pretty much made a fool of myself back there, didn't I?"

"I don't want to discuss what just happened over my sister," she said. "I want to know more about the fight at the singing. Were you still angry with Dathan? When he left?"

"Nope. All settled."

"What about Elsie? Were you angry with her because she was with Dathan?"

He picked up his hat off the floorboard and tried to punch it back into shape, but the hat reverted to its squashed appearance. "I thought a lot about Elsie when I was over there." He gestured. "Crazy place. People driving down the road, drinking a Coke, and suddenly a bomb goes

149

off, and the guy next to you, the eighteen-year-old kid from Little Rock, has no legs anymore. When I went, I wanted to see something besides this valley." He waved toward the surrounding mountains. "Those, too. I thought there must be something better outside." He shook his head. "There isn't. So when . . . when everything fell apart, I thought I'd come back. Give it another try. See if some of that peace that the bishop preaches about is for real."

"Rupert." Rachel laid a hand on his arm. "I can't begin to imagine I know what you've seen over there, but—"

"Not just seen. Done."

Her throat clenched with compassion for this broken young man. "I've seen violent death, too. It stays with you."

He nodded. "That it does." Rupert blinked back welling tears. "Sometimes I think I never left that godforsaken place. I can still taste the sand, you know. It gets into everything: beans, coffee, in your eyes, your ears, and mouth."

"But you're home now," she said gently. "You have a life ahead of you. You have to let all that go."

He shook his head. "I dream about it. Night after night. There was this cute little kid, ten, maybe twelve. Hard to say, because they don't get enough to eat, and they're skinny and short. Anyway, his name was Malmud or Mamud, something like that. We called him Manny. He was a shepherd. Just this little kid off all by himself with this flock of goats and sheep. He'd gotten a thorn in his foot and it got infected. Looked awful. Our medic dug the thorn out, patched him up, and gave him some antibiotics. His mother was so grateful that she sent a basket of bread to us as a thank-you. Manny brought it. And it was good bread, flat, but really tasty. Then he stopped coming around. We found out later that the bad guys caught him. Left the basket on his mother's doorstep with Manny's head in it as a warning not to be friendly with Americans."

Tears ran down Rupert's face and he made no effort to hide them. "We thought we were doing a good thing, keeping the kid from losing his foot. And we got him killed. We should have just taken a few shots at him. Then he might still be alive."

"Or the infection might have turned to gangrene and killed him," Rachel said. "You didn't hurt him. It was evil that took that innocent child's life. You can't blame yourself."

Rupert scoffed. "Sure, you can. People you would never guess could do terrible things, do."

"Like Dathan? You think he's the one who harmed Elsie?"

He shrugged. "Can't say. Maybe. Maybe not."

"You never said how you got to the singing that night."

"Wagon. Why?"

"I'm just trying to get a clear picture of that night in my mind. Do other young Amish think Dathan did it?"

"Most do. Which makes me wonder why you're pestering me." He picked at something on his hand. Dried blood, maybe. "Not everybody. Not Lettie. She thinks the best of everybody. Even me," he added, his voice barely above a whisper.

"And who does Lettie think killed Elsie?"

"Why don't you ask her that yourself?" Rupert jerked open his door. "Enough questions."

"Don't go. I'll drive you home," Rachel said.

He snatched up his hat. "I think I'd rather walk. I think I've said more than enough. Any more questions, ask Dathan." Rupert got out, put his hat on his head, and walked away without looking back.

"Rupert, please!"

He didn't answer.

She felt more confused than ever as she called Evan. To her relief, he picked up. At the sound of his voice, she nearly started crying. "It's so good to hear you," she said. "I wish you were here with me."

"Me, too," he answered. "You don't sound so good. I guess it's pretty rough on the family, finding Elsie like that."

"Worse than you can imagine." She filled him

in on all that had happened, including her odd conversation with Rupert. Evan listened without interrupting. It was one of the things she loved best about him. He was a good listener. "But he lied to me about fighting with Dathan, so how can I trust Rupert now?"

"You can't. He sounds messed up to me."

"I'm afraid Lettie likes him."

"You've got to put a stop to that. From what I heard, Rupert is suffering from PTSD. Not good. Sometimes these guys get over it, but it can take years. It's not something you'd want your sister to have to deal with. Not to mention that he could well have killed Elsie in a fit of jealousy. He probably saw plenty of bloodshed in Afghanistan. From what I heard, he was out in the mountains and was one of the few survivors of his platoon. Not a good scenario."

"I think Rupert has suffered a lot, but I don't think he's capable of killing Elsie. Certainly not if he loved her. And I think he did."

"Men kill the women they profess to love all the time. You know that family disputes are the most dangerous situations for a cop to walk into."

"I can't put my finger on it, but he just doesn't seem the type to me. He loses his temper, yes, but to actually do real harm to someone? If he was fighting with Mike today because Mike said something rude about Lettie, then he was defending her."

"Maybe. Or maybe it's another example of Rupert's inability to control his emotions. Seems like he's a loaded gun ready to go off to me."

"But he chose to come home. He wants to join the church, to be Amish again. If he had murder in his heart, could he do that?"

"Stay away from him, Rache. It's bad enough you're running around the countryside asking questions of regular Amish. Have some faith in Lucy. I told you, she's a good cop. She'll find Dathan and get answers."

"She thinks he did it. So do most people here."

"But you don't?"

"I don't know, Evan. I don't think Dathan did it. But I'm trying to keep an open mind." Her phone beeped in her ear and she glanced at the screen. "Hey, Lucy's calling so I'm going to go. Maybe she has news about releasing Elsie's body to the family."

"I'll try to call you tomorrow. Watch yourself, darlin'. I love you."

"Me, too." She quickly switched to Lucy's call. "Lucy? It's Rachel. I hope you've got some good news."

Her mother was still awake when Rachel arrived back at her parents' home. It was late enough that everyone but Lettie and her father were in bed. Lettie met her in the hall. She was carrying a basin with a towel thrown over it, but Rachel didn't have to guess what was in it. "*Mam*'s been sick again."

"*Ya. Dat* wanted her to come home from Aunt Hannah's hours ago, but you know our mother," Lettie said. "Stubborn."

"I'm afraid it runs in the family," Rachel answered. She was about to ask Lettie about the fight earlier in the day. She wanted to know what Mike had said that had made Rupert so angry. But Lettie looked as though someone had run her through an old-fashioned wringer-washer machine, so she decided it could wait until tomorrow.

"I was going to get her nausea meds," Lettie explained. "She wouldn't take them earlier. Said she didn't want to get 'hooked' on them."

" 'Hooked'? On nausea medicine?"

Lettie shrugged. "You know *Mam*. No convincing her otherwise. Medicine is for weak people. And she jumped down my throat for suggesting it."

"Don't complain. At least she speaks to you."

"*Ya*, she does. All the way home she fussed about Rupert. Said if he wanted to be Amish again, his behavior wasn't showing it. She thinks he'll break his father's heart again when he runs back to the English."

"Don't worry, I'll see that she takes her medicine. You go on to bed."

Lettie yawned. "Thanks. And thanks for getting

Rupert away before Uncle Aaron could eat him alive. I know he shouldn't have been fighting again, but—" Her eyes widened as she realized what she'd just said.

"I know about the fight between Dathan and Rupert," Rachel said.

"*Atch*. Who told you?"

"It doesn't matter. The thing is I know, and it doesn't look good for Rupert to constantly be getting into fights."

"I know. But it isn't his fault. People provoke him. He's been through a lot."

"Lettie!" their mother called weakly from the bedroom. "Bring me a clean towel."

"I'll go," Rachel said. "You get to bed. We can talk more about this tomorrow."

Twenty minutes later, Rachel crept out of her mother's bedroom and closed the door. She'd gotten her to take the medicine and take a little water. Then she'd been able to help her into a clean nightgown and wash her face and hands. She'd sat by the bed reading to her until she'd dropped off to sleep.

Rachel dropped the towels and washcloths and the soiled nightgown into the washer, thankfully a fully modern one and not a wringer type such as her *mam* had used when Rachel was a child. She made a final walk-through of the house to see that the doors were locked, the windows closed, and then retreated to the porch for a bit of air before going up to the room she shared with Lettie.

Her father was sitting on the porch. "Your mother?" he asked. "This wasn't a good day for her, but she thought her place was at her brother's house in their time of sorrow."

"She's better. Sleeping now. No fever, just exhausted and nauseated."

"For that we need to be grateful," her *dat* said. "I was glad to hear your friend the police lady was able to have Elsie's body released. The funeral in the morning will give her family some peace."

"She promised me that someone would bring the body to the house sometime after midnight."

"*Goot.*" Her father sighed. "As *goot* as such a thing can be."

"Trooper Mars told me that the cause of death was cerebral hemorrhage due to blunt force trauma to her temple. That means—"

"I know what it means, daughter. I may be a farmer with only an eighth-grade education, but I read the newspapers. Terrible. Terrible. Your Uncle Aaron is not the easiest man to have as part of our family, but he is a father who loves his children. He doesn't deserve to have such a thing happen to his family. Neither does your Aunt Hannah."

"It was a single blow to the head," Rachel explained. "And someone tried to help her. They bandaged her injury. She lived for a while, but whoever it was, they didn't seek medical care for her."

"Foolish," he said. "A waste of a precious life."

"She might have died anyway. But we'll never know that. Maybe if they'd gotten her into surgery right away . . ."

"An accident it could have been. Lots of ways besides violence. She could have fallen. I suppose the horse could have kicked her. But if it was an accident, why wouldn't Dathan do the right thing? And how could he bury her like that, without prayers, without her family around her? It doesn't look good for him."

"No," Rachel agreed. "It doesn't."

"But now, he must know that her body has been found. Why hasn't he turned himself in to the police? Where can he run? In two weeks, every Amish community in the country will know what happened and be watching for him."

"What if it wasn't an accident?" she wondered out loud. "Lucy thinks that they argued and she was killed in the fight. Maybe he was jealous of someone else. Maybe she'd told him that she wouldn't marry him and he lost his temper."

"I wouldn't like to think that, that one of our own could do such a thing. But I know that such a thing is possible. Anger is a poison in a man's veins. Wherever he is, he deserves our pity and our prayers."

"I am praying for Dathan. And for Elsie."

"Maybe he needs your prayers more than she does," her father suggested. "If he did kill her in a fit of rage, his conscience will tear him apart. And our Elsie is safe in the arms of a loving and all-knowing God."

"Did you ever think that maybe the way we bring up our children puts them at risk?" Rachel asked. "We're protected, sheltered from the world's evil. Maybe we do them a disservice by not teaching them to defend themselves."

"*Ne*, daughter. Never think that. The Bible tells us to turn the other cheek. When the martyrs of old were burned at the stake, they prayed for their tormentors. And when savages swept down on our farms and tomahawked whole families, most of our men would not raise an ax or a rifle to take their lives in turn. Nonviolence, love, trying to live by the example of Jesus. That is the only way for us . . . the only way we Amish know."

CHAPTER 10

It was just before eleven in the morning when the long line of horses and buggies started pulling away from the Amish cemetery. Elsie was buried in the same cemetery where her body had been found.

Rachel and her sister-in-law Ruth were assisting Rachel's mother back to the family buggy. She was weak this morning and unsteady on her feet. Rachel had guessed at breakfast that she was feeling poor, but nothing would do but that she took her place at the graveside and stand through the two-hour service in her black church clothing, cape, and bonnet. And although Rachel had offered to bring a folding chair for her *mam*, she would have none of it.

Elsie's funeral had brought most of the long-time residents of Stone Mill together, including Amish from most of the church communities and Englishers. Noticeably absent were the Benders, Dathan's family.

"I wonder why they didn't come?" Ruth whispered to Rachel. "Too upset that their son and brother is missing?"

"Or feeling guilty," Rachel's mother replied weakly. "They may believe Dathan killed Elsie and can't face her parents."

Rachel didn't comment. Together, she and Ruth helped Rachel's mother step up into the back of the Mast buggy, where Amanda and Lettie were waiting to see that she got safely home to bed. The week's events seemed to have taken a heavy toll on Esther Mast, both physically and emotionally.

Rachel couldn't help feeling concerned. Her mother had seemed much better on Saturday, but now it was evident from her color and lack of strength that she was much worse. Cancer was a terrible disease, but the doctors had been so hopeful, and they'd all been so sure that she would be able to make a full recovery. Esther Mast had always been a strong and active woman, and her attitude was good. And there were certainly enough people praying for her. Rachel tried to push back the fear that hovered at the back of her mind. Logically, she knew that even with the best of modern care, not every woman survived breast cancer. Whether or not she was a good person, much loved and needed by her family, had little to do with the outcome.

"I will rest a little and then we will go to your Aunt Hannah's and sit with them," her mother announced.

Rachel assumed the message was for her.

"Ask your sister if she is going there now," their mother said.

"I think so," Rachel answered. She was shaken by the finality of seeing Elsie's unpretentious pine coffin lowered into the ground and thinking what a waste her death was. Such a kind and beautiful soul . . . to have her life cut short so violently. Other than a few tears, Rachel had managed to hold her emotions in check all morning, but she needed a little time alone to clear her head. Being an emotional wreck wouldn't do Mary Aaron and her family any good, and the most positive thing she could do for her younger cousin was find out what had happened to her and why.

Rachel had left her Jeep out on the side of the road because she'd guessed that there would be a lot of people at Elsie's funeral. But she hadn't guessed that this many would come. Her Aunt Hannah and Uncle Aaron and, of course, Mary Aaron, were well known in Stone Mill and throughout the valley. But Rachel suspected that a few of the non-Amish had come out of curiosity rather than to share the family's mourning. She'd noticed a few hangers-on here that she doubted had ever sat through a sermon before, let alone one that lasted so long. If she'd been a gambling person, which she wasn't, she wouldn't have bet ten cents that a redneck like Roy Thompson would have shown up here.

Rachel's father untied the driving horse and climbed into the front seat of the buggy, where two of her younger siblings, Sally and Levi, were waiting. Rachel wanted to speak to her father before they left, so she walked around the buggy, but before she could get his attention her cell phone vibrated.

"Tell your sister that her pocket telephone is ringing," her mother said from the interior of the buggy. "I don't know what is so important that she couldn't leave it at home while we buried poor Elsie."

Rachel swallowed her urge to offer a defense. True, the buggy sides were thin, but her mother must have hearing as acute as an owl. And so few people had her cell number, Rachel wondered who it could be. Everyone she knew was either here, or knew where she was this morning. Even Lucy had come, in full dress uniform, and remained through the entire service. That meant a great deal to Rachel and said a lot about her character.

Rachel turned away to check the screen of her cell and was surprised to see that it was Evan. "Hey, I'm still at the cemetery," she said quietly. "The funeral service just ended."

"I hoped it would be over before now. Listen, I've only got a moment. This is probably a terrible idea on my part, but I thought you'd never forgive me if I knew and didn't tell you."

He hesitated. She waited, watching her family's buggy pull away.

"Rachel, a body was just found on the road not too far from the cemetery. The passerby who found him and called in the accident identified the dead man as Dathan Bender."

"What?" Rachel suddenly realized that she'd raised her voice and an Amish couple nearby was staring at her. "Sorry," she murmured to them. And then to Evan, she whispered, "Dathan Bender's body has been found?"

"There's a good possibility. A friend on the desk passed the word to me. I'm not even sure if Lucy knows yet. But you can't say that I passed this on to you. Or that anyone did. The troop will probably call her in, but it has to go through regular channels. Otherwise, someone will guess that my source passed on confidential information."

"Where is he? Who found him? What happened to—"

"Easy, easy. Let me tell you what I know. But you have to promise not to do anything crazy. This is serious, Rache. I can get in a lot of trouble for telling you this."

"I understand." Her breath was coming in deep gasps and she tried to control it, but her heart was pounding and she felt light-headed. "What happened to Dathan?"

"The man who called 9-1-1 said it looked like a hit-and-run to him."

"Who called it in?"

"I don't have that information. Apparently, the guy was reluctant to give his name."

"Where's the body?" she asked.

"On Log Church Road near Elijah's Gap. Not far from the old stone bridge."

She knew exactly where he was talking about. "Was Dathan driving the wagon?"

"Nothing was said about a horse or wagon being involved. I got the impression that the victim was just walking along the road when he was hit."

"But why would he be on foot if he had the horse and wagon? And there's hardly ten cars a day on that road. How could he have been struck and killed?"

"I don't know. It's definitely weird, but this whole thing has been weird from day one."

"And why would Dathan be walking on the road this morning?" she asked, thinking out loud.

"He could have been coming to the funeral. It's common behavior for killers to attend the funerals of their victims. Hide in the woods and watch from afar. There was a case in Harrisburg recently where a man shot his wife and two kids. The police searched everywhere for him, and the idiot showed up at the funeral wearing a wig and a fake mustache."

"No, I don't believe it's Dathan," Rachel said. "I'll have to have proof before I believe it."

"Well, if it is him, this may well be a dead end on Elsie's case. With them both gone, we may never know what happened. More murders go unsolved than you realize."

"I hope for the family's sake that we do get some answers." She glanced up. People were staring at her now. She started walking away. "Thanks for letting me know. I owe you." She cut through the woods to where she'd left her Jeep on the road. "What would I do without you, Evan?"

"Probably get into more hot water than you already have. I've got to go. Don't make me sorry I called you."

"I won't. I promise."

Rachel said good-bye and slid the cell back in her pocket. Glancing back toward the cemetery, she saw Lucy striding away from the grave, speaking into her cell. Rachel knew that if she didn't get to the scene before the troopers started cordoning off the area where the body was found, her chances of seeing if it really was Dathan were probably slim. Lucy's personal vehicle, a gold Subaru, was still blocked in by departing cars and buggies, but Rachel guessed she'd manage to have people move quickly if she was responding to an official call.

Rachel needed to get to her Jeep. She doubted Lucy knew the shortcut from the cemetery to the old logging road that would lead her cross-country to Elijah's Gap. Rachel picked up her skirt and began to run.

She reached the Jeep and got in, looking over her shoulder to see if anyone was watching. No one was and she put the Jeep into gear, but then she wasn't sure which way to go. Cars and the buggies blocked the drive and the roadway. She edged off the shoulder, looking for a break so that she could pull onto the blacktop. A pounding on the passenger's window startled her.

"Unlock the door. Let me in," Mary Aaron said.

Rachel hit the Unlock button on her door.

Mary Aaron slid into the passenger's seat. "Where are you going in such a hurry?"

Rachel stared at her. "How did you . . ." She shook her head. "Never mind." Apparently Mary Aaron had seen her undignified departure from the cemetery and had run her down.

Mary Aaron, in full dress clothing, including the black bonnet and cape, must have been a sight, racing between headstones. "Don't your parents need you?" Rachel hedged.

"*Ne*. They've got the elders and their wives driving back to the house with them. Now, *vas is*? What are you hiding from me?"

Rachel saw her opening and cut off a pickup to get out on the road. "I wasn't hiding anything," she protested. "I'm just trying to get ahead of Trooper Mars." She stole a glance at her cousin as the Jeep crawled down the road. "They've found a man's body. It may be Dathan's."

"Dathan's dead, too?" Mary Aaron groaned.

"That's what I'm going to find out," Rachel explained. "It was reported that he was hit by a car over by Elijah's Gap. The body's still there. It was just called in."

Mary Aaron removed her black dress bonnet and cape and pushed them into the back. "Well, what are you waiting for? Let's go."

"You're coming with me?"

"Elsie was my sister." Her cousin snapped her seat-belt buckle in place. "Step on it."

Rachel took the shortcut just to find a state police patrol car parked at an angle across the north end of Log Church Road. She hadn't been quick enough. The officer, a grizzled veteran named Ronnie Curley, stood by his vehicle, palm raised for Rachel to stop. She'd had contact with Trooper Curley before and she hadn't liked what she'd seen of him. Any man who'd been on the force as long as Curley should have made the rank of sergeant by now, but Curley hadn't ever made it higher than corporal and had twice, according to Evan, been called up for less-than-admirable behavior. He wasn't a bad cop, but neither was he a particularly good one. And he definitely wasn't a fan of Rachel's.

She braked and backed up, unwilling to take

the time to attempt to charm Curley into giving her more information. With a wave in her rearview mirror, she backtracked a quarter of a mile and turned onto a rutted lane that led to an abandoned farmhouse. "A long way to walk," Mary Aaron offered.

"Not really." Rachel downshifted and drove through the deep grass around the ruins of the house and the roofless stone barn. Some other farmer was growing hay in the back field, and it had recently been cut. Bales lay scattered across the expanse of meadow. Rachel put the Jeep into four-wheel drive and cut a path between the bales, avoiding the low ground and keeping to the high, sending a rabbit running for its life. On the far side of the field were the remains of a wooden gate. Rachel stopped the Jeep and jumped out. "Give me a hand," she said.

Together, they dragged the rotting boards out of the way, got back in the vehicle, and drove through. There was a short stretch of overgrown weeds and small trees, and then another logging road plunged into the thick woods. Rachel took the abandoned track. The road here was hard and rocky, littered with small branches and fallen acorns, and the trees formed a thick canopy of leaves overhead.

The road ended at a fallen tree. "Now what?" Mary Aaron demanded.

"Now we follow the stream on foot," Rachel

answered. "It leads to the stone bridge at Elijah's Gap. The road crosses it. We can be there before anyone sees us." She glanced at Mary Aaron. "Unless you'd rather wait here?"

"Forget that."

A quarter of a mile later, Rachel scrambled up the bank from the rocky streambed under the bridge. Mary Aaron was only a few yards behind her, gamely keeping up despite her heavy church clothes. Rachel didn't need to climb all the way to the blacktop, for which she was grateful.

To her right, not more than a hundred feet away, a man's battered and bloodstained body lay sprawled, facedown, in the weeds on the slope. He was Amish, all right: homemade denim pants, work boots, a blue shirt, and suspenders. And standing on the edge of the road over the body was Trooper Lucy Mars.

Lucy caught sight of Rachel and Mary Aaron just as they saw her. "What are you doing here?" she shouted. "You can't be here."

"Is it Dathan?" Rachel asked, walking slowly toward her. "You aren't sure, are you? You need someone to make a definite identification. You don't know what he looks like, and you don't even have a photo. Mary Aaron can definitely ID the victim. And if it's not Dathan and he's Amish, chances are she can still ID him."

"How did you find out about this?" Lucy asked

in her most authoritarian policewoman voice. "How did you get past the roadblocks?"

Rachel struggled to come up with something that wasn't a lie, but wouldn't incriminate Evan.

Mary Aaron, a little out of breath from their mad dash up the creek bed, came to her rescue. "It was Amish who found him, wasn't it?"

Rachel looked back at Mary Aaron. Evan hadn't told her who had discovered the body. She wasn't sure how much he knew. "Where did you hear that?" she asked Mary Aaron in *Deitsch*.

"Because there's an Amish man standing on the bridge," her cousin replied in the same dialect. "Look. I think it's Dathan's brother-in-law."

Rachel turned around to stare at the man. Her cousin was right. He was a good distance away, but it certainly looked like Charles Schumacher.

"What did she just say?" Lucy asked Rachel, her tone impatient, and maybe a little flustered. "I'd appreciate it if you spoke English."

Rachel switched back to English. "You can't keep anything secret from the Amish," Rachel said to Lucy, which wasn't untrue. "News travels fast in the valley. We call it the *Amish telegraph*."

"Amish telegraph or not, you can't be here," Lucy answered.

"Why not?" Rachel indicated the Amish man on the bridge. "Do you know who he is?"

Lucy frowned. "He gave his name as Charles Schumacher. Why are you asking?"

Mary Aaron sighed.

Lucy glanced from Rachel to Mary Aaron and back again. "What is that supposed to mean? Isn't he Charles Schumacher?"

Rachel studied the dour man on the bridge. It was Charles, all right. Same raggedy black beard and close-set eyes. Charles was staring at them just as intently. "Yes," she said to Lucy. "He's Charles Schumacher."

"And?" Lucy was clearly losing her patience now.

Mary Aaron folded her arms and looked Lucy straight in the eye. "Did he tell you that he's married to Dathan's sister, Agnes?"

Lucy made a game attempt but couldn't quite hide her surprise. "Dathan's brother-in-law?"

"The same," Rachel put in.

"You're probably wondering why he didn't tell you," Mary Aaron said. "Especially since he lives with Dathan. Lived."

"Maybe because there was no love lost between him and Dathan?" Rachel moved closer to the body. "An odd coincidence, don't you think, Trooper Mars? That Charles would be the person to find Dathan when no one else could? Convenient."

Lucy was listening, arms crossed over her chest.

"Charles has been married to Dathan's only sister for ten years," Mary Aaron explained, casting a glance in the man's direction. "It was common knowledge that he was trying to force Dathan off the farm."

Rachel nodded. "Charles has a lot to gain by Dathan's death and would have had plenty to lose if Dathan married Elsie and brought her home to live on the farm."

The policewoman's mirrored aviator sunglasses provided a perfect mask, but Rachel could see the trooper's lips firm and the muscles in her cheek tighten. "Are you hinting at a life insurance policy on Dathan?"

Rachel shook her head. "The Amish don't believe in insurance."

"They . . . we think it shows a lack in trusting God," Mary Aaron explained. "But with Dathan dead, his sister, Agnes, will inherit the farm when the widowed mother dies."

"And she's not in the best of health," Rachel said. "She's had several heart attacks and has some sort of chronic blood condition."

"The truth is, Charles spent the last ten years making Dathan's life miserable," Mary Aaron continued hotly. "Charles bullied him and physically abused him when he was a teenager and hadn't got his full growth. Elsie told me so. She said Charles used to whip Dathan with a leather shaving strap. And she said that Dathan promised that when they were married, she wouldn't have to live under the same roof as Charles and Agnes."

"He was going to insist they leave?" Lucy asked. "Could he do that?"

Rachel nodded. "Dathan was the only son. That's a big deal among the Amish, especially those who still make their living from the land. A husband is supposed to provide for his wife."

"Elsie told me that Charles didn't treat Dathan's mother well either," Mary Aaron added. "That she was afraid of him and only let him stay on because Dathan was still a boy when Agnes married. The Benders didn't have much. And they never would have been able to survive without a grown man to do the heavy work."

"Sounds like this is going to get complicated," Lucy admitted. She exhaled slowly and glanced around, her gaze lingering on the body. "Maybe I do need some help in dealing with your people."

"You might," Rachel agreed. "Because few would ever tell you those things about what went on in Dathan's house."

"I thought you were supposed to be gentle people."

"Most of us are," Mary Aaron said. "And I'm not saying Charles had anything to do with this. I just think you need to know all the circumstances."

"I don't understand why your community isn't more cooperative," Lucy said.

"We have a long history of distrusting the

world," Mary Aaron explained. "We try to take care of our problems amongst ourselves."

"But your people knew that Dathan was being mistreated and let it go on?" Lucy's phone vibrated in her hand.

"This is a conservative town, both Amish and Englishers. More than a few use corporal punishment to control their unruly children."

Lucy glanced down at her cell phone and then back to where the body lay. "You may as well take a look and confirm that this is Dathan Bender. But I warn you, it's not a pretty sight. His face and the side of his head are bad."

"I understand," Mary Aaron said. "I'll do it. His mother deserves to know as soon as possible if this is him."

"If you're the one to notify the next of kin, I could go with you," Rachel offered to Lucy. "We both could."

"Someone from the troop is standing by to go tell them once we have confirmation. He's had a lot of experience, and I think he speaks a little Dutch."

"*Deitsch*," Rachel corrected her. "What we speak is a particular Germanic dialect."

"I'll allow Mary Aaron to come close enough to the body to make an ID. But I see no need for you to view the body close-up, Rachel."

"I have to stay with my cousin," Rachel replied. "You get us both for the price of one, or not at all."

Lucy Mars sighed. "You know, you're getting to be a pain in the neck." Her gaze narrowed. "How'd you say you knew about this?"

Rachel didn't answer and the policewoman looked down the road again. "Let's get this over with before Detective Starkey gets here and I end up losing my job."

Rachel glanced at Mary Aaron. Her cousin nodded and gripped her hand. Together they walked up the stony slope to attempt a definite identification of the unfortunate victim.

CHAPTER 11

The sun was just setting Tuesday evening when Rachel pulled her Jeep out of her Uncle Aaron's driveway and headed toward the town of Stone Mill. Worn out from the funeral and a doctor's visit, Rachel's mother had turned in early, and Rachel wanted to do a little paperwork. Leaving her business in town to stay at the farm while her *mam* had her cancer treatments proved easier than she'd thought it would be, almost too smooth. Ada, Hulda, and Mary Aaron seemed to run the guesthouse with the precision of a Swiss clock. And Rachel wasn't sure if she should be pleased, or feel a little superfluous in her own establish-ment.

Mary Aaron, in the passenger side, fastened her seat belt.

Rachel had planned on going to Stone Mill House alone, but when she'd stopped by to check on Mary Aaron and the family, Aunt Hannah had suggested she take Mary Aaron with her to the B&B. Her aunt thought that Mary Aaron needed to get away from the house with the constant stream of mourning visitors, and their constant talk of Elsie, for a few hours.

Rachel could understand why Aunt Hannah was worried. Although Mary Aaron was making an effort to act normal, it was plain to Rachel that her cousin wasn't herself. Not that the last couple of days hadn't been enough to deeply affect all of them. Hardly an hour after they'd seen Elsie lain in the ground, they'd had to identify Dathan's battered body.

Mary Aaron hadn't shed a single tear at the accident site. She'd studied the dead man and positively pronounced that it was Dathan Bender, confirming his brother-in-law's statement. She hadn't broken down, and she'd shown less emotion than Trooper Mars had. What was different was that Mary Aaron had grown increasingly silent throughout the day. She'd answer direct questions, but she wasn't initiating conversation, and she refused to be drawn into a discussion of Dathan's possible hand in Elsie's death.

Another odd thing was her unusual state of disorder. Mary Aaron was always neat and tidy. Whether getting in hay, sewing at a quilt frolic, or canning tomatoes, Rachel could always count on her cousin to look attractive and put together. But at the funeral, Rachel had noticed that Mary Aaron appeared disheveled. And tonight she was wearing an everyday work dress that Rachel was certain she'd worn for several days running. Tendrils of hair had come loose from

178

her bun and dangled beneath the back of her *kapp*, and her sneakers were muddy. Rachel wasn't a psycholo-gist, but she didn't need to be a professional to guess that Mary Aaron, the most well-adjusted person she'd ever known, was deeply depressed.

"Rae-Rae? Are you listening to me?" Mary Aaron asked. "How did Aunt Esther's doctor's appointment go this afternoon?"

Rachel blinked. "Sorry, I was woolgathering. The visit went well, actually. I think I told you they warned us that the chemo would be a rough one this time, but *Mam* doesn't seem to be recovering her strength as she usually does. So I called Dr. Belkin's office late this afternoon and asked if they could squeeze her in."

"And what did she say?" Mary Aaron asked. Marjorie Belkin was her local family physician as well as Rachel's, her mother's, and her sisters'.

"Dr. Belkin said she'd had a phone consulta-tion with *Mam*'s oncologist this week and that her extreme fatigue was to be expected. Her vitals were good, and the blood tests remain encouraging."

"*Goot*," Mary Aaron said. "That should make you feel better."

"I suppose so, but I can't help being concerned." Rachel glanced at her cousin. "*Mam* says it's all in God's hands and she doesn't worry about it."

"That's what my mother says about Elsie's

death. That she's with our Lord and we should pray for her soul and let her go."

"I miss her, too," Rachel said, switching to low beams as an old truck approached them, going well below the speed limit. "I can't imagine what you're going through."

Mary Aaron stared out her window into the falling dusk. "Everyone says the same thing. 'She's in a better place.' Or, 'Elsie's death was part of His plan. She's with the angels and if we are faithful, we'll see her again in heaven.'" Mary Aaron's voice cracked. "How can I hear that and wonder if it's not true?"

"It's the bedrock of our faith," Rachel said. As the truck rolled by, she thought she recognized the driver as Buddy Wheeler. She raised her hand to wave, then was embarrassed to see that it wasn't Buddy. The guy she didn't recognize waved and grinned.

"Who was that?" Mary Aaron asked.

Rachel shrugged. "So back to what you were saying. I think it's natural to question our beliefs at times like this. It doesn't mean we're wrong."

"But what if we *are* wrong?" Mary Aaron's plea was passionate. "What if our backward beliefs and behaviors lead to innocent girls like Elsie dying? What if ours isn't the only way to follow in the footsteps of Jesus, the way the bishops tell us? And what if I never see Elsie again?"

Rachel shivered. "Mary Aaron . . ." She found

her cousin's hand and gripped it. "I don't know what to say. Sometimes, all you can do is trust and—"

"Trust?" Mary Aaron turned back to face her. "What if Elsie trusted when she should have fought back? Or run?"

"I don't think we'll ever know."

There was a long silence between them. And then, seemingly out of nowhere, Mary Aaron asked, "When did you decide that you didn't want to be Amish anymore?"

Rachel's reply caught in her throat. They were walking on uneven ground. The doubts Mary Aaron was struggling with were the same ones that she'd personally fought with for years. But saying so might unduly influence Mary Aaron. Wasn't that what everyone said? It wasn't good for her to spend so much time with Rachel because she might lure her away from the church? "Is this about Elsie's death?"

"It's been on my mind for a while, but after Elsie . . ." She sighed. "I guess losing Elsie has really made me question what I want."

"I left the church years ago. I think I've made my peace," Rachel said. "Mostly. I know I still believe. Maybe not everything our Amish church teaches, and not the part about men being in control, but in God and in His Son, Jesus. I do believe in the power of prayer, and I believe there's a plan."

"But you didn't feel comfortable in the old ways," Mary Aaron said, making it more of a statement than a question.

"I felt like I had to learn more about the world. I was desperate to study further than eighth grade. I wanted to go to college. To see what was out there, but . . ."

"But what?" Mary Aaron urged.

Rachel drove several miles and was entering the town limits of Stone Mill when she finally answered. "I made my choice, but I struggle with it every day. And I wonder if I made the right choice. It's complicated. And sometimes, I feel like I'm caught between the Amish life and the English life. And I'm not sure if I'll ever feel completely at ease in either one."

Mary Aaron didn't say anything.

"I hope we did the right thing today. Going to see Dathan's body," Rachel said, changing the subject for one almost as touchy. "That can't have been easy for you." Rachel felt uncomfortable herself when she saw someone dead, and she wasn't really Amish anymore. She wondered how much the old superstitions and unspoken customs clouded her psyche.

"We had to know," Mary Aaron said. "But I don't think he just happened to wander out in front of a car and get himself killed."

"Me either," Rachel agreed. As they passed the Black Horse Tavern on Main Street, she spotted a metallic-gold Subaru Outback parked at the curb near the entrance. She braked and pulled into the next parking lot. The bakery was closed at this hour, as were most of the businesses in town. Stone Mill shut down early in the evening. The Black Horse and the bookstore were the exceptions.

"What are we doing here? The bakery's closed," said Mary Aaron.

"We just passed Lucy's car on the street in front of the Black Horse. The gold one with the Rutgers decal in the back window. I want to see if anything came back on Dathan's autopsy yet. It's probably too soon, but it doesn't hurt to ask. You can wait here. I'll just be a few minutes."

"*Ne.*" Mary Aaron put her hand on the door handle. "If you're going into the tavern, I'm coming with you. I've always wanted to see what it looked like."

Rachel stared at her. "Are you sure? Your father will come unhinged if he knows you've been in a bar."

"My father has his opinions. I have mine. I didn't say I was going to drink peppermint schnapps, but I'm almost twenty-five. I think I'm old enough to walk into a tavern."

Rachel eyed her skeptically. An Amish woman in the Black Horse? That would be all over town by morning, and probably prime gossip at half the Amish churches by next Sunday. "Maybe this isn't such a good idea," she said. "I could always call Lucy."

But Mary Aaron was already out of the car. Rachel hurried after her cousin.

The Black Horse was one of the oldest continually running taverns in that part of the state. It was all stone, heavy beams, fire-blackened brick, and scarred pine floors. A wooden bar ran the length of the room with a massive stone fireplace taking up one wall. Most of the floor space was taken up with booths constructed of wide boards, aged to a dark walnut hue, leaving a small area where five round wood tables and an assortment of mismatched chairs stood shoulder to shoulder. A wagon-wheel chandelier hung over the bar, and each booth boasted a single dented wall lamp, old enough to have been converted from gas to electric.

Rachel couldn't help smiling as they walked in. The interior of the Black Horse was dark enough that, while Mary Aaron's Amish dress might draw attention, she doubted anyone would recognize her.

A group of three regulars sat at one of the round tables. The bartender stood nearby talking to them. The only other customer was a lone woman sitting in the farthest booth from the door. Rachel waited long enough for her eyes to adjust to the dim lighting and then went to where Lucy Mars was just finishing a mug of beer. A second mug, empty, stood by her elbow. Rachel didn't know how long the policewoman had been there, but she appeared to have thrown off her professional façade. She was no longer wearing her police uniform. Instead, she was dressed in jeans, cowboy boots, and a plaid flannel shirt.

"Rachel." She waved with an enthusiasm Rachel hadn't seen in her before.

"Trooper Mars."

"Please, call me Lucy. We're there, don't you think?" She tapped the table. "Have a drink with me. Have two."

"Okay." Rachel motioned to Mary Aaron, and they slid into the booth across from Lucy. The trooper put two fingers to her lips and whistled shrilly, startling Rachel and Mary Aaron. "Another round here," she called to the bartender.

The man ducked behind the bar. "What will it be, ladies?" he called.

"Another Otto's for me," Lucy said. "Have you tried Slab Cabin, Rachel? It's good."

"Yes," Rachel agreed. Slab Cabin was a local IPA and was excellent. "I'll have the same. And can we have a root beer for—"

"I'll have Red Mo if you have it," Mary Aaron said.

Rachel's mouth gaped open. She had no idea Mary Aaron knew what Red Mo was. Or how she could have known unless she'd sampled the ale.

Mary Aaron's smile was sly. "You don't know everything I do, *Cousin*."

Rachel slid her attention from her cousin to Lucy. "Bad day, wasn't it?"

"Very bad day." Lucy's head bobbed a little as she set the mug down on the table and used a forefinger to wipe at the moisture ring the mug had left on the dark pine surface. "I got reamed out big-time when Detective Starkey arrived. Thinks highly of himself. Filling in for Evan. Assigned temporarily from Harrisburg out here to the sticks. Let me assure you that Detective Sparky . . . *Starkey,*" she corrected, "definitely was not pleased that I'd let the two of you identify the body. He was so unhappy with what he called my 'poor and unprofessional judgment' that he insinuated I might not even be on the case when I go in to work Thursday. Have tomorrow off," she added.

She wasn't slurring her words, but they weren't exactly sharp either. Rachel wondered how many beers she'd had before the two empties on the table.

"I'm sorry," Rachel said. "We didn't mean to get you into trouble."

"What do they expect? I'm not a detective. They want you to make decisions, and then they come down hard on you when you do." Her shoulders slumped.

"Any word on the autopsy?" Rachel asked.

The bartender came with three mugs. The red ale was Mary Aaron's. Lucy waited until he'd placed the order on the table, wiped the surface with a clean towel, and gathered up the two empties.

"Prelim says the victim was hit and killed by a motor vehicle. Sparky's theory is that Mr. Bender killed Miss Hostetler, either accidentally or in the heat of an argument." Lucy waved her hand expressively as she spoke. "This morning, Bender was on his way to her funeral when he was overcome with guilt and deliberately stepped out in front of a car."

Rachel frowned, thinking that sounded more than a little far-fetched. "Anyone report hitting . . . something? If it was an accident, it would have been reported."

Lucy shook her head slowly in an exaggerated motion. "Not if his tags were expired." She ticked off on her fingers. "Not if she was uninsured. Not if he has a habeas out for back child support. Not if she was somewhere she wasn't supposed to be."

"Or . . . anyone report seeing a vehicle that looked like it had hit someone?" Mary Aaron said.

Rachel sipped her beer. "Doesn't that sound like an absurdly pat explanation?"

Lucy slapped her hand on the table. "Of course it's too pat! But it wraps up this investigation in a tidy knot, and our Detective Starkey-Sparky is free to take his vacation without the clutter of a multiple homicide investigation file on his desk. He's off on an island holiday, I'm directing traffic at an SPCA Neuter Your Dog and Adopt a Guinea Pig Day, and our bearded informant has just inherited a farm."

Mary Aaron closed her hand around her mug. "Amish don't commit suicide."

"Sure they do," Lucy replied. "A man who hanged himself over in the next county just after Christmas. Something Beiler, wasn't it?"

"All right. Maybe some do," Mary Aaron allowed. "A very, very few. But not conservative boys like Dathan Bender. And the James Beiler you're thinking of was in his eighties, had some kind of incurable cancer, and his wife of sixty years had just died. Besides, he wasn't Amish, he was Mennonite."

"Mennonite, Amish," Lucy said with a sigh. "It's a little confusing sometimes. Especially when the women wear those little white hats." She touched the back of her head.

"Prayer *kapp*," Rachel murmured and took another sip of her ale. It was good, but she was more of a wine person, and even then she never had more than a glass or two. Old habits died hard. "Dathan would never have committed suicide."

Lucy leaned on the table. "Detective Starkey seems pretty confident."

"I'm telling you, he's wrong," Mary Aaron insisted. "I know these people. Knew."

Rachel noticed that her cousin hadn't touched her drink.

"You think Sparky's wrong. Rachel probably thinks he's wrong," Lucy said.

"And what about you?" Rachel asked. "Do you agree with Detective Starkey's theory?"

Lucy shook her head, then closed her eyes. Suddenly she seemed about to burst into tears, and Rachel wondered if she should have ordered the root beer for the trooper.

Lucy took a moment, then opened her eyes. "In my opinion," Lucy said, "which counts for nothing, compared to Sparky's, is this whole thing looks fishy. How did the vehicle hit him hard enough to kill him in the first place? The driver had to slow for that one-lane bridge with the stone walls on either side. He would have then really had to step on it. And that's not all." Lucy took another big sip and blinked. "Not by half."

Mary Aaron opened her mouth to say something, but Rachel nudged her ankle and she remained quiet. She pushed her glass back without tasting the Red Mo.

"Mr. Bender's wrists," Lucy continued. "Marks on both of Mr. Bender's wrists. Well, one worse than the other. Marks that could have been made by rope or tape or something. Starkey said it was pavement burns, but I don't buy it. They were similar on both wrists. Too similar. How could the victim have road burns around both wrists? In the same place? It doesn't sit right with me."

"What did the medical examiner say?" Rachel asked.

"Nothing except that he died from head trauma, and there were internal injuries as well. Could be weeks before we get the full autopsy report. The good news is that the body'll be released tomorrow so the family can have the funeral Thursday."

"That is good news," Rachel said. "But you're not going to end the investigation while you wait on the report? You'll keep asking questions?"

"I'd like to," Lucy answered. "I would. But . . ." She reached for her mug again. "Have to follow boss's orders."

"He's not my boss," Rachel said, sitting back. "I can ask questions."

"You can and you should," Lucy said, lifting her glass in salute. "Because there's more to this than Sparky thinks. I'll bet my badge on it."

Convincing Mary Aaron to go home instead of coming with her wasn't easy but Rachel managed. It was already late, and Charles Schumacher and his wife were probably in bed, but Rachel knew that she wouldn't get a wink of sleep if she didn't satisfy her curiosity by asking Dathan's brother-in-law a few questions. Fortunately, she was already wearing Plain clothing. All she had to do if the Schumachers were still up was to tie a kerchief around her head.

Lucy's ring of keys hung heavy in her pocket. Rachel dug those out and shoved them in the glove compartment. She would rather have driven Lucy home herself, but Lucy wasn't budging from the booth, so Rachel satisfied her conscience by getting the bartender to promise to see her safely home himself. It had been Mary Aaron who'd demanded and gotten Lucy's keys.

"I may be unprofessional and display unprofessional judgment, but I'm not stupid enough to drive when I've consumed a six-pack," Lucy had announced as she handed the keys over to Mary Aaron.

It was nine twenty when Rachel turned into Dathan's mother's lane. The house looked dark, and she was just about to give it up and back out of the driveway when she saw a bobbing light in the yard. She continued on and stopped near the barn.

Charles Schumacher raised his lantern so that the light shone on her face. "What are you doing here?" His tone was not friendly.

"Milking a little late, aren't you?" Rachel asked in *Deitsch*, through the open window. Charles held a bucket of milk in his free hand. She couldn't see his face, but she had no doubt that he was frowning at her.

"Visiting a little late, aren't you?" He set the bucket on the ground. Charles was bareheaded and he wore only suspendered trousers and a short-sleeved shirt, despite the coolness of the evening. "What do you want?"

"I want to offer my condolences on Dathan's death. It must have been a shock to you, finding him like that when . . . What were you doing at Elijah's Gap this morning? Coming to Elsie's funeral?"

"*Ne.* I wasn't."

"May I ask what you were doing?" She got out of the Jeep.

"I answered the English police questions. Don't know why I should repeat it all to you."

"I'd appreciate it, Charles. I'm just trying to keep all the facts straight."

"No secret. I was looking for my wagon. Dathan took my horse and wagon. My horse came back sometime last night. Standing in the yard when the sun came up this morning. No harness. Looked healthy. Somebody had been looking after him. So I told the wife, 'You tend to the chores. I'm going hunting for my wagon.' " He took a step toward her. "You got a problem with that?"

"*Ne.*" Rachel shook her head. "No problem. Just seems a little . . . odd. Everybody in the valley at

Elsie's funeral, and you happened to trip over your dead brother-in-law's body in the road."

"Don't matter what it looks like. That's what happened. What was I supposed to do? Walk on by? I did what anybody would do. I went to a phone and called the police."

"*Ya.*" She nodded again. "I suppose anybody would do that. But why didn't you tell the dispatcher or the trooper that it was your brother-in-law's body you'd found?"

He picked up the milk bucket, then set it on the ground again. His body movements were quick but stiff, almost like a robot's. "I don't like dead people. I was upset. Anybody would be upset to see him like that. Never found a dead man in the road before. And who's to say I didn't tell her? Maybe the trooper didn't hear what I said."

Rachel thought on that a moment. She just couldn't get a read on Charles. She knew she didn't like him, but that didn't mean he had anything to do with Dathan's death. Or Elsie's. "Could I ask where you were Friday night?"

"You can ask, but I don't have to answer." He was quiet for a minute, long enough for Rachel to think he really wasn't going to answer. Then he spoke again. "Got nothing to hide. I shot a deer. It run off and I was tracking it."

Rachel wondered if Charles was telling the truth. She'd expected him to say he was home with his wife. Could he really have been tracking a wounded deer? It was a good alibi if he was lying. How could anyone challenge it? "And that's what you told the police?"

"*Ya.* That's what I said. That's what I stand by. They can ask my wife. You can, too, if you like. Agnes will say just what I said. Now, go on with you. I've got work to be done." He seized the handle of the milk pail and hurried toward the house, milk splashing on his trousers with every step.

I'll leave, Rachel thought as she walked to her Jeep. *But I'm not done asking questions. Not by a long shot.*

CHAPTER 12

"I know I should have stayed home tonight, but I just couldn't." Mary Aaron sat down on the porch step beside Rachel and wrapped her arms around her knees. "I can't breathe there."

"Did you tell your mother you were coming here?"

Mary Aaron edged closer and laid her head against Rachel's shoulder. "I told *Dat*. He was still up. He walked me most of the way here."

Rachel slipped an arm around her, but she didn't say anything. What was there to say? She believed in heaven, but here, now, sitting on her father's porch, she wasn't certain what that meant. How could she comfort Mary Aaron with platitudes when she was filled with so much doubt?

It was late, after midnight. Everyone in her parents' house was sleeping. Lettie was sleeping with their *mam*, which suited Rachel fine. The bedroom she shared with her sister was perfect for two, but crowded for three. Rachel even had an extra nightgown to lend Mary Aaron, so here they were, sitting on the front porch in their nightclothes, wide awake, despite the hour.

"There's the Little Dipper." Rachel pointed out the faint stars, twinkling silver against a navy-blue firmament. Only part of the Big Dipper was visible, the rest hidden by a partly cloudy sky.

"It's nice, knowing that it's always there, isn't it?" Mary Aaron said. "Something that stays the same when everything else changes."

"*Ya*, it is," Rachel agreed. "When I was small, *Dat* used to sit out here with us kids and point out the constellations. Let's see, it's September, so I'm guessing somewhere up there are Capricornus, Cygnus, Equuleus. I used to be able to identify them all. At least with *Dat*'s help," she mused.

"Elsie liked the stars." Mary Aaron stared up at the sky. "She used to open the window of our bedroom when we were supposed to be in bed. She'd lean way out and watch for falling stars. Once we saw more than a dozen in one night."

Rachel leaned forward, cupping her chin with her hand. "Wherever she is, I hope she sees a whole rainbow of stars."

The chirp of crickets and the buzz of night insects were interrupted by louder footsteps and the creak of a cabinet door opening in the kitchen. "Somebody's up." Rachel motioned for Mary Aaron to stay where she was and she went to the screen door.

A hobbling form in a long white nightgown

196

materialized in the shadows. The kitchen faucet ran.

"*Mam*? What are you doing up?"

Rachel's mother turned with a start and Rachel opened the screen door.

"Can't a woman get a glass of water in her own kitchen without someone making a fuss?" the older woman grumbled in *Deitsch*, making it obvious it was a general comment, rather than one meant directly for Rachel.

"Sorry. I didn't mean to startle you," Rachel said in the same dialect.

Esther hobbled toward the door, water glass in hand, but when Rachel tried to give her mother her arm for support, the older woman brushed her off. "Who's that?" her mother asked. "Mary Aaron? Didn't know you were spending the night."

Mary Aaron stood up and smiled at her. "Aunt Esther. *Ya*, I hope it's no trouble."

"And what trouble would you be, child?" The older woman walked slowly over to a rocking chair and eased herself down. "You know you're always welcome here, day or night."

"Thank you," Mary Aaron said.

Rachel swallowed the lump that rose in her throat and went to stand by the porch railing. "We couldn't sleep. We were just sitting here, looking at the stars."

"No wonder you couldn't sleep, Mary Aaron,"

her mother said, sipping her water. "Terrible thing. First your blessed sister and then that young Dathan found dead. Terrible."

"It doesn't seem real," Mary Aaron admitted.

"Death is real enough. Comes when we least expect it. The Bible tells us that each of us has a certain number of days, but it does seem like Elsie's days were cut short by some evil." She made a sound of disgust. "And the English police expect us to believe nonsense about Dathan killing her and then himself. Do they think we are stupid?"

"You don't believe it either?" Rachel asked, surprised to hear her mother voice the very thoughts that were going through her own head.

"Know rubbish when I see it! Hear it. That boy wouldn't jump out in front of a car on purpose. And he'd never harm a hair of Elsie's head." Her mother leaned forward in the rocking chair, seemingly speaking to Mary Aaron alone, but Rachel knew better. Her mother was communicating with her in the only way she could. "Somebody needs to get to the bottom of this. Find out the truth. Not for justice. Justice will come in the Lord's time. But for peace."

Mary Aaron crossed to her aunt's side and knelt beside her. "You think finding out how Elsie and Dathan died will give us peace?"

"The peace of knowing the same thing won't happen to my Amanda or Lettie or you." Rachel's *mam* set down the water glass and laid a hand on Mary Aaron's head. "I worry about my girls and my nieces, and every other girl in this valley. Not just Amish, but every child. Even that young woman at the bookstore with all those holes in her ears."

"I keep thinking the same thing," Rachel said. "But I don't know how to find out what happened. I've been going around in circles for days, upsetting people, and getting nowhere."

Rachel's *mam* nodded and looked down at Mary Aaron. "Never thought any of my children were quitters. If a person really wanted to find out, they'd ask questions."

"I *did* ask questions," Rachel assured her. "But everywhere I turn, I hit a stone wall. You know how everyone is around here. Private. Nobody wants to admit to seeing anything."

"Trouble is," her mother announced, "people give up too easy. Some folks, God blessed them with a good mind and a heart to go with it. And God expects us to make use of every gift He gave us. Me, I'm too weak to hardly get out of this chair, but if I had my health, I'd ride that path that your sister and Dathan took when they left that frolic. I'd keep doing it. I'd put myself in Elsie's seat in that wagon. I'd want to know everything they did and everything they saw that night."

"*Mam*, Mary Aaron and I drove up and down the road that night," Rachel said. "I walked the road the next day. There's nothing there to tell us what could have happened to them."

Her mother pretended to ignore her. "If it was me doing the seeking," she continued, "I'd go up to every farm along the road, talk to every soul in every house. I'd find out what they saw that night. Night, that's what a person has to take into consideration," she went on. "A body would have to go at night, not in the daytime. Just about the same time Elsie and Dathan were riding that road. And no foolish motor Jeep. A thinking person would drive a horse. I can't do it. But the right person, a smart person with a good heart, if they put their mind to it, I'm sure they'd come up with the truth."

It was late the following afternoon when Rachel finally got the household in order and was free to slip out. Her mother was sleeping. Amanda and Lettie were busy in the garden, and Sally was gathering eggs in the henhouse. Supper had already been planned, and the girls would be able to handle it without their eldest sister's help.

Knowing she'd better take the opportunity to go while she had it, Rachel ran back upstairs for her keys to the Jeep. When she pushed open her bedroom door, she halted in surprise.

Mary Aaron stood in the center of the bedroom wearing jeans and Rachel's *Paul Simon, Graceland: 25th Anniversary* T-shirt. Her cousin's shining hair, which was usually braided and pinned up under a scarf or *kapp*, was secured in a high ponytail and topped with a worn Penn State ball cap.

"Mary Aaron?" Rachel stood in the doorway and stared as if her cousin were some kind of apparition. *"What are you doing?"*

"Shhh!" Mary Aaron rolled her eyes and put one hand on her hip. "You want to bring the whole household up here?" She waved Rachel into the room. "I was just trying it on. I wanted to see what it felt like."

"Mary Aaron—"

"*Ne,*" Mary Aaron interrupted. "I don't want to talk about it." She turned her back and shrugged out of the T-shirt.

"I just—"

"Not now and probably not later," Mary Aaron said firmly.

"I came up to get my keys. Everything's quiet downstairs. I was going to head out."

"Then get them. I'll catch up with you. Just give me a minute."

"You're coming with me?"

"Of course, I'm coming with you." Mary Aaron tossed the ball cap on the bed.

Rachel took one more look at her cousin in the jeans and beat a hasty retreat. A few minutes later she was headed out the front door when Mary Aaron called to her in English.

"Wait up!"

Rachel stopped and turned. Mary Aaron trotted down the stairs, hair pinned up under a spotless *kapp* and wearing Lettie's Lincoln green dress and matching apron and cape. Rachel guessed that the black stockings and black tennis shoes were Mary Aaron's own. "Quite a change," Rachel remarked.

"Told you. I don't want to talk about it."

"Does Lettie know you're wearing her new dress?"

"Not yet, but I'll tell her when we get back. I spilled tomatoes on my dress when we were canning this morning."

"Oh, *well* . . . that explains the jeans and ball cap perfectly," Rachel replied.

Mary Aaron cut her eyes at Rachel but didn't take the bait. "Where are we going?"

"We're doing what my mother said I should. We're going to retrace the route that Elsie and Dathan took again, and this time we're going to talk to everyone at every house, until we learn what happened to them."

The first farmhouse they stopped at was an Amish one. The houses and farm buildings were set back a long way from the road. "Young Mose Heiser and his wife, Wilma, work the farm," Mary Aaron explained as they drove up the gravel lane. "Mose Sr. lives in the *grossdaddi* house. He's a widower."

They passed a young man in his late teens, early twenties, cutting weeds with a scythe, and pulled into the barnyard.

Young Mose's wife, a pleasant, sturdy woman in her early fifties with bright blue eyes, met them in the yard and led them to the garden, where her husband was picking tomatoes with the help of several children. An older man, whom Rachel supposed was Mose Sr., seemed to be directing the harvest from a wheelchair under a shade tree.

"Nope, didn't see anything out of the ordinary Friday night. We usually turn in early," Young Mose said when Rachel explained her reason for stopping. "And you can believe these kids of ours are in their beds early. Cows have to be milked five thirty in the morning, sharp."

"Awful thing," Wilma said, wiping her large red hands on her apron.

"What's that?" Mose Sr. cupped a hand to his ear. "What did she say?"

Young Mose repeated Rachel's question for his father, then, "Do you have the batteries in your hearing aid, *Dat*?"

"Saving them for Sunday church." He tugged at a full snow-white beard. "Better them youngsters had been home in their own beds. They'd be alive then, wouldn't they? I don't hold with late-night frolics and such. Too worldly."

"Thank you," Mary Aaron said. "If you do hear of anything, we'd appreciate if you'd let us know."

"What? Speak up, girl!" Mose Sr. shouted. Wilma repeated what Mary Aaron said, and the old man nodded.

Mary Aaron smiled at him. "Elsie was my sister, and you can understand that the family wants to know what happened that night."

Rachel directed her next statement to Wilma. "We noticed that some of the mailboxes on this road were damaged that weekend. Yours seemed to have survived." When they'd turned in the driveway, Rachel had seen that the Heiser mailbox was securely entombed in a three-by-three-foot solid brick pillar.

The woman chuckled. "Too much work to try to knock it down. My husband's a mason by trade. You saw our mailbox. He put that up five years ago."

"Seven," Mose Sr. corrected. "Seven years last March. A solid mailbox."

"I'm sure you're right, Father Heiser," Wilma soothed. "But some of our neighbors didn't make out so well."

"Not Amish what done it," Mose Sr. declared. "That was the work of the devil's hands. Idle hands."

"But you don't know who damaged your neighbors' mailboxes?" Rachel asked. "Didn't hear anything?"

Wilma and the younger Mose shook their heads. "Happens all the time," Mose said. "Young folks, Englishers in trucks running up and down the roads at night, drinking alcohol and making mischief. That's why we put up a sturdy mailbox."

Rachel and Mary Aaron thanked the Heisers and returned to the Jeep. But as Rachel was turning it around in the yard, the young man who'd been scything weeds around on the far side of the driveway whistled to catch their attention.

Rachel braked. "Who's that?" she asked Mary Aaron.

"Young Mose and Wilma's son Joseph. I think they call him Joe."

"You or me?" Rachel looked at her cousin. "I'm afraid if both of us get back out, we'll catch someone's attention out back. My guess is that Joe isn't looking for any attention from his family."

"I think he likes you better. He can't take his eyes off this Jeep."

Rachel got out and went over to where Joe was continuing to swing the scythe in powerful, steady strokes. He was a short, muscular boy wearing blue jeans and a fairly new pair of cowboy boots. "Afternoon," she said and proceeded to introduce herself and explain why she was there.

He paused and wiped the sweat from his forehead. "Sorry about your cousin and her boyfriend. Not something you expect to have happen right here in our valley."

"No," Rachel said, speaking to him in English. "You don't. And that's why Elsie's sister and I are helping the authorities find out just what happened."

"I didn't know her too well. Elsie. She was a pretty girl, always had a smile."

"She did, didn't she?"

Joe glanced around. None of the other family members were in sight. "I keep thinking about what happened. Or *didn't* happen. Dathan was a good guy. Not the kind who would hurt anybody. He had that little dustup earlier in the evening at the singing with Rust, but that wasn't like Dathan. He didn't like to fight. And he would *never* take his own life."

"Not even if he'd done something he was ashamed of?"

"*Ne*. Nothing would be worth going to hell for all eternity. Maybe it was an accident that killed Dathan. But I'm telling you, he didn't step in front of a car."

"Were you at the singing?" she asked.

Joe considered a moment and then nodded. "I was, but I took Clara home early. She's my girl. Her mother and father are just warming to the idea of me, and I want to keep on their good side."

"Did you see the fight?"

He shook his head again. "*Ne*. Heard about it,

though. There were a lot of people. And . . ." He shrugged. "I don't know what my parents told you. But . . ." He offered an apologetic smile. "Older folks don't always see everything that goes on. They're the best. I respect them, but . . . you know how it is."

"There was something you remember about that night? Something unusual?" Rachel pressed. Joe seemed like a young man who had something more to tell her, if only she could convince him to say it.

"Well, like I said. There were a lot of people at the singing. Clara and I left early, because stuff happens after the chaperones go up to the house." He raised an open palm, rough with calluses. His fingernails were short and squared off at the tips. "I'm not judging. But Clara and I are serious in our faith. We don't drink." He leaned on the handle of the scythe. "So I drove her home and came back here and put the horse away. But later . . ." He hesitated and then went on. "After *Mam* and *Dat* were asleep, I snuck out to meet her." He shook his head. "Not what you might think. We don't do anything that we shouldn't. We want to call the banns this fall and get married. That stuff can wait."

She smiled to herself, appreciating the young man's honesty, and understanding how hard this must be for him to say to her. "So you and Clara met each other later?"

"*Ya.*" He pointed toward the road. "In that little grove of cedar trees not far from our mailbox. Just to talk."

"And you saw something that night after the singing?"

"I don't know if it means anything. And you can't tell anyone that I told. I can't get Clara in trouble. We were talking about who we wanted in our wedding party when this pickup came barreling down the road. Real fast. It nearly ran this little car off into the ditch."

"Can you tell me anything else about the truck? Make? Color?"

He thought for a moment. "Green, I think. *Ya,* it was green. Older. I couldn't say what kind."

"Did you get a look at the driver? How many people were in the truck?"

"I think there were two, but it was dark. We just noticed, 'cause it was going so fast." He shrugged again. "It's not much, but it's all I know. And it might be something important."

There was no one home at the second farm. At the next, Mary Aaron told Rachel to stay in the Jeep and let her do the questioning. "I know the wife. The husband, Clarence, is as strict as they come. Scarf or no scarf on your head, you're not Amish and you're driving this vehicle. He won't say two cents to you. And if he won't talk, neither will she."

As she waited impatiently for Mary Aaron to return, Rachel studied the farmyard and buildings. The Yutzis were an industrious lot. The barn, sheds, and chicken houses were old, but well cared for. The cows were sleek, and the horses in prime condition. The garden looked to have been laid out with German precision, and the dogs and children looked smart and well behaved.

Mary Aaron's expression was grimly resigned as she got back into the Jeep. "*Ne*, the Yutzis saw nothing out of the ordinary Friday night. Clarence thinks I'd be better off home with my mother instead of running up and down the road bothering folks with foolish questions." She fastened her seat belt and pulled a face. "He said that I was to tell you that if you want to solve a mystery, you should find out who smashed his mailbox."

The fourth house on the route had originally been an Amish homestead that had been purchased recently by Englishers from Boston. Accustomed to the normal Amish farms with neatly painted fences, mowed lawns, and carefully weeded gardens, this place made Rachel want to shake her head in disgust. The occupants weren't exactly hopeless, but they were clearly in over their heads. Fences sagged, the garden was overgrown, and a red tractor stood mired up to the rim in a ditch. The square, stone farmhouse had boasted a front porch, but the new owners had removed that for some reason and replaced it with concrete-block steps.

Surveying the barnyard, Rachel saw an array of animals that would have done justice to Noah. A pair of llamas stood in the shade of the windmill, a miniature horse trailing a rope grazed on the weedy lawn, and an obese, potbellied pig sprawled in the center of the yard. A clowder of cats, of various colors, breeds, and sizes, accompanied by a long-haired rabbit, milled and mewed around the back stoop.

"Let's hope they're friendly," Rachel whispered to Mary Aaron as they walked around an overturned push lawn mower and a basket of wormy peaches to reach the back door.

"The people or the cats?" Mary Aaron asked.

"Both."

A tall, thin woman wearing an ankle-length maroon skirt, dreadlocks, and a *Free Tibet* T-shirt answered Mary Aaron's knock. She listened politely to what Rachel had to say and then shook her head.

"Can't help you. Never left our place Friday. We had friends here for a birthday celebration, and they stayed over to go to West Virginia with us. Had a march on Sunday. Maybe you saw it on TV. Friends Against Fracking? We didn't get back until Tuesday morning. That's when we heard about the deaths. Horrendous. We never expected violence here practically on our doorstep."

A cat began climbing Rachel's ankle and she tried to dislodge it subtly.

"Who is it?" A man about the same age as Ms. Tibet came to stand behind her. He was completely bald, with wire-framed glasses and tube-like earrings that stretched his earlobes to the size of quarters. Rachel wished Mary Aaron had remained in the Jeep. She didn't need her getting ideas.

"This is my husband, Sidney," Ms. Tibet explained. "Sidney, this is . . . Excuse me, what did you say your name was?"

"Rachel. Rachel Mast. And this is Mary Aaron Hostetler."

"And what can we do for you?" Sidney asked.

"I'm acting as an informal liaison between the authorities and the Amish community," Rachel explained. "You may recognize me from the Civic Association. I chaired Stone Mill's Winter Festival this year."

"Oh, yes. We went to that. Refreshingly back-to-roots affair. Remember, Sidney? We found that fantastic potter." She looked pointedly to Mary Aaron. "And this is your cousin?"

Rachel bent to brush off a feline attack on her other leg. "Yes," she answered. "My cousin."

"She's asking people about Friday night, the night those Amish kids were killed. I told her we were out of town," the wife explained.

"Must have been a crime wave," Sidney said.

"Some Neanderthal smashed our mailbox that weekend. I'm beginning to think we should have bought a farm in Maine."

"Too many mosquitoes," his wife said.

"Did you make a complaint about your damaged mailbox?" Rachel asked. "File a police report?"

"No, we didn't," Sidney replied. "I would have to be in far more distress before I'd call the cops."

Rachel nodded. "Thank you so much for your help. I'll mention your mailbox to my fiancé when he returns from Washington. He's a detective with the state police. I'm sure he'll be eager to provide any assistance he can."

"Sorry we can't be of more help," the woman said. "I see our cats like you. It shows, when someone is sympathetic to our little furry friends. I'm always looking for good homes for some of them, if you'd—"

"No, thank you," Rachel said, backing away. "I have as many cats as I can care for now."

"We adopt them from the pound and take in strays. There's always a need," Ms. Tibet insisted.

"You might ask that Amish man," Sidney called after them. "The one who comes with the horse and wagon and leaves in his truck. He came through Friday afternoon. I remember because we were barbecuing in the yard. Saw him."

Rachel turned around. "There's a man in a horse and wagon who leaves in a truck?" She studied him. "Who? Where's the truck?"

"Must keep his truck back there." He pointed vaguely in the direction of the road. "Down and across the street. There's a dirt road that leads to an abandoned lumber mill. There's a log across the lane, but he just drives around it, through the weeds."

"Do you know his name?" Mary Aaron asked.

Sidney shook his head. "Never spoke to him. Just see him coming and going most nights." The man shrugged. "He might have seen something."

Rachel thought for a moment. "Do you know what time you saw him? After dark? Before dark?"

"Before dark," Sidney answered. "Like I said, we were grilling. Steaks. Four. Four thirty, maybe?"

Ten minutes later, Rachel and Mary Aaron had parked the Jeep out of sight, in the woods, and were traversing the dirt road that led to the old lumber mill. "Who could be keeping a truck hidden in the woods?" Mary Aaron asked.

"No idea."

"What are we going to do if we find this truck?" Mary Aaron looked ahead.

"I don't know," Rachel answered. Her mind was going in ten directions at once. An Amish man keeping a truck hidden in the woods. Surely this had something to do with Elsie and Dathan going missing. But how? Lucy said the vehicle that hit Dathan had been big, likely a picku truck. Was this the truck that had hit and killed him? "See if we can figure out whom it belongs to?"

"Like if he left his name on it?" Mary Aaron asked.

It may have been an attempt to lighten the mood, Rachel wasn't sure. "He may have left his registration in the glove box, or maybe a receipt or something."

"And if he didn't?" Mary Aaron pushed.

"Then we wait for him."

"We're going to sit in a truck in the woods and wait for someone to come along?"

Rachel shrugged. "Have you got a better idea?" She stopped and pointed at the pickup cab just visible through the trees ahead of them. "And wouldn't you know it? It's a green truck."

CHAPTER 13

Twilight slowly fell on the valley, the mountains and the endless expanse of old-growth trees and weathered rock all absorbing the light from the setting sun. As evening crept in, the woods seemed to come alive with rustling, snapping of twigs, and the chirping of frogs and crickets.

"How long are we going to sit here?" Mary Aaron asked, keeping her voice low.

"Until the owner of this truck comes to claim it," Rachel whispered back. They'd been sitting in the cab of the green pickup for the better part of an hour, and not seen nor heard a soul at the abandoned sawmill. There was no registration in the glove box and not a single slip of paper on the floor or under the seat that might indicate whom the vehicle belonged to. Rachel had taken down the license plate number though, thinking that if all else failed, maybe she could get Lucy to run it.

"And if he doesn't come? Will we sit here all night?"

"Maybe."

It had been easy to park the Jeep a few hundred feet away, where it couldn't be seen from anyone driving up the overgrown lane from the road. Rachel hoped that if the owner came, he wouldn't notice her tire tracks in the grass.

Mary Aaron shifted on the seat. She was behind the steering wheel and had less room to stretch out. "Will your parents be wondering where you are?"

"They know I'm still trying to find answers. You heard *Mam* last night." Rachel ran her finger along the dashboard of the old truck, drawing a line in the dust. It didn't appear as if anyone had sat on the passenger's side in a long time. "They won't worry about me."

"*Atch*, I think they'll still worry. I imagine parents worry their whole lives about their children. But your *mam* and *dat* know they can't tell you what to do." Mary Aaron sighed. "I try to imagine what that would be like. To make up your own mind: when to come home, when to eat, what to wear. For most of us here, the women, at least, we live under our parents' roof, by their rules. Then when we marry, we have a husband's wishes to answer to."

"It's the way it's always been, the way it still is for most women in the world," Rachel mused. "Not just Amish, but women everywhere."

Mary Aaron stared out into the woods. "Supposedly it's what God intended. But who says that? The preachers. The bishop. Good men, but *men*."

Rachel studied her cousin. "You sound more like a college Englisher than an Amish woman about to be baptized. Next thing you know, you'll be protesting in front of the mayor's office, carrying a sign."

Mary Aaron suppressed a giggle. "I don't think the mayor of Stone Mill has an office. Doesn't the town council meet at the bookstore?"

"You know what I mean." Rachel hesitated and then went on. "You're not having second thoughts, are you? About being baptized? Marrying Timothy? He told me he wanted to post the banns for you two this fall, but you haven't wanted to talk about it."

"Timothy should keep quiet. I just need some time to think this all through. Baptism and marriage are big steps." Mary Aaron shook her head. "Before I know it, we'll have a house full of children."

"But you love Timothy, don't you? And you want children."

"You're a fine one to be asking these kinds of questions." Mary Aaron turned on the truck's bench seat to face Rachel. "How long have you kept poor Evan dangling on a baited fishing line? I don't think you're completely sold on marriage yet either."

Rachel ignored Mary Aaron's attempt to turn the conversation into one about her. "What other choices do you think you have?" she asked. "Do you want to leave the community? Go out in the world? Live on your own?"

Mary Aaron shook her head. "*Ne. Ya.* Maybe." She lifted her hands and let them fall to her lap. "I don't know. I can't picture myself living anywhere but Stone Mill, among the people I love. But then I get to thinking that I've never lived anywhere else or made my own decisions. How do I know I won't regret it if I do what everyone in my family expects me to do without seeing what other choices are out there?"

"I think—"

Mary Aaron raised a hand in warning, and Rachel fell silent.

They both turned their heads. From a distance came the repetitive sound that might have been a horse and wagon coming up the lane. Rachel rolled the passenger-side window halfway down. There was no doubt. A horse and vehicle were coming their way.

Rachel ducked down and motioned for Mary Aaron to do the same so they wouldn't be spotted in the cab of the pickup.

A male voice cut through the stillness of the clearing. "Easy, boy." There was a creak of a leather harness and the crackle of leaves crushed by wheels and a horse's hooves. The voice was too low for Rachel to make out who was speaking, but he was using *Deitsch*. Then footsteps became audible, and the driver's door opened from the outside.

The man jumped back with a cry. Mary Aaron slid over to the center of the seat.

"What are you doing here?" The figure raised his fists and took a martial arts stance, not seeming to recognize them.

"Rupert?" Rachel got out and hurried around to the driver's side. "Rupert!" She shrank back when he turned fast on her. "It's Rachel. Rachel and Mary Aaron."

It seemed to take a moment for him to understand what she was saying, and then he lowered his hands, coming to his full height. "What are you doing here?" he demanded again.

"What are *we* doing here? What are *you* doing here?" Rachel kept a safe distance from him. She had no doubt that Rupert could be dangerous, perhaps even lethal, with whatever hand-to-hand training he'd received in the Marines. But she had no intention of fighting with him. If he took one step in her direction, she'd run. And she hoped Mary Aaron would do the same. "Is this your truck?"

He didn't respond.

Rachel glanced away with a sigh, then back at him. "You weren't honest with me, Rupert. And that's a problem. If the police come to question you again, it isn't going to be friendly. You could be in big trouble."

"You should go," he ordered. "Now."

Mary Aaron slid out of the truck. "Rupert, please. Help us find out what happened to my sister." She spoke calmly, quietly, as if he were an injured animal. "You and Elsie were friends. You cared about her. I know you did."

"Friends?" He drew the back of his hand across his mouth. "We were more than friends. I loved her. I would never hurt Elsie."

"So why haven't you been truthful with me? What are you hiding, Rupert?" Rachel followed Mary Aaron's lead and gentled her tone. "Why did you lie to me about your fight with Dathan over Elsie?"

"Because it would make me look like a suspect!" he snapped. Then he stared at the ground and when he spoke again, it was barely above a whisper. "And because I didn't do it." His hands became fists at his sides. "I didn't hurt Elsie."

"Okay. So, why the lies?"

"I didn't lie. Just about the fight."

"You lied about how you got to the singing that night," Rachel said. "You told me that you went to that singing in a buggy."

"I said in a wagon."

"All right, a wagon. But that's a lie, too. Someone saw you drive away from here in that truck." She pointed.

"I didn't take the truck to the singing. I went

somewhere else first. Then I came back and took the wagon I'd left here in the woods." Rupert suddenly stiffened and stared at Rachel, narrowing his eyes. "I don't have to answer to you. I'm done with questions."

"I'm not letting you go without getting some answers, Rupert." Rachel dropped her hands to her hips. She wasn't afraid of him now, and she was starting to lose her patience with him.

He set his jaw. "You want to grill somebody about running the roads? Why don't you talk to Dathan's brother-in-law? Men like him"—he pointed randomly, his motion jerky—"they ought to be home with their wives."

Mary Aaron spoke, her tone gentle. "Rupert, no one wants to cause you trouble if you didn't do anything wrong. It just looks suspicious. Someone told us that a green truck ran a car off the road near here the night Dathan and Elsie disappeared." She pointed. "Just down that way. We're asking questions to try to find out what happened to Dathan and Elsie. If you had any feelings at all for her, and you didn't have anything to do with her death, you should want to help."

"You already know everything I know. I got into it with Dathan that night, but it was over when they left. I would have cut off my right arm before I would hurt a hair on Elsie's head. I don't have the faintest idea what happened to her, but I can tell you one thing. What's going around, this talk that Dathan jumped in front of a car and killed himself? That's nuts. Dathan was a good kid, but he was a goody-goody. He wouldn't so much as touch a drop of beer or a cigarette. He would have been scared to lose his immortal soul by committing suicide."

"So what do you think happened to Dathan?"

He shrugged and shook his head at the same time.

Rachel thought for a moment and then asked, "Why the truck?" She pointed. "This *is* yours, isn't it?"

"*Ya*, it's my truck." Another shrug. "When I get headaches . . . when I start remembering stuff I'd rather forget, I like to drive. I open the windows, turn up the radio, and just drive. But I don't run people off the road. I keep it here because obviously I don't want anyone in my parents' church to know about it."

Rachel exhaled. "You should have told me you were out in a truck Friday night."

He threw his shoulders back. "I don't have to tell you everything I do. If the cops want me, they know where to find me. I'm not hiding, because I didn't do anything wrong."

He brushed past her, got into the truck, and started the engine. Rachel stood where she was as Rupert backed the truck off into the brush, turned it around, and took off down the lane.

Above the roar of the motor, she heard the *crack* of glass in the back of the truck.

"Beer bottles," she said, half to Mary Aaron and half to herself.

"*Ya*," Mary Aaron agreed. "There were dozens of them. Empties in the bed of the truck. I noticed them when we got in."

Rachel stared after the taillights that were growing steadily smaller in the distance. "What do you think about what he said about Elsie? Do you think he's telling the truth?"

Mary Aaron nodded. "I think so. I think he really did care about her."

Rachel led the way back to the Jeep; they both got in. She backed up and then pulled forward, and as she did, she heard the clang of bottles from the back of her Jeep. When she heard the sound, she braked hard and the bottles clinked again. "Beer bottles!" she declared, smacking the steering wheel with the palm of one hand. She turned to Mary Aaron. "Beer bottles," she repeated. "When I was walking the road the other day, I found a lot of beer bottles. In the ditches. Along the road. A couple smashed, maybe against mailboxes."

"Were they Bud Light?" Mary Aaron asked. "That's mostly what was in the back of Rupert's truck."

"Not the same brand I found on the road."

"If Rupert's drinking like that, maybe he doesn't remember what happened that night."

"Maybe." Rachel hit the gas.

"Where are we going?"

Rachel gripped the wheel. "If an Amish man is buying beer in town, I have an idea someone will have noticed."

Mary Aaron grimaced as they pulled up in front of Fine Wine & Good Spirits, a state-operated liquor store on the seedier side of Stone Mill. The place had been an institution in the valley as long as Rachel could remember. Constructed of concrete blocks painted an ugly orange and then allowed to fade and peel for decades, it had all the appeal of a low-rate dungeon, complete with barred doors and windows. The parking lot had once been gravel, so it had its share of bumps and low spots, which filled up with rain and snow and provided a constant supply of mud and mosquito hatchery, depending on the season.

"Wait here," Rachel said to Mary Aaron. "I'll make this quick."

Two young men on the bench outside the single door stared at Mary Aaron, and she stared back. "And *why* are we here?" she asked, sounding doubtful.

"I'm going to try to find out if Rupert came in Friday night. And if he did, how much beer he bought. Did he buy enough for one person or a couple of dozen?"

"We don't know that there was drinking at the singing," Mary Aaron defended.

Rachel turned her head and cut her eyes at her cousin. She'd been to a few parties in the days when she still wore a white prayer *kapp*. Alcohol was often available. Even drugs. *Rumspringa* could be dangerous for young Amish men and women *sowing their oats*. "Really?"

Mary Aaron sighed. "Okay, so there may have been drinking. But Dathan and Elsie didn't stay late, and drinking alcohol always goes on late. Any drinking that went on had to have been late. After the older Troyers went to bed. But I don't know what drinking at the Troyers' would have to do with Dathan and Elsie."

"I don't know that it does. I just think it's important for us to know exactly what happened and the exact times that the people we've talked to came and went." She rested her hands on the steering wheel. "I don't think Rupert is being completely honest with us. He wouldn't look me in the eye when he spoke."

"You said yourself, he's been through a lot." Mary Aaron sat back in her seat. "Do you think he may have had something to do with their deaths?"

Rachel shook her head. "I don't know. Rupert might be innocent. But he's not stable, or he doesn't seem as if he is."

"He wanted us to question Charles. I wonder

why." Mary Aaron thought for a moment. "He's not a very nice person. Nothing like Dathan."

"If not being nice was a crime, there'd be a lot more of us incarcerated."

"Not me, I hope."

Rachel chuckled. "No, Mary Aaron. Definitely not you."

Her cousin laughed with her, then folded her arms and hugged herself. "Is it wrong to laugh? To go on like nothing happened? When my sister's dead?" She shuddered. "I don't know. It doesn't seem real. Either I want to cry my eyes out, or I don't want to think about it. But then I feel so guilty when I do forget about it for a few minutes."

Rachel reached out and touched Mary Aaron's arm. "But we aren't going on as if nothing happened. We're trying to find out how Elsie died and why. We can't let anything, even mourning Elsie, keep us from finding out the truth."

"*Ya*, that's what I keep telling myself. But I—"

Knuckles rapped on Rachel's window and she jumped. Lowering the window, she studied the skinny boy who stood there. He was wearing an Ocean City, New Jersey sweatshirt and a ball cap, the brim turned backward. He had small eyes and a prominent nose, and if he'd started to seriously shave yet, it didn't show. "Yes?"

"I rode all the way down here on my bike. Four miles. My stepdad wanted me to buy him a six-pack, but now that I'm here, I realize I left my ID at home. Can you help me out? I'd make it worth your while. Buy you a six, too."

"You want me to buy beer for you?" Rachel frowned, looking him over again. "How old are you?"

"Twenty-two."

"Right." Rachel shook her head. "Go home and come back when you're legally of age and can buy your own. Or, better yet, don't come back at all. There are better ways to spend your money."

"I'm twenty-two. I swear it. Come on, what will it hurt you to do me a little favor? I'm talking one six-pack."

"No way."

The boy muttered something under his breath and struck the door halfheartedly with his fist as he walked away.

"He looked closer to seventeen than twenty-one," Mary Aaron observed.

"Eighteen, tops. I've seen him hanging around at Howdy's Garage and Tow. I think he's a nephew or something. I've heard Howdy giving him a hard time." Rachel opened the Jeep door. "He's harmless."

Mary Aaron got out on her side, still eyeing the boy crossing the parking lot. "I'm coming with you," she said.

"You're not."

"We're doing this together, aren't we?"

Rachel glanced away, then back at her cousin. "If your dad finds out I took you into a liquor store, he'll nail my hide to his barn door."

"Mine, too. But I'm of age, Rae-Rae. You're not *taking* me anywhere. I'm going in myself."

As Rachel walked toward the door, she muttered, "Why do I think this is a bad idea?"

Inside, a small television blared a sitcom with a canned laughtrack that Rachel thought had gone off the air years ago. The clerk slouched on a stool behind the counter, an open can of grape soda pop in his hand, a big bag of potato chips open in front of him. She thought she recognized him from the grocery store, or somewhere in town. He was somewhere between thirty and fifty, shaggy-haired, and obviously a hearty eater.

"Hi," Rachel said, approaching the register.

The clerk caught sight of Mary Aaron and inhaled a mouthful of pop. In a frenzy of choking, he coughed, spraying grape soda on the counter, and two trickles of soda ran out of his nose. Eventually, he got his breath and his face turned from puce back to its normal shade.

"Don't you have Amish customers?" Rachel asked sweetly.

The man waved in Mary Aaron's general direction. "Men, sure. Not women. At least not in that getup."

"That's good to know," Mary Aaron supplied smoothly. "We have some questions to ask you about Amish customers."

The clerk cleared his throat. "I get paid to sell whatever comes over the counter. Not to answer questions."

"We saw underage kids outside your door." Rachel pointed.

"Can't keep 'em off the property." He wrinkled his nose. "Free country and all that."

Rachel refrained from the remark that rose on her tongue. A smart aleck. Just what they needed. "We're helping with the investigation of the deaths of two young Amish people. I'm sure you heard about it."

He scowled. "What's that to me?"

"Talk to us or the police," Mary Aaron said. "Your choice."

"Cops can talk to me all they want," he replied. "Got nothin' to say to them. Don't know anything about the murders except what I read in the paper." He reached for his bag of chips. "Now, do you want to buy something or not? We don't allow anybody to just hang out in here."

"I just have a couple of questions," Rachel said.

"Told you. I'm not answering any questions." He returned his attention to the TV.

"Suit yourself," Mary Aaron said. "But don't be surprised if Trooper Mars of the Pennsylvania

State Police takes you in and puts you in a lineup when you least expect it."

Rachel grabbed her cousin's arm and steered her out of the store. *"Lineup?"* she hissed at Mary Aaron as they went out the door.

"I read about it," Mary Aaron defended. "Isn't that what they always do with shady-looking guys like him? Put them in a lineup?"

"Mary Aaron, you have to be a suspect to—" Rachel cut herself off. She wasn't in the mood to explain the whole thing just now. "Just get in the Jeep. Please."

"Sure you won't change your mind?" the kid in the *Ocean City* sweatshirt called to them as they cut across the parking lot. "You get me a case of Bud, there's ten in it for you."

"Sorry," she said, following Mary Aaron to the Jeep.

In the Jeep they sat there in silence for a moment while Rachel tried to think what else to do. Another truck pulled up in front of the store, and the kid in the parking lot walked over to try the same trick on the two guys in the cab. They exchanged a few words and then the two men went into the building. The boy's shoulders slumped and he started back for his seat on the rickety bench.

Rachel rolled down her window. "Hey! Come here."

The kid strolled over. "Change of mind, hon?"

"You here a lot?" she asked him.

He shrugged. "Some."

"I'm not buying you beer, but there's twenty dollars in it for you if you answer a few questions."

"Shoot."

Beside her, Mary Aaron made a small squeak. Rachel ignored her. "Do you know Rupert Rust? Used to be Amish. He drives a green pickup."

"The guy in the fatigue jacket? Was Amish, then joined the Marine Corps?"

"That's him. Do you remember if he was here last Friday?"

"Yeah, the jerk was here," the kid answered without hesitation. "Wouldn't buy me any beer, if that's what you're asking. Told me to go home to my mother. Threatened to call the cops on me if I didn't clear out."

"You're positive?" Rachel fished a twenty from her wallet and waved it in front of the boy. "Did Rupert Rust buy alcohol for himself Friday night?"

"Yup. Two cases. Bud Light. I told him light beer was for wussies." He held his hand out for the twenty-dollar bill.

"Was anybody with him?"

"Nope. All by himself. Got no friends, as far as I can tell. It's cool that he fought those sand monkeys and all, but he's a little scary."

"You know what time it was? When you saw Rupert here?"

The boy shrugged.

"Well, was it late afternoon, early evening, after dark?"

The kid sighed. "Six, maybe. It wasn't dark yet. I remember because he was wearing Amish clothes under the jacket. But not the big hat."

Rachel handed him the money. He grabbed it and walked away, jamming it in his pocket.

"He could have said thank you," Mary Aaron said as Rachel started the engine.

Rachel looked at her. "What do you think the chances are that it's just a coincidence that Rupert came here in Amish clothes, and bought two cases of beer the night of the singing? He must have taken it to the Troyers'."

"Maybe he drank them himself," Mary Aaron suggested.

"He didn't drink that much himself." Rachel backed out of the parking space. "Not in one night, at least."

"Where to?" Mary Aaron buckled her seat belt. "Home?"

"Yes, but just for a pit stop. I'm not satisfied that we've found out all we need to."

"You shouldn't have given that boy that much money. He'll just spend it on beer."

Rachel shifted into drive. "Maybe he will, but if he does, it's his decision. Ours is to keep asking questions until we find answers."

CHAPTER 14

"I don't know why we couldn't have come in the buggy," Mary Aaron grumbled. "It would have been a lot more comfortable."

"You said you wanted to know everything they knew that night. You wanted to ride home from the Troyers', just like Elsie and Dathan did. They were in a *wagon,* not a buggy," her brother said.

"I'm just following my mother's advice," Rachel said to her cousins. "*Mam* said that I should do exactly what they did Friday night. That way we'd see and hear most of what they did."

It was a little after nine, and John Hannah, Elsie's twin, was driving the horse and wagon in the direction of the Troyers' farm with Rachel and Mary Aaron sitting on the hard wooden bench seat beside him. Rachel's original intention, when they'd left the liquor store, was to go home and borrow her own *dat*'s horse and wagon, but Mary Aaron had suggested they start from her house, because it had been Dathan and Elsie's destination the night they went missing.

John Hannah had caught them harnessing the horse and had insisted on coming with them. "It's dangerous out there," he'd said. "Especially at night. After what happened to Elsie and Dathan, I'm not taking any chances with you two." Before they'd left the barn, John Hannah had grimly tucked a wooden baseball bat under the seat.

Rachel and Mary Aaron had stared at one another, but neither had commented. John Hannah was one of the mildest-mannered and sweetest of her male cousins, and if he thought they needed something for self-protection, Rachel wasn't about to argue. She'd never known him to get into a fight, but he certainly hadn't intended to use the bat to play baseball.

As they rode along in the dark, Mary Aaron and John Hannah were still sniping at one another in typical brother-and-sister exchanges. It seemed a little lighthearted, considering they had just buried a sister, but Rachel knew that both were truly grieving and the mild-mannered arguing was a way to ease the tension they were both feeling. Rachel tried to shut them out and concentrate on the homes and woods that pressed in on both sides of the road. It was a dark night, and there were no streetlights. A single buggy passed them near the lane that led to the old sawmill, and Rachel couldn't help wondering if Rupert's truck was there. Or was he driving around, trying to ease one of his headaches? The air was cool. Autumn came quickly to the mountains and she was glad that she'd worn a jacket and taken a lap blanket from the tack room.

"How well do you know Titus Troyer?" Rachel asked John Hannah when there was a lull in the chatter. John Hannah and Titus were close in age, but not from the same church community. "I understand he was a friend of Dathan's."

"I've asked around. Nobody has anything bad to say about Titus. He's a little churchy to suit me."

"Yet he hosted a singing where kids drank alcohol," Rachel said.

"A lot of young folks around here are *rumspringa*. It's expected that they experiment with the sins of the world before they choose the Amish life," he said. "You can bet there were no drugs on the property and that the drinking was limited to a little beer. That's as far as Titus would let things go."

"Kids shouldn't drink alcohol," Rachel insisted. "Some of them are underage, which means they're breaking the law."

"I didn't say I approved of it." John Hannah flicked the reins over the horse's back and the animal picked up its pace. "I'm just telling you how it is, or how I think things probably went. But the drinking usually happens late, and Dathan and Elsie left early."

"Lettie came home early, too," Rachel mused.

"And you said you did," Mary Aaron said to her brother. "You took Dora home."

"Not Dora, her sister," John Hannah corrected.

"Anna Mary. I like a lot of girls. And I'm not ready to pick just one."

Rachel drew the sleeves of her polar fleece jacket down. It was chilly in the open wagon. "You think Asa Troyer knew what was going on at the bonfire?"

"The drinking? Doubt it."

Rachel stared out at the darkness. The wagon didn't have battery-operated lights like a buggy would, but John Hannah had hung lanterns from the front and the back of the wagon. It was a cloudy night, with no moon to speak of, and mist lay low to the ground on both sides of the road. The fields and woods that surrounded them were blacker than black. Occasionally, a pair of eyes would gleam in the darkness, some yellow, some red and glimmering. It should have been relaxing, rolling along at the horse's easy pace, but it wasn't. There was something a little scary about their surroundings tonight, almost spooky. She wondered if Elsie and Dathan had thought the same thing Friday night.

They had almost reached the driveway that led up to the Troyer farm when John Hannah reined in the horse. "Look over there," he said.

Rachel stared into the dark, but she couldn't make out anything farther than fence posts on the side of the road. The horse perked up its ears, flicked its tail and mane, and nickered. An answering whinny came from the darkness.

"Hey!" John Hannah called.

There was no answer, but seconds later, battery lights switched on and Rachel saw that a horse and buggy had pulled off into a clearing in the trees. "Hey, yourself," came the shouted answer in the *Deitsch* dialect. "Who's there?"

"John Hannah Hostetler." John Hannah clicked to the horse and guided it into the same area, effectively penning the horse and buggy in. "Titus? Is that you?"

"*Ya*, it's me," came the answer.

But Rachel was already climbing down and making her way over to the buggy. Titus got out. "It's Rachel Mast," she said, trying to see if there was anyone else still inside. Behind her, she could hear Mary Aaron.

"What are you doing out here?" Rachel asked.

"I went to visit someone, but her father wouldn't let her out of the house. A lot of people are spooked by what happened to your cousin."

"So you're just sitting here?" Rachel asked.

"*Ya*. Watching the road." He shook his head. "Can't get it out of my mind. They were right here, Dathan and Elsie. Safe. And then . . ." He sighed. "I just can't imagine what could have happened to them."

"That's what we're trying to find out," Rachel replied. "We were coming to see if you were still up. We have a few more questions for you, if you don't mind."

"*Ne.* I don't mind." Titus shuffled one foot. She could make out most of his face in the buggy lights. He looked as if he'd missed a lot of sleep.

"Some things you told us about Friday night weren't quite right," she said.

"Such as?"

"There was beer at the bonfire, wasn't there?" Mary Aaron came to stand at Rachel's shoulder. "Come clean, Titus. We're not going to take it to the bishop."

"Or your father," Rachel finished.

"Tell him what you like." Titus's voice was tight. Not angry, but clearly, he was upset.

"I'm guessing that it was Rupert Rust who supplied the beer," Rachel said.

Titus straightened his shoulders. "I don't tell tales on others."

"We're not trying to get anyone in trouble. We're just trying to figure out what happened. Was Rupert drinking heavily?" Rachel asked. "Did he leave here drunk?"

"Rupert didn't have a drop. Gave it up months ago. Said it was bad for his demons. Made them louder in his head." Titus removed his hat and tossed it into the buggy. "Creepy, huh?"

"Was he driving his green truck that night? The old one that he hides up at the abandoned lumber mill?"

Titus hesitated. "*Ne.* He was in a wagon. If he'd come up here in a truck, my father wouldn't have liked it. I heard that Rupert has a truck, but he didn't bring it here Friday night."

"But he and Dathan did get into a fight that night, didn't they?" Rachel insisted. "Something you didn't tell us last time we were here."

"I didn't want to get anyone in trouble. Rupert's a little weird, but he wouldn't do anything to hurt anyone. And he thought the world of Elsie. I can't believe he'd ever do anything to her. Rupert just wants to come back, you know. Outside, it was bad for him. Real bad. He really wants the Plain life."

"Can you tell me when Rupert left?"

Titus hesitated, and then said, "Right after the fight."

Rachel glanced at Mary Aaron, who met her gaze, then returned her attention to Titus. "*Before* Dathan and Elsie?"

Titus nodded.

"Like, how long?"

Titus thought for a moment. "Half hour, maybe."

"A half an hour would be enough time to get to the pickup at the sawmill," Mary Aaron whispered to Rachel as they walked back toward the wagon where John Hannah was waiting for them.

"That's what I was thinking," Rachel agreed.

The ride home was uneventful, unless you counted the herd of deer that ran across the road ahead of them and nearly spooked the horse. The three of them didn't talk much. What was there to say? Rachel felt as though she was back at the beginning. She had lots of suspicions. The fact that Rupert left before Dathan and Elsie certainly had her wondering again. But she still had no solid clues. She felt as though she was at a dead end. She doubted that the police had anything more. And if someone didn't come up with some idea, Elsie's and Dathan's deaths would just be one more ghost story to add to all the others here in the valley.

"Is that too warm for you?" Rachel adjusted the faucet so that a mix of hot and cold water sprayed on her mother's hair, or what was left of it. She, Lettie, and their mother were in the main bathroom of the farmhouse on the lower floor.

"Tell your sister that it feels good," *Mam* said to Lettie. "It's just the right temperature. My scalp itches, and the warm water and shampoo ease me."

"*Mam* says—" Lettie began.

"I heard her." Rachel glanced at her sister. Lettie's damp hair was wrapped in a thick white towel, and her eyes twinkled with mischief. "I can hear you, *Mam*," Rachel said.

Her mother ignored her. "Is Mary Aaron coming back to spend the night again tonight, Lettie?" she asked. "She's welcome here anytime, but I saw her leave just before breakfast. Did she go home? Her mother may need her."

Rachel squeezed the water out of her mother's thin hair. Bald patches were appearing at the back of her head and on either side. Her mother had always had such thick dark hair, but what was left was quickly turning to silver-gray with darker threads running through it. "Hand me that conditioner," Rachel said to Lettie.

Rachel poured out a generous amount and gently rubbed it in. Her mother sighed with pleasure as Rachel continued to massage and rub her scalp. "Mary Aaron went home, but I think she was going to Stone Mill House to check on things at some point today."

"Some people in the community worry about Mary Aaron spending so much time at the B&B around all those English," their *mam* commented. "Maybe in this terrible time of mourning, she'd be better off at home on the farm with her family."

"Mary Aaron's an adult," Rachel said patiently. "She can make her own decisions. She's been a godsend for me this summer, but if she didn't want to be there, I'd find another solution."

"Enough. Tell your sister she can rinse it out now," their mother said.

"It's better if we let the conditioner sit on your hair for a few minutes," Rachel advised.

"Rachel says—" Lettie began.

"I heard her. I'm not deaf," their *mam* said. "Hand me a towel, Lettie."

Lettie rolled her eyes and handed a towel to

Rachel, who wrapped it around their mother's head. "Not long," Lettie said. "We'll just leave it five or ten minutes."

"All right, all right." Their mother settled herself onto the closed toilet seat. "You know, just because your cousin is a capable young woman with a strong will doesn't mean that she shouldn't have our extra attention now. Mary Aaron loved her sister dearly, and now that Elsie is gone, Mary Aaron needs gentle handling. She needs her family, all of her family, to get through this. She needs our prayers above all."

Lettie nodded. "*Ya*. I have been praying for Elsie and for the family."

Rachel put an arm around Lettie's shoulders and hugged her. "We all miss her."

"You have to remember that Elsie is with God now," their mother said. "I know you miss her, but she is in a better place. And we will see her again." She folded her work-worn hands in her lap. She'd lost weight since she'd become ill, and her hands were thinner than Rachel had ever remembered them. Still, they were strong hands, she told herself, the hands of a survivor.

Lettie removed her own towel and began to comb out her long hair.

"I'm still really confused about what your sister has or hasn't found out about what happened that night," their *mam* said.

"They had to have met someone on the road,"

Rachel said. "One of the neighbors saw a green pickup truck, an older truck, on the road. Rupert Rust has a green truck that he parks out by the abandoned sawmill."

"He wants to join the church, he'll have to get rid of that motor truck," their mother remarked.

"He used to go with Elsie, and he and Dathan didn't get along," Rachel continued. "That makes Rupert someone to look at."

Their mother shook her head. She pulled off the towel and handed it to Lettie. "I don't think Rupert would hurt anyone. He saw enough violence across the water where the Englishers sent him to shoot at foreigners. He's messed up in his head, but I've known him since he was a babe. He's no killer."

"I agree. Rupert would never have harmed Elsie," Lettie insisted. "He's a good person. He wants to live right. That's why he came home to the valley. *Mam*'s right. He's mixed up, but he's really sweet."

Rachel rested her balled hands on her hips and glanced from one of them to the other. Lettie looked the most like their mother of any of them. She'd be a real beauty if she smiled more and didn't take herself so seriously. It was clear to Rachel that Lettie had a thing for Rupert, so it was natural that her sister would defend him. But it surprised her that their *mam* thought he was innocent as well. Their mother was far more astute than Lettie. And she was an excellent judge of character.

"Lots of old green pickup trucks," Lettie said. "And the neighbors must know Rupert's truck if they knew it was there. No one said it was Rupert, did they?"

Rachel shook her head.

"Then if the bad person was in a green truck, it had to be another green truck," their *mam* suggested. "So, maybe your sister who wants to play Englisher detective should see who else drives a green truck that would be on that road at that time of night."

"There must be a dozen old green trucks around here," Rachel protested. "You want me to check them all out?"

"If I was playing detective," their mother replied, "I would get in my motor car and start driving around and asking more questions. I would find out who owns those trucks and where they were Friday night." She ran a hand through her hair. "Time to rinse this stuff out. I've more to do today than sit here in this bathroom in my nightgown." Lettie took their mother's arm and supported her as she walked back to the sink. Rachel reached for the faucet, but her mother put her hand over it first. "A person who wanted to see right done wouldn't give up so easily."

Rachel swallowed the lump in her throat. "I'm not giving up, *Mam*. Mary Aaron and I have talked to everyone we can think of. We rode around in the dark last night, hoping to—" She exhaled. "I feel like I'm going around in circles." But almost at once she remembered what Rupert had said about seeing what was up with Charles. What was he insinuating? He'd suggested that Charles was on the roads at night. Why?

"They never found the wagon, did they?" Lettie asked.

"*Ne.*" Rachel hesitated. "Charles said that his horse came home and he was out looking for the wagon when he found Dathan's body by the road."

"So someone who wanted to play Englisher detective should look for the wagon. Horses are great for going home if they're loose. But the horse didn't unhitch itself, and it didn't take off the harness. If your sister wants to help, she should find the wagon. Find the wagon, and find whoever hurt Elsie and Dathan."

"Just like that," Rachel said as she turned the water on. "Find a wagon in this valley. How many wagons do you think there are? A hundred? More?"

"Maybe your sister will find the wagon wherever the green truck lives," their mother suggested.

"I've been looking and looking and asking and asking and I've gotten nowhere," Rachel said. "Am I supposed to go from one farm to the next, asking to see if they have a wagon? And how would I know it was Charles's wagon if I found it? Most wagons look alike." She finished rinsing her mother's hair and wrapped it in a towel again. "I don't know what to do next," she said. "If you have any ideas, I'd like to hear them."

"Tell your sister," her mother started. "That—"

"*Ne!*" Lettie interrupted, startling both Rachel and their mother. "I'm tired of playing this game, *Mam*. Rachel has given the last five months of her life to us. She's done everything she can to help you. Can't you speak to her?"

Their mother opened her mouth and then closed it. Moisture clouded her eyes. She reached a hand out to Lettie. "I don't know if I can," she said hoarsely.

"Well, I've had enough," Lettie flung back. "I'm not doing this for you anymore. It's not working. Rachel isn't coming back to us. But she's still your daughter. And my sister. And I'm tired of seeing you hurt her."

"Lettie, please," their *mam* croaked.

"*Ne.*" Lettie shook off her mother's hand. "Maybe I'll go to the B&B and stay with Mary Aaron. And maybe I won't come home. I'll just live there."

CHAPTER 15

Once her mother's hair was washed and she was dressed in anticipation of a visit from friends, Rachel walked out into the apple orchard. It wasn't far from the house, but it would give her privacy to make a few phone calls while remaining near enough to hear if anyone needed her. It had been a bountiful year; the trees were heavily laden with fruit and the apples were beginning to ripen. The sun was warm on her face, but it was a cool day, and she was glad that she'd thrown her mother's knit shawl around her shoulders.

At moments like this, it was easy to forget the violence that had touched her family, and let the peace of the farm wash over her. She'd always felt close to God in her mother's orchard. The orchard had been a wedding gift from her father to her mother. He'd carefully planted all of the original trees: Lodi, Granny Smith, Jonathan, Orleans, and Ben Davis. Over the years, her *dat* had added Rome, and Arkansas Black, a wonderful apple that would remain firm and delicious all winter, Winesaps, and Deacon Jones, as well as pear and nut trees. But it was the apples that her mother loved best. Her *mam* was famous for her cider, apple butter, and apple pies, pies that always won raves from the customers at auctions and community dinners.

Her father had fashioned a wooden bench in his workshop and put it out here in the orchard for Rachel's mother. And it had always been family tradition that when she was here, knitting, writing letters to friends, or reading, none of her nine children would bother her unless the house was on fire or the bishop was coming up the lane. Rachel made her way to the bench, lovingly crafted of cedar and carved with hearts and tulips in the old Dutch patterns. It was so peaceful here that she took several deep breaths and inhaled the sweet scent of ripening apples and the crisp odors of the coming autumn.

Why couldn't I have been content with a life like this? she wondered. But a restlessness of spirit had pulled her from this idyllic spot and thrown her into the English world. And now that she had fulfilled most of her goals in life, she discovered that the old joys tugged at her heart. She wasn't Amish anymore, but she doubted that she would ever shake the person she'd once been. Was there a place between the English and the Amish that would be right for her? Or, as her mother liked to say, had she thrown out the butter beans with the shells? She was certain that she loved Evan, but would she ever feel the peace and the contentment with him that her parents shared?

In any case, she hadn't come out here to dwell on her own insecurities. She'd wanted a chance to ask for help. Resolutely, she rang Lucy's cell.

"Rachel," the trooper said.

"Hey. I was just checking in." Rachel gazed out over the orchard. "Wondering how the investigation is going."

"Sorry. Nothing new that I'm aware of. I'm back on the road. Evening shift tonight. As far as I know, everyone at the troop seems to be satisfied with the scenario Detective Starkey laid out. Dathan and Elsie quarreled and he killed her in some sort of tussle. Then, he felt so guilty that he committed suicide the morning of her funeral. If you think about it, it makes sense. It wouldn't be the first time I've heard of such a case."

"Not this time. I'm positive. It didn't happen that way," Rachel insisted.

"I understand where you're coming from," Lucy said patiently. "But what you think may have happened isn't fact, it's conjecture. We can only go with the evidence we have. With the little evidence we have, this is a plausible conclusion."

Rachel thought for a moment, not sure how much she wanted to tell Lucy. She felt like Lucy had been very understanding, that she was on her side, that maybe she even thought the detective was wrong, too, but Lucy was still a cop and cops had to stick together. "Lucy," she said, deciding to trust her instinct. "I've been talking to some people, and there are reports of a driver in an older-model green pickup driving erratically along the road near the Troyer farm Friday night. Someone told me that he saw a green pickup run a smaller car off the road. Maybe the truck ran Dathan and Elsie off the road, too."

"There was no report of an accident that night. And the horse came home just fine. You and I both know what happens when a horse-drawn vehicle meets a car on the road, Rachel."

"Okay, but maybe someone in that truck saw something that night. Saw Dathan and Elsie driving home. We haven't found a single person who saw them after they left the singing." Rachel pushed a fallen apple with the toe of her sneaker. "Come on. How many older green pickup trucks can there be in the valley? Do you think you could help me find out whom those vehicles are registered to? Just . . . I don't know, look it up?"

"I can't do that." Lucy sounded annoyed, and a little indignant. "I could lose my job over something like that." She hesitated. "But if you found the owners on your own, I might be able to help you check them out. When I was off duty, of course."

"Thank you," Rachel said. "I mean it."

"I'm sympathetic, Rachel. Really. If I were making the decisions on this investigation, I wouldn't be so quick to seize on an easy solution. And I'd take a closer look at the brother-in-law."

"You're not the first one to tell me that," Rachel said.

"You'll have to come up with something solid or they won't listen," Lucy continued. "The detective in charge is gearing up to go on vacation, so this case is really on its way to the filing cabinet."

"You mean it's closed?" Rachel asked.

"No, not exactly. But it's definitely not going anywhere for the two weeks he's away. They're waiting for final autopsy reports, but no one's pacing the floor over it."

"Then it's up to me," Rachel said. "And I appreciate any help you're willing to give me."

"I'll do what I can, but I won't break rules." Lucy gave what could have been a chuckle. "Well, I *will* bend them a little. And you already know I can behave at least slightly inappropriately."

It took Rachel a moment to realize what she was talking about. The Black Horse Tavern the other night. "You were fine. We're all stressed out."

"I just wouldn't want you to think . . ." Lucy stopped and started again. "I don't usually . . ."

"Lucy. It's fine." Rachel smiled. "And don't worry. I'd never mention running into you in a tavern. We both have a reputation to uphold in this town. What either of us do off duty is our own business."

"Thank you." She sounded relieved.

After she and Lucy ended their conversation, Rachel called Evan. She assumed she'd just get his voicemail, so she was surprised when he picked up.

"Hey," he said, sounding pleased she'd called. "I was just going to call you. I'm counting the days here. Missing you."

"And I miss you," she said, surprised by the emotion welling up in her throat. Mary Aaron was right, she wasn't quite ready to tie the knot, but she certainly cared for Evan. Loved him.

"How are you?" he asked. "I keep thinking about what you must be going through. I don't like being so far away. I came close to walking out on the course twice this week."

"Don't do that," she said. "You've worked so hard, and a lot of people are depending on you. You can't just quit on account of me."

"I know, I know, but . . ." He trailed off, his deep voice thick with emotion.

"I'm fine," she said. "Well, maybe not fine, but I'm okay. Dathan's funeral yesterday was awful. Almost worse than Elsie's, maybe because it was the second in a week. How are you doing?"

Evan sighed. "I'm no scholar. But you knew that. Fortunately, most of what they're teaching us is straightforward common sense. These guys giving this course on terrorism in hometowns are sharp, and they've been dealing with what we hope we'll never have to. I'm learning a lot."

"See. I knew you would. And it will be wonderful for your career."

They were quiet for a moment, just enjoying being together, even if they couldn't be together. Then Evan asked, "How is your mother doing?"

"Holding her own. Some days are hard for her, but emotionally, she's tough. I'm still praying that she'll beat this."

"If anyone can, your mother will. You come of strong stock."

"Let's hope so. I don't know what *Dat* would do without her. Or what I would do. She's the heart of this family."

"I know how much you love her," he said. And then, "Okay, tell me what's happening with the investigation. Because I know that's why you called."

"Not true. I called because I needed to hear your voice," she defended. But then she smiled. He knew her so well. "And to talk about the case."

She filled him in as briefly as she could without leaving out anything important. She'd been afraid that he'd warn her against interfering in the detective's casework, but he surprised her. He took her side. "So you agree with me?" she said. "It's all too neatly wrapped. Both dead. No apparent witnesses. No one saw anything. Just chalk it up to murder-suicide."

"Detective Starkey might be right," Evan replied. "But you need more than circumstantial evidence to close a case. And this one isn't even a week old."

"That's what I was thinking."

"So how can I help?" Evan asked.

Rachel sighed with relief. "You don't think I'm chasing a wild goose?"

"Honey, I've learned the hard way that your hunches are good ones. I've seen Amish suicides, but never by jumping in front of a car. It's too odd."

"And it's odd that whoever hit him, just kept going. I mean, that's illegal. If Dathan jumped out in front of the driver, the driver wouldn't be at fault, and he would report it. You don't leave a dying or a dead man on the street."

"Lucy said people hit and run for all sorts of reasons: a habeas, expired tags or insurance."

"Yeah." He drew out the word. "But it doesn't happen often."

"And the explanation is awfully handy for the detective's theory," she added.

"Okay, the circumstances are odd, we both agree," Evan said. "So what's your theory?"

"I don't have one yet. But I'm sure Dathan's death and Elsie's are connected. Not by murder-suicide, but by a third party. My guess is that whoever killed Elsie killed Dathan." She told him about the green truck that was seen on the road near the Troyers' and about Rupert's truck and the fact that Lucy said he had an alibi but had refused to say who could vouch for him. "I thought I'd start by checking out the older green trucks in the valley," she said. "I was hoping you could help me find them through registrations: name, address, that sort of thing."

"You don't want much, do you?" There was a brief silence on the other end of the line, and then Evan said, "Look, I can't call Headquarters and tell them to give my fiancée access to private information." He hesitated. "But I do know somebody at Motor V who owes me a favor. I'll see what I can do."

"Thanks, Evan. I knew I could count on you."

"Right. Because you know the only crazy one around here is me, crazy about you. Be careful. Don't take any chances. Because if you're right and someone murdered the two of them, how many more is he willing to kill?"

"Or she," Rachel cautioned.

"Or she. But Elsie died due to blunt trauma. Your perp is likely a man."

"I was thinking the same thing. Elsie obviously died first. What if those marks I saw on Dathan's wrists mean he was tied up? What if—"

"Whoa, don't get ahead of yourself. So, you need to come up with a motive. The perp would have to have had opportunity and the physical strength to deal with the two of them. This

Charles, the brother-in-law, might fit that bill. Does he have an alibi for Friday night?"

"I'm taking a good look at him," Rachel said. "Lucy is suspicious of him as well, mainly because he's the one who discovered Dathan's body and because he has a motive."

"You said he inherits the farm now," Evan said.

"He sure does. Well, through his wife. And I'm still not sure I trust Rupert Rust. He was in love with Elsie, and he argued with Dathan Friday night. It came to blows. Rupert has a history of violence, and he doesn't seem entirely stable. Mentally. I don't think Rupert would have hurt Elsie, but it's a possibility."

"Jealousy. That's a powerful motive. Lots of women killed by their ex-boyfriends."

"Rupert already has a bushel basket full of troubles, though," Rachel said, as much to herself as to Evan. "I'd hate to accuse him and then find out he's innocent."

"We don't like to ever accuse anyone who's innocent," Evan replied. "But if there's somebody ruthless enough to kill the two of them, you need to use caution. I don't want to get a phone call about you."

"I'll be careful. But I can't just let whoever did this walk. It wouldn't be fair to Elsie and Dathan."

"I'm not asking you to. I'm just asking . . . I'm telling you not to put yourself in danger. Listen, I've got to run. I can't be late for this next lecture. But you take care of yourself. And tell your mom that she remains in my prayers."

" 'Bye, Evan."

" 'Bye, Rache. I love you."

"I love you, too," she said.

"I'll be home soon," he promised.

"Not soon enough."

As Rachel walked back toward the house she became aware of the crying of a baby. There were several horses and buggies in the farmyard, her mother's visitors. The wails came from the nearest. Her brother Levi held the horse as Agnes Schumacher assisted her mother down from a buggy. Hiding her surprise at finding them here, Rachel stepped forward to greet them.

"I hope it's not too much for your mother, to have our quilting circle here," Agnes said. "Charles cut the head off some chickens this morning, and we made a nice soup to bring her."

"Nothing like chicken soup to cheer a body," Dathan's mother said. Both women were all in black, except for Agnes's white prayer *kapp* under her black church bonnet. Inside the buggy, the baby screamed louder. The poor thing had screamed through Dathan's funeral, too.

"Can you manage this soup, Mother?" Agnes asked as she lifted a stainless steel pot from the floor of the vehicle.

"I'll take it," Rachel offered, reaching for the

pot. "My, you made enough soup for half the community."

"Esther has a houseful of children yet," the older woman, Martha, said.

"It's very kind of you, I'm sure," she said. Where did these women get the strength? Rachel wondered. Their son and brother buried the previous day, and they were concerned with helping someone else. If it were her, she'd be a basket case, not cooking for the sick. But it was the Amish way. The bishop preached against expressing too much grief for the loss of a loved one because it showed a lack of respect for the Lord's will.

"*Mam*, here's your sewing basket," Agnes said. "Wait while I get Baby Charles."

"I'm going in," the mother said as she trudged away, carrying her sewing things.

Rachel hoped that someone would get Baby Charles before he screamed his lungs out. She'd always loved small children, but this one had a particularly loud and piercing shriek. Bad enough, she noticed, to set the horses' ears to twitching and to cause them to shift nervously from side to side and roll their eyes.

"Baby Charles is teething," Agnes said. She looked as though she'd been awake all night. There were dark bags under her eyes, and her sallow complexion seemed almost ashen. Life hadn't been particularly kind to the woman, and it showed. In spite of her earlier impressions, Rachel felt a stab of sympathy for her. It couldn't be easy being married to Charles.

Baby Charles let out another howl, tiny fists and feet thrashing. Rachel involuntarily stepped back. She didn't know whom the infant took after, but despite the red and angry face and the tears streaking his chubby cheeks, Charles Jr. was a beautiful child, with bright blue eyes and thick, curly blond hair. She could only hope he wouldn't have his father's sour disposition.

Rachel rested the heavy pot of soup on her hip and then remembered Levi. "Take this inside for me, please," she said to her brother. "I'll tie the horse." There was plenty of room at the hitching rail for another animal, and it only took a few seconds to secure it.

"Maybe I'd best try and feed Baby Charles, before I take him in," Agnes said. "His crying may wear on your poor mother."

Lines at the corners of her eyes and mouth told Rachel that she was stressed. "No need to worry," she said. "*Mam* adores babies. She won't mind."

Ignoring the suggestion, Agnes climbed back into the buggy, cradled Baby Charles, and pulled a shawl over the baby for privacy. "You may as well get in. Wind's picking up."

Rachel walked around the buggy and got into the front seat beside mother and child. "I'm so sorry about your Dathan," she said. "How is your mother holding up?"

"Better than I am, I think." Agnes spoke loudly so that she could be heard over the baby's shrieks. "She has her faith to sustain her." She rocked and patted him, and eventually he must have begun feeding because his screams became sniffles and an occasional sob.

"I don't know how people bear the death of those dear to them if they don't have God in their lives," Rachel said. She kept her eyes averted. "My sister Lettie tells me that your brother had been baptized and was strong in his beliefs."

"*Ya*, he was." Agnes patted the baby's back and shifted to a more comfortable position for them both. "Dathan was always a good boy. A thoughtful son and brother. He would have made a good husband for poor Elsie."

Rachel wanted to ask about the relationship between Dathan and Charles, but it didn't seem the right moment. She sensed that Agnes was wrestling with more than just a fractious infant. "Does Baby Charles have any brothers or sisters?"

"One, a half brother by Charles's first wife. He grew up with his mother's parents, so I've never had the mothering of him. Charles and I lost several babes after we were first married. And then we went a long time before I got in the family way again. He is my greatest blessing, Baby Charles. But he has always been a fussy baby. First his stomach woes, and now his teeth. But he does thrive, praise God."

"Yes," Rachel agreed. "He does. He's a fine boy."

"Charles doesn't always have patience with him. Perhaps it's been so long since he had a young one. You can't blame a child for crying when they're in pain."

"No, you can't." Rachel glanced into Agnes's face and was amazed to see how the woman's features softened as she spoke of her son. *Love can work miracles,* Rachel thought. There was little beauty in Agnes's thin mouth, long nose, and narrow-spaced eyes, but her countenance took on a glow when she looked down at her nursing baby.

"It really is kind of you and your mother to come to see my mother," Rachel said softly. "When you are mourning your own loss." She hesitated. "And carry so heavy a burden."

"I do." Agnes nodded. "I do."

Baby Charles's sobs had now changed to satisfied grunts and sighs.

"He was hungry," Rachel said.

"*Ya*, he was." Agnes looked at Rachel and then glanced around, as if looking for someone. The skin on her thin lips was peeling, and the corner of her mouth looked sore.

"Have you been well?" Rachel asked. "How is your own health?"

"It's not my back or my stomach that pains me." Agnes met Rachel's gaze, and she could see the uncertainty and embarrassment in Agnes's red-rimmed eyes.

"Sometimes it helps to share our worries."

Agnes nibbled at her lower lip, biting away another section of skin and leaving a raw spot. "I was thinking that I should go to the bishop for guidance, but he's not always great in matters like this . . . women's matters."

Rachel waited, not saying anything.

"My Charles likes to go deer hunting."

Rachel nodded, wondering where this was going.

"He goes every Friday night. Only, he must be a poor shot, because he never brings home a deer."

Rachel frowned. By Agnes's tone, she got the idea that Agnes didn't think her husband went hunting on Friday nights. What was she getting at? "Was he hunting last Friday night?"

Agnes nodded. "He was. At least he said he was."

"The night that Dathan and Elsie disappeared."

Agnes lowered her head, not making eye contact. "*Ya*, that night."

"But it's a habit, nothing out of the usual for Charles to go hunting on a Friday night?" Rachel asked. "Has he always done that?"

"Just the last six months."

Rachel stared out the windshield of the buggy

into the familiar barnyard. "Bow season's just started. Not gun season yet."

"That's what I said," Agnes said. "I told him that he should leave those deer alone until fall. We didn't need the game wardens coming around and making trouble." She rocked back and forth on the seat, cradling her child beneath the cape, wordlessly crooning to him. "I sing lullabies to Baby Charles when he's feeling poorly," she murmured. "Charles thinks it's sinful. You should only sing hymns. And you should only sing them during worship service. But my mother sang lullabies to me when I was a baby. I don't think it's a sin, do you?"

"No," Rachel said. "I don't."

"Another thing. When Charles came home on Friday night, he smelled like alcohol." She gave Rachel a piercing glance. "I know what alcohol smells like. I was *rumspringa* once." Her smile seemed sad. "A long time ago."

Rachel drew in a breath. "Are you afraid that Charles had something to do with Dathan's death?"

Agnes stiffened. A guarded look came over her face. "I shouldn't have said anything. I said too much." She shook her head. "I shouldn't be talking to you about Charles. He is my husband and the head of my house. He would never do anything wrong. He would never harm my brother."

Jerked from his comfort, Baby Charles began to fuss again.

"I think he may be unwell. He feels a little feverish. He needs to be home in his own crib," Agnes said brusquely. "Tell *Mam* that I'll pick her up in two hours." She waved at Rachel. "Untie my horse. I'll be back for her or I'll send Charles. Pay no attention to what I said." She motioned again, making a flapping motion with her hand. "Best you don't come around any-more to our place. Charles doesn't like it."

Rachel turned to get out of the buggy, but then looked over her shoulder. "Tell me the truth. You do think he knows more about Dathan's disappearance and death than he said."

"*Ne*. Get out. And leave us alone. We have a right to mourn in peace without you interfering."

Agnes gathered up the leather reins and Rachel scrambled down. She untied the horse and watched as Agnes turned the buggy and drove out of the farmyard. As they went down the lane, Baby Charles was crying again.

CHAPTER 16

Rachel watched until the buggy disappeared around the bend and then returned to the house. Her thoughts were racing. If Charles hadn't been hunting Friday night, what *had* he been doing? Why did he lie to his wife and to her? Was it possible he'd had something to do with Dathan and Elsie's deaths?

Agnes had told her to forget what she'd said, but the information was much like Pandora's box. Once opened, it couldn't be shut again before possibilities spilled out. Agnes was clearly troubled by Charles's alibi, and her distress clearly suggested that she was telling the truth. She suspected that her husband was hiding something, and with good reason. The hunting alibi wasn't a good one, obviously, if he never brought venison home for the table. The obvious conclusion was that Charles wasn't hunting. She wondered how she could find out what he was really doing on Friday nights. On this past Friday night.

As she entered the kitchen, Rachel heard a murmur of feminine voices from the parlor. She went down the hall and peeked in. Her *mam* was seated in a big rocker, and her visitors were scattered around the room, each with a sewing project in hand. Most of the women were in formal black, in deference to the funerals they'd just attended. Their bonnets had been laid aside with their capes, and they wore white *kapps*. Her Aunt Hannah, however, wore her hair covered with a navy wool scarf. Her dress, in contrast to the others, was dark blue with a matching apron over it. Everyday work clothing. The apron was patched, proof of good service.

Aunt Hannah must have walked across the field from her house, Rachel thought, because she hadn't seen her uncle's buggy in the yard. Rachel said hello to the women, gave her aunt a hug, and asked her mother if there was something she could fetch for them from the kitchen.

"I think some of Amanda's fresh-squeezed lemonade would be lovely," her mother announced to the room. "And some of those ginger cookies that Lettie baked this morning. Our Lettie has a hand with cookies. So light they practically float off the plate."

"A pretty girl, your Lettie," Dathan's mother offered. "And so devout. You'll have no trouble finding her a husband." Her sideways glance at Rachel might have been interpreted as *unlike this older one.*

Rachel smiled dutifully. No doubt she was beginning to resemble an old maid, or what passed for one, among the Old Order Amish. Today she was wearing one of Amanda's dresses, which was an unflattering shade of brown. She was taller than Amanda, but her younger sister was heartier. Not only was the dress too short by Amish standards, but it was also too wide. She'd twisted her hair up on the back of her head, and topped it with a blue paisley men's neckerchief. It went without saying that she hadn't bothered with makeup. Not that she ever used much, but she was teetering on the downward slope of *plain* today.

"I hear your Lettie has her eye on a young man." An elderly woman glanced up from the baby gown she was hemming. "That Rust boy, the one that came home from the Englishers."

"I don't know where you heard that," Rachel's *mam* said. "My husband wouldn't have it. We're happy for the Rusts that they have their son back, but my husband would never approve of such a match. Rupert Rust has a long way to go before he's a member of the faith community again."

"I'll just get the lemonade," Rachel said. Her mother smiled but avoided eye contact with her. Stubborn to the roots, Rachel thought.

"Where's Agnes?" Dathan's mother, Martha, asked. "She said she was coming right in."

"*Atch*," Rachel responded. "I'm sorry. I meant to tell you. Agnes thought Baby Charles was feverish. She decided to take him home. She said she'd be back to pick you up in two hours."

Martha frowned. "We weren't staying that long. Two hours is too much of a strain on your mother. That foolish daughter of mine. Nothing wrong with that child of hers. Every baby gets a little feverish when they're teething."

One of the other women spoke up. "Don't worry, Martha. My place isn't two miles from yours. We'll drive you home."

But Dathan's mother would not be appeased. "Agnes should at least have had the decency to come in and tell me herself. I wouldn't have stayed if I'd known she wasn't. She'll ruin that child, fussing over him. My children always ran a fever when they were cutting teeth. My little Dathan . . ." She broke off and covered her mouth with her hand. "My Dathan . . ." she whispered and her shoulders trembled.

"He's in a better place," someone murmured.

"Safe in the Lord's arms," Rachel's mother intoned. An echo of agreement rippled around the room, and someone murmured something about what a fine funeral Dathan's had been.

Aunt Hannah rose from the sofa, setting her knitting down. "I'll give you a hand, Rachel."

Rachel waited for her in the hall. "It's good to see you," she said, giving her aunt another hug. "I've been praying for you."

"Don't stop. I need all the prayers I can get."

Aunt Hannah sighed and straightened her shoulders.

She was a round woman, usually quick with a smile, but she seemed to have aged ten years in the last week. Rachel's heart went out to her. "It was good of you to come. You know if *Mam* wasn't sick, she'd be with you at your place, doing everything she could to help."

"I know she would, but honestly, Rachel, I was glad for an excuse to get out of the house. I've cried until I have no tears left, and I just feel empty inside. It was all I could do to stand there at Dathan's grave yesterday after burying my Elsie only two days before."

Rachel nodded.

"Elsie's passing has been so hard on your uncle. He's angry, and the anger eats at him. I try to tell him that we have to accept God's will, but it doesn't make it any easier to bear." She caught Rachel's hand in her work-worn one and squeezed it. "Mary Aaron is my worry now. Our Elsie is with the Lord, and I know she's safe, but Mary Aaron . . ."

"We all have to grieve in our own way." Rachel kept her voice down so what was being said wouldn't carry to an eavesdropper. "I know Mary Aaron has taken Elsie's death hard."

"It's not that," her aunt said. "That would be expected. Death is a terrible thing for the young. They haven't had to live with it as an older person has. But I was worried about Mary Aaron before we lost our Elsie. I've been worried for months." She looked up at Rachel. "Do you know that she's gone to Stone Mill House to stay?"

Rachel considered it for a moment before responding. "*Ya*. She said she was going to stay the night tonight, but I just assumed that she was giving Hulda a break. The two of them have worked out a good system. I wouldn't have been able to stay here with *Mam* had it not been for Hulda and Mary Aaron." She met her aunt's concerned gaze. "It's not unusual for her to stay over when Hulda's—"

"This time she took a suitcase," Aunt Hannah said, cutting her off. Tears welled suddenly in her eyes. "She never does that. And she told her father that she didn't know when she would be home. She said she had a lot of things to think about. What is it that she can't think about in her own home? I'm afraid this is serious." She gripped Rachel's arm. "Has she said anything to you about not joining the church?"

"What?" Rachel's eyes widened. Taking her aunt's hand, she pulled her into the bathroom and closed the door behind them. This was not the kind of conversation she wanted anyone to overhear. "Not joining the church? *Ne*, she's never said a word about that to me."

"She's been struggling with her decision for months. You know she's past the time when most of our girls are baptized. Timothy has been urging her to join the bishop's classes, but she keeps giving him excuses."

Rachel considered her aunt's words. It was true. Mary Aaron hadn't been her usual happy-go-lucky self in months. And Rachel had been so wrapped up in her own problems and caring for her mother that she hadn't been as attentive to her cousin's needs as she should have been. "Aunt Hannah, you know I would never urge Mary Aaron to leave the faith," she said. "I've never said anything that would make her think that I wanted that."

"*Ne, ne,* I know you wouldn't," her aunt assured her, her eyes still teary. "I know you, Rachel. You're a good girl. You care about Mary Aaron."

"I love her like a sister." Truthfully, Rachel felt closer to her cousin than to any of her sisters, but she'd never admit to such a thing aloud.

"*Ya,* you do love her. And she loves you. She's considered you more of a big sister and a friend than a cousin since you came back to us. But my Mary Aaron is very strong-willed. You're mistaken if you think you or anyone could make her leave *or* join the church." Her Aunt Hannah shook her head. "My daughter is an adult and she can make her own decisions. This is a choice we all have to make. It isn't an easy one, to give up the pleasures of the world, but for most of us it's not a sacrifice but a blessing."

"You know I know that," Rachel said, gazing into her aunt's eyes. Mary Aaron was considering leaving the Amish? How could that be possible? And how had it come to this without her realizing it?

Hannah reached up and stroked Rachel's cheek, fighting another wave of tears. "You're wise beyond your years. Sometimes I wish your mother had your wisdom."

"*Mam* has only ever wanted what was best for me. She just never understood that it wasn't this life."

Hannah made a clicking sound between her teeth. "She's like my Aaron, too set in her ways. Sometimes a willow must bend in the wind or it will break. It would break my heart if my Mary Aaron left, but so long as God gives me speech, I would never stop talking to her. And I wouldn't care what your uncle or the bishop had to say about it."

Rachel smiled. "I can just see you defying Uncle Aaron."

Hannah sniffed in disregard. "He's the head of my family and the father of my children. I respect him, but like any husband, he can be foolish. A man doesn't always see the right path to follow. That's why God knew he needed a wife to point out the way."

Rachel hugged her. "You were always fierce in defending your children."

Her aunt gave a small groan. "Would that I could have been there to defend my Elsie."

Rachel hugged her tighter. "I'm so sorry, so very sorry. But I'll find who hurt her. I will. I promise you."

"*Goot*." Hannah wiped under her eyes, and Rachel tore off a section of toilet tissue and handed it to her. "As far as Mary Aaron." Hannah blew her nose. "I wanted you to know that if the worst happens, if she does decide her life lies outside of the community, I will never blame you."

Rachel pressed her lips together. "But a lot of people will."

"*Ya*, you're right." Hannah tossed the toilet tissue in the trash can. "And sadly, your uncle may be among them. I'm sorry for that."

"But she can't have made a decision yet. Maybe I can go home and spend the night. We'll have a chance to talk. I've been missing my own bed, and my mother seems to be having a good day."

"You are a blessing to her, you know, a *goot* daughter. Esther appreciates it, even if she won't say so."

"I'm here because it's the right thing to do. *Mam* and *Dat* and the younger ones need me. I'm not doing it for appreciation."

Her aunt managed a chuckle, though her eyes were still teary. "I know that, and so do they. But I wanted you to hear it from me. You care very much for your mother, and we all know it. Esther knows it." Aunt Hannah sighed. "I should get back. Hand me a washcloth. I can hardly go back in there looking like this. What will they think?"

"That you're mourning the loss of your daughter, probably."

"*Ya*, I suppose. I shall never have an hour or a day that I don't miss her. But she is safe, and it is my living children I must worry about. If you'll go and talk to Mary Aaron, I will rest easier tonight. Let her know that I want her to stay among us, but if she can't, she will still always be my precious daughter." She paused and then went on softly, "And tell her that it was a hard decision for me, too."

Rachel turned to her aunt, completely taken by surprise. "I didn't know you'd ever considered not joining the church."

"You young folks don't know everything. I met someone who wasn't Amish . . . someone I cared for very much." She reached for another piece of toilet tissue and dabbed at her eyes. "For months I wrestled with indecision, and finally, after much prayer and many, many tears, I had to tell him that it wasn't to be. So I know . . . how difficult it can be. But tell her, that from the time I looked into my firstborn baby's eyes, I have never regretted my decision to stay."

· · ·

Later in the day, after making arrangements with her father and sisters to be gone for the night, Rachel phoned Mary Aaron at the B&B. She checked to see if she needed to pick up anything from Wagler's Grocery and told her she was coming home for the night. She gave her cousin the excuse that she wanted to sleep a night in her own bed. She knew Mary Aaron too well to announce beforehand that she wanted to talk to her about something serious.

Wagler's was busy as always, as it was the only full-service grocery in the valley. Rachel was going to take a basket, but then she took a cart instead, knowing that she always picked up more than she expected to as she made her way up and down the aisles. Polly, the owner, was at one of the registers, and she waved. Rachel waved back. She'd have to remember to choose another line at the checkout. Polly was a dear, but she liked to talk and Rachel needed to get home. If Rachel went to Polly, she'd be an extra fifteen minutes getting out of the store.

Rachel turned her cart to the produce section. Most of the customers were locals, both English and Amish. There were only two she didn't recognize, a woman in a suit and heels, and an older man. Her friend Coyote's husband, Blade, was at the orange display patiently restacking the fruit that had rolled into the lemon bin. In the cart was an infant car seat, cradling a new-born, and perched in the child seat was a grinning toddler triumphantly waving an orange over his head.

Rachel stopped to admire the children and to tease Blade about the spilled fruit. "You're not supposed to take them out of the bottom of the stack," she said.

"Try telling that to Badger," Blade said as he retrieved another orange, this time from the lime bin.

The child's name wasn't really Badger. It was Bradford or Bradley. Rachel couldn't remember which, but she knew that Coyote had told her that he was a foster child whom they were attempting to adopt. The couple collected children the way some people collected objets d'art. But despite Blade's rough exterior, the gold earring, and the full sleeve of tattoos, he was a devoted father and a regular churchgoer. Any fortunate child who found his way to the apartment over the pottery shop would be assured of a good education, caring parents, and love.

"Oh, hey, we're really sorry about your cousin and her boyfriend. We would have come to the funeral, but one of the kids had a doctor's appointment with a specialist in Philadelphia. Coyote's not even back yet; she stayed over to get supplies for the shop."

"Thanks. Tell her to give me a call when she gets home."

"I will, and if there's anything we can do, just shout."

She sighed as she moved on to the dairy section. She never saw Blade or Coyote when she didn't wonder if she would regret not marrying years ago. She wasn't too old to become a mother yet, but her years were definitely numbered. *If I wait much longer,* she thought, *Evan and I might have to resort to adopting.* And that would be all right too, because she did want children. She just thought she wanted to be settled in mind and body before she had them.

She was just rounding a corner piled high with a display of cereal when a tall man came from the next aisle over and nearly collided with her cart. "Roy! Sorry," she said automatically, although she didn't feel that she was completely at fault. "I wasn't paying attention."

"Yeah, well, that's why they give driver's licenses."

Not a particularly witty remark, but Roy Thompson wasn't known for his IQ level. Roy wasn't a big fan of hers or she of his. Rachel had had dealings with Roy before; he did bodywork on cars. He was good at what he did, but she always got a little creeped out when she had to do business with him. He'd had his share of run-ins with the police, lived in a run-down shack out of town, and worked as little as possible. He was wearing a black muscle shirt that had seen better days, torn jeans, down-at-the-heel motorcycle boots, and a matching leather vest with OUTLAW stamped in gold ink. On his head was a battered cowboy hat with a rattlesnake-skin hatband. Rachel suspected the snakeskin, like the motor-cycle attire, was Roy's attempt to attract the opposite sex and add to his reputation as a would-be tough guy.

He didn't linger but muttered something under his breath, grabbed the steaks out of his cart, and hurried away. She pushed her cart around his abandoned one and continued on. But she hadn't gone more than two aisles before she came upon Buddy Wheeler, leaning on a broom, deep in conversation with his cousins, Wynter and Duck. By their body language, the three seemed to be at odds about something.

". . . told you he could fix it," Duck was saying heatedly as he pounded Buddy on the shoulder with his fist.

Wynter spotted Rachel first and elbowed Duck. He stopped in mid-sentence and looked away. Wynter's face flushed, and she glanced at her brother and then back at Buddy before pasting a phony smile on her face. "Rachel."

Duck, a stocky guy in coveralls with dark hair, sideburns, and a grease-stained ball cap, shoved his hands in his pants pockets and backed up several steps. He wasn't much taller than Wynter. His clothes were dirty, his beard as straggly as an old Amish man's.

"Hey, Wynter. Buddy." Rachel nodded to Duck. She didn't really know him, only of him. She glanced in the direction Roy had gone, suddenly suspicious. Something told her that a moment before, this group had been a foursome. "Saw your pal Roy leaving." She pointed in the direction he'd gone. "He seemed in a hurry. Everything okay?"

"Fine," Buddy piped up, not sounding like everything was fine. He shook his head. "Nothing wrong." He kept shaking his head.

Duck wiped his mouth with the back of his hand and stared at his feet.

"You know my cousin Duck?" Buddy asked. He was the tallest of the three by six inches, and wearing a WAGLER'S GROCERY apron and hat. His jeans were wrinkled, but clean, and his athletic shoes were threadbare and the left one had a hole in the toe.

"My brother," Wynter supplied. She had a cart containing a single bag of colorful cereal with marshmallows in it, some prepackaged bologna, and two loaves of cheap white bread.

Rachel looked back at Duck. He was a friend of Roy Thompson's, she was sure, because she'd seen Duck riding in Roy's truck with him before. He was wearing a holster on his hip that held a hunting knife. Rachel couldn't see the blade, but by the size of the leather-wrapped handle, it was definitely too big to be sporting in a grocery store.

"Heard your boyfriend was out of town," Wynter said. "Too bad, what with what happened to those Amish kids." She glanced at Buddy and then back to Rachel. "But I guess the cops have already figured out what happened."

"They're still investigating," Rachel said, trying to study each one of them without making it too obvious. Something was clearly going on here. The question was, what? Were they trying to shoplift? "These things take time."

"Right," Buddy said. "But they must know what happened. The Amish guy doing whatever he did to her and then offing himself."

"You think that's what happened?" Rachel asked.

"How would we know what happened?" Duck raised his shoulders. One cheek bore a suspicious lump, and as she watched, a small dribble of tobacco juice dripped out of his lower lip. He captured the drop with his tongue and sucked it back in. "These Amish, they ain't what everyone thinks, all goody-goody. They get into trouble just like everybody else."

"So, what do they think?" Wynter pressed Rachel. "I mean, if the boyfriend jumped in front of a truck after his girlfriend turned up dead, he must have been guilty, wouldn't you say?"

"I wouldn't say anything yet," Rachel replied. Out of the corner of her eye, she spotted Polly coming their way. "You'd better get back to work, Buddy. Here comes your boss."

"Shoot." Buddy began sweeping vigorously. "You guys gotta go," he told his cousins. "Now," he whispered harshly.

Rachel made her escape, going in the opposite direction of Wynter and Duck. She finished picking up everything on her list and checked out. Polly had thankfully given over her register to a young woman who was both efficient and too busy to do more than offer the standard, "Thank you. We appreciate your business."

Rachel took her two bags and walked out to the Jeep. She was loading them in the back when Hulda pulled up in her golf cart. Her neighbor was as dapper as ever today in pin-striped slacks, a cashmere twin set in soft lavender, and leather clogs. She had obviously just come from the hair-dresser, and she was wearing sparkly nail polish that matched her sweaters.

"Rachel, darling," Hulda said. She threw open her arms and Rachel returned her hug. "How is your mother?"

Rachel took the time to fill her in on her mother's progress and listened while Hulda gave her a rundown on the current guests who had checked in since Rachel had been there. As pressed for time as she was, she couldn't show Hulda less than her full attention. Her neighbor had been such a help, stepping in to trouble-shoot at the B&B and to make savvy business suggestions. The senior might have been in her nineties, but she had more energy than most people half her age.

"I'm off to State College to see friends, but Mary Aaron has everything in hand," Hulda assured her. "One of the cleaning girls called out sick today, but Mary Aaron arranged for that girl Chelsea to fill in. She's taking college courses online, and she's available most afternoons."

Wynter and her brother, Duck, came out of the store, walked past where Rachel and Hulda stood, and got into a beat-up black compact that was sporting one yellow door. As Wynter backed up and pulled out of the parking lot, Rachel saw the girl watching her in her rearview mirror.

"Now, there's a piece of work." Hulda waggled her finger at the departing vehicle. "She worked for us for about twenty minutes. Three days, actually. Trouble, if I ever saw it. Sneaky. And the brother? I've never heard anything good about him."

"Did you have to fire her?"

Hulda puckered her lips. "Didn't need to. She

didn't come back after the third day. No notice. Just never showed up again. Except to demand her check. You know, she has the reputation for suing businesses. She filed a case against the bookstore. Claimed she slipped on the marble floor. Ell said she saw her fall and it was nothing but an act."

"Did she get any money?"

"With George's lawyers?" Hulda chuckled. "Poor old George may be on his way out, but he's still as sharp as a hat pin when it comes to legal matters. But his lawyers found out that she'd sued at least two other businesses, every time for a fall. She claims headaches and backaches. Won a pretty penny from a theater over in State College, but it won't fly here."

"She came to Elsie's wake. And Dathan's funeral. I couldn't imagine why; the food, I suspect. The brother wasn't with her though."

"Duck? There's a bad one. He spent two years in Harrisburg for assault when he was hardly more than a kid. His real name's Deiter. The 'Duck' is supposed to be a pun on the last name, I suppose," Hulda explained. "You know, Duck Feathers."

Neither of them laughed.

"Roy Thompson was here, too," Rachel said. "All of them were acting strange. Like they were up to something."

"More than likely, they are. There's another

sorry case. Roy's mother wasn't much, and the father was a thief and an alcoholic. I don't think he ever had much of a chance. Not like Duck. He had decent parents. They used to be Amish back in the day. His granddad is, still. Ada's relations. So Duck and Wynter come of good stock. But they were raised elsewhere. Been living with John Miller as of late, because Duck got in so much trouble in Harrisburg."

"Does Duck work around here?"

Hulda scoffed. "Work? Not if he can help it. He mooches, mostly. Supposedly helping around the grandfather's farm, but mostly he just runs the roads, drinks too much, and takes advantage of that softheaded Buddy." She flashed a smile. "Well, I best get my crackers and cheese and get on the road." She slung her handbag over her shoulder. "You just passing through town?"

"Actually, I thought I might spend the night at home." Rachel closed the tailgate of her Jeep. "Missing my bed."

Hulda gave a wave and walked away, headed for the main entrance of the grocery store. "Well, stop by for a cup of tea in the morning, if you have time. I miss you, Rachel."

"I miss you, too."

Rachel was still thinking about how thankful she was for her family and friends when she pulled out of the parking lot and headed for home.

CHAPTER 17

Rachel was awakened by a loud purr and a rough, wet tongue across her cheek. She jerked awake, and her seal point Siamese, who let out a blood-curdling yowl, leapt off the bed. Rachel yawned and closed her eyes, taking a moment to remember where she was and what day it was. Thursday? No, Friday.

Friday. A week since Elsie and Dathan had vanished, she remembered sadly. It seemed like much more time had passed. The whole thing was unreal. And being unable to find out what happened to them, after she'd promised that she would, was frustrating.

Bishop, the cat, meowed again. Rachel opened her eyes and focused on the old-fashioned wind-up alarm clock on her nightstand. Seven fifteen. She reached for the clock and brought it closer to be certain of the time. She needed to get up. Mornings didn't come as early here at Stone Mill House as they did at the farm, but early enough.

She threw back the quilt and, ignoring the cat's pleading for attention, began a hurried preparation for her day. Some visitors rose early, and Rachel liked to be on hand, when she was home, to greet them and try to make their stay here special. She loved the house and the town, and she hoped that each person who stayed at Stone Mill House would carry away a sense of history and of home. Being an innkeeper was the last thing Rachel had ever expected to do when she'd left Amish life for the English world so many years ago, but welcoming people to the house, town, and valley had become her passion.

Without the income from the B&B, maintaining a two-hundred-year-old house would have been financially prohibitive. She'd risked everything: emotionally, physically, and every cent she had, to bring Stone Mill House back from the brink of ruin, and she liked to think that she'd taken big steps in rescuing the town of Stone Mill from economic decay as well. Tourism brought life back to the local businesses and provided employment for the youth, both Amish and English. Times had been particularly difficult in the isolated valleys of heartland America the last few decades, but Stone Mill was coming back strong. She'd made a lot of promises to a lot of people who believed in her, and she had no intentions of letting them down.

Good smells were drifting from the kitchen as Rachel came down the front stairs with Bishop in her arms. She unlocked the front doors and pushed the screen door open far enough for the Siamese to slip through, then inhaled deeply of the crisp September air. "Stay out of traffic," she warned the cat. Not that there was much traffic on this street or that Bishop had the energy to wander far. Soon enough, he'd show up at the kitchen door demanding to be let in.

She stood there for a moment, taking in the picturesque peace of green lawns, curving brick walks, and stately trees beginning to assume their fall colors, before turning back to the morning's chores. How could anything so terrible as Elsie's and Dathan's violent deaths happen in such a tranquil place? She took another deep breath and murmured a silent prayer for strength and the wisdom to solve this mystery. Finding out what had happened to Elsie and Dathan wouldn't bring them back, but it would soothe some of the ache in their families' hearts.

Rachel pulled the doors closed, and the old iron lock clicked with a satisfying sound. Guests wishing to use the front entrance were welcome to do so between eight in the morning until ten at night, but the air was too cool to leave the wooden doors standing open. As much as she would have liked to, she couldn't stand there and muse. She had work to do.

And maybe the routine of everyday life would steady her.

When she'd come down, the guest floors had been quiet. Maybe everyone was still abed,

Rachel thought. As she turned from the front entranceway, Mary Aaron came down the steps carrying a basket of dirty linens. Rachel stared. Mary Aaron was wearing a pair of her jeans, her favorite blue sweater, and her new running shoes. Her waist-length hair, uncovered, was pulled back in a ponytail again. Rachel didn't know what to say.

"Close your mouth," Mary Aaron said. "You'll catch flies."

Rachel put a hand on the antique rosewood chair that stood by the stairs. "We really need to talk," she managed, still in shock from the transformation that seemed to come so easily to her cousin.

"*Ne.*" A dimple appeared on Mary Aaron's chin when she smiled. "I told you last night, I don't want to talk. About anything. I just want everyone to leave me alone. I need time to think. Time to just . . . be."

"Has Ada seen you dressed like that?" The jeans fit Mary Aaron really well, maybe better than they fit Rachel. She didn't mind Mary Aaron borrowing her things. She wore Mary Aaron's dresses herself occasionally, but seeing her dressed like a twenty-something Englisher again was unnerving.

Mary Aaron shifted the basket to her hip. "I was in the kitchen earlier. Coffee."

"Did she . . . say anything?" Rachel motioned to her cousin's attire.

Mary Aaron shrugged. "She didn't bat an eye. Just reminded me to tell you that she thinks the dryer vent is clogged again. She says the lint will set the house on fire and burn us all to a crisp."

Rachel couldn't resist a chuckle. Her housekeeper was not a fan of modern conveniences. She used the refrigerator and freezers reluctantly, refused the coffeemaker and food processors, and wouldn't lay a finger on the vacuum cleaner or the house phone. The washers and dryers she regarded with greatest suspicion. The complaint about dryer lint was one that Rachel heard at least once a week. "I'll look at it," she promised. "But I think it's fine." Ada thought an electric dryer was a terrible waste of money. Who would pay to dry laundry that the sun and wind would dry for nothing? Ada's opinions affected the Amish maids who helped out in the house, and they all expected the dryer to dry the clothes in far less time than it possibly could.

"A guest is in the dining room," Mary Aaron said. "He wants to know a scenic route to State College. I told him there was only one road over the pass, but he wants to ask you."

"Sure," Rachel said. "What's his name?"

Mary Aaron shrugged again. "An Englisher." She lowered her voice. "They all look alike to me."

Rachel watched her cousin walk away. She wanted to tell her that by noon every Amish household in the valley would know that Aaron

289

Hostetler's daughter was wearing English clothes, but Mary Aaron knew that as well as she did. Rachel understood why Mary Aaron might want to try wearing the clothes, but why now? Couldn't she wait? This would bring down a rain of grief, affecting not just her and her family, but the whole community. But Rachel held her tongue. As Hannah had said, Mary Aaron was stubborn. When she was ready, she'd reach out. And when she did, Rachel would be there for her. Until then, she'd have to be patient.

The visitor who wanted directions was Lester Barbour, who'd stayed with them several times before. Rachel waved him to a small table, poured him coffee, and brought a plate of blueberry scones hot from Ada's kitchen. She answered his questions, provided him with a detailed map of the county, and told him where he and his wife could visit an Amish farm to buy specialty cheeses. Afterward, she checked the dryer vents, found that they were working properly, and retreated to her office to pay a few bills and check for inquiries and reservations on her computer.

There was always more to do than time to do it, not only for Stone Mill House but for the town and the business association. A note on the Kenton Dairy calendar over her workstation reminded her that she had promised to write new material for the Winter Festival brochure. And it was supposed to have been submitted to the committee on Tuesday. There were two requests for donations to local youth groups, and a plea from her church for restoration of a stained-glass window. She wrote three checks, and sent an email to a third-grade teacher accepting an invitation to act as one of the judges for an essay contest on Stone Mill history. It was after eleven when she walked out to the mailbox.

It seemed as though fall had come overnight. Squirrels were scampering all over the lawn in a frantic last-minute effort to bury as many acorns as possible, and she could hear the bleat of her goats from the pasture. The sun was warm, but the temperature lingered at sixty. The postman must have come by a few minutes early because she'd missed the outgoing mail. There was a note from a couple who'd spent their honeymoon at Stone Mill House, the electric bill, and an unstamped, white business-sized envelope with her name handwritten across the front.

Curious, she tore it open. The envelope contained a single sheet of paper. A printout. Listed were the names of registered owners of green trucks, 2010 and older, along with addresses, all within the Stone Valley zip code. There was no note, but Rachel knew who had made it happen. She looked at the list for a moment, took a deep breath, and fished her cell phone out of her jeans pocket. When Lucy answered, Rachel told her what she'd just found in her mailbox.

"Who sent it?" Lucy asked.

"I don't know." Which was true. She *didn't* know who'd actually sent it, only who was responsible.

For a moment, Lucy didn't answer. In the background, Rachel heard a dog barking. "You're in luck," Lucy said with a note of warmth in her voice. "I just agreed to switch shifts with someone, and I've got the day off. I'll be by shortly. We can divide up the list and go door-to-door."

"I appreciate this, Lucy."

"I want this case solved as bad as you do. It's just that there are things I can do, and things I can't. But today, I'm all yours."

"Sure you don't want a cat?" the woman asked. She had a toddler on her hip and was wearing a T-shirt that said SUPPORT YOUR LOCAL MIDWIVES. She appeared to Rachel as if she would need the services of one before Christmas. Three or four other kids were running around the yard. One was up a tree, hanging from his legs from a branch, while one of his whooping brothers tossed water balloons at him. A golden retriever, tail wagging, pressed hard against the woman's knee. A little girl carrying a fat cat in a striped doll dress shrieked with laughter and chased a sibling through a flower bed and around the corner of a house.

"Or maybe I could interest you in a kid?" the woman teased. She was tall and slim, pretty in a natural way, with dark wavy hair and bright blue eyes. Behind her stood a large two-story log cabin, so new that Rachel could still smell the fresh-cut cedar and see piles of sawdust at the side of the yard.

The green pickup that Rachel had come to ask about stood at the end of the driveway with a FOR SALE sign in the front window. Smaller lettering on the poster read: NEEDS TRANSMISSION. WILL TRADE FOR FIREWOOD.

The truck had been immaculate for a fourteen-year-old vehicle, the green paint on it was unscratched, and it didn't have a single dent. And it clearly hadn't been moved in a month. "Paul's father took good care of that truck," the woman had informed her. "Kept it in his garage. My husband used it for driving back and forth to work, but the transmission went out." She'd laughed at the misfortune. "At least we inherited the truck and didn't buy it. Easy come, easy go."

"I have enough cats," Rachel said. "And I'll have to pass on the children, too."

"I could let you have an excellent deal on a six-year-old." The woman grinned. "He eats any-thing you put in front of him." She pointed at the tree where a small boy was making his way doggedly up the branches. "Climbs like a monkey."

"No, thanks," Rachel said. "It was nice to talk to

you." She got back into her Jeep and carefully turned the vehicle around. She didn't want to run over any dogs, cats, or children.

It was almost dark, and this was the sixth place she'd checked out, all without finding a single suspicious person of interest. She drove a short distance from the Walkers' home and pulled over at a roadside spring. There were more than a half dozen of these spots in the valley. Pipes coming out of the hillside produced an endless flow of clean, cold mountain water, available without charge to anyone passing by. She splashed water over her face, drank deep from cupped hands, and leaned against the front fender of the Jeep for a few minutes until finally, she took out her cell and called Lucy.

"I talked to five registered owners or their family members. One house was empty. The truck was in a shed, obviously abandoned, and from the dust and cobwebs on it, it hasn't run for a long time. I saw four more of the trucks on my list. One went to South Carolina a month ago with a fertilizer salesman and the truck owner's wife. The owner said he hoped he never saw the truck or his wife again. The salesman was welcome to her. I'm just getting nothing we can use to lead us to Elsie and Dathan's deaths or disappearance. The others all checked out one way or the other; nobody seemed the least bit suspicious to me. Everyone was very cooperative."

"No better here," Lucy said. "I ran into a guy with a green truck with a habeas out on him. He kept apologizing to me when I had to call an on-duty trooper to take him in. I felt bad for him. Apparently, he'd lied to his wife and told her that he'd taken care of it, but he hadn't. The wife was so mad that by the time the officer arrived, the poor guy seemed almost relieved to get in the patrol car." Lucy chuckled.

"And then," she continued, "another place, really run-down, trash piled around the back door, a pack of dogs running loose, looked promising. The woman who answered the door had had a few too many and definitely wasn't helpful. The truck in question was in the barn, and she was so reluctant to let me see it that I thought we had a lead. Turns out, the truck hadn't been involved in anything shady last Friday night. The tags and insurance were expired. She thought I was going to lock her up. I just told her to get some insurance on the Internet and get the thing tagged. And she wasn't going anywhere. She said that her worthless husband was a long-distance truck driver, and he always takes her keys when he goes on the road to keep her from getting a DUI."

"And you're sure the truck hasn't been out in the last week?" Rachel asked.

"They'd left the window down and some barn swallows had built a nest behind the wheel on the front seat. The babies were only a couple of days old, but I doubt that the driver of that truck seen running a car off the road was riding around the countryside sitting on a nest of barn swallow eggs."

Rachel laughed. She could picture the nest with the little birds craning their necks for worms. "It sounds as though I've wasted your time."

"Not at all. This is the way police work goes," Lucy explained. "Forget TV or the big screen. Just ask Evan. Detective work is slow and mostly boring. You just keep hitting dead ends until you don't."

Rachel sighed. "I know. You warned me. I was just hoping we'd come up with something."

"I did bump into Rupert Rust," Lucy said. "I told him we needed to know his specific whereabouts after he left the party Friday night. I told him we'd have to take him in if he couldn't produce an alibi."

"And?" Rachel said. At this point, she honestly didn't think Rupert had anything to do with the deaths, but she would like to have put a line through his name in her head, just the same.

"He left the party with a girl."

"Who?"

"He said he wasn't ready to say, but he'd talk to the girl. See if she'd be willing to speak with us. He said without her permission, he couldn't give her name. Said her parents wouldn't approve." Lucy made a sound on the other end of the line, like she was thinking. "I hate to say it, but I think he's telling the truth."

Rachel thought he was, too. And as much as she hated to admit it, she had a good idea which girl Rupert might be referring to. She exhaled, suddenly tired and just plain worn out. "So, shall we call it a night?" she asked Lucy.

"I think so. I've got to take my dogs for a run, and I've got to be to work early. Maybe tomorrow, one of us will come up with a better idea."

"I really appreciate your help, Lucy. It means a lot."

"No problem. Stone Mill is my home now, too. And they still might be right, you know. It could have happened just like the detective thinks. Dathan could have killed her, and then not been able to live with himself." Lucy's voice became softer. "I know you don't want to think it, but even the Amish sometimes do unthinkable things. We're all human."

"*Ya*," Rachel agreed. "We're all human. But I've got a gut feeling that that's not what happened."

"Well, if you have a hunch, stay with it until you run out of options," Lucy encouraged. "If you ever get bored with inn keeping, I think you'd make a good cop."

Rachel was only three miles from her mother's home and headed in that direction when her cell rang. She pulled off the road into the first driveway she came to and glanced at the screen. She didn't recognize the number. "Hello?"

"Rachel." Her sister Lettie was practically yelling into the phone.

Rachel's heart skipped a beat. "What's wrong?"

"Nothing. Can you hear me?"

"If you lower your voice a little, I can."

Lettie gave a huff, but spoke at a reasonable volume. "*Mam* isn't feeling good. I think she's trying to do too much."

"Where are you calling from?"

"The barn."

"I meant, from whose phone?"

"You're not my father," Lettie said. "What I called for is that *Mam* says she'd love some sorbet. Orange or lemon. They carry it in a round tub at Wagler's Grocery. She says that her stomach's upset and the sorbet always helps. Do you mind picking some up for her on your way home?"

Rachel saw no need to tell her she was almost home already. "Sure. I won't be long. Lettie, is this your cell?"

"Just get the sorbet, Rachel. Hold the big-sister lectures."

Before she could ask anything else, Lettie hung up. First Mary Aaron in jeans, and now Lettie with a cell phone. Amish life certainly wasn't what it was when she was a kid. Rachel pulled back onto the blacktop, made a U-turn, and headed back to town. Twenty minutes later, she was headed back out of town with a quart of orange sorbet on the passenger seat.

Earlier, she'd been considering going by the Benders' farm, and the inclination still nagged at her. It would be out of her way, but it was Friday night. Agnes had specifically said that it was Friday nights when her husband went *deer hunting*.

She glanced at the bag on the seat. With the heater on, the ice cream would be melting. But after all the driving and all the questions she'd asked and having gotten no leads today, a few more minutes wouldn't hurt. And sometimes hunches paid off.

A mile outside of town, Rachel switched off the heater in the Jeep and turned left, instead of right toward home. There were fewer farms and more woodland near the mountains. The road the Benders lived on was narrow and twisty. A skunk scurried across in front of her and she slowed the car. The stench was heavy, and she could imagine what it would be like if she had hit the thing. "Go in peace," she called after the animal. Full dark had fallen, and stars were beginning to appear in the night sky. Out here, without any town or highway lighting, she could see more stars than she could remember seeing in a long time.

On a whim, Rachel pulled off into a farm field

near enough to the Benders' driveway to see lights, but not close enough for anyone from the driveway to see her Jeep. She didn't even know why she was stopping. She was just *going with her gut,* as Lucy had suggested. She turned off the engine and the lights. She got out of the vehicle and stood leaning against it and staring up at the light show above. The air was chilly and filled with the spicy scent of fir and pine. There was a full chorus of mountain breeze playing off the trees and rippling the tall grass on either side of the road, as well as the buzz of insects, the clamor of frogs, and the *who-who-who* of an owl. Now the wild things would come out: rabbits, squirrels, weasels, deer, foxes, and bears. The previous year a record-sized black bear was shot only a mile up the mountain from here. Rachel could imagine furry bodies stirring and moving through the forest, padded feet stepping soundlessly on the pine needles and old leaves.

The faint sound of a car engine cut through her reflection, and Rachel glanced at the road to see headlights coming toward her. The vehicle wasn't coming fast; it stopped a few hundred feet away. Rachel stood silently watching, wondering what the driver was up to. And then, a figure moved out of the wood line and approached the car.

She heard the distinct sound of a woman's voice, but it was too far away to make out her words. There was the *click* of a car door. As the car door opened, the overhead light came on. A man wearing an Amish hat and clothing slid something long into the backseat and then got into the front. It wasn't until he got inside that Rachel saw who it was. Before she could react, the door slammed shut, the light went out, and the car pulled away.

CHAPTER 18

The car made a U-turn and Rachel watched as the taillights receded around the bend in the road. It was too dark to get a good look at the car, but it was small, definitely a compact model. And there were only two people visible inside, Charles and a female driver. Rachel had seen the silhouette of her hair. And by the glow of the cigarette hanging out of her mouth, Rachel would venture that the woman wasn't Amish.

Rachel jumped back into the Jeep and started it up. She glanced at the paper bag on the seat, then reached over and gave the container a squeeze. The sorbet was melting fast; it would be beyond salvageable soon. But she could always buy more sorbet.

Pulling onto the road, she accelerated to catch up with the vehicle. She didn't want it to be obvious that she was following them, but she hoped to find out who was in the car and where they were going. It didn't take long. As she came over the crest of a hill, the compact was stopped in the road ahead of her. A herd of deer was running across the road in front of the vehicle. She slowed, creeping up behind them.

Just as they started moving again, she got a good look at the vehicle. It was an old green Ford Focus. In the back window was a decal with a winged creature on it. Rachel couldn't make out the writing underneath, but she did get the first four numbers of the Pennsylvania tags. The vehicle continued on, going no more than thirty miles per hour. Realizing that to remain behind them would draw attention, Rachel waited until they reached a straight stretch of road and passed them. Now she was ahead, definitely where she didn't want to be if she was the one following them. "This detective stuff should come with written directions," she muttered half-aloud.

Rachel continued on until she came to the next crossroad. Right went in the direction of town. Straight ahead led down the valley, and the left turn didn't go far before the road became gravel. There were few farms on the road, and acres of state game land. The only thing after that was an abandoned gravel pit and a small mobile home park crowded between a narrow hollow and a rocky hill. Park Estates was hardly luxury living. There were less than a dozen trailers, fewer than the count of hunting dogs or vehicles up on blocks the last time Rachel had been there.

What to do? Just on the far side of the cross-road was a visitors' area for hikers entering the state game lands. There was a tiny parking lot surrounded by thick evergreens. Without hesitation, Rachel drove into the lot, shut off her lights, and made a U-turn so she was facing the road.

The compact stopped at the stop sign and turned left toward the gravel pit and Park Estates. They were still moving slowly. Rachel wondered why. Was it that the deer herd had spooked them, or were they looking for something or someone? She waited as long as she dared and then followed. She thought about trying to drive with her lights out, but the road was too rough for that. If she wasn't careful, she'd blow a tire and have to call for assistance. Besides, Charles and the driver might get suspicious.

Rachel checked the time on the dashboard. If she was going to make it back to town to buy more frozen sorbet for her mother, she didn't have much time before the grocery closed. But she had to know what the two of them were up to. It didn't take long for the taillights to come into sight again. Would they turn in at the quarry or one of the game land pull offs? No, the car kept going until they reached the dead end and turned left onto Park Estates Drive. Rachel wondered if she should stop now or follow them in and see which mobile home they were going to. There weren't that many homes there. She knew an older woman, Blanche Willis, her neighbors, the Blatts, and Buddy Wheeler. That left, at most, eight or nine trailers, probably less.

George O'Day, who owned the park, had made some improvements in the last year or so, but it was still basic housing and a long way from town.

Curiosity won out and Rachel made the turn into the mobile home park. She saw at once that the pot-holed lane that had led into the park had been replaced with blacktop. The community was only one street long with a turnaround at the end, but the entrance had stone pillars and a white picket fence, and the blacktop continued on past each trailer. Rachel saw the Ford pull up in front of a mobile home with a small front yard two doors down from Buddy Wheeler's place. Rachel drove to the far end of the street and stopped in front of a trailer with the lights off and a trampoline in the side yard.

The couple got out of the car. As the overhead light came on, Rachel got a good look at the man. It was Charles, all right. The woman, a short brunette, led the way up the sidewalk. She unlocked the door and they both went in. The porch light went off, and another light came on in the front of the dwelling.

What was Charles doing with this English woman at the trailer park? He wasn't deer hunting, that was for sure. Rachel didn't like Charles, but she was still reluctant to make the obvious assumption. If Charles was cheating on his wife, though, he probably wasn't responsible for Dathan's and Elsie's deaths, which would cut her list of *persons of interest* down considerably. Being an adulterer would make Charles a snake, but not a murderer. Rachel wanted to march up to the door and confront him, ask him outright if he was with this woman last Friday night. But common sense won out over emotion. She'd come back tomorrow and question the woman. That was the smart choice.

Rachel glanced at the digital clock on her dashboard again and her heart sank. Wagler's would close in sixteen minutes and her mother's sorbet was now completely melted. Could she get there in time? Probably not. Out of desperation, she punched in the number of the grocery, and sighed with relief when she heard Polly's distinct voice. "Wagler's Grocery, how can I help you?"

Twenty-five minutes later, Rachel headed out of the store parking lot with two tubs of sorbet, orange and lemon. Polly waved from her own vehicle. The joys of living in a small town where the owner of a business would ring up your order, put it on the B&B tab, and wait in her car until you arrived to pick it up. After a day of small disappointments, getting her *Mam*'s treat raised Rachel's spirits. Tomorrow morning, she'd go and have a talk with the woman at the trailer park.

The following morning, Rachel and Mary Aaron made the turn onto Gravel Pit Road. Rachel had spent the night at the farm and hadn't been able to get away until breakfast was cleared away and the house set to order. Her mother had announced that she was tired and had decided to spend the day in bed. That would have terrified Rachel normally, but what was normal anymore? Besides, her mother definitely looked better this morning than she had in days. And she had eaten a full breakfast of eggs, bacon, canned peaches, and toast.

Before leaving, Rachel had tried to corner Lettie to speak with her privately, but apparently Rachel wasn't the only Mast girl with gut feelings. Lettie dodged her all morning, seeming to sense that Rachel had questions for her of a personal nature that went beyond a contraband cell phone.

Giving up on the private chat with Lettie, Rachel went to the farmers' market for Ada, and when she'd dropped the fruits and vegetables off at the B&B, Mary Aaron had gotten into the Jeep. She was wearing a lavender Amish dress, black stockings, a jean jacket, and a scarf instead of a *kapp*. "I'm coming with you," she proclaimed.

"You don't even know where I'm going," Rachel had replied, taking a cue from Ada and making a point not to comment on Mary Aaron's ensemble.

"I'm coming."

Neither said a word for five minutes, then Mary Aaron piped up, "Pull over. I want to drive."

"You want to drive? You don't have a driver's

license," Rachel protested, looking at her cousin as if she'd lost her mind.

"I have a learner's permit."

"Since when?" Rachel asked.

"Does it matter? Come on, pull over. I need practice. And you'll have to sign that I drove with you and how far."

Rachel brought the Jeep to a stop. "Are you sure you want to get a driver's license?" All she could think of was that her aunt was right; Mary Aaron intended to leave her faith. And the idea made her sad, for some reason.

"I'm getting a driver's license. I'm not in training to be a go-go dancer."

Since they were both speaking in the *Deitsch* dialect, the last statement came out odd enough to set Rachel's head spinning. She threw up her hands and traded seats with Mary Aaron.

To her surprise, her cousin managed the shift smoothly and drove the Jeep down the road as if she'd been doing it for years.

"Exactly how did you learn to drive?" Rachel asked, not expecting an answer.

"Hulda and Timothy. Hulda, mostly. She's a better driver than he is."

"Timothy drives?"

Mary Aaron shrugged and grinned. "He tries."

"Don't tell me you've been sneaking out with my Jeep nights you sleep over and I'm in bed by nine?"

Mary Aaron looked hurt. "Would I do that without asking? We've been using Hulda's dead husband's car. It's been sitting in her barn for years, but her grandsons keep it tagged and in shape."

"The 1966 Jaguar?" Rachel blinked and stared at her cousin. "You're putting me on, right?"

"We only take it out at night. That way I wouldn't have everyone see me behind the wheel, and she wouldn't have to listen to her family tell her not to."

The thought of Mary Aaron, complete with cape and bonnet, hot-rodding around the mountain roads at night in Hulda Schenfeld's husband's classic E-Type Jag was almost more than Rachel could comprehend this morning. "You've lost your mind, haven't you? You're completely off the leash," which, translated, came out to some-thing like off the *halter*.

Mary Aaron giggled. And Rachel found herself laughing with her. They laughed so hard that the Jeep started to veer off the road, and Mary Aaron braked. They came to a stop, and Mary Aaron leaned her head against the wheel and the two of them laughed as they hadn't in a long time.

The blast of a car horn brought Rachel back to the moment. "Move over," she instructed Mary Aaron. "We're blocking the road."

Mary Aaron turned and looked at the indignant driver behind them. She leaned out the window and shouted in English, "Sorry, my bad." She steered the Jeep off to the shoulder and held up her fingers in the peace sign as the man drove past. Glancing back at Rachel, she said, "See, that's why horses are better. People who depend on horse power aren't in such a hurry." And then she paused, wiped her tearstained cheeks and asked, "Why are the Englishers in such a hurry? We all end up in a grave. Why hurry to it?"

"Good question. I don't have a clue."

"It's what I thought. They probably don't know either. So I did that man a favor, gave him a few more minutes to enjoy this beautiful fall day." She cut the engine, got out, and walked around to Rachel. "Okay, you can drive."

"We needed that laugh, didn't we?" Rachel said as she took over control of the vehicle once more.

"So why are we going to the trailer park?" Mary Aaron asked as she buckled herself in and closed the door.

Rachel filled her in on what had happened the night before.

"Hulda said Charles was a runaround," Mary Aaron told her. "He did the same thing with his first wife."

"Hulda told you that?" Rachel asked, again surprised. "Why didn't you say something?"

"I don't gossip." She offered a wry smile. "Not too much. And it might not have been true. But Hulda said that she'd heard that one of the waitresses from the diner was playing footsies with Dathan's brother-in-law. She said he's always liked Englisher women."

"Interesting."

As Rachel drove into the mobile home park, she noticed Buddy sitting on his front step smoking a cigarette. He looked up, saw her, stubbed out his cigarette, and hurried inside. "Weird," she said as they crawled by. "What's up with him?"

The compact car in front of the trailer two doors down was exactly where Rachel had last seen it. It was the same vehicle; she was certain of it because the back window bore a MOTHER OF DRAGONS decal with the drawing of the winged dragon she had seen the night before. The car was a Ford Focus. What she wasn't expecting was that the car was blue, not green as she had thought.

A woman came around the mobile home with a pot of pansies in one hand and a spade in the other. Rachel parked right in the middle of the road. "Coming?" she asked Mary Aaron as she got out.

"*Ne*. I'll sit this one out."

Rachel approached the woman. She looked to be in her early to mid-forties, chubby, a plain face, cheerful smile. She was a brunette, and she wore her thin hair hanging down her back. "Good morning," Rachel called.

"Good morning." She set the plastic pot of pansies beside a garden gnome. There was another gnome by the back door. Rachel wondered if this was a natural breeding ground or if these two had migrated from the ones in the Blatts' yard across the street. "I'm Rachel Mast." Rachel offered her hand and the woman shook it. "I have the B&B in town."

"Right. You used to be Amish. We haven't met." She shrugged. "I just know who you are. I'm Andrea Tucker. Everyone calls me Andy. Are you collecting for something?" She was wearing a plaid cotton shirt and jeans. Her athletic shoes had clearly seen better days, and her cat's-eye glasses were taped at one hinge. "I'm afraid you've caught me between paydays."

"No," Rachel said. "I don't want money. I'm helping the police with the investigation of the deaths of that young Amish couple. Elsie Hostetler was my cousin, and I'd appreciate any help that you could give me."

"Oh." She eyed Mary Aaron nervously. "Yes, I heard about that. I'm so sorry. Your cousin. How terrible." She glanced at Mary Aaron again. "But I don't see how I could help. I don't know anything about the accident."

"Accident? Did Charles tell you it was an accident that killed Dathan?"

Her face went white. "Charles," she stammered. "I don't know any Charles. I'm sorry. I have to go. My . . . my oven. Something's in the oven. It might burn."

"You do know a Charles. Charles Schumacher."

"No. No, I don't. I'm sorry. I have to go."

She turned to make her escape, but Rachel moved to block her way. "Please. This could be important. I know that you picked up Charles from the woods near his house and brought him here last night. So there's no use—"

The woman burst into tears. She pointed to Mary Aaron in the car. "That's his wife, isn't it? We're just friends, that's all. Nothing is going on between us. He's just my friend."

Across the street, a woman stepped out on her porch and stared at them.

"Could we go inside?" Rachel asked. "I don't want to make a scene for your neighbors."

"All right," the woman sniffled. "Just please don't hurt me."

"I would never hurt you," Rachel assured her. Mary Aaron started to get out of the Jeep, but Rachel shook her head. "I'll be right out," she called to her.

Mary Aaron nodded and settled back into her seat.

Rachel and Andy went into the mobile home. It was neat as a pin inside. The sparse furniture was old but tasteful, and pots of African violets bloomed everywhere. A cat slept in a basket beneath the living room window. The woman motioned to a beige sofa. "Please, have a seat." She pulled a tissue from a box set inside a crocheted cover and dabbed at her eyes.

Rachel found her sympathies very much in favor of Andy. She wasn't what she'd expected.

Not in the least. "You say that you and Charles are friends," she said.

Andy nodded and sniffed. She sank into the only chair, a deep brown recliner. "He comes into the diner sometimes for lunch, and he sits in my section. He's a good tipper, Charles is. He always leaves two dollars, even if he just has coffee. A lot of men will leave you a couple of quarters. But Charles is always a gentleman."

"We are talking about Charles Schumacher, right?" Rachel leaned forward. "You realize that he's married, don't you? Charles? He has a wife and a baby boy."

"He told me. It's not a very happy marriage. She's not a kind person. She doesn't treat him right. He's such a sweet man. But you know, they marry for life. There's no chance of him divorcing her. The Amish think divorce is a sin. They never divorce."

"No, they don't," Rachel answered. "So why are you seeing Charles behind his wife's back?"

Andy drew in a shuddering breath. "Parcheesi," she managed. "We play Parcheesi, and sometimes Dutch Blitz. Charles is good at Dutch Blitz. He taught me how to play. Do you play?"

Rachel wondered if, like Alice, she'd tumbled down a rabbit hole. "Dutch Blitz? Yes, I know how to play."

"I'd never even heard of it. But Charles told me how much fun it was. And he bought me my own deck of cards. Wasn't that nice of him? We never do anything nasty, nothing to be ashamed of. We just play games and eat pizza. I like the self-rising kind that you cook in the oven. They don't deliver out here. Pizza. I mean, I suppose we could go to the Black Horse, but theirs is frozen, too. They certainly don't make it from scratch."

"So you're telling me that you pick up Charles and bring him here to *play card games?*" Rachel didn't know what to think about the woman's story. It was just weird enough to be true. "And that's all you do?"

Andy stared at her lap and her face grew red. "Sometimes Charles likes to brush my hair, but that's all. We don't kiss or touch or anything like that. I told you, he's sweet. He's just lonely . . . and so am I. He's tied to that woman, and she never laughs or wants to do anything fun. So we talk and play games." She looked up at Rachel. "Are you married?"

"No, I'm not. But I'm engaged."

"You're pretty. And you have an education and that big house. You probably don't realize it yet, but there aren't many sweet men in this world. I know. You should have seen my last husband. He was a—" She bit off her words. "A rotten toad. Every time he got drunk he'd use me for a punching bag. He broke my jaw the last time. It took that before I finally got some sense and left him for good." She folded her arms and rocked back and forth. "But Charles isn't like that. He doesn't want to fool around, and he doesn't drink at all. Neither of us do. We just like to laugh and play games."

"Was Charles here last Friday night, the night that young couple disappeared?"

"Yes, I pick him up every Friday night."

"What time?"

"Usually about nine now, as soon as it's good and dark. His wife goes to sleep early."

"And what time do you take him home?"

"Different times, one, sometimes a little later if we're playing a good hand."

"Not earlier? He was with you from nine to one last Friday night?"

Andy reached for another tissue. "No, it was later that night, more like two thirty. I remember because last night he told me he couldn't stay past midnight because they got up at four o'clock, and his wife would complain if he had trouble waking up. I dropped him off a little after twelve last night."

"Do you have a truck or access to a pickup?" Rachel asked.

"A truck? No."

"Were you with Charles Tuesday morning?"

"No. I wasn't in town. I got a couple days off and went to my sister's. She lives in State College. She wants me to move there, but I don't know. I'd hate to leave Charles. I can give you my sister's number. You know, if the police want to check."

"Does Charles have a truck or a car?"

"Charles?" She laughed. "No. He doesn't know how to drive. Going fast scares him. Last night, when we were coming home, this herd of deer jumped out in front of us and it scared him half to death. I had to drive like a granny all the way home. He definitely doesn't have a car."

"Moving might be the best thing to do," Rachel said. "For you to move to State College before Charles's wife finds out he's been coming here with you. She might not believe the part about you two being *just* friends. Agnes does have a bad temper. I wouldn't want to be you if she does find out."

"You're probably right," Andy replied sadly, looking down at her hands. "It's not like I have a palace here. But I'll miss Charles. He treats me the best of any guy I've ever met."

Rachel thanked Andy and made her way back to Mary Aaron. As they headed out of Park Estates, Rachel spotted Buddy. He was in his backyard this time. "There he is again," she said, leaning to get a better look at him.

He made eye contact and hurried toward the rear of the trailer.

"Weird," Mary Aaron remarked. "Doesn't he drive a truck?"

"A blue one."

"So, where is it? If he's here, where's his truck?"

"Good question." Rachel threw the Jeep in reverse.

CHAPTER 19

Rachel knocked on Buddy's door. She could hear voices inside, one female and one male. Buddy had hightailed it inside when he saw her drive by again. "Open the door, Buddy!" Rachel said. A big dog started barking.

"We know you're in there," Mary Aaron shouted.

The voices went suddenly silent. The dog continued to bark.

"Come on, Buddy," Rachel said, attempting to be heard above the racket. "We know you're home. We saw you. We just want to talk."

The barks grew louder, followed by frantic scratching on the inside of the door. Buddy's voice rang out. "Get down! Shut up! Get in your bed!" The dog gave a few more halfhearted barks and then several whines. "Go!"

The animal went quiet, and Rachel could hear the woman again. It sounded like she was arguing with Buddy.

"Buddy, open the door," Rachel repeated, knocking again. Mary Aaron climbed up on a cooler on the deck and peered in a narrow window.

"I see her," Mary Aaron said. "It's that weird

Englisher girl who came to Elsie's wake. Wynter, Buddy's cousin."

The door creaked and opened a few inches. Buddy glared out at Rachel. "What do you want?"

"Where's your pickup, Buddy?"

His eyes widened, and a stunned expression spread over his face. "I . . . I just, um—"

"Keep your mouth shut, Buddy," Wynter shouted at him. "She's not a cop! You don't have to talk to her!"

"I don't want to make trouble for you," Rachel told him. "But if you don't answer my questions, Buddy, the police will be here."

"Just tell us where the truck is," Mary Aaron put in.

"And then we'll be on our way," Rachel said. "We only—"

"Tires!" Buddy blurted. "Tires. Needed new tires. It's . . . it's at Howdy's."

"Buddy, what'd I tell you?" yelled Wynter. "Duck's not going to like it, you talking to people."

"Your truck's green, right, Buddy?" Rachel asked.

"No, no, not green," Buddy stammered. "Blue, it's blue. Howdy's putting new tires on my blue truck. Why you wanna know what color my truck is?" he asked.

"That's all we needed to know. Have a nice

day," Rachel told him as she backed away from the door. "Sorry to have troubled you." And to Mary Aaron, under her breath, she said, "Let's go."

"I think he's lying," Mary Aaron said when they got in the Jeep.

"Me, too," Rachel said. "The question is, why?"

"Right," Mary Aaron agreed. She looked over at Rachel. "What did you find out from the woman?"

Rachel shifted into second gear. "Charles comes here with her on Friday nights when he tells his wife he's hunting." She elaborated on what Andy had told her.

Mary Aaron listened to the whole story and then asked, "And you think she's telling the truth?"

"I do. It's just kooky enough to be the truth. Most people aren't smart enough to lie convincingly." She exhaled, feeling frustrated. "I could be wrong, but I don't think that Charles had anything to do with Dathan's death. And I was so sure . . . I guess I was sure he might have been."

"Okay, so if Charles isn't our guy, how about Rupert?" Mary Aaron asked. "He has a truck. He fought with Dathan earlier, and he might have been jealous of Dathan and Elsie."

"Lucy told me that she questioned him and he has a solid alibi. He says he was with some girl that night, and the girl can confirm it, if necessary. He just doesn't want to say who it is, if he doesn't have to. If he's telling the truth, then he's innocent. I was looking for motive and the ability to commit the crime. Rupert had both, but . . . I'm just not sure he would do such a thing." Rachel glanced at Mary Aaron. "Did you want to go back to Stone Mill House or home?"

"The B&B."

A horse and buggy passed them. A woman and several children were visible inside. Rachel and Mary Aaron waved and the occupants waved back.

Rachel stole a quick glance at Mary Aaron. "Are you sure you don't want to talk . . ." she ventured.

"About what?"

"You know about *what*. About what's going on with you."

"*Ne*. I still don't want to talk. I'm working it out in my head."

Rachel tried not to show her impatience. "Fine, but I want you to know that I'm here if you need me. Anytime."

"I know that." Mary Aaron adjusted the visor. "So are we going by Howdy's Garage and Tow and check up on Buddy's story?"

"I think we should."

Mary Aaron frowned. "I wonder why Wynter didn't want him to talk to us. That seemed strange, didn't it?"

"*She* seems strange," Rachel said, thinking out

loud. "And it's strange that she'd come to Elsie's wake."

Mary Aaron turned to look at Rachel. "You know, Buddy was at the graveyard when Elsie's body was discovered."

"He was, wasn't he?" Rachel mused. "But so was Rupert. And his father. A lot of people were there, including that English boy Rupert got into a fight with." She looked at Mary Aaron. "You think that means something, that Buddy was there?"

"I don't know. Maybe. This is hard," Mary Aaron said. "I wish Evan were here. He'd know what to do."

Rachel sighed, afraid she had a headache coming on. "I wish he were here too."

They didn't say any more until they got to Howdy's. It was closed. There were no cars there, other than those behind the chain-link fence left for repair or waiting to be picked up. The shade was down on the door. "He should be open," Mary Aaron said, looking out the Jeep's window. "Saturday's a busy day for a garage."

"Unless Howdy has something better to do." Rachel pointed at a hand-lettered sign taped to the door. It read *GONE HUNTING*. "*Atch*," Rachel said. "Opening day?"

"Antlered deer. Bow," her cousin replied. "John Hannah and Alan both bow hunt. I don't think they were going out today, though. Because of

Elsie. They were sticking close to home in case *Mam* or *Dat* needed them."

Rachel looked around. "You see Buddy's truck? I don't see it."

"There's a blue truck out there, but it looks brand new."

"Buddy's is definitely not new." Rachel slid the Jeep into first and crept forward, still checking out the garage. "I guess it could be in one of the bays." The garage doors were shut. There were windows, but they were high and narrow. "Wonder if anything is open around back?"

Mary Aaron rolled her eyes. "Just pull the Jeep up to the garage doors. If I climbed up on the hood, I could see inside."

Rachel shook her head. "That would be a sight. I can always stop back tomorrow and just ask Howdy." He lived in a small bungalow on a long lane behind the garage.

"Or we could ask his wife," Mary Aaron suggested. "Maybe she's home."

"*Ne*. If he went hunting, Sis went with him. She doesn't let him out of her sight."

"Ah, one of those jealous types."

"Exactly." Rachel parked the Jeep, got out, and walked around to the back of the building. Howdy was fifty-something, weighed well over four hundred pounds, had long braids, was missing his front teeth, and wore long johns year round under his greasy coveralls. The man was

323

honest and had a good heart, but he was hardly a guy who had women lined up to steal him from his wife of thirty years.

Rachel peered through the fence. Besides the new blue Chevy, there was a tractor out back, an orange Honda of indeterminate years, a boat trailer missing a front wheel, and large stacks of used tires. There was also a doghouse with a lazy pit-bull mix sleeping in it. "Hi, Killer," Rachel said. The dog opened one eye, then closed it. He never moved.

"Maybe he should have Sis out here," Mary Aaron ventured. "She'd be a better watchdog."

Rachel chuckled. She tried the back door that opened into the garage, but it was locked. There was a window, partially obscured by a calendar.

"Are you going to pick the lock?" Mary Aaron asked.

Rachel turned and gave her a look. "No, I'm not going to *break in*. That would be dishonest."

"And sneaking around trying to look in windows, that isn't?"

"I just want to confirm Buddy's story. If he told the truth, then there's no reason to be suspicious of him. I don't want to sic Lucy on him if I don't have to."

Mary Aaron grimaced. "Buddy Wheeler always seems suspicious to me. Why do you think his girlfriend left him?"

"She did? When?"

Mary Aaron shrugged. "Back in early summer. June, maybe. I heard he was really brokenhearted over it. Didn't date any other girls for long time."

Rachel dragged one of the used tires over and climbed up on it. She could see in on an angle, giving her a partial view of the first bay, which was empty. The rest of the garage was dark. "There's something up on a lift. Doesn't look like a truck, though. I guess I can check tomorrow with Howdy," she said.

Back at the B&B, Mary Aaron got out. "Don't worry about me," she said. "I'll be fine. We'll talk when I'm ready." She stood there for a moment with the door open. And then she leaned in. "Who do you think the girl was?"

"What girl?" Rachel asked.

"The girl Rupert is claiming is his alibi. Maybe you should ask him. Maybe he'd tell you even if he doesn't want to tell the police."

Rachel sighed and stared out the windshield. "*Ne*," she replied. "I know who to ask."

Saturday night was a date night for many of the Amish young people, and Lettie was out. Their *dat* said she left before supper and presumably would be in before ten, but volunteered nothing more. Rachel didn't want to ask her mother whom Lettie had gone out with, because discussing her sister's activities would have been an intrusion of privacy. Her mother wouldn't have told her if she knew. Rachel understood that her parents, especially her mother, would be worried about Lettie's safety after what happened to Elsie, but tradition was stronger than forbidding her to go or prying into her dating life. Lettie, like Mary Aaron, was of legal age to do as she pleased.

But Elsie had been, too, Rachel reminded herself. So she asked Amanda, who made a face but told her that Lettie was going to a singing with some girlfriends. Sally chimed in with the information that Lettie was supposed to be in by ten, but she usually was late. And if *Dat* and *Mam* were asleep, according to Sally, her big sister got away with it.

Their mother had been well enough to have dinner with them at the kitchen table. One neighbor had sent a loin of fresh pork baked with apples, while another had provided a huge pot of baked beans. With Amanda and Sally's help, it had been easy to pull a big dinner together. Rachel's buttermilk biscuits hadn't burned, and there were slaws and salad left over from the noon meal. They'd all sat around the table, and it had been like old times. Well, for everyone but her. She'd taken her usual place with Sally and Levi at the children's table. But as they told each other of the day's activities and planned for tomorrow's worship service, the years fell away, and Rachel felt again the warm contentment that she'd had growing up.

Her brothers surprised everyone by offering to clean up after supper, and Rachel, her sisters, and parents retreated to the porch, where they sat watching dusk fall. Their *dat* had led them in a prayer, and they listened while he read from Psalms.

By nine thirty, her mother was tucked into bed and the kitchen was tidy and ready for the Sabbath the following day. Rachel's father paused on his way up to bed to ask Rachel if she'd join them at church, and she agreed, sensing it was important to him. Service was three hours long, but somewhere between the sermons, the hymns, and the restless shuffling of feet and the crying of children, Rachel sensed she could refill her well of inner peace. She needed to think, and she needed to pray. She couldn't imagine a better place to renew her spirit and try to gather the strength to continue on in her search for the answers concerning her cousin's death.

It was almost ten when Rachel crept out of the house in her stocking feet and closed the kitchen door quietly behind her. She sat on the step just long enough to put her sneakers on and then hurried down the lane. Near the spot where the driveway met the road, there was a group of cedars. Rachel parted the boughs, spread her blanket on the ground, and sat down to wait for Lettie.

She didn't have long to wait. Around ten thirty, Rachel heard the horse's hooves on the blacktop a while before they reached the lane. She got to her feet and peered through the branches. A wagon rolled toward her in the silvery moonlight, and for an instant, a shiver passed down Rachel's spine. The thought that this might not be Lettie but the ghosts of Dathan and Elsie made her shiver. But she knew better. Elsie and Dathan had left this world for a better place, and it was the living Rachel had to worry about.

As horse and wagon drew closer, Rachel could make out a couple on the front seat. They were sitting close together, too close for proper behavior. Rachel kept her eyes focused on them as the driver reined in the horse. Lettie and the boy sat in the wagon whispering to each other, and then he gave her a chaste kiss. When he tried to pull her into his arms again, Lettie said, "*Ne*, I have to get in."

He got down and came around to help her out of the wagon. Rachel got a good look at his face then. As she'd suspected, Lettie's companion was Rupert Rust. He walked to the edge of the lane with Lettie. They exchanged a few words that Rachel couldn't make out, and then he walked back to the wagon. Lettie stood in the driveway until he drove away.

Once Lettie started up the lane, Rachel came out of the trees and hurried after her. Her sister let out a little shriek.

"Ohh! Don't do that!" Lettie gave her a small

shove. "You scared me half out of my wits. I thought . . . I thought—"

"You thought what? That Elsie's killer had you? What's wrong with you? If you're going to sneak out with a man, and *that* young man, the least he could do would be to see you safely to your door."

Lettie began walking faster. "I told him not to. *Dat* might find out. He wouldn't like it. They don't approve of Rupert."

"And with good cause. He's a world of trouble, Lettie. You have no idea how much—"

"*Ne,* I won't hear it." Lettie whirled on her. "You don't know him. None of you do. We're supposed to forgive. What he did was wrong, joining the military. He should never have left us. But he knows that now. He's repented, and he's paid for what he did time and time again. He wants to come home. And he wants a life here. And I'm going to help him find it."

"And if *Mam* and *Dat* forbid it, what then? Will you go against them?"

"If I have to. I love him, and he loves me. That's all that matters."

"No, it's not all that matters. You didn't come home with Joanna last Friday night, did you? You lied. You were with Rupert, weren't you?"

"What if I was?" Lettie's face was pale in the moonlight, her fingers balled into fists at her sides. "You don't understand. Nobody does."

"He told Trooper Mars he was with a girl, but he didn't say who. Were you with him? Or are you lying now to protect him?"

"Do you think I'd do that?" Lettie asked. The anger was gone from her voice, and she sounded hurt. "Do you think I'd protect Rupert if there was the slightest chance he'd hurt Elsie? I loved her, too. But Rupert was with me that night. We left the singing after Dathan and Elsie." She caught Rachel's hand. "Is he really a suspect? Do people *really* think he's a murderer?"

"He killed people when he was a Marine. You know that. If he could do it then, he might—"

"*Ne*, he wouldn't." Her tone was firm. "He put all that behind him. God has reached down and touched him. He told me that he'd never kill a living thing again, not even a snake. His father wanted him to cut the heads off chickens and he couldn't do it. He said he waded in blood, and he believed he'd lost his soul. But he's found it again here."

"And you believe him?"

"I do. And you would, too, if you knew him. He has his period of redemption, a year, maybe more. He wants to get a steady job, maybe at the mill. In time, maybe everyone will forget what he did." She squeezed Rachel's hand. "And maybe we can have a life together, Rupert and me."

"Lettie, I know he bought alcohol for the kids at the singing the night Dathan and Elsie went missing."

"That was a mistake. He was doing it because he thought it would make people like him. But I made him promise that he'd never do it again. And believe me, anyone drinking that night was old enough to know better. He didn't buy much, and it was just beer. It wasn't like they were drinking and driving."

They walked up the lane together in the darkness. "It's still against the law for anyone under twenty-one."

"I know. But it won't happen again."

"Apparently, there's a lot that went on that night you didn't tell me," Rachel admonished.

"*Ya*, maybe I should come to you, but I didn't want to get into trouble. And I didn't want to get him into trouble." Lettie's hand was trembling. "Do people think he could commit murder?"

"You're telling me the truth now?"

"*Ya*, I am."

"Did you see the fight between him and Dathan?" Rachel asked.

"I did. It was Dathan who started it, not Rupert. He saw Elsie talking to Rupert and he got in his face. Dathan shoved him. He called Rupert out, said he wasn't as tough as he let on. Rupert didn't want to fight, but the second time Dathan put his hands on him, Rupert lost his patience and hit him." She shrugged. "It wasn't much of a fight. Other kids broke it up."

"What happened after that?"

"I tried to calm Rupert down. The two of us sat behind the barn, and I put ice on his face. We just sat and talked and then he drove me home."

"And that was after Dathan and Elsie left?"

Lettie nodded. "*Ya*. After maybe half an hour, maybe more."

"So you and Rupert took the same route as Elsie and Dathan. But you didn't see them?"

When Lettie didn't respond at once, Rachel pulled her hand from her sister's and took hold of Lettie's upper arms. "You *did* see them? And you didn't say anything to me or to the police?"

"*Ne*, I didn't actually see them." Lettie sounded as though she was about to cry.

"What exactly *did* you see?"

"We saw a wagon. It might have been Dathan's wagon, or it could have been another wagon. But we didn't see them. The wagon was empty."

"What do you mean, *empty?*" Rachel demanded.

"You know the old Zook farm, the one where the house burned down years ago? The drive-way's all grown up. Anyway, when Rupert and I drove by the lane, we noticed a wagon."

"Was the horse still hitched to it?"

Lettie nodded. "Yes, but they weren't in the wagon. We thought . . . we thought maybe they'd gone for a walk or . . . maybe they were . . . oh, I don't know. We don't tell on each other, you know that."

"But this is important. It could be a clue to their disappearance. You should have told me or the police. I can't believe you saw the wagon and didn't tell anyone."

"I wasn't sure it was *their* wagon. Lots of kids drive wagons on Friday nights." Lettie sniffed. "I'm sorry. I wanted to tell you, but Rupert said it would get Elsie in trouble. When she was just missing. Then . . . then it seemed too late to say anything."

"So you didn't follow your own sense of what was right and what was wrong?" Rachel accused. "You kept quiet to suit Rupert?"

"I knew you wouldn't understand," Lettie muttered sulkily.

Rachel rested her hands on her hips. "Are you committed to this relationship?"

Lettie nodded. "I am."

"And is he?"

"I think so. It's hard for him to say how he feels. He knows people don't trust him. He's not even sure he can trust himself. But he just needs time. And he needs someone to care about him."

Rachel exhaled slowly. "I suppose it would be a total waste of my time to warn you that Rupert might bring you nothing but heartache."

"If someone had told you that leaving the

church would bring you heartache, would it have made a difference?"

Rachel pulled her sister close and hugged her. Lettie began to cry.

"Don't you understand?" Rachel murmured. "He might not make it, Lettie. He might be too damaged to ever fit in here again. And if he is, are you willing to leave with him? Abandon your faith for this man?"

"*Ne*. I won't do that," she sobbed. "I . . . I couldn't. I already told him that. I'll never leave."

Rachel rubbed her sister's back, still holding her. "But you're planning a life with someone who gets into fights over other girls? Someone who's so messed up that a car backfiring sends him facedown on the ground?"

"That's why he needs me." Lettie peered up at her. "He doesn't know how to heal. But I can help him. I can save him, Rachel. I can save him from the demons that rip him apart."

"You need to talk to *Mam* if you're serious about this."

"Not yet," Lettie said. "Promise me you won't say anything. This is my life, not yours. You don't have a right to interfere. Promise me."

"If you can promise me you won't do anything rash."

"I promise." Lettie pulled away. "But you can't tell on me. You can't. I'll never forgive you if you do." She turned and walked quickly up the drive.

Rachel stared after her. Okay, it wasn't Rupert who killed Elsie, and it wasn't Charles. Had she hit a dead end?

Or . . . did Joe make a mistake about the color of the truck in the dark, just as she had when she thought Andy's car was green, when, in fact, it was blue? Rachel stood there in the dark for a few moments, oblivious to the chill in the air, thinking.

Maybe she needed Evan to get her a list of owners of blue pickups in the valley. Tomorrow, she'd be in church most of the day, but she'd be home by late afternoon. She'd call Evan then and plead for his help again. Because she wasn't giving up, not now, not ever, until she found out who was responsible for Elsie's and Dathan's deaths. The answer had to be out there some-where, and if she kept asking questions, she'd find it.

CHAPTER 20

Rachel bowed her head and closed her eyes as the preacher's words floated in her head. She felt so at peace here, today, seated on the women's side of the worship service between her mother and her Aunt Hannah. She didn't come often; usually she stayed home with her mother while the rest of the family went to service. She'd been worried that the long day today might tire her mother, but her *mam* appeared well, almost radiant. Three different elders had offered sermons today, the bishop and both preachers, so church was running longer than usual. This was the second session of preaching, after the break for the shared midday meal. Rachel guessed that it was somewhere between two and three o'clock, but it really didn't matter. There were no set rules about how longthe services might run.

Strange how church days sometimes seemed long and boring to her. Not so today. She treasured every moment. It was what the bishop had asked them to do, to cherish their loved ones and to give thanks to God for every blessing, because we could so quickly lose the ones closest to us. Elsie and Dathan's names had been mentioned only once, but everyone knew that their thoughts and prayers centered on the families and bringing them peace and acceptance. "They sit in His holy presence, basking in the light of His countenance," Preacher Reuben was saying. "And those of us who remain faithful will be with them again." He went on to warn them against anger and remind them to pray for all those involved, because those who had done harm to us deserved forgiveness.

Rachel opened her eyes and glanced sideways at her Aunt Hannah. She had remained so strong, but Rachel knew she had to be in great pain at the loss of her daughter. All of her friends and all of her children were here with her today to support her, all but one. Rachel had seen her aunt searching for one absent face. Mary Aaron hadn't come to wor-ship. Mary Aaron was going through a spiritual crisis, Rachel got that, but her mother needed her. She should have come to church whether she wanted to or not. Her sister hadn't been in her grave a full week.

Rachel tried to push thoughts of Mary Aaron and her personal struggle away. This wasn't the time. And it wasn't her place to judge her cousin. She hadn't wanted to attend church when she was fighting her own battle, trying to decide whether to go or stay.

Today, Rachel had come to service in one of her mother's dresses, a sister's black stockings, and a scarf of her own choosing. It was easier to blend in and not be a distraction if she looked like everyone else. The skirts and dresses she wore to the Methodist church wouldn't be suitable here. She wasn't trying to look Amish, but neither did she want to offend anyone by dressing too fancy. It had apparently worked, because everyone at the service treated her like everyone else. She'd helped to serve the midday communal meal, and she'd shared in the laughter and familiar talk as well as the chores.

Rachel looked over at the men's side, where her father sat beside her Uncle Aaron. The two had never been especially close; Uncle Aaron was too severe for her father's taste. But her uncle was grieving, and Rachel's *dat* had been quick to step to his side. He might think the man too stern in his ways, but her *dat*'s heart went out to a brother-in-law's pain. Good men, both of them, Rachel thought, and they had each taught her so much about life.

How she wished Evan were here. She'd intended to call him about the blue trucks, but it would have to wait. She had completely forgotten that he'd told her she couldn't reach him by phone until he headed home. The last section of the class was classified, and the participants traveled to an undisclosed location for the final days of the program. No contact by phone was allowed. She was so proud of him. He'd worried that he wouldn't be able to keep up with the amount of material or pass the physical and mental tests. Evan hadn't been one whom academics came easy to, but he was determined and when he put his mind to something, he never quit until he reached his goal. If he had to study twenty hours rather than four or five for an exam, he did it. Evan was a special person, deeply caring and understanding, and she knew how fortunate she was that she'd found him. She loved him with all of her heart, but that didn't stop her from wondering if they could ever close the gap between her world and his. She desperately wanted—

"Rachel," her aunt whispered. "The hymn. Stand up."

"*Atch.*" She quickly rose to her feet as every voice rose around her. Her mother offered her a heavy German hymnal, but Rachel smiled and shook her head. She knew the words. Sung without accompaniment, the slow dirge rose in volume until it echoed off the rafters of the barn. Men's voices from across the dividing aisle and the high, sweet notes of children seated with their mothers and sisters blended in an outpouring of praise. The sound of the ancient hymn flowed over Rachel and seeped under her skin, raising gooseflesh on her arms and filling her with the joy of God's grace.

The hymn was a long one, and when the final

notes drifted through the open doors into the crisp September day, tears were running down Rachel's face. Most Amish services were held in church members' homes, but the Millers' house was small and their old stone barn large. Hand-hewn rafters cut from virgin timber more than two hundred years ago stretched overhead, so high that the roof was lost in shadows. The walls were stone, and the floor wide-plank pine with the marks of centuries of hard work and passage, but the air was sweet with the scent of new timothy hay, and every surface had been scrubbed, whitewashed, or raked to make the interior of the barn fit for worship. And who could complain of a service held in a stable, when the Bible told them that the Son of God was born in one?

Aunt Hannah handed her a handkerchief. Rachel nodded thanks and wiped her eyes. She wished she'd thought to bring tissues, because she needed to blow her nose, but she'd never dirty her aunt's hand-stitched hankie. And then, the strangest thing happened. Her mother reached over and patted her hand.

Rachel looked into her face, and for an instant met her mother's loving gaze. A sob rose in Rachel's throat. Everyone was getting to their feet for another hymn. Her mother leaned over her head to Aunt Hannah. "Tell her not to despair, but to trust in the Lord. He made her smart and different for a reason. If she has faith, He will lead her to the truth."

The women around them were singing loudly. Rachel stood, but although she was familiar with the hymn, she couldn't manage to get the words out. Her aunt put an arm around her and whispered in her ear, "Your mother says—"

"I heard her." Rachel muffled her crying with the handkerchief. She glanced at her mother, who was now standing erect and singing lustily. But Rachel knew the smile was for her, and her spirit soared. "I love you," she murmured.

Esther Mast stared straight ahead, her lips moving to the words.

"She loves you, too," Aunt Hannah whispered. "She's just too stubborn to say so."

Two hours later, Rachel stood in what had once been the driveway of the Zook house looking at the wagon tracks in the tall grass. Someone had been there recently, and that someone had driven a horse, because the horse had left definite proof. "Is horse manure enough solid evidence, Lucy?" she said aloud, dialing the policewoman's cell phone.

"Stay there. I'm not more than ten minutes away," Lucy said when Rachel had explained what she'd found and where she was. "But I'm on duty, so it will have to be a quick stop."

Rachel scanned the undergrowth. Had Dathan

and Elsie been here? And if they had, why had they left the wagon and walked away? The tall grass made for poor walking. There were a lot of briars and an outcropping of rock, a good hiding place for rattlesnakes. Snakes like to sun themselves on the stone on a cool day. Rachel kept a distance from the rocks. Snakes were mostly dormant at night. Dathan would have known that, but would they have taken the chance and walked over them? She didn't think so. If a couple stopped here to share a few kisses, there would have been no need to leave the wagon. But Lettie had said the wagon had been empty. It didn't make any sense.

"Those are definitely wagon-wheel tracks," Rachel explained when Lucy arrived a few minutes later.

"Unfortunately, it's not really evidence. Any wagon or buggy or who knows what could have been here." Lucy looked older and more formidable in her uniform, what with the boots and tall hat. And she sounded more serious as well. "And I'm not sure how credible a witness your sister is," she went on, "being that she first said she didn't see anything, and now, a week later, remembers seeing a wagon with no one in it that she thought was Dathan Bender's."

"I know how this seems, but I think she's telling the truth. And the timing was right for this to be evidence that Elsie and Dathan stopped here."

Lucy kicked at the weeds. "Not much of a spot for a romantic stroll in the moonlight."

"No," Rachel replied. "But there was something else I wanted to ask you." She went on to tell her about the car that she'd believed green that was actually blue. "So I'm thinking that maybe the guy I talked to might have been wrong about the color of the truck that was driving aggressively along this stretch on Friday night. I still think the truck could have had something to do with Elsie and Dathan's disappearance." She stared out at the grass wondering if this was the place Elsie had been harmed. "We checked out all the green trucks, but we didn't check blue ones." She looked back at Lucy. "Do you think it's a waste of time to have a look at blue ones?" She thought about Buddy's truck. There was no way he could have had anything to do with Elsie's and Dathan's deaths. But his behavior had been strange. Even for Buddy. And where was his blue truck if he didn't have it and it wasn't at Howdy's?

"Absolutely not. We get a report of a robber who stands six feet tall, but when we finally catch him, he's only five and a half. He just looked bigger from the business end of a gun. And eyewitnesses, don't get me started on them. The person who swears they are positively certain they can identify a suspect can be off on age, race, even the sex of another person. And a group of witnesses can all give different statements. Humans are fallible. And many times people say what they think the questioner wants to hear."

Rachel nodded and then looked up at her. "You think you could help me get the list?"

"Nope. Same reason as before. What I *can* do is try to find out where the case is right now. I've heard nothing, but Detective Starkey is in Aruba now. With him out of the office, I think I can get some information. I'm sorry. I wish I could offer more help."

A call came over Lucy's radio, and the trooper moved toward her car to respond. "Got to run," she said after responding. "A truck turned over and forty pigs are playing havoc with traffic on the highway. If you get that list of blue trucks, let me know. I won't be off again until next weekend, but I'd be glad to give you a hand checking out the trucks then."

Without Evan's help or Lucy's, Rachel felt that her chances of getting the list of blue trucks wasn't good. Not good, but not impossible. She wasn't giving up. If she couldn't get the information from Evan, maybe she knew someone who worked in Motor V, or maybe Hulda or George did. She'd just have to keep trying.

In the meantime, there was one blue truck she *could* track down. She got back in the Jeep and headed for Howdy's.

If Sis was surprised to see her at their door late on a Sunday afternoon in Amish clothing, she didn't show it. "Whatcha need, Rachel?" the woman asked. "We don't get much call for towing broke-down buggies." She grinned at her own joke.

Rachel chuckled. "I'm sure you don't. Is Howdy home? I need to ask him something."

"What about?" Sis opened the door a little wider. She was wearing bib overalls and a pink cowgirl shirt with fake pearl buttons on the cuffs. She rounded out the outfit with fringed pink cowboy boots. As far as Rachel knew, Sis hadn't grown up on a ranch, didn't own a horse, didn't ride. She was one of Stone Mill's more interesting charac-ters, but everyone liked her, at least everyone who didn't have their eye on Howdy.

"I was just wondering about a new set of tires for my Jeep. Buddy Wheeler said he got a good deal on truck tires this week. Some kind of sale."

"Buddy Wheeler buy new tires from us?" Sis scoffed. The woman wore her hair in pigtails. They were inky black and tied with rawhide laces that had little bells that jingled when she moved. Rachel wondered how that worked out if you were stalking deer. "Buddy Wheeler don't have the money to buy a gas cap, let alone tires. When Howdy sees him, it's to patch up a blown tire or put on a new muffler. He goes through mufflers like a house afire." She peered at Rachel with a puzzled expression. "He buy new tires from somebody else? Must have been on tick. You see him, you tell him he still owes us for that head gasket last fall. He keeps promising, but Howdy never sees a red cent."

"So you don't have Buddy's truck in your shop?" Rachel asked.

"My meat's about to burn. Come on in." Sis retreated to the stove, which wasn't far. The back door opened into the kitchen. A big pot of greens was boiling on the stove, and beside it was a cast-iron frying pan full of venison steaks. The ceiling was low, and the peeling wallpaper straight out of the '70s. "You hungry? You're welcome to stay for supper. Fresh venison. Shot yesterday."

"Thank you, but I ate at church. You know we always have a big midday meal on worship days. I couldn't eat another bite. Really."

"Howdy! Howdy, get out here! Rachel Mast wants to know the price on new tires for her Jeep!"

Howdy came through a curtained-off doorway that Rachel guessed led to their bedroom. He was clad in clean overalls with his long under-wear beneath them, and stockinged feet. His socks were hunter orange. He rubbed his stubbly chin. "Give you a great deal, Miss Rachel. When you want to come by?"

"Next week, maybe the week after," Rachel stalled. There would be no getting out of it. Whether she needed them or not, she was probably getting new tires. "I was thinking of winter ones," she said. "Something good for these roads when the weather gets bad."

"I can fix you right up," Howdy assured her. He pulled out a chair. "We're just fixing to eat. You want something?"

"I asked her already," Sis said as she forked the steaks onto two plates. "She says she ain't hungry. Had a big feed this afternoon with the Amish. I'm guessing that's why she's dressed thata way." She pointed at Rachel with the big fork.

"Sorry to hear about that little gal." Howdy plopped himself into an oversized chair at the table. "Aaron Hostetler's daughter. She's kin to you, ain't she? You think that Amish boy killed her?"

"No, I don't," Rachel said.

"Buddy Wheeler told her he bought new tires off us this week," Sis said.

Howdy shook his head. "Lies like a dog, that boy."

Sis heaped greens on the plates. The kitchen smelled of grease and motor oil. "I just made a pan of biscuits," the woman said. "You sure you don't want one? Them big ones out of the freezer section. Better than homemade any day."

"No thanks." Rachel backed toward the door. "I'll be in touch about those tires."

"Fix you right up," Howdy promised.

"And you see that good-for-nothing Buddy, you tell him he still owes us four hundred dollars. No checks. I want cash this time," Sis insisted.

Rachel made her escape and returned to her Jeep. Inside, she rested her hands on the steering wheel. So Buddy hadn't told the truth about his truck being at the garage. Where was it if it wasn't at Howdy's? And why had he lied?

Rachel drove back down the drive from the garage. She checked her phone for messages. She'd called Mary Aaron at the inn just before she'd left the Zook property, but her cousin hadn't returned the call. Which was weird. Mary Aaron always called back right away.

Rachel called Stone Mill House again. It rang four times and then went to voicemail. Perplexed, she listened to her own voice telling callers that they'd reached Stone Mill House and to please leave a number and someone would call them back as soon as possible. She hung up, waited two minutes, and then tried again with the same result. Was Mary Aaron outside? She decided to call Hulda and see if her cousin was over there.

"Mary Aaron?" Hulda said. "I haven't heard from her all day. Expected her over here at lunchtime. I've been right here."

"Hmm. She wasn't in church today," Rachel said, thinking out loud. Was Mary Aaron just ignoring her calls because she didn't want to talk to her? She tapped her foot nervously against the floorboard.

"She hasn't been herself lately, that's for certain," Hulda said. "But she's had good reason, and so have you. I'm sure it's nothing. I'll just walk over there and ask her to give you a call."

"I've called a couple of times in the last hour and got no answer."

"Maybe she's in the grape arbor or the garden."

"No, I don't think so. It's Sunday," Rachel said. "Amish don't work on Sunday."

"Picking flowers hardly counts as working," Hulda said.

"I'm over at Howdy's Garage and Tow. Maybe I should come home."

"Honey, what did I say? It's no trouble for me to go over. And if she needs help, I'm glad to pitch in. It gives me something to do other than to tell these worthless children of mine what they are doing wrong at the emporium. They don't like it. I don't like it. I should have sold the whole thing years ago. I knew there wasn't one of them smart enough to screw in a light bulb, let alone run a business."

Deciding to wait on the call before she headed back to her parents' house, Rachel got out of the Jeep and walked around it. Her tires were in good shape, but they weren't heavy-duty winter tires. Maybe she could have these four taken off and saved for next spring. They were too good to trade in or throw away. She wished she hadn't used the tire excuse to pry information out of Howdy's wife. At least she didn't have to feed tires or clean their litter box like the kitten she was talked into. Or the goats.

Rachel wondered how long it could take for Hulda to have Mary Aaron call back. They must be outside. But Hulda had a cell. She might be ninety-something, but the lady was up to speed with high-tech. Hulda was a blessing. Of all the neighbors she could have had, she couldn't imagine anyone better.

Two buggies went by; the occupants waved. One adorable small boy in a straw hat peered at her from the rear window of the second buggy. Rachel tried to retrieve the sense of calm she'd had when she'd left church that afternoon. She'd been really calm for the first time all week. And maybe, finally, there'd been a breakthrough with her mother.

Another Amish family came down the road in an open wagon. The mother held a small baby, and the back of the wagon was filled with red-haired children from toddlers to early teens. "Hello, Rachel!" they all shouted in *Deitsch*. She greeted them in return. It was such a serene afternoon. The sun was out, there was a light breeze, and there wasn't a cloud in the crystal-blue sky. She was simply keyed up over the whole week's frustrations. Mary Aaron would call back, and they'd have a good laugh over her worries.

Her cell finally rang and she answered too loudly.

"It's Hulda."

Rachel didn't like the sound of her neighbor's voice. "What's wrong?"

"Mary Aaron's not here at the inn."

"What do you mean, she's not there? She's supposed to be on duty."

"No, Rachel. She's gone." Hulda sounded as if she was about to burst into tears. "And it's all my fault."

CHAPTER 21

When Rachel got to the B&B, Hulda was standing on the back porch sobbing. Hulda Schenfeld, who'd lost half of her relatives to Hitler's madness, never cried.

Rachel put her arms around her. "Sssh, shhh, tell me."

"I'm afraid something terrible has happened. She . . . she took the car last night. Nobody's seen her since."

"Took the car? Took it where?"

Hulda shook her head. "I don't know. But it's my fault. I gave her the keys to the Jag. Told her to take it anytime she liked. She's a safe driver. She'll have no trouble passing the test. We've been practicing for months."

"Hulda. Where did Mary Aaron go? She wouldn't just take off and leave the B&B. Where is she?"

"I don't know. Mrs. Roth, second-floor corner room, told me she didn't see Mary Aaron today. And that high school girl who comes in to vacuum on Sunday afternoons said the office was locked and Mary Aaron wasn't here. No one's here but the guests."

"She's actually *missing?*" Rachel let her go, taking a step back. *"Missing since last night?"*

"Do you think she's run away?"

A chill ran down Rachel's spine. "I hope so," she blurted. The alternative was too frightening to consider.

"But I don't think she has," Hulda said, gaining control of herself. "No, it's not like her. She wouldn't leave Stone Mill House unattended. And she wouldn't want us to worry." She looked around. "Do you have a hankie?"

Rachel ducked inside and grabbed a section of paper towel off the roll. She brought it back. Hulda nodded gratefully and blew her nose.

"She would never have taken the car if she didn't intend to come back," the elderly woman said.

"But you told me she takes it all the time."

"This is different. She goes out at night sometimes, but she's never gone more than an hour or two. At first, I went with her, but then she didn't need me. I didn't mind. She knew she had permission to borrow the Jag whenever she pleased."

"But if she has a driving permit, she needs a licensed driver with her."

"Stuff and poppycock. There are lots of things we're supposed to do. I'm as much to blame as she is. Probably more. I'm the elder and I should know better."

"Do you think she'd leave the Amish life without telling us?"

"I don't know about that," Hulda admitted. "But I don't think she's made up her mind."

"She *has* been wearing my clothes," Rachel reminded her.

"Trying them on. Seeing how they feel. As far as the driver's license, she said that in America, you're really not an adult if you don't have a license. She wanted to see if she could really get it, but she didn't know whether she wanted to actually drive. At least that's what she told me."

"I couldn't get her to talk to me about it." Rachel opened the kitchen door. "I'm going up to her room. See if she left her prayer *kapp*."

Every Amish girl that she'd ever known had made a show of leaving the *kapp* when she left the faith. Rachel had. She'd washed and starched and ironed her *kapp* and left it lying on her bedspread in the center of her bed. Everything in her room was just so, the floor swept, the dresser empty. She'd left her dresses, too, but it had been the *kapp* that had been such a powerful symbol. She'd left a note for her parents as well. Had Mary Aaron left one?

Mary Aaron's room was one that was sometimes used as an overflow for guests at holidays when the B&B was full. It was on the second floor, in the back, and had only one window, a wide-cushioned window seat, and one wall of exposed stone. There was no attached bathroom, and Mary Aaron used a larger guest bathroom at the end of the hall. Rachel hurried through the house and up the flight of steps with Hulda on her heels.

At Mary Aaron's door, she tried the knob. It turned easily, and she flipped on the light switch. The room looked as though Mary Aaron had just run downstairs for a snack or had stepped across the hall for a shower. Her Amish clothing hung in the closet. Her purse lay on a nightstand. A pair of black athletic shoes stood beside a large empty shoebox from Zappos. An illustration on the side of the box showed brown cowboy boots with a low walking heel. Mary Aaron's name and the B&B address were on the address label. Rachel looked in the closet and under the bed. No boots were visible. Had Mary Aaron walked out of the B&B in cowboy boots?

Beside the bed stood an opened can of root beer and a bag of potato chips. Rachel knew that Mary Aaron had a fondness for root beer and chips. When she was here, the two of them often shared some before bed. Beside the chips was a pink-and-white-flowered makeup case. Rachel opened it. It contained no makeup, just a toothbrush and tube of toothpaste.

"Why wouldn't she take her purse?" Hulda asked. "Maybe she just took her wallet."

"Maybe." Rachel picked up the black purse

and opened it. A black wallet filled most of the interior. There was also an eyeglass case. The eyeglasses were prescription, but Mary Aaron only used them for reading and computer work. She could see fine at a distance. Rachel inhaled. "In for a penny, in for a pound," she said and opened the wallet. There were four tens, two twenties, and several fives and ones. "She intended to come back," Rachel said, scared now. "If she was running away, she would have taken her wallet."

In one final invasion of privacy, Rachel opened the top drawer of the walnut dresser. Mary Aaron's *kapp* and a pile of bobby pins lay waiting for her. She had intended to come back. Rachel knew it.

"You don't suppose she could have had an accident?" Hulda said. "And she's lying in a wreck in some ravine?" She clapped a manicured hand over her mouth. "Oh, no, I didn't say that." She dropped onto the antique four-poster bed. "What if I've killed her with my stupidity? We have to call the police. Tell people to start looking for her."

"You know what the police will say. The same thing they said about Elsie and Dathan. That she ran away to join the English." Rachel slowly closed the dresser drawer. "I guess we have to start with who saw her last."

"If she was here yesterday afternoon, Ada should

have talked to her, discussed this morning's breakfast plans." The housekeeper didn't come on Sundays. Peggy Grimes, who worked in the kitchen at the high school, put out a cold breakfast for the guests on her way to church. But Rachel or Mary Aaron always consulted with Ada about the pastries and available fruit.

"I'll drive over to Ada's and ask her," Rachel said. "Maybe Mary Aaron told her where she was going."

"Do you want me to come with you?" Hulda dabbed at her eyes with a balled-up tissue she'd taken from her pocket. "I feel like I should be doing something. If anything's happened to that girl, I don't think I could stand it. That sweet Mary Aaron, she's just like a daughter to me."

Rachel headed for the door, refusing to speculate what terrible thing could have happened to Mary Aaron. Right now, she had to stay level-headed. She had to find her. "If you want to help, stay here while I go and talk to Ada. Someone has to be here for the guests, and Mary Aaron might come back on her own. You can call me on my cell if she does."

"And if Ada doesn't know anything?"

"I don't know." In the doorway, Rachel turned back. "It wouldn't hurt if you would pray for her."

"You don't need to ask," Hulda said. "I'll warn you, I may not be Amish, but I come from praying stock. And I'm a powerful pray-er."

• • •

Rachel's housekeeper and her extended family were just finishing up supper when Rachel came to the kitchen door. Ada answered it; she must have seen Rachel.

"I'm sorry to bother you on a Sunday," Rachel said, through the screen door. "But I'm concerned about Mary Aaron. I was wondering if you had any idea where she might have gone last night?"

Ada tilted her head, opening the door, indicating Rachel should come in.

It was a visiting Sunday for Ada's church, and the long kitchen table was elbow to elbow with daughters, grandchildren, nephews, nieces, brothers, sisters, and children of all sizes. Evening meals were customarily simpler ones for most Amish families in the valley, but not so with Ada. Kettles of soup, roasted pork, cold chicken, macaroni and potato salads, bread, rolls, rice pudding, several kinds of pies and *strudelsand*, a four-layer German chocolate cake, beckoned and beguiled the fortunate visitor or relative. Not only was her housekeeper related to half the families in the valley, she fed many of them on a regular basis.

"Have you eaten anything?" Ada asked. "Sit down and have a little something."

"I can't, Ada. I'm looking for Mary Aaron."

The kitchen chatter faded and curious faces turned toward Rachel. Ada scowled and raised a finger. "Eat, eat," she ordered her guests. She nodded toward the door and the two stepped back onto the porch and out of earshot of the table. "Now, what is this nonsense about Mary Aaron?" she demanded in *Deitsch*.

"She's not at the inn and she's not at home. I'm worried about her."

"Probably no need to worry," Ada assured her. "You know she has a bad case of *rumspringa*, but it will pass. She is Aaron Hostetler's daughter. Have you ever heard of a Hostetler leaving? She isn't going anywhere."

"She didn't return to Stone Mill House last night, where she was supposed to be. I was hoping that you'd know where she was going."

"Didn't come back to the B&B?" Ada frowned with concern. "You sure she didn't go home to her mother's?"

Rachel shook her head.

"That isn't like her, is it?" Ada folded her arms over her chest, thinking. "Yesterday, she said she was going out to John Miller's place. Was going to take him an apple pie and a pan of gingerbread. Those Englishers you had staying this week hardly ate a thing. Afraid of gaining a pound."

"Which John Miller?" Rachel asked. There were several in Stone Mill; Miller was a common Amish surname.

"Elderly. Lives a ways down the valley. John was a second cousin to my father. Sad case." She lowered her voice. "Only had two children, and they both left. One to go Mennonite, the other to God knows where. Grandchildren turned out to be worthless. Bad blood there someplace." Ada pursed her lips. "Nothing wrong with John. His wife was a little strange. She was a Zook from out west somewhere. Died young. Seventy-eight, I believe."

"So this John is a widower?" Rachel asked. She wanted to know why Mary Aaron would suddenly decide to pay a visit to someone she barely knew, but there was no rushing Ada. She'd tell it her way or not at all. "Is John a relative of the Hostetlers?"

"Lands, no. Haven't you heard a word I said? He was a second cousin to my father."

Then Rachel remembered something. "Wait. Is John grandfather to Wynter Feathers? English girl."

"That's her. And her good-for-nothing brother, Deiter. Why that one's not in jail or in the ground, I'll never know."

"Deiter?"

"He goes by Duck. You must have seen him with his cousin Buddy Wheeler. John raised Buddy a few years, all of them at one point or another."

"So Wynter and Duck are John Miller's grand-children?"

"Didn't I just say so? She and Deiter live off

John. Neither one has ever held a job, as far as I know. Bad business, both of them. They supposedly take care of him, but it's more the other way around if you ask me. Buddy never amounted to much, but at least he works some."

Rachel tried to think. Had Mary Aaron decided to do some investigating on her own? Was that why she had made up the excuse of taking a pie to John Miller? So she could ask him about his grandchildren? "About what time did you see Mary Aaron last?" Rachel asked Ada.

"Let's see." Ada glanced up at the slatted porch ceiling. "I left Stone Mill House late yesterday. I was doing up these cakes for today. It's my niece's birthday and she favors German chocolate cake. I think I left a little before six. She was on her way right after me, I think." Ada's brows raised. "I didn't ask how Mary Aaron was getting out to John's with the pie. I suppose John Hannah drove her. It's quite a ways by buggy. Poor ground, John's farm. Rocky. Hard to grow much on that hilly ground. He never prospered. He should have never married that Ohio Zook, my father said. You know the farm, don't you?"

"I think I do." Rachel hesitated. "I think I'll ride out there. Maybe John would appreciate something more substantial than pie. Could I take him some of your potato salad?"

"I can do better than that. Let me fix up a decent meal for him. There's roast chicken that wasn't touched, and I've got enough stuffed cabbage to feed the town of Stone Mill twice over." She headed for the kitchen. "You give John my best, and tell him to come visit anytime." Her shrewd eyes filled with concern. "I have a lot of respect for John, but those grands are bad apples. I hope Mary Aaron's not messed up with them. They'll lead her astray. And when you find her, you can tell her that I said so."

Armed with the excuse of Ada's stuffed cabbage, Rachel set out for John Miller's farm. A few directions from Ada had been all that was necessary. It wasn't that far, no more than eight miles as the crow flies, but farther on twisting mountain roads. The thought that Mary Aaron might have had an accident with the Jag worried her. These were no roads for an inexperienced driver at nightfall. She'd just go up and check out the Miller place and ask a few questions. What harm could it do?

CHAPTER 22

The road to John Miller's farm was as dangerous as it had been the last time Rachel had been out this way. There were so many curves that she couldn't go more than thirty miles an hour. Until it got too dark to see, she stopped at every overlook and place where the mountain fell away next to the blacktop. Sometimes there was a low guardrail. Usually not. She didn't see any signs that a vehicle had run off the road, but as the daylight failed her, she became more and more concerned that Mary Aaron was lying in the bottom of some ravine, injured . . . or worse.

By the time she pulled into the wooded lane that ran back to the high meadow where John Miller's homestead lay, night had fallen and it was too dark to make out anything other than the area illuminated by her headlights. She'd hoped to find Hulda's car pulled up on the side of the dirt driveway or parked in the farmyard, but there were no motor vehicles. Did that mean that Wynter and her brother were away? It was dark enough that lights should have been on in the small two-story stone farmhouse, but she saw none. Surely, eight o'clock was too early for John

Miller to be in bed. Maybe no one was at home and she'd driven out here on a wild goose chase.

But if old John Miller had no information for Rachel, she had no idea where to look next. She refused to believe that Mary Aaron would just take off without leaving a note to let her family know she was all right.

Rachel parked and got out. Several dogs began to bark, one with a deep-throated bellow. A smaller dog ran up to her. From the sound of the barking, the other was probably in the house. The dog circling her Jeep was a beagle, loud, but hardly aggressive. Rachel tossed him a dog biscuit that she regularly carried in her Jeep to pave the way when she stopped at Amish farms. Using the biscuits, she could usually make friends with the doggy residents quickly.

"Good evening!" she called in *Deitsch.* "Anybody home?" She took a flashlight from under her Jeep seat and shone the beam around the farmyard. Near the house was a small structure, probably a woodshed. To her left was a stone barn, doors sagging, most of the stone badly in need of repointing. One wall of the barn was in the process of falling in. She could make out the outlines of other outbuildings, possibly a corncrib, a chicken house, and a small stable. A buggy stood in the open shed, and a horse hung its head out the top of a Dutch door in the stable and snorted a greeting. "Hello!" she tried in English. No answer.

She wondered if she should have a look around. She was just about to walk around the big barn, when the front door to the house opened and a figure made its way down the crumbling stone steps. Accompanying the man was a much larger dog. Rachel couldn't make out the breed, but the animal pressed close to the man's side, and he kept a hand on the dog's back.

"Wynter? Deiter?" the man called in *Deitsch*.

"*Ne*," she answered. "It's Rachel Mast."

"What? You'll have to speak up." He raised his hand from his grip on the dog's coat and tapped his ear. " 's not so good!"

Rachel repeated her name and used the flashlight to safely cross the yard to where he waited. The massive dog at the man's side watched her and continued to bark. "I'm Rachel Mast," she said. "I have the bed-and-breakfast in town. Your cousin Ada sent some supper for you."

"Hush, dog," the man ordered. "Down." His companion stopped barking and sat. "Who did you say sent supper? You'll have to speak up. I don't hear so well."

"Ada Hertzler! She sent you food!" Rachel flicked the beam of light across man and dog. The animal appeared to be a mixture of Newfoundland and maybe Rottweiler. The man was tall and lanky, with a long gray beard and Plain clothing that had seen better days. He had a bony chin and a long nose. His eyes were open, but they showed no reaction to the light. *He's blind,* she thought. *That's why there are no lights on in the house.* "You're John Miller, right?" she said when she reached him.

"*Ya*, that's me." He smiled. "Least I was when I woke this morning."

Rachel repeated her excuse for coming.

"Ah, well, nice to meet you, Rachel Mast. I thought maybe you were Mary Aaron Hostetler. Don't get much company up here."

"Is she here?" Rachel asked.

"Is who here?"

Rachel raised her voice until she was practically shouting. "Mary Aaron. Was she here today?"

"Wait," John said. He dug into his trouser pockets and came up with a hearing aid. "Wait until I put in the batteries." In the other pocket he found batteries. Rachel waited patiently while he inserted the batteries and then put the hearing aid in one ear.

"Can you hear me now?" Rachel asked.

"I better, as much as this blasted thing cost me." He motioned to her. "Don't just stand there. Come inside. Getting nippy out here."

Rachel followed him into the dark house, again using the flashlight beam to see where she was going. The dog resumed its vigil by its master's side, and the beagle fell in behind them, bringing up the rear. In the front room, the man went to a table, fumbled with matches, and lit a kerosene lamp. Yellow, flickering light illuminated the room. The furniture was sparse and old-fashioned, even for an Amish home, but it appeared clean and orderly. A cross-stitch family tree adorned one plastered wall. In the corner of the room was a potbellied stove, but it wasn't lit. The parlor was chilly, and Rachel kept her jacket on.

"Don't bother with lamps when I'm here by myself. No need. The dogs find their way with their noses." John motioned to a Victorian-era settee with a stiff wooden back. "I haven't seen Ada Hertzler in a month of Sundays, and now she sends me supper two days in a row. If we weren't kin, I'd think maybe she was interested in marrying me." He laughed at his own joke and settled his long frame into a ladder-back chair. "Mast. Rachel Mast. You're that Mast girl that ran off to the English and then came back, aren't you?"

"I am," she said.

"So you're kin to Mary Aaron. Nice girl. Sat and talked with me. Like I said, I don't get much company up here. It was kind of her to stay so long."

"She and I are first cousins," Rachel explained. "So, she *was* here last night?"

"*Ya*, she was." He proceeded to list the food that Mary Aaron had brought.

"Did she come in a car?"

"A car? Now, why would she do that?" John removed his wool hat and placed it on the table. "Oh, you mean, did she have a driver? *Ne*, not that I heard. I assumed she came by horse and buggy. She's Amish, so I wouldn't expect any different. I did say to her that it was a long way for her to drive up here. But she didn't mention a driver." He tugged thoughtfully at his beard. "She made me coffee. Good coffee, too. Wynter, that's my grand-daughter, she makes the worst coffee you ever put in your mouth. Weak as rainwater. Usually I make it myself. My Alma could make good coffee, but Wynter is pretty hopeless in the kitchen. Sandwiches, cereal out of a box. Cheap bologna. Potato chips. Her mother never learned how to cook, and Wynter never had any interest in learning."

"Wynter lives here with you?"

"Supposedly. Comes and goes, same as her brother. At least she don't see me go hungry when she *is* here. Not like Duck. Nothing but a lazy cadger, always trying to pry money out of me. Send him to the store, he comes home with nothing and no change. Don't even feed and water the horse or the chickens. Only let them come back here because they promised to help out."

From the looks of the farmyard, Rachel didn't think the two were much help. She tried to imagine how a blind man would manage on his own.

"It was foolish of me to agree to have 'em here. But I lost what sight I had, and the truth is, I get lonely up here without my wife," John continued. "Wynter said Duck had changed, wanted to straighten out his life. Might even come back to the church, she told me. But it was all lies, just like last time and the time before that. I thought being back on the home place might give him roots, help him find his way. I'm a silly old man to think so. Once the tree is bent, there's no straightening it. Duck's useless to himself and anybody else. And Wynter's not far behind him. God help me, I must have failed them somehow."

Rachel wanted to ask about Mary Aaron, but she sensed that John needed to talk and she tried to keep from interrupting him. "Have they been here today?" she asked. "Your grand-children?"

"Maybe, can't say for sure. Didn't have my hearing aid in. And they pretty much sleep all day. Prowl around at night. They don't spend any time with me when they are here. They got rooms in the back of the house, and there's a back staircase. Like I said, those two come and go. I sleep in the kitchen, warmer that way, and I know where everything is. I heat with wood, same as I always did."

The guide dog stretched out at John's feet. The beagle sat by the doorway that Rachel assumed led to the kitchen and other rooms of the house.

"Were they here yesterday? Maybe when Mary Aaron was here?"

John shook his head. "They might have been here earlier, midday maybe. Like I said, you can't depend on them. Alma and me raised them both for a while. Their cousin Buddy, too. But they didn't want any part of our ways. None of my grandkids did. Don't know why. Did a lot of praying over it." He shook his head again. "Broke the wife's heart, it did. Heartache is all they ever gave her. And she tried her best to keep them on the narrow way. But the world is mighty powerful. Takes some of our young folk, no matter how hard you try to hold them to the faith."

Rachel wondered what church community John belonged to. She wanted to ask, but the Amish were touchy when it came to personal questions. It wasn't like any Plain community to let an older person try to manage alone, though, especially one without his sight. He seemed like a nice man, and she couldn't help being concerned for his safety.

"Can I offer you some coffee?" John asked. "I believe there's some of that gingerbread Mary Aaron brought. I hid it in the sauerkraut crock. That Duck's got a sweet tooth. Anything good, he finds it and eats every crumb. Awful good gingerbread. My wife made good gingerbread."

Rachel politely refused the refreshments and

got to her feet. John seemed lonely, and she felt guilty about rushing off without staying to visit, but she felt a sense of urgency that she couldn't explain. "Can you tell me what time Mary Aaron left last night? No one has seen her today, and I'm getting a little concerned. It's not like her to miss church."

"She didn't make worship services?" John pressed his lips together in concern. "A shame. She said she was going. Asked me if I'd like to go with her. Said her church group was a good-hearted one with a fine bishop." He shrugged. "I'm too far away for her to run back up here and fetch me. I used to go to one of the local district churches. We had a solid community, but most of the folks have moved away. Hard to make a living farming these days. Harder for a blind man with knees that ache when it rains. It was different when my Alma was alive. We never missed a church Sunday."

"So what time did she leave?" Rachel pressed.

"I don't know, exactly. Sometime around seven. I remember her saying something about sunset and needing to get on."

Rachel got to her feet. "Well, I don't want to keep you up. I'll just get that food that Ada sent out of my Jeep."

"You tell her it's appreciated. And you come back anytime you're up this way. You seem like a fine young person, even if you did run off to the

English. And you tell that Mary Aaron she does make good coffee. I'm sure you'll find her at home when you get back. Such a sensible young woman. Make some man a wonderful wife, that girl."

Fifteen minutes later, Rachel had delivered the promised supper and made her farewells to John. He was a lovely man, and she intended to see if someone in her mother's church community couldn't reach out to him.

Rachel got into her Jeep and made a U-turn in the barnyard, but her nagging worry wouldn't let her leave the Miller farm without at least looking around. She stopped at the head of the lane, slipped on a jacket she'd left on the backseat, and put her cell phone in the pocket. Then she took her flashlight and began an inspection of the farm buildings. It was hard going because the weeds were high and the structures overgrown with greenbriers and wild roses. It was a dark night with no moon in sight, and it was difficult not to get tangled in the waist-high grass. At least it was until she stumbled into an area where the grass had been crushed by a vehicle. Rachel's heartbeat quickened. A car or a truck had passed this way. She followed the tracks.

From up on the mountain came the plaintive cry of a coyote, and Rachel shivered. The air was chilly, the wind coming down from the heights bitter for September, but the real cold came from within. The tracks were small, definitely not a truck. They could have been made by Hulda's old Jaguar, and they led behind the big stone barn and attached sheds.

Abruptly, she came upon the Jag. She'd almost stumbled into it, because it was nearly hidden by brush. She turned the flashlight beam on the vehicle, willing it to be some sort of mistake . . . an old rusted junker . . . not Hulda's car at all . . . a vehicle that couldn't be the one Mary Aaron had been driving.

Her foot tangled in the briars and she stumbled forward, arms windmilling to catch her balance. She fell and the flashlight rolled away, struck something metal, and the light went out. Feeling foolish, she pulled her cell phone out of her jacket pocket and used that light to get her bearings as she unwound herself from the briars. Thorns cut into her bare legs, and she wished she'd taken the time to change out of the Sunday service dress and into jeans back at the B&B. She caught her breath as she ran the light over the car. She made her way to the driver's door, pushing aside the branches of the maple sapling that had been piled against it.

Rachel let out the breath that she'd been holding without realizing it. The interior of the vehicle was empty, but on the seat lay one of Ada's serving dishes with the red and white tulip design. And a blue head scarf. A small sound of dread escaped her throat, and she quickly clenched her lips together.

She shone the beam around her, looking frantically for Mary Aaron. She didn't see anyone, but she did catch a glimpse of a blue pickup. Buddy's. He lied to her about where it was. He lied to Mary Aaron and she must have called him on it. She must have found out *why* he'd lied.

No, Rachel screamed silently. *Not Mary Aaron.* Frantically, she scrolled for Lucy's phone number and dialed. Nothing happened. Rachel tried again. The call wasn't going through. No bars. She wasn't getting a signal up here. "Come on, come on," she whispered, moving left a couple of feet, then right. "Please." She put in the number a third time with the same results.

What to do? Should she continue her search for Mary Aaron or go for help?

"Hey!" A man's voice came from somewhere behind her.

Instinctively, Rachel spun around and ran back along the tire tracks. Pounding feet thudded behind her. She stumbled once, caught her balance, and ran smack into a broad chest and two brawny arms—arms that closed like a vise around her.

"Just couldn't mind your own business, could you?" a voice said in her ear.

She knew that voice. Buddy's.

"Let me go!" She struggled, kicking and striking

out at him, but he was too strong for her. He pinned her arms to her sides and held her. "Where's Mary Aaron? What did you do with her?" Now she was terrified. If Buddy's was the blue truck that ran the little car off the road, if he was the one who had killed Elsie, and Mary Aaron had figured it out . . . Tears filled her eyes.

"Dang it, Rachel." Buddy gave her a shake. "Why couldn't you let it go?"

"Got her?" the other man demanded, running toward them.

A bright light blinded her.

"Shine that thing someplace else," Buddy complained. "Stop it, Rachel. Behave yourself and you won't get hurt."

Rachel found herself trembling, not with fear, but with rage. She wanted to lash out at him, but knew that further struggle now was useless. She forced herself to stop fighting him. "Your grandfather knows I'm out here. He'll wonder why—"

"Shut up! The old man's gone to bed," the man with the light said, cutting her off. "He took out his hearing aid and he won't know nothing until the sun comes up."

"What are we going to do with her, Duck?" Buddy pleaded. "This is getting worse and worse. I don't want—"

"It's not up to you, now, is it?" Duck said. "Put her with the other one until I can figure this out."

"Mary Aaron? She's here?" *She's alive?* Rachel felt another hard hand on her; he was checking her jacket pockets. "Don't touch me!" she protested, jerking away.

"Just wanna make sure you don't have a knife or something worse on you," Duck said as he retrieved her fallen cell phone from the grass. She'd dropped it when Buddy grabbed her. "Looky here. Fancy phone for one of you Amish girls."

"She ain't Amish," Buddy said. "I told you that. She left."

"Well, she looks Amish, don't she? Long dress. Black stockings."

"You can't do this. Not two of us. You'll never—"

"I told you to shut your mouth," Duck growled. He shoved her cell phone in his pocket.

"That's mine," Rachel said. "You can't take my phone."

Duck laughed, his face illuminated by his flashlight. "Finders, keepers."

"We ain't going to keep it," Buddy said.

"Speak for yourself." Duck chuckled. "Mine's almost out of minutes. This one will be good for a long time."

"It's not right," Buddy muttered. "I ain't no thief."

Duck shrugged. "She lost it, I found it. That ain't stealing. Way I see it, she was the one trespassing in our granddaddy's field. Come on. I ain't standing here all night."

"I guess you'll have to come with us, Rachel," Buddy said apologetically. "Now, don't make a fuss and nothing bad will happen."

"Where's Mary Aaron?" Rachel repeated.

Duck gave her a shove forward. "You going to walk nice, or do I have to knock some sense in you first?"

Rachel made her move. She broke free of Buddy's grip and ran. If she could reach the trees, she knew she'd have a chance that they couldn't find her in the dark. She'd always been a runner, and she gave it all she had as she fled across the overgrown field.

It wasn't enough. Duck was fast.

She'd gone maybe a few hundred feet when he tackled her and knocked her facedown on the ground. For seconds, she lay there, sucking in air, trying to regain her senses. Then he jerked her to her feet and twisted her arm behind her back.

"Walk!" he panted, as breathless as she was. "And if you try anything else, so help me, I'll break your leg."

CHAPTER 23

Halfway across the field, Duck stopped abruptly, ripped the tie cord out of the bottom of her jacket, and used the nylon to tie her wrists behind her back. "That's better," he said.

Not better for me, Rachel thought. She winced as he yanked the cord tight. "That hurts," she protested.

"Too bad for you."

"Come on, Duck." Buddy hurried to catch up. "No need to be rough with her."

"Shut up!" Duck snapped. "She brought this on herself."

"No, she didn't," Buddy argued, punching his cousin in the shoulder. "It was you. You had to throw that beer bottle at the wagon."

"That was an accident. And you're as much to blame as me. You were driving the truck. If I go to jail, you get the same sentence." He jabbed Buddy with a finger. "And don't you forget it!"

"It was an accident, Rachel. I swear it," Buddy insisted. "We never meant to hurt her."

Rachel suddenly felt light-headed. He was talking about Elsie. She'd already guessed he was responsible, but somehow hearing him say it . . . "How could you do such a thing, Buddy?" she demanded, getting in his face. "How could you kill an innocent person?"

Buddy shrank back. "I . . . I didn't. He's the one who did it."

Duck shoved her. "Another word out of you," he said to Buddy, "and I'll make you sorry you were born."

"Idiot," Buddy muttered. "You were always an idiot."

Duck let go of her long enough to swing a fist at Buddy. Buddy dodged him and took off into the darkness.

Duck seized Rachel by her arm and dragged her forward. The flashlight beam bobbed, but she caught glimpses of rocks and trees and high grass. She could tell that they were moving uphill, maybe back toward the house, but she couldn't be certain. The darkness, the violence, and the revelation that Duck and Buddy had killed Elsie . . . and probably Dathan . . . had left her rattled.

Suddenly, a stone structure loomed in front of them and Buddy appeared, out of the darkness, running ahead. The small building was rooted in the stony ground, backed up against a steep rise, perhaps a story and a half high. A shallow stream spilled out from under the front wall and water soaked her shoes. They splashed through it. Two whitewashed steps led to an old board-and-batten door. A springhouse, she realized. And if this was the springhouse for the Miller farm, they couldn't be far from the house and barns.

"Open the door," Duck ordered. Buddy moved up the steps and slid back an iron bar. Years, weather, attacks by black bears—all had taken their toll on both door and latch. Deep claw marks scarred the thick oak, but Rachel could see that it was a formidable obstacle for a four-legged intruder.

Buddy swung the low door open and shined his flashlight through the doorway. Duck shoved Rachel again. "Get inside," he ordered.

The steps were steep and uneven, and Rachel struggled to climb them without the use of her arms for balance. Her heart was pounding. She could feel something wet dripping from her nose. Blood. At some point in the confrontation, she must have also bitten her tongue or the inside of her mouth, because she could taste blood. Being trapped like this was bad. Bad.

But her fear wasn't for her own safety as much as for Mary Aaron's. *Please, God, let her be in here,* Rachel prayed silently as she stumbled up the stone steps. *Let her be alive.*

At the top of the steps, Duck pushed her through the opening. Cobwebs dragged at her face. The floorboards sagged under her feet, and she smelled dampness and rodent droppings. Buddy's flashlight scanned the room.

"Rachel!" Mary Aaron cried.

Rachel caught a glimpse of her cousin, sitting on the rotting floorboards, her back against a wooden post, ankles and wrists wrapped in tape. Mary Aaron was awake and alert, her eyes wide, her expression fierce. She was wearing a pair of jeans, a flannel shirt, and a puffy vest that Rachel recognized from her own closet. And the cowboy boots. There was a water bottle between her knees.

"This has gone far enough!" Mary Aaron shouted at the men. "It's all over, guys. Time you turned yourselves in. If it was just an accident, the way you said, Buddy—"

"I told you, I didn't hit her with the bottle," Buddy protested. "It was him."

"Yeah, so what?" Duck retorted. "Who was driving the truck that flattened the guy?"

"Dathan was getting away," Buddy argued, turning to Rachel. "I didn't mean to kill him. I was just trying to knock him down to—"

"Shut up!" Duck repeated. "Quit running your mouth and tie her up."

Buddy yanked off his ball cap and threw it on the floor. "I don't know what you're thinkin' here, Cousin. First the girl, then him, and now these two? It ain't right."

"It ain't right we spend the rest of our lives in the slammer for an accident either, is it?" Duck said. "Do you know what those places are like?

It won't be some little wimpy jailhouse. It will be state. And I've been there. I know what it's like. And I won't go back."

"But we won't go to jail, right?" Buddy's tone took on a whine. "We're takin' off. We're going to North Dakota? Plenty of jobs up there in the oil fields. Start over. Make some real money, isn't that what you promised?"

Duck stood there, staring at Buddy. "You've got to be the stupidest guy in the state. You just told them our plan!" He gestured to Mary Aaron and Rachel, who was moving toward her cousin. "You think we can just leave them to run their mouths? They know about the truck."

"Not just me," Mary Aaron said. "I called Trooper Mars. I left a message on her voicemail. I told her about the truck and the dent in the front. You think there's no DNA on the truck in the shed? You think the police won't find out how you killed Elsie and kidnapped Dathan and killed him, too? It's over. It's all over, and the only hope you have of not being locked up for the rest of your lives is to surrender right now. Get a good lawyer and explain how it was all an accident."

Duck glared at Mary Aaron. "You left a message, she'd have long been here. Tape that one's mouth," he said to Buddy, pointing to Mary Aaron. "She hasn't shut up in the last day. And put that one there." He indicated Rachel and then the pole Mary Aaron was leaning against.

Rachel didn't think, she just moved. She lowered her head and charged Duck. She hit him full in the stomach, and he staggered backward. "Scream!" she shouted as she gained her own balance and ran toward the door.

"Catch her!" Duck yelled.

"Don't hurt her!" Mary Aaron shrieked. "You hurt her and—"

Buddy slammed into Rachel and they both went down. Rachel's head hit against the floor hard and the room spun. Mary Aaron's screams were suddenly muffled, and Rachel felt herself being lifted up off the floor and shoved back against the same beam that her cousin was tied to.

Cursing, Duck sat Rachel down, slapping her hard across the face. Her head rocked back. "Give me that tape," he barked to Buddy. He ripped off a section and taped her ankles together. Mary Aaron's protests continued while Rachel tried to catch her breath and clear her head. She was going to have to be smart here, she and Mary Aaron, or she was afraid they were both going to end up dead. Buddy, she could deal with, but his cousin? Duck was mean. And deadly.

"*Grossdaddi*'s gonna hear them," Buddy warned.

"Is not. He's deaf as a stone. He won't hear nothing," Duck argued. "This springhouse is too far from the house. So, yell your head off," he told Rachel. "It ain't going to do you any good."

"But he might hear. If he puts his hearing aid in," Buddy said.

"If he does, I've got plenty of tape left." Duck spun the roll of duct tape on his finger. "He's old. He couldn't do nothing to us. He doesn't watch himself, he'll end up the same as them."

"But he's our grandpa. You can't tie your grandpa up," Buddy worried anxiously. "And you shouldn't have hit her like that. You're not supposed to hit girls."

Duck stood upright, wiping the dirt and cobwebs away from his mouth. "Yeah, and you shouldn't have sent that dude flying with your truck. Broke his back, probably. Crushed his skull. But you did, didn't you?"

Buddy's flashlight beam jerked, and light spilled across the floor. Rachel saw that some of the boards were missing. Below was only darkness and the rush of running water. She began to shiver uncontrollably as damp and dread seized her. Then she felt Mary Aaron's fingers brush hers, and Rachel slowly got control of her panic.

Buddy was near to tears. "I didn't mean to do it," he blubbered. "I keep telling you that. He was getting away, and I just had to stop him. But I never touched the girl. I tried to help her. I bandaged her head. I didn't think she was going to die."

"Why didn't you just call the paramedics when

you saw that Elsie was injured?" Rachel begged. "Why did you take the horse and wagon?"

"We got scared," Buddy said. "I wasn't thinking straight."

"You want to tell truths?" Duck laughed. "Truth is, you were drunk out of your head that night. It was your idea to go bash some mailboxes."

"But it wasn't my idea to throw beer bottles at horse and wagons." Buddy looked to Rachel. "I didn't think she was gonna die. She was awake and talking when we brought her and him and the horse and wagon back here. We were just figuring out how to get out of town before we cut them loose. But then the horse got out through a break in the fence and . . ." He hung his head. He sounded as if he was trying not to cry. "And then she did die," he said, softer than before.

"Oh, Buddy," Rachel sighed. "So you buried her in the Amish graveyard? Did that seem like the right thing to do?"

"She was dead, wasn't she?" Duck snapped. "But that one was Buddy's idea." He hooked a thumb in Buddy's direction. "Seemed smart at the time."

"We tried to tell Dathan it was an accident," Buddy explained as he retrieved his cap and tugged it on. "We didn't want to hurt either of them. It was just fun and all. Duck and me were smashing mailboxes, like you do. Sort of a game. But then he threw the bottle."

"And killed Elsie," Rachel exhaled, still in disbelief that such grief could have come from such a foolish act. How many lives had Duck ruined with that beer bottle? "But if killing Elsie was an accident," she said, looking at both of them, "why kill Dathan, too?"

Buddy broke down. "When she died, Dathan went crazy. Wouldn't listen to reason. Kept shouting that we'd murdered her and we were going to prison."

"So you killed him with your truck," Rachel demanded, "and you turned a drunken accident into a double murder."

"I'm sorry." Buddy was sobbing. "I'm so sorry. I never wanted to hurt anybody. We were just—"

"Will you shut up!" Duck shouted, grabbing Buddy's arm and dragging him backward. "It's too late for all that. Get out of here."

"Is Wynter back yet?" Buddy wiped his snotty nose with the sleeve of his brown camo Carhartt jacket.

"She will be."

"And then we're heading to North Dakota, right? To get them oil jobs?"

"Oh, yeah, you can count on it." Duck followed Buddy out of the springhouse and jerked the door shut behind him.

Rachel heard the iron bar slam into place, and the springhouse descended into blackness again.

"Get this tape off my mouth," Mary Aaron

mumbled. Apparently she'd loosened it enough so that Rachel could understand her. She wiggled as close as she could get to Rachel, leaning against her.

Even though Rachel's hands were tied with the cord from her jacket, and she couldn't see a thing, she was able to grope with her fingers to catch the edge of the duct tape on Mary Aaron's mouth. It was difficult to maintain her grip, though, because Duck had tied the cord so tightly that most of the feeling was gone in her fingers. "This's going to hurt," she warned.

"Just get the tape—Ouch!" Mary Aaron jerked back as Rachel ripped off the tape. "I hoped you'd figure out where I went when I didn't come home, but I didn't expect you to come alone."

"You would have made it easier if you'd left a note where you were going and why." Rachel strained at the cord on her wrists, but all it did was to tighten the knots. "What made you come up here to John's farm last night? And don't tell me to bring him pie."

"Buddy lied about getting tires put on. On his blue truck. And I knew that Wynter and Duck were staying here and that they were close with Buddy. I came looking for Buddy's truck. I never suspected they were all in on it. I didn't find the truck." She motioned with her chin. "But I *did* find Charles's wagon. It's in the barn."

"Truck's in the back." Rachel shifted her

weight. There seemed to be a nail head coming through the floorboard directly under where she was sitting. "How do you know it was Charles's wagon?"

"There were bloodstains on the seat and floor," Mary Aaron said, clearly making an effort to remain detached. "And somebody had gone to a lot of effort to hide it. They piled hay on top of it. It's got to be Elsie's blood," she finished softly.

Rachel's tone was gentle when she spoke. "Why didn't you tell me you were coming up here, Mary Aaron? I'd have come with you."

"I thought it was safe enough with John here. And like I said, it hadn't occurred to me that Duck and Wynter were in on the whole thing. I just thought maybe one of them knew something about Buddy, not that they were involved in Elsie and Dathan's deaths."

"But you were concerned enough to leave a message on Lucy's phone."

Mary Aaron groaned. "Duck was right. I made that part up."

Rachel leaned the back of her head against the pole for a second. "So you *didn't* call Lucy?"

"I tried. I tried to call you when I found the wagon, and then Trooper Mars. But I couldn't get a signal."

"Whose phone did you use?"

"John Hannah's."

"Where is it?"

"Buddy took it."

"They took mine, too." Rachel exhaled. Her head was pounding and her nose had started to bleed again. And she was tied up. But she wasn't ready to give up. She just had to think. She just had to figure out how to get Mary Aaron and herself out of this. "Mary Aaron. What were you thinking? And look at you! You're wearing my clothes. What are you doing?"

Mary Aaron sighed loudly. "Making a mess of my life, obviously."

Rachel didn't respond.

"So," her cousin asked. "How did they get *you?*"

"I came up here looking for you. I talked to John, and then on the way out, I stopped to look around for Hulda's car. I honestly didn't think you were here. I was afraid you'd run off the road with it last night. Had a terrible accident."

"I didn't wreck. I know how to drive."

"Then I discovered the Jag," Rachel went on. "But Duck and Buddy caught me." She looked toward Mary Aaron, even though it was too dark to see anything. "Have you seen Wynter? It doesn't sound like she was with Duck and Buddy, but it would be too good to be true to think she might be able to help us."

"*Ne*, I haven't seen her since this morning. But she's part of it. She knows what happened. I heard Buddy tell Duck that she knew where John hid his savings. He doesn't believe in banks.

389

Apparently Wynter's the thief of the group."

"She intends to rob her grandfather?" The nail was still digging into Rachel's thigh and she shifted to another position. The pins-and-needles sensation in her hands was fading, replaced with a dull ache. "I didn't ask if they'd hurt you. Are you okay?"

"Duck hit me. I hit him in the elbow with an ax handle."

"Why didn't you use the other end?"

Mary Aaron managed a halfhearted chuckle. "There *was* no other end. The ax head was missing. I tried to get away by climbing a ladder to the hayloft in the barn. I would have made it, but the ladder rungs were rotten. One broke and I fell about ten feet to the floor. I did something to my right knee. It's all swollen, and I don't know if I can put any weight on it. Buddy had to carry me to the springhouse. But he's not so bad. He gave me his coat last night so I wouldn't be cold."

"That vest has a rip in it," Rachel said. "It was new."

Mary Aaron sighed again. "Sorry."

"You should be. And you're going to have to buy me a new one once we get out of this mess." She looked down at her cousin's feet. "Apparently you've got a Zappos account now."

"You get us out of this and I'll buy you two down vests," Mary Aaron told her. Rachel heard her shift her weight. "This didn't work out like I thought it would," Mary Aaron went on. "I wanted to find the truck with evidence that they had been involved in Elsie's murder and solve the case. Like you did before." She sounded as if she was about to cry. "I wish I was home in my own bed."

"Me, too," Rachel admitted. They were quiet for a moment, and then she said, "Are you?"

"Am I what?"

"Leaving."

"This springhouse? I hope so."

Rachel swallowed. Her mouth felt dry, and she could still taste blood. "I meant, are you leaving the church?"

"I don't think so. Jeans aren't as comfortable as they look when English girls wear them."

"Can you be serious? We're in a bad spot here." *We could die,* Rachel thought, but she didn't want to say so. Saying so would make it all the more real. "Are your hands taped, too?" she asked.

"*Ya,* but there's a trickle of water leaking in through the back wall of the springhouse. I've been soaking the tape when—"

"Shhh!" Rachel cautioned. Something scraped on the steps beyond the door. The latch squeaked. A beam of light flashed across Rachel's face. It was a more powerful light than the flashlights had been earlier.

"It's just me," Buddy said. "Don't be scared. I

brought you a blanket. The temperature's dropping outside. We might get frost tonight."

"I'm thirsty," Rachel said. "Could you give me a drink?"

He picked up the water bottle from between Mary Aaron's knees. Rachel hoped that Buddy wouldn't notice that the tape around Mary Aaron's mouth was gone. Buddy unscrewed the bottle cap and held the bottle to her mouth. Rachel took a long drink, coughed, and shook her head.

"No more," she said. "Thank you for the blanket. I am cold. But aren't you going to get in trouble with Duck for bringing it? He won't like it."

"Duck don't tell me what to do." He spread the blanket over their laps. "Besides, he went to check on our grandfather. To make sure he's asleep. Duck won't find out I'm here. I'm not stupid."

"I can see that," Rachel reasoned. "But he's the boss. He's the one who started all this. He threw the bottle and killed Elsie. You said he did."

"He threw the bottle. It was an accident. But the bottle hit the girl right in the head. It was awful, dented her skull in."

Mary Aaron uttered a tiny whimper.

"I'm so sorry. We were just drinking like we do, messing around, throwing beer bottles, hitting mailboxes. We never intended to kill anybody. Not a girl. Not anybody."

"But it happened," Rachel said. "And now all this. But you're just making it worse, Buddy. You know that, right? If you tell the truth, people will listen. Elsie was Amish. So was Dathan. You know how the Amish forgive. If you say you're sorry, if you mean it, they won't insist on you going to jail."

"I can't go to jail. You heard Duck. Bad stuff happens in there. Bad stuff happened to him. He was different before he went to Lewisburg. He just ain't the same. But he's my cousin, like a brother to me. I gotta look out for him."

"You have to look out for yourself, Buddy," Rachel argued. She hesitated and then went on. "You know Duck wants to kill us, right?"

"He won't really kill you. He's just scared because he's on parole. He's afraid they'll send him back for a long time. He said we would work it all out, and stuff just got out of hand. That girl, she shouldn't have died. She was awake and talking to me."

"What did she say? Did she ask you for help?"

Buddy shrugged. "It didn't make much sense. I know some *Deitsch*, but she was just jabbering. Something about her father and getting home on time. I thought she'd be okay in the morning and then we'd let them go."

"But you took them away from the scene of the

accident? You took the horse and wagon," Rachel said. "Why?"

"Duck was scared somebody would come along. And I'd had a few beers and I didn't want a DUI. We brought them here. Just until we sobered up and got our plan worked out. I never thought she would die. Then Duck said we couldn't let him go, because he'd tell."

"How did Dathan get from here to where he was killed?"

Buddy grimaced. "I said it wasn't safe here. Wynter said so, too. We were gonna take Dathan to this guy Duck knew. Then when we were safe away from here, Duck's friend could let him go."

"But he got away?"

"Yeah. I don't know how. He was in the back of the truck. He was tied up. But he got loose. He jumped out and started running down the road. He was fast. I was just trying to catch up with him and I accidentally hit him. He just flew through the air."

"So why didn't you keep going to North Dakota then? Why did you stay?"

"It was Wynter. She said the truck was evidence. Cops would stop me before I got across the state line. We needed a new car or to get my bumper replaced. That's what we were working on when you saw us in Wagler's."

"So Roy Thompson was going to do the

bodywork and then you were heading to North Dakota?"

"Yeah. Wynter said she knew where *Grossdaddi* had a couple thousand dollars stashed. She wasn't going to take it all, just enough for expenses. You can make a fortune out there, working on the oil wells. We can make a new start."

"But there won't be any new start if Duck kills us," Rachel said. "You know my fiancé is a state trooper. A detective. You murder us, and the authorities will hunt you down no matter where you go."

"I won't let him hurt you. The other stuff, that just piled up. But we'll leave you here. And tomorrow, when we're a long way off, I'll just call 9-1-1 and say that you're up here. Nobody else needs to get hurt."

"That's not going to happen. You know that, right, Buddy? Duck's going to kill us. And he might kill you, too," Rachel insisted.

"No, you don't know him like I do. Duck's family. He's smart, and he cares what happens to me and Wynter. Thousands of guys up there in North Dakota. Nobody will find us. And if they try, we'll just slip over the border to Canada. I've always wanted to see—"

The door flew open. "You idiot! What are you doing back in here?" Duck filled the doorway. He was wearing a headlamp now. "I told you—"

"You can't keep tellin' me what to do," Buddy protested. "We're in this together. Gramps okay?"

"He's sound asleep. I told you he'd never hear them yelling."

"I think—I think we need to leave for Dakota tonight—tonight," Buddy stammered. "Right now. Just leave Rachel and Mary and go."

"We will," Duck said. "As soon as we clean up the loose ends. We can't leave witnesses, not now that you blabbed where we're going."

Wynter appeared in the doorway behind Duck.

"Wynter, tell—tell him he can't do this," Buddy pleaded. "He's got this crazy idea we can kill Rachel and Mary Aaron. I can't—"

"I got it, Duck," she said, cutting Buddy off. "Right where I thought it was."

"The money?" Buddy asked.

"Oh, yeah, and what I went to town for. He sold it to me, all right."

Rachel's breath caught in her throat as she saw a flash of metal.

"You heard Duck," Wynter said as she pointed a revolver at Mary Aaron. "No witnesses."

CHAPTER 24

Sweat beaded on Buddy's face, despite the chill of the stone enclosure. "You can't—we can't—"

"Shut up, Buddy," Wynter interrupted. "We end this now and nobody knows what happened to Elsie Hostetler. Everybody thinks that Dathan killed her and then himself. There's nothing to tie us to either of them."

"But you can't kill Rachel and Mary Aaron. I won't let you do it. It ain't right. I'm not a murderer," Buddy yelled in Wynter's face. He looked to his other cousin. "Tell her, Duck. Tell her that's stupid. We're not shooting anybody."

Duck backed toward the door, his voice soft, manipulating. "She's talking sense, Cuz. This will never be finished if we don't tie up all the loose ends."

"They stuck their noses where they didn't belong," Wynter said, "and now they pay for it. Consequences to everything."

Rachel couldn't make out Wynter's face, but her tone was cold, almost emotionless. It was as though Wynter could talk about taking human life as easily as taking out the trash. Rachel tried to suppress her anger so that she could reason with the three of them. "You guys haven't thought this out," she said. "You'll never get away with it."

"You'll have to face a higher court," Mary Aaron said, forgetting that she was supposed to be gagged. "John Miller's a God-fearing man. He didn't raise you to be killers."

"And look where he is. An old man sitting here on this worthless farm, never seeing nothing, never getting anything. I gave up worrying about what he thinks a long time ago," Wynter answered.

"There's got to be another way," Buddy said.

"You have the brains of a turnip," Wynter taunted.

"He's not the stupid one," Rachel said. "He's the only one who realizes the consequences of what you're considering. He's not ready to risk his immortal soul for you."

"Everybody's got an opinion, don't they?" Wynter said, swinging the gun around to point the barrel at Rachel. "I'm not happy about this. Duck isn't. But it's the only way to get free of this mess."

"Buddy, please. You have to do what's right," Rachel begged. "Don't listen to them. They don't care about you. When the police arrest you, Duck and Wynter will blame everything on you. It will be your word against theirs."

Buddy swung around to look at his cousins. "You wouldn't do that, would you?"

"Let's take this outside," Duck said.

Buddy stood between Mary Aaron and Wynter's gun. "Stop waving that thing around before it goes off," he warned her.

"I think you're scared," Wynter said. "And you're the one who's supposed to be the mighty hunter. Don't you shoot stuff all the time?"

"Deer, rabbits, not people," Buddy answered. "And not women."

"Outside," Duck barked.

The three of them filed out of the springhouse, leaving Buddy's flashlight where he'd put it on the floor. Someone slammed the door and slid the bar. Rachel could hear their voices raised in anger. One of them, Buddy, she supposed, was crying again.

An ominous phrase raised the hair on the back of her neck.

". . . the old mine shaft." Duck's voice. "Nobody will ever find . . ."

Frantically, Rachel attempted to free her hands from the bindings. The nail head beneath her dug into her hip again. This didn't seem real. She had to hold it together. If she gave in to hysteria, she'd be useless. Below, Rachel could hear the spring, flowing continually out of the rock and earth of the mountain. Above her, in the rafters, there were high-pitched squeaks. Bats. She hated bats. She could imagine their tiny, leathery wings brushing against her face and their scratchy claws—"There's a nail sticking up, poking me," she told Mary Aaron, trying to get her mind off the bats.

"I don't think that's our biggest problem right now."

Rachel almost smiled.

"I've been watching Netflix. In the movies, this is when the hero policeman shows up," Mary Aaron whispered. "Evan would be good. Or Trooper Mars. I'd settle for any of them."

"Don't panic," Rachel replied. "We'll think of something."

"Too late for that. Can you move over a little? Away from me?"

"Maybe. A little. Why?" Rachel asked.

"I've been soaking the tape on my wrists for hours, in the water trickling behind us, and it's a lot looser. Maybe if I can borrow your nail, I can get it off."

"My nail?"

"The one poking you."

Rachel squirmed away from the post back toward the wall. The beam from Buddy's flashlight wasn't much help because it wasn't pointed right on them, but at least it wasn't pitch dark. Mary Aaron dropped sideways onto the floor and searched for the protruding nail. "It's right there," Rachel urged. "On my left."

"Found it." Mary Aaron was breathing hard, her movement obviously painful. "There. Got it." Quickly, she reached for Rachel's wrists.

Rachel's heart drummed against her ribs. It sounded so loud that she wondered why they couldn't hear it outside. Any minute they were going to be back. She just knew it. "Hurry," she whispered.

"Doing my best. Sit still. Can you bend your arms a little closer?"

Seconds became minutes. Now Rachel was sweating. If she didn't get loose soon, Duck or Wynter would come back in and shoot them like fish in a barrel. Of course, if she did get loose, what then? She didn't have a gun or a weapon of any kind. How would they—

"There."

The cord came undone and Rachel clutched her wrists. Immediately, sharp pain shot through her fingers. Her hands felt numb. How could she defend them if she couldn't use her hands? Mary Aaron began to work on Rachel's ankle binding. "There's a little window on the far wall. If you break the glass, I think you can squeeze through. Climb out and run. Into the woods. They won't find you on the mountain."

"I'm not going anywhere without you," Rachel said.

"I can't run. I don't even think I can walk, Rae-Rae. I'm telling you, my knee's bad."

"I'm not leaving you," Rachel insisted.

"Your father's right. You're as stubborn as your mother." Mary Aaron ripped loose the tape on Rachel's ankles and used the post to pull herself upright. She tried to take a step, gasped, and let out a groan. "I definitely can't walk on it," she said. "And I won't get far hopping like a rabbit. Go now, before they come back. They won't shoot me if they think you can identify them. There wouldn't be any reason to shoot me."

Coming to her feet, Rachel rubbed her hands together hard, willing feeling to return. She wasn't sure she agreed with her cousin's logic. "I won't leave you."

Mary Aaron grasped her arm. "I'll be all right. And I'm not afraid to die. It's fine. If I die, I'll be with Elsie."

"You're not baptized yet. How do you expect to get to heaven if you're not baptized?" Rachel didn't believe that, but it was what the bishop taught and she needed an argument. She had no intention of allowing Mary Aaron to sacrifice herself so that she could get away.

"That's a minor detail," Mary Aaron replied. "I'm sure I can clear that up once I get there."

"I'm not leaving you," Rachel insisted. "Is there anything in here I can use to hit them with? You've been here in daylight."

"Over by the door there's a broken butter crock. It's in pieces, but the base must be pretty heavy."

"Okay, so here's the plan." Rachel leaned down, picked up the blanket, and tossed it behind

402

them so neither of them would trip on it in the dark. "You wait behind the door. When one of them comes in, you slam the door on the others. I'll hit them with the pottery."

"And what about the other two?" Mary Aaron was already crawling toward the door. "Watch the floor. Half the boards are rotten and some of them are missing."

"I don't think Buddy will hurt us, no matter what they say," Rachel whispered. "With any luck, Buddy won't be the first one in the door."

"What about the gun?"

"Pray that Wynter comes in first. I'll hit her with the crock and you slam the door on whoever's coming in next. Wynter'll drop the gun. You grab it."

"Me?" Mary Aaron's voice sounded childlike. "I don't know anything about handguns."

"You've used a rifle. I know the boys take you hunting. It's easy. Don't point it at anything you don't want to kill."

"I don't know if I could shoot someone," Mary Aaron murmured.

"Hopefully you won't have to," Rachel answered, trying to figure out where the best place to stand was. "We have to fight back. Defend ourselves. It's our only chance. They think we're tied up. We'll take them by surprise. If we put up a good enough fight, I think they'll run away."

Rachel stripped off her jacket. If she had to fight one or two of them, she'd need to move freely. She picked up Buddy's flashlight and sighed at her own stupidity. *The flashlight.* If she needed a weapon, this was a far better one than some broken pieces of crockery. When Mary Aaron reached her spot behind the door, Rachel flicked the beam over to find the broken crock. The base was intact, thick, and almost ten inches across. She snatched it up and shoved it into Mary Aaron's hands. "I'll use the flashlight. You use this," she said, handing her the crock. She turned off the flashlight. Darkness would be to their advantage.

"Is it wrong to pray that we can hurt them?" Mary Aaron whispered.

"Pray they won't hurt us."

They were barely in position when Rachel heard the murmur of voices and footfalls on the steps. The door creaked open. Rachel brought the heavy flashlight down on the first figure to come through the door. Mary Aaron threw her weight against the door to try to close it. Wynter screamed and tumbled to the floor. Wood cracked. A man barreled through the entranceway, shoving Mary Aaron aside. Rachel swung the flashlight again, striking his shoulder. He whirled on her. It was Duck. He was holding the gun in one hand, a flashlight in the other.

Rachel caught sight of Wynter, on her hands

and knees. Mary Aaron brought the butter crock down on her back. Wynter shrieked as one hand and then a knee plunged through the rotten floor.

"Don't hurt them!" Buddy charged into the room.

Duck swore.

Rachel heard a loud *pop. I'm going to die,* she thought, preparing herself for the blow. But she felt nothing. Somehow, Buddy was between her and Duck.

"Oh." Buddy sounded surprised as his body rocked back.

"Buddy?" Duck screamed.

Buddy exhaled as he sank to the floor.

"What did you do?" Wynter cried, struggling to get free from the floorboards. "You shot Buddy. You idiot, you're supposed to shoot her!"

Rachel switched on Buddy's flashlight just as an object hurtled through the air and struck Wynter in the back of the head. Wynter sagged forward and collapsed, partially suspended between the rotten floorboards.

Rachel stared at Duck. He raised the gun again. He was less than six feet from her.

"Nice try," he said, shrugging. "Too bad for you."

John Miller's big dog came out of nowhere. Growling, it burst through the open doorway and launched itself on Duck, knocking him to the floor. The handgun went flying. On hands and knees, Mary Aaron scrambled after it. Duck yelled as the massive animal pinned him down, teeth snapping inches from his face.

"Down, boy." John's soft voice was infused with threads of steel. "Easy now," he ordered in *Deitsch*.

Still uttering deep growls, the dog backed off its victim and retreated to its master's side.

Duck sat up. He was trembling and his face was white in the glare of the flashlight as he got to his feet. "What you think you're going to do, old man?" he demanded. "You can't stop me. I—"

A cold, metallic *click* resounded through the springhouse. It was a sound that many people might not recognize. Rachel wasn't certain if she was imagining what she'd heard . . . if it was a desperate product of her imagination. But when John eased back the second hammer, she knew exactly what he was holding. A twelve-gauge shotgun. Her *dat* had one just like it that had once been his *dat*'s.

"You're blind!" Duck shouted. "You can't shoot me!"

"Let's see," John said. "Or you can get on your knees, hands on your head." Rachel thought he looked like an avenging angel standing there in his white nightgown with his long white beard and shoulder-length gray hair.

"You're blind and you're deaf," Duck spat, but he must have been scared, because he followed his grandfather's directions.

"I may be blind, but I'm not dumb. And I kept my hearing aid in tonight. I heard you. I heard Wynter take my savings from under the floorboard in the attic, and I heard you say you were going to murder these girls and throw them down the mine shaft."

"Gramps . . ."

"Enough, Deiter. You've said enough," John said. "Rachel, are you all right?"

"I am," she said as she passed her flashlight to Mary Aaron and crouched over Buddy's sprawled form. She placed her fingertips over his mouth and felt nothing. His chest was a blossom of dark red. "He's not breathing," she said, her voice trembling. He took the shot point-blank. "Buddy's hurt bad. Duck shot him." She knew she should try to do CPR even though his eyes were open, his pupils fixed. And there was so much blood seeping from the hole in his chest. As she got to her knees over him, she tried to remember how many com-pressions you were supposed to do before giving a breath. But every instinct told her that it was too late, that everything that made Buddy Wheeler alive and human was gone, that even now, his soul was rising somewhere into the dark night.

"You shot your own cousin?" John asked.

"It was an accident," Duck growled. "It's not my fault. Just stand aside and let me pass. You owe me that much. I'm your grandson. Your blood."

"I owe you nothing," John said. "Mary Aaron, you okay?"

"I am."

"You know how to use a shotgun?"

"I do," she said.

"I'm going to hand this to you and I want you to take good aim on Duck's knees," John said. "If he moves so much as a finger, blow his leg off. He won't run far then."

Rachel glanced at Mary Aaron. She nodded as John passed the shotgun to her.

"I don't want to hurt you," Mary Aaron said to Duck. "But I'm nervous. See how I'm shaking. If you do anything to frighten me, this gun is going to go off." She pointed it directly at Duck's knees.

John then knelt beside Rachel and laid a gnarled hand on Buddy's face, closing his eyes.

"Should I do CPR?" Rachel's voice trembled.

"He's gone, child," John murmured. "He's beyond your help."

Wynter was sobbing.

"I'm so sorry," Rachel said, sitting back, panting hard. "He wasn't a bad man."

"Just a foolish one." John exhaled a long, shuddering breath, got to his feet, and took the shotgun back from Mary Aaron.

Rachel put her hand out. "Give me my cell phone," she told Duck. "Give it to me," she repeated.

"Gramps . . ." Duck pleaded. "You don't have to do this. Just let me go. You don't want me to go back to prison."

"But I do," John said. "I want them to lock you up where you'll never hurt anyone again. You and Wynter both."

His granddaughter remained on the floor, weeping bitterly, making no effort to extricate herself from the floorboards.

"Buddy died for Rachel," Mary Aaron said. "He jumped between her and Duck. He saved her life."

"Then there is hope for him," John said. "God have mercy on his soul." He motioned to Rachel. "Back out of here. You, too, Mary Aaron. Dog, come. We'll lock these two in here until we can get the police."

"And the paramedics," Rachel said. "Mary Aaron's knee is hurt, and Wynter may need patching up."

"I should have run those two out long ago," John said. "But I was a foolish old man. I kept thinking they'd change. Maybe Buddy would be alive if I had."

"You can't blame yourself," Mary Aaron said. "And if you hadn't come when you did, Rachel and I would both be as dead as Elsie."

"They killed her, didn't they?" John asked.

"*Ya*," Mary Aaron answered softly. "They admitted it. It's a long story. It started out with Buddy and Duck having too much to drink."

"That figures." John handed the shotgun to Rachel. "Bet you know how to use this."

Rachel accepted it.

John turned his attention to Mary Aaron. "Let me help you down the steps. I'm blind, but I'm not helpless." He locked the springhouse door. "You stay!" he said to the dog. "Guard the door. That will hold them."

"I may have to drive down the mountain to get a phone signal," Rachel said as she backed out of the springhouse, John and Mary Aaron behind her.

"You take your time," John said. "What's done is done. We've got all the time in the world to pick up the pieces and try to go on living."

EPILOGUE

December . . .

"It's snowing," Mary Aaron said as she walked into Rachel's mother's kitchen. She was wearing a navy-blue dress with a matching navy apron, black wool stockings, and her white *kapp*.

Of course, two days ago, Rachel had seen her in jeans and a sweater, a headband in her hair. Her cousin was still finding her way, and the whole family was trying to be as supportive as they could. No one wanted Mary Aaron to leave the faith, Rachel least of all, but they all knew they needed to give her time, and trust her to make the right decision. At least that's what Rachel kept telling her aunt and uncle.

"I left my boots by the back door," Mary Aaron told Rachel. "Didn't want to track snow all over your clean floor."

"A little snow, what could it hurt with this mob?" Rachel's mother went to Mary Aaron and hugged her. "Your mother? How is she?"

"Good," Mary Aaron said. "She and *Dat* went to visit Alan's girlfriend's family. It looks serious between them, and you know my mother has

411

been pushing for more grandchildren. Wanting to know when Alan's marrying, when I'm marrying."

Rachel chuckled as she took a cast-iron pan of biscuits out of the oven. "That sounds familiar." She was eager to return to her own home, and eager to be part of the B&B again, but she would miss many things about being in the heart of her childhood home.

"Does that mean us?" Evan asked, leaning over her shoulder to look at the biscuits. "I can assure you, Mother Mast, it's not my fault we haven't given you one or two. Rachel's the one who's dragging her feet."

Rachel turned back to the stove, certain that the warmth in her face wasn't all from the oven. She swatted at him with one of the hot mitts she pulled off her hand and he retreated. It was so good to have Evan back in her life every day, and so good to see her mother's health making such steady improvement. She'd finished her last round of chemo and her doctors had declared her cancer-free. Rachel wasn't naïve; she knew the cancer might return, but for now, they had much to be thankful for.

Rachel's father and the boys came into the kitchen and took their places at the table. Their *dat* wasn't in his usual place at the head of the table, though. He'd given that spot to John Miller, who was becoming more a member of their family with each passing day. But no one was taking her mother's seat at the opposite end of the table. As her energy returned and color came back into her cheeks, Esther Mast had taken back the reins of the household.

The following morning, Rachel would be returning to Stone Mill House for good. With her *mam* herself again, there was no reason for Rachel to remain here at the farm any longer. And since John and his dogs were temporarily installed in the downstairs bedroom, the house was fairly crowded again. Her mother and Ada had hotly contested which of them would take John into their home, but Esther had won out, because John wouldn't come without his dogs. That, and Rachel's father had insisted that, come spring, it would only take a little work to set the *grossdaddi* house in order. The two-room log dwelling sat only a few hundred feet from the Mast farmhouse, far enough away to give John his privacy, but close enough to make him part of life here.

It turned out that John still had a fine herd of Southdown sheep, a breed that Rachel's father had long wanted to raise. John had seventy years of experience, and by bringing his herd to the Mast farm, he would ensure that he wouldn't have to sit idly in a rocking chair and be dependent on the family's charity.

"There is no talk of charity," Rachel's mother had declared, ending the contest between her and

Ada over where John would live, before it came to blows. "John saved Rachel and Mary Aaron's lives. And my grandmother on my mother's side was a Miller. I'm sure we're as much kin as you are, if we were to track it back," she'd told Rachel's housekeeper. "John comes to us."

John had protested being uprooted from his farm, but not wholeheartedly. With Buddy lost to him and Duck and Wynter behind bars, he was ready to make the move. He knew he couldn't live alone so far from others in the community any longer. And in the months since he'd come, Rachel had come to value his wisdom and good-heartedness. He and her father hit it off at once. Her *dat* had lost his own father years ago, and he still missed having an older man to confide in. John Miller had fit into their lives as comfortably as an old shoe.

"Is that turkey ready?" Rachel's father asked. "I'm starving."

"You're always starving," her mother replied. "Girls." She clapped her hands and Amanda and Lettie hurried to bring the salads and the bowls of mashed potatoes and vegetables while Rachel brought the biscuits to the table. Mary Aaron got the ham from the refrigerator and her *mam* got the butter and pickles.

"Any more trips coming up?" Rachel's father asked Evan.

He shook his head and winked at Rachel.

414

"No, sir. I'm not going anywhere again without Rachel. I'm afraid she'll get into trouble without me."

"Amen to that," Esther declared. "And it's time the two of you stopped sock-footing around and set a wedding date."

"*Mam!*" Rachel protested. They had, actually. The previous night. She and Evan just hadn't announced it yet.

"Actually, we have set a date," Evan said.

Rachel looked at him and raised a finger to her lips. "But we're not saying when."

"You two!" Mary Aaron laughed.

"Come on, everyone," Rachel's mother said, motioning to them. "Let us break bread together."

Rachel and Evan exchanged looks. He smiled and she smiled back at him. Soon they would be building their own traditions, starting their own family rooted in love and faith. It wouldn't be the way either of them had been raised, but together they would find a path that was best for them. She took her place at the children's table beside her sister Sally.

Samuel closed his eyes, lowering his head to begin the time of silent prayer.

"Wait, Samuel," her *mam* said. And she turned in her chair to face the children's table. "Rachel, come join us. Squeeze right in there on the bench between Lettie and Evan."

Rachel stared at her mother. "You mean . . ."

Tears filled her eyes. "You want me to sit with you?"

"*Ya*, daughter, it's been long enough, don't you think?"

Their gazes locked, and Rachel saw the love in her mother's eyes that she'd always known was there.

"You are part of this family, and you will always be," her *mam* said. "Come, sit here with me, where you belong. And be quick about it before the biscuits get cold."

Center Point Large Print
600 Brooks Road / PO Box 1
Thorndike, ME 04986-0001 USA

(207) 568-3717

US & Canada:
1 800 929-9108
www.centerpointlargeprint.com